GLACIER'S
EDGE

ALSO BY R. A. SALVATORE

THE WAY OF THE DROW

Starlight Enclave

THE LEGEND OF DRIZZT BOOKS

SAGA OF THE FIRST KING

TALES OF THE COVEN

FORGOTTEN REALMS

GLACIER'S EDGE

A NOVEL

R. A. Salvatore

HARPER Voyager

An Imprint of HarperCollinsPublishers

HarperCollins books may be purchased for educational, business, or sales promotional use. For information, please email the Special Markets Department at SPsales@harpercollins.com.

Harper Voyager and design are trademarks of HarperCollins Publishers LLC.

A hardcover edition of this book was published in 2022 by Harper Voyager, an imprint of HarperCollins Publishers.

FIRST HARPER VOYAGER PAPERBACK EDITION PUBLISHED 2023.

Designed by Michelle Crowe
Frontispiece and opener art © Aleks Melnik / Shutterstock

Library of Congress Cataloging-in-Publication Data has been applied for.

ISBN 978-0-06-308600-5

23 24 25 CPI 2 3 4 5 6 7 8 9 10

This is for everyone who's taken this long and wonderful journey beside me, most especially (of course), my wife, Diane, who's been there from the start, giving me the support, the time, and the space to chase a dream. This is my life's journey, and for everyone sharing the road—family, friends, publishers, and of course, the readers—thank you.

CONTENTS

GLACIER'S
EDGE

PROLOGUE

He sat in the dark and the quiet. And the cold. Even though he was wearing his Boots of the Winterlands, imbued with a dweomer to protect him in severe cold, Jarlaxle couldn't ignore the seeping discomfort finding its way to his bones, a chill beyond even the capabilities of his protective garments.

This time, he knew that the energy of the Weave wasn't failing, as it had, up here at least, soon after he and his friends had arrived at the top of the world near the Qadeej Glacier.

It was simply *that* cold around him.

He was sitting at the bottom of his pit created by his portable hole, ten feet below the frozen floor of the great chamber above. When he first fell in, the icy tornado had been swirling about him and he hadn't been able to close the hole to create a true extradimensional space. So instead he had merely created a pit, a barely sheltered pit covered and mostly filled by the swirling ice chips that had engulfed him and each of his friends up above. Freezing traps aimed like arrows for those who had dared enter the chamber of the slaad lord—and Jarlaxle was fairly certain that the monster that had come against them was indeed exactly that. Its presence, the sheer gravity of the being, was undeniable. With Catti-brie, Zaknafein, and Artemis Entreri, Jarlaxle had assembled a powerful fighting force, one that he had expected could get him out of almost any circumstance.

But that immense dark slaad that seemed as much smoke as flesh and bone had toyed with them.

Only Jarlaxle's pit and his remarkable hat, which he had expanded into a giant and sturdy umbrella above him, had kept him from being encased or crushed.

Which was all well and good, except his friends didn't have portable holes or magical hats.

The resourceful drow took a long, deep breath and reminded himself to have patience. The cavern above him was quiet, but he wasn't in any hurry to learn whether the slaad monster had departed. Long hours had passed before Jarlaxle even dared create a spark of light. After his vision had adjusted to the sudden brightness, he peeked around the umbrella, put his hand against the block of ice that had come down beside it and cramped him into this tight corner. It couldn't be solid, he guessed, not filling the entire hole, at least, for the air had not grown stale. He even thought he could hear, now and then, a slight whistle as the breeze blew through the chamber above.

Patience. He was in no hurry. He couldn't be, he told himself repeatedly, but his heart argued each time. His friends were out there, all of them, he believed, encased in ice. Preserved, he hoped, for he had witnessed other victims escaping the frozen tombs. But he couldn't be sure.

Patience, he told himself, and he tried not to picture Zaknafein and Catti-brie and Entreri in their tombs of glistening ice.

He reached into his belt pouch and brought forth some food.

Persimmons.

Persimmons with a block of kurit muskox cheese.

Jarlaxle's heart broke as he considered the delicacy, as he thought of Callidae, the city he had left behind only a few days before. The underground society had been everything he had hoped to find, and even more. Weirdly, Callidae had freed him of his fear that because he was drow, there was perhaps something wrong about him, something within him that even he could not truly trust. Callidae had shown him that Drizzt was not a fraud, and was not unique among the drow people—theories that both the controlling drow matrons and the prejudiced non-drow constantly advanced.

It was Lolth, not the drow. That's what he knew to be true now. Always, it was Lolth. The deceiver, the corruptor, the tyrant who held Menzoberranzan in her thrall through the punishing zealotry of her matrons.

And now, so soon removed from that greatest and most glorious revelation of Callidae, here he was, trapped under the ice, with three of his dearest friends possibly dead only a few yards away.

Persimmons.

Jarlaxle reached into his magical pouch again and produced a bottle of Scellobelee wine. His bracer brought a dagger to his hand and he flicked off the stopper, then cut into the block of cheese.

He toasted Callidae.

He toasted Zaknafein and Entreri and Catti-brie.

And he tasted again the delicacies of Callidae, and let them fill his thoughts and his hopes, and used them to renew his determination that it would not, could not, end like this.

Not now.

Patience.

WRAPPED IN A HEAVY BLANKET, DRIZZT SAT ON THE CHAIR set on the lawn in back of the Monastery of the Yellow Rose, the cold wind sending a flurry of snow dancing wildly in the air all about him.

He watched the departing form of Grandmaster Kane, and smiled around the edges of his pipe when the old man began moving in what seemed a combination of a dance and pursuit, angling about to catch the large snowflakes on his tongue.

Kane was doing that for his benefit, Drizzt knew, given the discussion they had just concluded, one convened over a particularly flavorful herb in the pipe Kane had brought for Drizzt.

Kane had spoken about the various ways in which people trap themselves in their own narrow vision, of how they let worries of what might be, or what might come to be, rob them of so much of their lives.

Like the snowflake-catching dance, the grandmaster was teaching.

He was always teaching.

"Where are you, my love?" Drizzt asked the wind. He was facing north in his chair, and his mind's eye took him out beyond his vision, took him to places of perpetual snow and cold, almost as if he might imagine to reality an image of Catti-brie, Jarlaxle, Entreri, and Zakna-fein sitting about a blazing fire, sharing tales and laughing at their day's grand adventure.

The flurry at the monastery lessened soon after, one area of clouds off in the north parting just enough for Drizzt to note some of his favorite star formations. He let his entire being fall into that distant cluster of twinkling lights, in that moment achieving complete meditation.

He came out of it smiling, thinking of his many star-filled nights on Kelvin's Cairn in Icewind Dale. How many times had he thought a friend lost, or had his friends thought him lost? Undoubtedly, one day, those fears would prove true.

Undoubtedly.

It was the reality the Companions of the Hall had all accepted years ago, decades ago, a lifetime ago—quite literally for the other four of the group.

What if she was lost to him forever now? What if his beloved Catti-brie would not return?

"Then I will make sure Brie knows her mother as completely as if Catti-brie was with her every day," he vowed, and despite the dark thought that he could not escape, Drizzt found that he was smiling, that he was content and accepting.

"But she'll be back, my Little Brie," he added, turning his gaze to the huge monastery, wherein his little girl was fast asleep.

He puffed on his pipe, then pulled it from his mouth and bit at a particularly large snowflake that drifted in a snake crawl in front of his face.

He didn't catch it.

Drizzt laughed and looked at the pipe Grandmaster Kane had brought out to him. He had little experience with such implements, and little desire for them, but this one had proven quite soothing—perhaps too much so.

Or could there really be a "too much so" at this time? he wondered. He had been wrapping himself more frantically in fear for his wife the last tendays, he had to admit, ever since Kimmuriel had departed for the west and home.

"What did you do, Grandmaster?" he asked the wind, which again did not answer.

Or maybe it did, because Drizzt lost himself in its mournful song and the fanciful dance of fluffy snowflakes. He was in the here and now, in the moment, and even when he tried to focus again on his wife and friends who had gone into the cold north, he kept falling back to this time and this place.

Which is exactly how Kane said it should be.

He would trust in his friends and Catti-brie. He wouldn't let helpless worry prevent his enjoyment of the moment in these beautiful Galena Mountains with his precious baby, Brie.

He wouldn't let his fears take him from the present.

Not now.

Patience.

SOME OF THE YOUNGER PRIESTESSES AND WIZARDS OF House Baenre had gathered in the gallery behind the choir screen in the main chapel and were now singing a series of quiet and introspective meditation chants and harmonies that Yvonnel had supplied to Myrineyl, Matron Mother Quenthel's daughter and the newly anointed first priestess of House Baenre.

In a darkened back corner of the grand chamber, Yvonnel let the sounds take her thoughts to a place of contentment and peace, a place of personal freedom from the storm of concerns that had been raging for so many months now, and even more so since she had worked with Quenthel on the great heresy against the Spider Queen goddess.

Yvonnel didn't entertain doubts about that action. The web she had helped create was a powerful and laudable statement.

More, the creation was a good thing. A thousand driders had ended their torment by diving through the magical disenchanting, curse-removing strands of that blasphemous web.

It was the future, not the past, now weighing upon her, as it did on Quenthel and Zeerith and so many other powerful players in the game of Menzoberranzan. What actions must they now take? Was it their move or Matron Zhindia's? Which faction, Lolthian or heretic, had time on their side?

There were no precedents for this, no illithid-gifted memories of Yvonnel the Eternal that her granddaughter and namesake could plumb to find some guidance. The city was quiet from afar, but on edge up close, in every house, in every alleyway, in every shadow. Very few of the powerful families had staked their ground here, and while Yvonnel and many others had an idea of which way a Matron Vadalma Tlabbar or a Miz'ri Mizzrym might lean, none was going to stake their very existence on the hopes of the potential executioner, be it Lolth or House Baenre.

Houses Fey-Branche and Do'Urden were with them, Yvonnel knew, although she feared that Matron Zeerith Xorlarrin Do'Urden might not be as solid an ally as supposed. Then again, such was always the way with the drow, wasn't it?

And wasn't that exactly what she was trying to change?

Houses Barrison Del'Armgo, Hunzrin, Mizzrym, and Vandree were likely in Matron Zhindia's court, although Zhindia should greatly fear the reversal of Matron Mez'Barris Armgo, for if that unpredictable leader of that mighty house, second in the city only to Baenre, threw her allegiance behind House Baenre, Zhindia's hopes and alliances would fall apart and she would find herself quite alone.

But that, too, was mere speculation. The drow armies had rushed back to Menzoberranzan and crawled into their respective holes. The events on the surface—the great and open blasphemy to Lolth by the most powerful house in the city—had all of them off balance, huddled, and fearful.

Which, of course, played right into Lolth's hands. Lolth rode chaos to power. She used fear and uncertainty to tighten her bonds on her devoted.

The song of the choir filtered about Yvonnel, calming her, reminding her that House Baenre was not sitting idly by, that her defenses were being strengthened, her new former drider force, the Blaspheme, already nearly fully outfitted for war.

Yvonnel and Quenthel had plucked the spiderwebs on the surface. There was no reason to slap the beast that was Lolth again.

Not now. Not *yet*.

Patience.

PART 1

THE BLASPHEME

In my many times of introspection, I find that I am often concerned with the notion of perception. Whether in politics or religion or the relationships of the various cultures and creatures of Faerun, there is always the matter of basic truths, of course, but more importantly, there is the matter of perception of those truths and where they will lead, and where they should lead. We are creatures guided by reason, by fact and logic, but we are, too, creatures guided by emotion.

Undeniably so, but separating the emotional from the logical is no easy task for most, myself included.

So I think about such moments that challenge us. How much worse is the cost of a battle if one you love is lost in the fight? And how less painful if all the casualties are distant from you emotionally?

The personal cost is not the same as the greater cost, for if a dozen were killed in the two scenarios above, then a dozen had been killed, and so the cost from afar should be considered the same. But we know it is not the same to different people. When an army returns from the bloodied fields, the news of the battle will be received much more viscerally and poignantly in a village where many were lost than in one where none were. And that will be felt differently in a large city where soldiers are lost than it is in those small villages.

Again, though, it depends on what city, on what people. If Clan Battlehammer went to war and a dozen dwarves were lost in a victorious campaign, they would rejoice in the outcome. Yes, they would salute the fallen, but with mugs raised solemnly within a sea of cheer. But if one of those fallen was King Bruenor, or one of the queens of Mithral Hall, the mugs would be raised solemnly within a sea of somber acceptance.

This is a maddening truth to me, but it is also an undeniable truth.

The blend of these two often-conflicting realities—logical and emotional—goes deeper than the mere perception of the world around us. I have come to believe that it goes a long way toward determining the type of person one might be. I am led inescapably to the belief that the level to which one can empathetically look past the personal to the pains and losses of the wider situation is a measure of one's heart and goodness.

Perhaps the only one.

I have met so many people who do not think something is troubling, or threatening, or terrible, and no amount of cajoling or explaining or presenting compelling evidence will move them from that dispassionate stance—until that individual or someone very dear to that individual is personally affected by the incident or assailant or disease.

As I watch the growth of Artemis Entreri, for example, I see that he has come to greatly enlarge his circle of caring. He has admitted friends into his personal group, and the widening of that circle has led him to see the pain of others even when such pain is not acute to him.

Empathy.

So often have I seen a lack of such, both in those selfish and tight with their hearts and, more surprisingly, in those who believe themselves firmly grounded in reason and verifiable fact. For how easy it is to get lost in thought, quite literally! And in those streams of sorting and calculating and hoping, how easy it is to lose sight of the reality that surrounds you.

We are all susceptible to this blurring of reality, this clouding of the physical truths about us while seeking the clarity of our philosophical eyes.

Similarly, we are all victims to our selfishness to one degree or another. We all narrow our perception too tightly at times and forget the truth: if a *person is in another place, how clearly do we appreciate that the world in that other place continues even when we're not there? Life continues in all its complexities and personal struggles, pain and joy.*

This existence, limited by our senses and thoughts and physical frailties, is not our dream, except collectively, which is hard to accept because our own experiences are so uniquely personal, and yet, at the same time, they are universal.

Bruenor often chides me that I overthink things, and here I am again, guilty. It is so easy to get lost in the philosophical, in the mysteries, in the unanswerable questions that are always there, somewhere, in your thoughts, ready to come forth whenever some event—the death of a loved one, a near brush of your own—starkly reminds you. This has been my uneven and confusing journey for some time, particularly since I returned from my transcendence of my mortal and physical self and glimpsed . . . possibilities.

For there I have been lost.

It took a drow psionicist, a man I've hardly considered a friend and never more than an ally about whom I remain suspicious and cautious, to refocus my sensibilities, to pull me out of the malaise of pondering the greater picture of my personal future and remind me that the world around me continues to spin.

To perceive beyond myself. To perceive beyond those in my immediate sphere.

To empathize with the wider world.

The road I walked those years in Menzoberranzan, and out of Menzoberranzan, has paved the way for others. As I became free of the grip of Lolth, as I became beyond her reach—no matter what she did to my physical being—so, too, can my drow sisters and brothers find their way. And I am called to help them. Whatever I may desire personally—my love for Catti-brie and our dear daughter; my joy when I am with my friends in these lands we have tamed and the good we have done for those around us; the simple pleasures of sitting on the back lawn of the Monastery of the Yellow Rose and allowing the stars to lift my spirits to the wide multiverse—my duty is now clear to me and the stakes could not be higher.

I cannot ignore the spinning wheels rolling and roiling all about me. Whatever my personal feelings—a sense of completion I do not wish disturbed—*I must shake them and understand that this particular journey is one that I in no small manner started, fanned, and pulled so many along with me.*

Menzoberranzan is going to war.

Drizzt Do'Urden is going to war.

—Drizzt Do'Urden

CHAPTER 1

What's in a Name?

Are you intending to stutter every time you try to say my name?" the tall and broad-shouldered drow woman said to the smaller man beside her.

"It is not a common name," the one who went by Dininae replied. "Mal'a'a'a'voselle . . ."

The warrior woman laughed and shook her head.

"What? It comes from the breaks in the name! They simply do not roll off my tongue so easily," Dininae dramatically explained. "The language was different back then, yes? Back when Menzoberranzan and Mal'a'a'a' . . . were young?"

"Mal'a'voselle," she corrected. "And yes, the language was different, but not so much so. I believe that you are merely stupid, or, worse for you, that you are teasing me."

"If we cannot find something to laugh about after the centuries of torment . . ."

"Millennia," Mal'a'voselle reminded him. "I lost count of the centuries centuries ago."

Dininae shuddered at that. He had served in the Abyss as a drider slave for a very short time compared to this warrior of old walking the Braeryn, the Stenchstreets, of Menzoberranzan beside him. In those long years, Dininae had not begun to get used to the torment of being a drider, the constant pain, the constant humiliation, the constant reminder by every demon he encountered that he was an abomination, that he was inferior, that he was unable to deny any demand or refuse to suffer any insult or torture. To do so would have created only more torment, and in the Abyss, that awful well of pain, both emotional and physical, was bottomless.

No, the last day Dininae had served as a drider had been no better, no more tolerable, than the first.

That abominable state of being could not numb with time, for wounds were never given opportunity to scab over.

As he considered that terrible truth, Dininae looked at the proud warrior walking beside him with renewed and heightened respect. A century had broken him, but she had endured at least twenty of those—thirty or forty centuries, perhaps!

"Are you sure that you're not just stupid?" the drow from another eon asked.

"When I look back at my life, I'm not sure of that at all," he admitted.

Mal'a'voselle stopped walking then, and several steps later, Dininae turned back to find her regarding him intently.

"Who are you?"

Dininae held up his hands as if in surrender, as if the question had no answer beyond that which he had already disclosed.

"Dininae?" she asked.

"Yes."

"Dininae what? Drow are usually proud of their surnames. I am Mal'a'voselle Amvas Tol. Even though my house was destroyed, even though my matron's choices cost me . . . everything, I remain Mal'a'voselle Amvas Tol."

"And I remain Dininae."

"Dininae what?"

"Dininae Stenchstreet, I suppose."

"I do not believe you. Do you know why I asked you to accompany me this day out of House Baenre?"

"My good looks, I assumed."

Mal'a'voselle's snort answered that.

"Among the Blaspheme, the name Dininae is spoken with respect," she admitted. "Not quite reverence, but true respect."

Dininae bowed. "For my good looks, I presume."

"For your speed and skill with the blades."

"I doubt I would survive for long in a fight with Mal'a'voselle Amvas Tol."

"You would be dead before you realized the fight had begun."

"Then it would seem that those regarding me highly are sorely mistaken."

"No, Dininae," Mal'a'voselle said, shaking her head and enunciating his name, stretching out each syllable, as if she continued to suspect that it wasn't his true identity—or not all of it, at least. "The drow have changed, as have the fighting techniques. In my time, many of the women, typically larger and stronger than the men, were the greatest of drow warriors. We were fast with the blades, but more than that, we were strong enough to drive through the inferior armor of our enemies. Now men dominate the warrior ranks, as all the women flutter about in their flailing obeisance to the Spider Witch. The fighting techniques employed by drow warriors have changed, that much is already obvious from our time in training with the Baenres."

"I wasn't in Lolth's Abyss nearly as long as you and those you most trusted," Dininae reminded her. "I fight in the style more suited to the Baenre trainers' desires. I watched the fighting styles of those trained at Melee-Magthere in these very techniques, and so I learned to mimic the routines."

"That much is true with many others of the Blaspheme, and indeed most were actually trained at Melee-Magthere. Among them all, however, Dininae stands as the most formidable. That's why I asked you to accompany me this day, and many days to come, likely."

"I am humbled," he said with another bow. "And I still don't want to fight you."

"Ah yes, but perhaps you will train with me. The enemies I will face will find openings, I fear, and though this Baenre armor I have been given is fine indeed, I do not wish to test it against a Melarni sword."

"I would be honored." He wasn't just saying that to flatter this drow who had seen the birth of Menzoberranzan. Mal'a'voselle was a force—she reminded him of the legendary Uthegentel Armgo, and already the whispers had begun that if that Second House sided with Baenre's enemies, she would one day find a blood duel against House Barrison Del'Armgo's current weapon master, Malagdorl, who was bred and trained in the spirit of Uthegentel (and indeed wore the armaments of that legendary warrior). Mal'a'voselle was wise to come to a warrior like Dininae to learn how to adapt to the new fighting styles.

"Honored enough to tell me your name?"

That didn't catch him by surprise. "Dininae," he said without hesitating.

"Dininae *what*? Dininae of what house?"

"None."

"Dininae, who learned to fight along the refuse of the Stench-streets?" she dubiously replied. "You taught yourself, and yet stand superior to those of the Blaspheme who also have not been dead for more than a century or two? And yet those other younger driders, almost to a one, were of noble birth? From the onset of Menzoberranzan, rare were the driders who were born as houseless drow, for why would Lolth or any ruling matron care enough to so torture a commoner?"

"It is not unknown."

"Ah yes, but rarer still would it be for a commoner to be more proficient with the blade than a warrior trained at Melee-Magthere, and to have almost certainly continued their training with a skilled weapon master after that."

"Still not as rare as a woman named Mal'a'voselle," Dininae quipped. "Yet here you stand."

The tall woman smiled widely. "Voselly," she said.

"What does that mean?"

"It means that you may call me Voselly. That's what they called me in those long-ago days, before I incurred the wrath of the matrons."

"I thought your nickname was Malfoosh."

The large woman stiffened, and for a moment, Dininae thought she would strike him.

"That was what they called me as a drider," she said, calming. "The demons of the Abyss called me that to mock me. You don't wish to mock me, do you, Dininae?"

"Of course not," Dininae quickly answered.

"Mal'a'a'a'a'a'a?" Voselly mimicked.

Dininae sucked in his breath, but the woman laughed heartily.

"It was a friendly tease, I did not mean to mock . . ." the man stuttered.

"If I thought it was anything more than that, I would have killed you. I accept your teasing in the spirit in which it was offered. But not Malfoosh—never Malfoosh. I am not an abomination anymore. I choose my name. I choose Voselly for those who are my friends."

"So, we are friends, then."

"Friends unless I discover that you are lying to me."

Dininae replied with a chuckle and a shake of his head, and could only hope that he had deflected the suspicion well enough with that.

KYRNILL KENAFIN MELARN TOOK A DEEP BREATH AND tried to steady herself when the curtains in her private chamber shifted on some breeze. She wasn't surprised when they fell back into place, revealing the nearly translucent specter of a young and extremely beautiful lavender-eyed priestess standing beside them.

What have you learned? she heard in her mind.

Kyrnill knew that she didn't have to audibly respond. She could feel the intruder in her thoughts. *Three nights . . . House Do'Urden . . . small but formidable force to test the defenses.*

And if they find weakness? the intruder demanded.

Matron Zeerith will fall.

Three nights?

When the light of Narbondel falls for the third time.

The specter nodded and offered a smile, which seemed to Kyrnill very unsettling, coming from a being that appeared more like a ghost than a fellow drow priestess.

Will you be there?

Kyrnill shook her head, but her expression gave away her uncertainty.

If you are, then be quick to hide, the specter warned.

The curtain swayed again. A torch on the wall nearby flickered and nearly went out.

The ghostly intruder was gone, from the room and from her mind.

Kyrnill exhaled and fell into a sitting position on the edge of her bed. She never liked these games of intrigue because she knew she wasn't very good at them. She generally tried the more passive route offered, letting others decide the often-fatal play. Such had been the case when her house, Kenafin, had merged with House Horlbar to form House Melarn. Kyrnill could have battled for the position of Matron Melarn and very likely won the title, but she had conceded it to Zhindia Horlbar, expecting that Zhindia would be killed in the ensuing chaos.

It hadn't happened, and as the years had slipped past into decades, decades into a century, Kyrnill's hopes to ever become again a house matron had also slipped. She was still the first priestess, outwardly seen as second to the throne.

But she knew better. Matron Zhindia wasn't ever going to let her ascend, particularly not now. Perhaps it had been cowardice, perhaps simple miscalculation, but Kyrnill understood more clearly than ever before that she had let her best and surely her safest opportunity pass.

THEY ENTERED A WIDE LANE OF TAVERNS AND BROTHELS, some of freestanding construction, others carved into stalagmites, and still others no more than walls of fabric hardly shielding the movements within.

Dininae knew this place from the days when he had been called Dinin, at that time the secondboy of House Do'Urden. He had come here often to play, to gamble, to fight—anything to break the monotony of his existence as the lowest noble of Matron Malice's court.

The Braeryn seemed quieter to him now, and quite a bit. At first, he figured that was due to recent events—the march to the surface, the brewing troubles, and the war with the demon hordes that had been fought here in Menzoberranzan only a few years before—but as he and Voselly continued their walk, he realized that no, that wasn't it at all.

The shelves were stocked, racks of dirty glasses piled at the end of every bar.

Which meant this wasn't a sign of decline. No, *this* day, *this* moment, the avenue was strangely empty.

He did see a few patrons and potential customers, some leaning on the bars, some standing with the prostitutes as if striking a bargain, a couple pitching bones in a small alley between two stalagmites that comprised a single tavern. But they were all so unnatural at it he didn't think them typical denizens of the Stenchstreets. He looked for insignia, and noted from the subtle revelations of their armor and weapons that these were not the downtrodden of Menzoberranzan, no.

Yet he saw no house markings, no emblems or crests.

And that made it worse.

"Are you at the ready?" he whispered to his companion.

"Of course. You see it, too?"

"I count six."

"At least eight."

"Ah yes, my favorite number, or so I was told from the moment of my birth," Dininae replied.

"Take heart, we've friends about," Voselly told him. "We need only hold our ground for a short while."

"Unless they also have friends nearby."

Voselly stopped and half turned, smirking down at him. She was about to say something, Dininae was about to shout something, when she suddenly spun about, bringing her trident sweeping across, angled downward with great force, driving aside a sword stabbing for her back. Her attacker unbalanced and fell forward just enough for Voselly to roll her shoulders and launch a devastating right cross that crunched into the man's face and snapped his head back viciously.

He was fully unconscious before he hit the ground.

Dininae had watched every movement, the sweep and the beautiful way Voselly had dropped her left shoulder back, essentially "throwing" the right hand with her left shoulder, resulting in such a long and truly devastating punch.

He silently reminded himself never to anger this woman, but that was all the time he had to consider anything other than the fight, which now came at him fast in the form of a pair of young men, or more pointedly, in a closing barrage of four waving and stabbing swords.

So quick was his draw that Dininae's swords seemed to simply appear in his hands, just as Zaknafein had taught him, drawing and stabbing in a single movement. His opponent to the right turned and slapped a sword across to deflect, but the other one had not anticipated the sudden attack and caught Dininae's left-hand blade right at the tip of his breastplate, where it slid up and jabbed into his throat.

Dininae would have finished him, would have nearly decapitated him, except that the other attacker was already countering with a backhand sweep with his blocking blade, forcing Dininae to fall back and turn fast to bring his left-hand blade slashing across to intercept.

He had one out of the fight temporarily at least, stumbling and gagging and falling off to the side, but another enemy leaped into the void and pressed forward fiercely, forcing Dininae back on his heels, his two swords working furiously to keep the four stabbing blades at bay.

Work for the rhythm, he told himself silently.

Zaknafein's litany.

Work for the rhythm, fall into the flow of the battle, discover the tendencies of your opponents. So Dininae did, and he was quite pleased with himself as he held his ground, anticipating each attack and deflecting, parrying, riposting even, or avoiding with a simple twist. After all of those years as a drider, he was still living up to Zaknafein's training, and living up to the compliments Voselly had just put upon him.

His shock broke him from that rhythm and that confidence when he sensed something coming hard for his head from behind.

Reflexively, he just folded his legs under him and dropped to his knees, tucking his chin as well and bracing himself.

But the missile—another enemy drow warrior—went over him, falling over the two attackers, who tried hard not to stab their poor flailing comrade in the collision.

With but a quick appreciative glance back at a laughing Voselly, Dininae sprang up and forward. He stabbed the thrown drow first, right in the kidney, and as that man crumpled in pain, Dininae blew past him, over him, seizing the initiative and driving back the two remaining attackers. He deftly employed an inside-out series of thrusts with his left-hand stabs, moving his hand in close and to his right hip and launching the attacks from there to force the stumbling, off-balance target to move out wider.

A final thrust sent that drow skipping back three strides, and Dininae turned fully on the drow to the right, blades rolling now as if to simply overpower the fellow.

Except, no, for Dininae broke almost immediately to go back out fast to the left, where that drow was charging, obviously believing Dininae fully involved with the other. The attacker came in with an offensive stance, one blade high, the other too far forward.

Dininae got past the tip of that blade easily, and lifted his left arm up high, blade horizontal to steal the chop of the drow's raised sword.

These were not houseless rogues. They wore fine armor.

But Dininae wielded Baenre swords, and with the momentum of both fighters bringing them fast together, that fine breastplate barely slowed the thrust of Dininae's right-hand blade.

The drow stopped abruptly, contorting weirdly.

Dininae stepped back, dropping his left shoulder to send his free sword cutting out hard behind him to stay the rush of the remaining fighter, while his right foot went up to the impaled drow's chest and pushed off hard, sending Dininae out and into a roll and throwing the mortally wounded attacker stumbling back and toppling over the first warrior Dininae had dispatched.

A flicker to the right had Dininae snapping his sword up, and just in time to deflect a hand-crossbow quarrel.

He looked all about, seeing drow flooding into the street, and at first thinking an army had come against him and Voselly.

But no, most of these were Blaspheme warriors, the fellow former driders, he realized. He looked to a smiling Voselly.

"They've been shadowing us?" he asked.

"I told you we had friends," she replied.

"You didn't say they'd be shadowing us."

The warrior shrugged. "Perhaps I wanted to confirm that which was told to me, and which I hoped to be true."

"That I can fight?"

"Yes, and perhaps you will soon find trust in me to tell me the truth about Dininae. You are no commoner. You are not self-taught in the arts martial. You attended the Academy and were trained by a weapon master."

She quieted as another large drow woman walked up, a fellow of the Blaspheme warrior who had spent millennia in the Abyss with Lolth and her demonic.

"What do you know, Aleandra?" Voselly asked.

"Your ambushers are fleeing."

"Let them go."

She nodded. "Yes, I gave the order already. But there is one other, a priestess of House Hunzrin. She wishes to retrieve these enemies who have fallen, to tend them that they will not die."

"Why does she care? Are these murderers of House Hunzrin?"

"No."

"Then?"

"She did not say, but my guess is House Melarn, of course."

"So House Hunzrin is trying to play a mediation role here and avoid a war," Voselly reasoned. She looked around at the five fallen ambushers, of which only one, skewered by Dininae, looked to be in mortal danger.

"Have her come and heal that one," Voselly decided. "And do with him as she will. The others come with us back to House Baenre. I would not overstep my authority here. Let Matron Mother Quenthel Baenre decide their fate."

Aleandra rushed away and began barking orders, while Voselly led Dininae back the way they had come.

"It was my kill," he said to her as they moved off. "You did not think the disposition of the fallen warrior should be my choice?"

"No," she answered simply. "I was once weapon master of the First House of Menzoberranzan. You are but a commoner, so you say. Why would I care what you wanted?"

Dininae stopped and let her move a few steps ahead of him, and stood there with hands on hips until she turned back.

"You mean to play the same games that decided our mutual fates in times past?" he asked.

"Your words have consequences. When I can trust you, I will respect you."

"Because I am a noble, you believe?"

"Because you will no longer be lying to me. Do not misunderstand me, warrior. I am as fearful as you regarding our disposition in this struggle, and regarding our future, if we even have one. We are the Blaspheme, so they have decided. We are Matron Mother Baenre's shock soldiers, her fodder. She will throw us against her enemies, no doubt, and will shed no tears when we are torn apart."

"Or Lolth will reveal her joke and revert us to a state of abomination," Dininae replied, admitting his deepest fear.

"It has crossed my mind. And that is why I intend to bring the Blaspheme tightly together beneath my command. Here or back in the Abyss, we stand together or we face torment—and actual death only if we are fortunate. But I like people who tell me the truth, Dininae."

She practically spat his sobriquet.

He didn't want to cross Voselly. He really didn't want to cross Matron Mother Baenre. And most of all, he didn't want to become a pawn in the grand scheming of the Demon Queen of Spiders.

But in the end, he was a Do'Urden, Elderboy Dinin Do'Urden, and in this most confusing and dangerous time, he simply couldn't discern how that truth would play.

YVONNEL'S SENSIBILITIES CAME BACK INTO HER BODY IN A quiet meditation chamber of House Baenre. As soon as she was whole again, body and spirit, she instinctively reached up and brushed away the squid-like tentacles that were set about her head, then shook her long white hair from her face and rubbed repeatedly, as if trying to further rid herself of the creepy touch of the illithid who sat before her.

"Should I be insulted, priestess?" that creature said in its gurgling, watery voice.

"I am surprised you recognized my movements."

"I did not. I felt your revulsion toward me."

"You must admit that you elicit such . . ." Yvonnel said, holding up a hand and offering a wide smile—two gestures she knew would be completely lost on this one, Methil El-Viddenvelp, the same mind flayer that had inserted the memories of Matron Mother Yvonnel the Eternal into her mind when she was still in Minolin Fey's womb.

"You sensed the exchange, I expect," Yvonnel said.

"I sensed that you trust Kyrnill Melarn," the illithid replied.

"Kyrnill Kenafin," Yvonnel corrected. "She is only Melarn because she had no choice when the houses were forced to join together as one. She never truly accepted that, particularly as Matron Zhindia has become more . . . zealous. And especially not now, if what we have heard regarding the conception of this city is true." Yvonnel considered it for a moment, and almost felt guilty for having initially reached out to Kyrnill those tendays earlier.

Only for a moment, though, for the information of Zhindia's attack would go a long way in stunting the appetite of those houses thinking to side with Zhindia's planned coup.

"Courage is often found in anger among the lesser beings."

It wasn't lost on Yvonnel that Methil included her in that group. She let it pass, of course, for Methil was an illithid and had no way of truly understanding the concept of conveying insult when merely, to his thinking, conveying the truth.

"Kyrnill walks a dangerous road. Matron Zhindia is not known for mercy."

Indeed, Matron Zhindia had a well-earned reputation for devising the most exquisite tortures ever seen this side of the Abyss. Her murder of Kyrnill's daughter Ash'ala Kenafin Melarn was said to involve maggots, a slow death of being eaten alive while soaking in a tub of her own feces and rothé milk.

The mere thought of it made Yvonnel sick to her stomach.

And made her hate the wretched fiend Lolth all the more.

CHAPTER 2

That Troublesome Sister

They fought along the southernmost way of the Braeryn, in sight of the Spiderfangs," the unexpected visitor to House Baenre reported to her sister, Matron Mother Quenthel.

Quenthel hardly heard the words of priestess Sos'-Umptu, as she was still trying to recover from the shock that her Lolth-loving sister had dared return to the Baenre compound after their heated falling-out on the surface, an argument that had included more than a few pointed threats.

"Lolth herself will come against you," Quenthel reminded her slowly and deliberately.

Recognizing her own words being thrown back at her, Sos'Umptu fought hard to suppress her fear and her anger.

"That is what you promised, is it not?" Quenthel asked. Beside her, the priestess Minolin Fey Baenre wore the look of a displacer beast after cornering a giant rat.

"I believe that you expressed your desire that Lolth would use your own body as her vessel to destroy this house. Your house. House Baenre."

"There is still time for House Baenre to correct our errors," Sos'Umptu said.

"*Our* errors? Or *your* error?"

Sos'Umptu tucked her chin and gave a quick curtsy.

"Continue with your tale of this fight," Quenthel told her. "They fought? Who?"

"Your soldiers, the Blaspheme and their leader, Mal'a'voselle Amvas Tol—"

"I am their leader," Matron Mother Quenthel corrected.

"The field commander, I mean," Sos'Umptu clarified. "I meant no disrespect."

"Didn't you, then?"

She ignored that. "The Amvas Tol warrior was ambushed along the avenue, but had cleverly set an ambush for the anticipated ambushers, so I am told."

"And who told you?"

Sos'Umptu swallowed hard.

"Matron Zhindia Melarn?"

"No, First Priestess Charri of House Hunzrin," Sos'Umptu admitted.

"Hunzrin soldiers ambushed my Blaspheme?"

"Who can really know? Priestess Charri came upon the fight as the ambushers—"

"The Melarni," Quenthel interrupted.

"The ambushers were fleeing, with several downed by the Baenre force. One was mortally struck by another of your Blaspheme warriors, but fortunately, High Priestess Charri was able to save the man."

"So, she and her house have taken sides."

"No," Sos'Umptu said emphatically. "High Priestess Charri, like many of us, is trying to avert a war. The wounded was a nobleman, a graduate of Melee-Magthere."

"A nobleman of what house?" Quenthel demanded.

Sos'Umptu hesitated.

"If she knew he was a noble, then surely Charri Hunzrin would know of which house, and surely Sos'Umptu would think to ask. House Melarn?"

"No," Sos'Umptu admitted.

"Speak it!"

"House Mizzrym," Sos'Umptu said.

Quenthel wore her surprise on her face. Beside her, Minolin Fey gasped.

"It cannot be," Minolin Fey said, but she quieted abruptly when the Matron Mother snapped a glare over her.

"Why are you so surprised?" Sos'Umptu asked. "This is what I tried to warn you about after your actions up on the surface. Your new soldiers, your Blaspheme warriors, openly walk the streets of Menzoberranzan. They were driders, Matron Mother! Abominations given to Lolth as punishment for their crimes against her, only to be stolen from Lolth by—"

"By us, yes," said another, and all turned to see Yvonnel Baenre enter the audience chamber. Beside her walked Velkryst, once a formidable wizard of powerful House Xorlarrin, but now Quenthel's consort here in House Baenre.

Sos'Umptu locked stares with this strange young woman, Yvonnel Baenre, the daughter of Gromph Baenre and Minolin Fey, whose status and power were not relegated by her birth order in the Baenre family tree. This one was different, powerful in magic both divine and arcane, and yet her high rank here—high enough to walk into the Matron Mother's audience hall without invitation—had been predicated on still more than that. Like Quenthel, Yvonnel had been given the memories of Yvonnel the Eternal, the great and old Matron Mother Baenre who had ruled Menzoberranzan for two millennia.

Sos'Umptu tried to hide her hatred for this young woman, whom she considered the epitome of an apostate. Once rumored to be the very avatar of Lolth in Menzoberranzan, Yvonnel had betrayed the Spider Queen, had betrayed House Baenre, had betrayed them all in the greatest act of heresy imaginable. Yet here she was, at the court of Matron Mother Baenre in the city's First House, walking in openly and speaking out of turn as if she were Matron Mother Quenthel's equal!

And thus, by implication, Sos'Umptu's superior.

"One of Matron Miz'ri's children attacked the Blaspheme?" Yvonnel asked.

"A nephew, I believe," Sos'Umptu answered.

"Trying to make a name for himself and garner the favor of Lolth, no doubt," Yvonnel said.

"Why would he not?" asked Sos'Umptu, turning her gaze and her words back at Quenthel. "Why would any of them not? Even if they do not wish to side with Matron Zhindia in any potential war, even if they fear the wrath of House Baenre, would not the other houses see soldiers of the Blaspheme openly walking the streets as a challenge to the goddess, and so as a way to find Lolth's favor?"

"Matron Miz'ri's nephew was not killed?" Quenthel asked.

"Charri Hunzrin saved him, I am assured."

"How many lie dead on that avenue?"

"None, Matron Mother," Sos'Umptu replied. "But Mal'a'voselle and her soldiers will soon return with several prisoners in tow."

"More Mizzryms?"

Sos'Umptu held up her hands. "I do not know. But I would not be surprised. Nor would it surprise me to learn that warriors of other ruling houses were involved. House Vandree, likely. Barrison Del'Armgo . . ."

"Not House Barrison Del'Armgo," Yvonnel said, walking up and taking the seat right beside Quenthel. She turned a catlike smile on Sos'Umptu, who narrowed her gaze in response.

Sos'Umptu fought hard to suppress her anger at the young woman—no, not a woman, she reminded herself. Yvonnel was only a few years old, or at least, only a few years alive. She had used magic to age her physical body into that of a young drow woman. So much about her was magically created or enhanced, even her choice of eye color.

Lavender eyes, so rare, and so connected to the greatest heretic of them all: Drizzt Do'Urden.

"What do you know?" Quenthel asked, cutting short Sos'Umptu, who was about to ask the same thing.

"I know that Matron Mez'Barris Armgo is not stupid. She'll not play her hand, one side or the other, until she has gathered much more information. She doesn't need the blessing of Lolth. She has an army at her command second only to our own—and only second because we have enlisted the eight hundred warriors of the Blaspheme as Baenre recruits."

"You underestimate the power of the blessing of the Spider Queen," Sos'Umptu insisted.

"And you overestimate it," Yvonnel retorted. "And if you don't believe that, you are a fool to come here. House Baenre spat in Lolth's face on the field under the open sky. We stole her driders from her chosen Melarni army, so you believe. We stole her driders from the very state of being driders. Do you entertain foolish hopes that there is a way to come back from that ultimate heresy in the eyes of the Spider Queen?"

Sos'Umptu didn't answer other than to stare—and to lick her lips. She stopped that as soon as she realized it, not wanting to let Yvonnel recognize her profound dread.

"Why *are* you here?" Yvonnel asked.

"I tend the chapel. That is my—"

"You lead the Fane of Quarvelsharess in the West Wall," Yvonnel corrected. "That is all."

"Priestess Myrineyl tends the Baenre chapel now," Quenthel said. "After your threats against me and this house on the surface, I elevated her to First Priestess of House Baenre."

"Tending the chapel of Lolth?"

"No."

"No? Not to Lolth?" Sos'Umptu asked incredulously. "Then to which god? Corellon of the elves? Or one of the dwarven gods for your new friend, King Bruenor, who murdered our mother? Are we all to grow beards?"

"Not to Lolth," Yvonnel answered, obviously interjecting before Quenthel exploded back at Sos'Umptu. "We'll see if a goddess or god earns the right to our chapel."

"Then what? To whom?"

"To Menzoberranzan," Quenthel answered. "A place of meditation and prayer to the city's hopes at the time of its inception."

"The fairy tale," Sos'Umptu returned, barely able to spit out the words. "The illithid trick!"

"I warn you now, sister," Quenthel stated very deliberately. "Once, I allowed you to speak to me in such a manner and walk away unscathed. I did so out of respect for your work in House Baenre these many decades. Once, but not again."

"Because you are the Matron Mother? But isn't that a position sanctioned by—"

"Because I am in command here, in this house," Quenthel cut her short. "And if you are so determined to threaten the house, I am bound to act. You came here with news that the war is escalating. Do you wish to leave of your own volition, or as a casualty of that war?"

Sos'Umptu looked from Quenthel to Yvonnel, and there, in the woman's lavender eyes—the eyes so akin to those of Drizzt Do'Urden!—the High Priestess of Lolth, the mistress of Arach-Tinilith, the once and longtime first priestess of House Baenre, the leader and first priestess of the Fane of Quarvelsharess saw without any doubt that if she spoke out of turn in the next moment, Yvonnel would kill her.

And Sos'Umptu knew without any doubt that Yvonnel could do it.

"You were given the Fane of Quarvelsharess by the generosity of House Baenre," Matron Mother Quenthel stated. "You were given your seat on the Ruling Council, the ninth seat added just for you, by my own beneficence. I have not taken either from you, and will not—not yet, at least. I expect the Ruling Council will be convened in the near future, before the war begins in full, if that is our fate, and know well that I will hear your every word on that important occasion, dear sister."

"That is not a threat," Yvonnel added, surprising both Sos'Umptu and, quite obviously, Quenthel. "We will all have to pick sides, it would seem. You are ally or you are enemy."

"But we need not pick right now?" Sos'Umptu asked, more than a little confused.

"We have not asked that of you," said Quenthel. "And we have not taken your outrage on the surface to heart. Indeed, it was reasonable outrage given that you, unlike we two, are not privileged with the actual memories of Matron Mother Yvonnel the Eternal, and given, well, the work of our entire lives previous. Trust me, trust us, when we tell you that this was not an easy choice for those who have risen under the shadow of the Spider Queen. I am Matron Mother because of Matron Mother Baenre's centuries of accumulating power within the framework of Lady Lolth's designs. Do you think I do not understand that?"

"You could have just joined with Matron Zhindia up there," Sos'Umptu said, her voice calm and quiet. "You could have assumed command of the entire demon, drow, and drider force, and paid back that wretched King Bruenor for all the harm he has caused us, for taking our great Matron Mother Baenre from us."

The Matron Mother sighed at Sos'Umptu's seeming lack of understanding. "No, I could not," Quenthel answered. "Not after I examined the memories of Yvonnel the Eternal. Not after I learned so viscerally and intimately that it has all been a lie."

"And now you will plunge the city into war, and half the drow or more may pay with their blood," said Sos'Umptu. "The other way was easier, I say, and equally just."

"No. Nor would Matron . . ." Quenthel paused and shook her head. "Nor would Zhindia," she corrected, "have accepted the alliance you propose. Not there and not here."

"Matron Zhindia is proud, but she is not stupid."

"I think her quite stupid," Yvonnel interjected. "But that is not the point. Matron Zhindia is a zealot, devout to all her faults, and Lolth would not accept us now because we cannot accept her."

What bothered Sos'Umptu the most in that moment of overt sacrilege was the smirk that grew on the face of Minolin Fey, a nobody, a minor priestess from a dying house who had been fortunate enough to be impregnated by Archmage Gromph, and more fortunate still when Lolth had blessed that pregnancy and had given to the ungrateful child, Yvonnel, such a tremendous gift as her namesake's memories and wisdom.

"You may visit the chapel before you leave," Quenthel told her. "First Priestess Myrineyl is doing wonderful work with it."

"No, she cannot," Yvonnel corrected, and she and Quenthel looked at each other. "Sos'Umptu is not ready to open her eyes and heart to our cause. She will simply make mental note of our improvements and use the images against you in the next meeting of the Ruling Council."

Sos'Umptu bit back her intended retort. She thought to question the true reason for her removal as first priestess of House Baenre, but she realized that she couldn't make her case. Myrineyl was Quenthel's daughter, but even if nepotism was the real reason, how could these heretics expect a devout Lolthian priestess like Sos'Umptu to continue to serve them in any capacity such as that?

"Whether she visits the chapel or not, Sos'Umptu will take great care at the next Ruling Council to listen more than she speaks. Isn't that right?"

Sos'Umptu didn't respond.

"You believe that everything that happens in Menzoberranzan is bent by the favor of Lolth," Quenthel reminded her. "And so, if we prevail, then obviously that is part of Lolth's plan. She is, after all, the Lady of Chaos, and what might please her more than to have an underground movement of zealots fighting to return her place of honor in Menzoberranzan?"

"It is the same dilemma as we found with Drizzt Do'Urden," added Yvonnel. "Lolth favored him. She loved him and all the chaos he wrought. Did he ever genuflect before her?"

"I do not believe he did," Quenthel replied. "And yet, he is still alive! And you, Sos'Umptu, were among us when we let Drizzt walk away free from Menzoberranzan. How do you reconcile that choice?"

"It was *not* my choice."

"No, it was mine, and Yvonnel's. Did you hear any arguments from the handmaidens? Did Lolth scold you in your prayers for our decision to free him?"

Sos'Umptu held her words. She realized that these two were getting an advantage over her here, were raising inconsistencies and unexpected twists to shake her off balance, and so they had. She wasn't about to let them see that.

"Visit the new chapel of House Baenre," Quenthel decided. Pointedly, she looked at Yvonnel, who should have had no say against the

Matron Mother, and Yvonnel nodded her agreement. "But do not forget what is expected of you should the Ruling Council convene. Because you are Baenre—*only* because you are Baenre—I am offering you time to meditate and pray on these swiftly moving events. We were rivals by birth, but never really so. I have always respected you, and always valued your advice. Again, I recognize that you cannot understand as clearly as we two sitting here before you. Mother's memories belong to me and to Yvonnel as if they were our own—indeed, they are our own because of the magic of the illithids, not Lolth."

"Or the deception of the illithids?" Sos'Umptu dared to interject.

"We will see," said Quenthel. "You are free to go, to the chapel or back to the Fane of Quarvelsharess, or wherever else you think wise. And you are free to return. You have my ear. I hope that I have yours."

Sos'Umptu gave a little bow and spun on her heel, quickly leaving the audience chamber.

She did pass by the Baenre chapel, but gave it only a quick glance, for Myrineyl was in there, and she could see with just that cursory look that many of the decorations she had so lovingly crafted in that place over the decades had been removed, particularly the spider murals and reliefs.

Sos'Umptu forced down her anger and resisted the urge to go in and assault the daughter of Matron Mother Quenthel.

"WHAT ARE YOU THINKING?" YVONNEL ASKED MINOLIN Fey, who was chewing her lip as she stood beside her powerful daughter and Matron Mother Quenthel.

"Do you trust her?"

"Of course not," Quenthel answered. "My sister's fealty is to Lolth and Lolth alone. From her youngest days, she was known as the most devout Baenre of all, even more diligent in her duties to the Spider Queen than our mother. She was never as cruel as Vendes and Bladen'Kerst, but I believe that Lolth favored Sos'Umptu over them, over all of us. Never once in all her years have I known her to take any action that would be contrary to Lolth's desires."

"My mother has spoken often about your . . . our, House Baenre's lost priestesses Vendes and Bladen'Kerst," Minolin Fey said, struggling to keep her thoughts clear and obviously more than a little nervous here. "They were among the most feared of Matron Mother Baenre's daughters." She sucked in her breath as she finished the thought, her eyes going wide and staring at Matron Mother Quenthel, clearly fearing reprisal for that last statement, which could very well have been interpreted as a slight.

"I never had the pleasure of meeting them," said Yvonnel.

Quenthel laughed heartily. "There was no pleasure missed, I assure you. I doubt that either of them would approve of our actions, and likely, they would have fought us on the surface. Of course, if Bladen'Kerst were alive, she would have succeeded Triel to this very chair as Matron Mother, and she, not I, might have been given the memories of our mother. And then none of this would have happened."

"Do you think those memories would have turned her heart as they have turned yours?" Yvonnel asked.

The wizard Velkryst laughed at the question, and when all turned to him, he explained. "I remember a day when no one would have dared ask such a question as that to the Matron Mother of House Baenre—I don't look back on that time fondly, of course, but I remember it."

"True enough," Quenthel agreed. "But then, if Bladen'Kerst had been sitting here and Minolin Fey had listed Vendes as the cruelest of all, Bladen'Kerst's mission for a hundred years thereafter would have been proving Minolin Fey wrong."

Again, Minolin Fey sucked in her breath.

"Be at ease, sister," Quenthel assured her. "You did not insult me, far from it. And to answer you," she said, turning to Yvonnel, "no, I do not see any conversion of Bladen'Kerst, or of Vendes, as a possibility. Perhaps if Triel had still held this chair, she would have come to our way of thinking, though I doubt she would have had the courage to so discard Lolth. But Bladen'Kerst? No. She was too far gone, had committed too many heinous crimes. She wasn't devoted to Lolth with the same depth as Sos'Umptu, but it was clear that both she and Vendes truly enjoyed the power Lolth gave to them, particularly the power to torture others. They reveled in it."

"Then I hope there are not too many like them throughout the city," Minolin Fey quietly put in.

Yvonnel didn't miss Minolin Fey's sheepishness here, nor the hopeful fact that Quenthel had referred to her as "sister." Though she was Baenre by her union with Gromph, that was the first time Yvonnel had seen any of the bloodline Baenres refer to Minolin Fey in a familial way.

That, she decided, was a good and important thing.

Quenthel snorted at Minolin Fey's remark, but Yvonnel was quick to interject. "That is a fine point and a critical question before us. Does a society—a closed and parochial society with little experience outside a secluded cavern—that has been trained for many generations, many centuries, in the way of Lolth, the way of chaos and cruelty and with the near absence of mercy, have enough people willing to step away from that darkness and unlearn almost everything that has been whipped into them collectively, as it was whipped into their parents and grandparents before them? Was the cruelty, the depravity even, of Bladen'Kerst and Vendes a matter of their hearts or a matter of resignation to simply not care, to simply make the most of the vile and inescapable circumstances surrounding them? I think that's an important question for us to remember as we go forward in trying to convince our fellow drow of better possibilities."

In that moment, Yvonnel considered the woman sitting next to her, the Matron Mother who had helped her create the great heresy and begin the turn away from Lolth. Was it a sincere and redemptive change of heart for Quenthel, or simply her easiest way out of the trap Matron Zhindia Melarn had built around the Matron Mother?

Yvonnel reminded herself that only a few years before, Matron Mother Quenthel had filled Menzoberranzan with demon hordes in order to stabilize her rule in a tumultuous time. Quenthel had just claimed that her sisters Bladen'Kerst and Vendes had traveled too far down the road of Lolth's evil ways, but had either of them caused more misery than the demon-bringer Quenthel?

Yvonnel didn't discount the power of the stunning revelations of the shared memories between herself, Quenthel, and Yvonnel the

Eternal, or the effect the exploration of those memories had enacted upon her, and hopefully upon Quenthel. But Yvonnel did not believe that she would have ever been capable of filling Menzoberranzan's streets with demon hordes as Quenthel had done.

Chaos begets order, she thought but did not dare say, for that had been Quenthel's justification for her litany of commands to bring forth the demon hordes, Yvonnel had later learned.

Yes, Minolin Fey had, no doubt inadvertently, asked a most profound and important question as the battle for the heart and soul of Menzoberranzan began to take shape: Could drow, could any society raised so completely within the web of Lolth, truly find and accept a new and better way of existence?

Could the woman sitting next to her, her co-conspirator against Lolth, the Matron Mother of Menzoberranzan who had recently filled the city's streets with hordes of demons in order to hold tight her power, truly convert?

"I do believe that you will find more men readily accepting the change than women," Velkryst said, drawing Yvonnel from her private concerns. "We were most often the ones on the wrong side of your Lolth-inspired snake-headed whips, after all."

She noticed Quenthel's scowl—one that the woman quickly seemed to mellow into a casual chuckle. This wizard Velkryst was cleverer than Yvonnel had thought, she realized in that moment. He was feeling around the edges of his relationship with Quenthel here. He had lived most of his life in House Xorlarrin, a powerful clan that was far more generous to men with regard to rank and station than any other houses. It had not been Velkryst's choice to come and join House Baenre and serve as Quenthel's patron. No, as with most such maneuvers by the more powerful houses, that arrangement had been made between Quenthel and Matron Zeerith Xorlarrin. While no doubt benefiting in stature by the move, Velkryst certainly had been given no say in the matter. He would go to live in House Baenre and serve Quenthel's every bedtime desire, and hopefully sire her children in order to tighten the bond between what was then the Third House, Xorlarrin-Do'Urden, and the First House, Baenre.

Had he found Quenthel attractive? Yvonnel wondered. Had he desired her in any way? If not, was the trade-off still worth it to him? He had, after all, likely sired the future Matron Mother of Menzoberranzan in Myrineyl.

Or was it simply a matter of resignation on his part, for such was life in the city of the drow? Had he ever been in love? Had *any* in Menzoberranzan ever truly known that most wonderful and powerful emotion of all?

Yvonnel had to think back to the earliest memories of her grandmother and namesake to feel any hints of such emotion in Yvonnel the Eternal. And even then, none of those memories matched the intensity she had felt when she had looked upon and come to know Drizzt Do'Urden.

"THEY ARE NOT MAKING A LIE OF MY LIFE," SOS'UMPTU Baenre told Matron Shakti Hunzrin soon after leaving House Baenre. She had not gone to the Hunzrin compound, in the section of Menzoberranzan known as Eastmyr—that would have been far too dangerous, for it was widely known that the Melarni were often there, including Matron Zhindia herself. Instead, Sos'Umptu had crossed through the Braeryn and past the fungi farm on the easternmost end of the great cavern, then out to the Isle of Rothé on the small lake of Donigarten. The Hunzrins controlled this area of Menzoberranzan, giving them far more power than their rank as the Eleventh House would indicate.

The meeting had been prearranged.

"Need it result in that?" Matron Shakti replied, surprising Sos'Umptu.

The Baenre leaned back in her seat and regarded the matron for a few moments. Shakti's closest ally was Matron Mez'Barris of the powerful Second House, the biggest rival of House Baenre, and she was also a frequent guest of Matron Zhindia Melarn.

"Why have you requested this audience?" Shakti asked. "When First Priestess Charri returned from her efforts in the Braeryn and told me of your request, I admit I was taken by surprise. It is not often that

Baenres and Hunzrins meet. Is Bregan D'aerthe finally failing House Baenre, then?"

Sos'Umptu resisted the urge to sharply retort. The Hunzrins were to the other houses, certainly to Mez'Barris Armgo, as Jarlaxle's mercenary band was to House Baenre, serving as merchants beyond the confines of Menzoberranzan. Shakti's question was absurd, of course, and the matron knew it, for Bregan D'aerthe had never been stronger, their bond with House Baenre never deeper.

Indeed, Bregan D'aerthe had recaptured Luskan from the hordes unleashed by Hunzrin trade.

"This is not about trade, Matron," she quietly answered. "It is about preserving Menzoberranzan."

"The City of Spiders," Shakti pointedly replied. "The city of Lolth. There is only one family trying to change that, it would seem."

"That is where you are mistaken," Sos'Umptu dared to point out.

"Ah, yes, House Xorlarrin, or should we call it Do'Urden now? If House Baenre is counting on Matron Zeerith Xorlarrin, then they . . . you, should prepare to be disappointed. At the first sign of defeat, she will preserve herself and her house, whatever gifts Matron Mother Quenthel might have bestowed upon her these last years. Matron Zeerith has ever been known as a windsock."

Sos'Umptu glanced at Charri, who stood to the side. Charri arched her eyebrows and shrugged, and even gave a little shake of her head when the normally reserved Sos'Umptu returned an angry glare.

"Can we stop with this inane probing?" Sos'Umptu asked directly. "Matron Zeerith is a windsock? What, then, of Matron Shakti Hunzrin?"

"Careful, High Priestess," Shakti warned.

"I sit on the Ruling Council, have you forgotten?" Sos'Umptu retorted. She knew she had the high ground here and the truth, for Shakti Hunzrin's own history was one of double-dealing, even against Lolth. "I am Baenre—yes, still, even after my argument with Matron Mother Quenthel on the fields above. I come to you in good faith."

"To betray your house."

"No, to begin the process of negotiation that we both know is the only way to save Menzoberranzan from catastrophe."

"To betray your sister, then, that you can assume the throne of House Baenre."

"Again, no," she ground out. "That is nothing I would ever want. I am the high priestess of the Fane of Quarvelsharess, the ninth seat on the Ruling Council. My duty is to Lolth above all—above family, above my house, above my very life. I have the ear of House Baenre as you have the ear of House Barrison Del'Armgo, and most importantly, of House Melarn."

"Matron Zhindia Melarn is not one to seek counsel or accept advice."

"True enough, but Matron Mez'Barris is. Without the forces of House Barrison Del'Armgo, Matron Zhindia cannot win. We can both agree that House Baenre has gone astray, but you above all know that such crimes against the Spider Queen can be forgiven, even rewarded if the end result is pleasing to Lolth."

"So, you intend to bring House Baenre back into the favor of Lolth. Why, then, this meeting? Why do you need me?"

"We haven't the time to do that and prevent a civil war."

"Tell me, then, priestess," Shakti asked, "is it Matron Mother Quenthel who needs to be convinced, or is it that strange creature Yvonnel who whispers into her ear?"

"Yvonnel, I would guess. But let me remind you before you entertain any thoughts of convincing with extreme means that Yvonnel was blessed in the womb by the avatar of Lolth."

"Convincing with extreme means?"

"Need I say it?"

"Assassination," answered Shakti, saying it for her. "Do you truly believe that you can accomplish your ends short of such measures?"

"She was blessed in the womb by the avatar of Lolth," Sos'Umptu repeated.

"If you insist," Shakti replied, her voice sounding rather like the purr of a cat that had cornered a mouse. "So, you don't want a war, you don't want to decapitate House Baenre, and you wish to remain devoted to Lady Lolth. Can you see why I'm still not sure what you think to accomplish?"

"I wish to manage a truce," Sos'Umptu replied. "One that keeps

House Baenre and House Barrison Del'Armgo in their current status, and elevates House Melarn to the third position. After her defeat on the surface, her failure with the heretics, and the general battering her house has taken in the more recent conflicts, Matron Zhindia would be a fool to refuse."

"She's the least of your problems with such an idea," Shakti said. "Everyone saw the heresy. Every house in the city knows now that House Baenre is vulnerable, that certainly after stealing driders from the Spider Queen they are not currently in Lolth's favor. And Matron Mez'Barris Armgo has never been a friend to House Baenre. Do you expect her to just accept your offers when considering the very real possibility that she could become the Matron Mother of Menzoberranzan, and Barrison Del'Armgo the First House?

"And what of the current Matron Mother?" Shakti went on. "Do you really believe that she will accept the elevation of House Melarn? You see everything in terms of Lolth—or think you do—but your sister better understands the levers of practical power. Matron Zhindia in the Third House would outrage Matron Zeerith and likely cost House Baenre a valuable ally. Matron Zhindia in the Third House will be seen as the victor in this rift, and House Baenre will be shown to be afraid of House Melarn. That, too, would soon enough lead to war, and one less favorable to House Baenre."

"Not if House Baenre is brought back from their actions."

"Redeemed from their blasphemy, you mean. Or perhaps we should better call it desecration, since Lolth's driders were so violated and vandalized."

Sos'Umptu started to reply but wound up simply exhaling, her shoulders slumping.

"Let me be clear here, High Priestess of the Quarvelsharess," Matron Shakti said in quiet and even tones, "House Hunzrin doesn't want this war any more than you do. That is why I sent Charri to the Braeryn when we learned of the impending ambush. That is why she saved the life of the Mizzrym noble. War is bad for business."

"But you want House Barrison Del'Armgo as the First House."

"I don't care either way. House Hunzrin is not the enemy of House

Baenre. I worked alongside both Matron Mother Triel and Archmage Gromph on important issues in the not-too-distant past. I hold no ill feelings toward Matron Mother Quenthel or even that strange Yvonnel creature. And what happened on that field above, while shocking, is between those two and Lady Lolth. No handmaiden of the Spider Queen, no answer of prayers by Lolth, has instructed me to go to war with House Baenre."

"But Bregan D'aerthe defeated your allies up above, your trading partners," Sos'Umptu reminded.

Shakti replied with a laugh. "Consider it from my perspective," she said. "Jarlaxle and his cadre of useless men have all that they can handle with the troublesome city of Luskan now, and with the many humans and dwarves and others who scrutinize his every movement. All of Bregan D'aerthe is up there—do you expect any of them to return here anytime soon? Who will House Baenre now call upon for trade outside the city, even trade up to the surface lands controlled by Jarlaxle and his friends?"

So concerned was she with the issue of obedience to Lolth, Sos'Umptu found herself caught completely off guard by that practical truth—and it was indeed a truth. In a roundabout way, the war up above had gone perfectly for House Hunzrin, even though their trading partners among the surface dwellers had been soundly routed and Matron Zhindia driven away in defeat.

"How do we avoid a war?" she asked the matron.

"We almost certainly don't," Shakti admitted.

"And thus, when it comes to us, what side will House Hunzrin favor?"

"All of them."

"Not whichever is seen in the favor of Lolth?"

Shakti laughed again. "That, I expect, is more the concern of the high priestess of the Quarvelsharess. But as one who has been on both sides of the Spider Queen's favor, as you previously alluded to, let me offer this one insight: Lolth doesn't much care about all the little rituals and acts of fealty and supplication that people like you fret over every waking moment. And Lolth likely cares less about who prevails in this war: Baenre, Barrison Del'Armgo, or Melarn. What Lolth cares about most of all, what thrills her and excites her, isn't the mountaintop, but the chaos of the scrambling creatures trying to get there."

As with Drizzt Do'Urden, Sos'Umptu thought. She looked upon Shakti Hunzrin with a benign expression painted on her face, very deliberately suppressing a snarl.

So many heretics . . .

"YOU HAVE MET WITH OUR FRIEND?" QUENTHEL ASKED Yvonnel when they were alone.

"I have."

"But you did not know of this attack on the Blaspheme. Do you think it freelancing by opportunistic others?"

"I knew nothing about it," Yvonnel said. "Likely it was just that, a strike against the Blaspheme in order to hopefully gain some favor with Lolth."

"The former driders of our Blaspheme are formidable," Quenthel said.

"Hardened," agreed Yvonnel. "Many have spent centuries in the Abyss. They fear nothing that can be done to them in this world, I am sure. And they seek battle. The large woman, Mal'a'voselle, was the leader of the group when they were driders in the service of Matron Zhindia. She seems no less eager for battle now. More so, I believe, for she can now turn her wrath against the forces of her eternal torturer."

"What did we do?" Quenthel asked, shaking her head, a question that both she and Yvonnel had asked many times since they had created the magical web to dispel the curse of abomination.

"What we needed to. And it's a good thing, because we're going to need them, and soon," Yvonnel explained. "It seems that Matron Zhindia is ready to begin the fight."

"House Do'Urden?" Quenthel said, suggesting the target. "Is that what Kyrnill revealed to you?"

"We have three nights."

CHAPTER 3

What Is Love?

Yvonnel Baenre lay back on her bed, trying to make sense of the world. Trying, somehow, to attach her unique life to the experiences of those around her. She had only been alive in this physical form, a female drow, for six years, but her memories were those of two thousand years of experience as a drow woman. Through magic she had aged her physical body into that of an adult. Through magic she had altered her appearance to that which she desired, right down to the lavender eyes she had given herself in tribute to a brave rogue who had so completely intrigued her: Drizzt Do'Urden.

But what had she missed? Even with the memories of Yvonnel the Eternal, the months of mental training under the tutelage of that horrible illithid, what did she not remember? What did she not know of the drow currently existing about her?

For so long now, she had tried to find the answers in the memories that had been given to her by the illithids, but the revelations she had found on the surface had, in an unexpected manner, shown her more of the ignorance in her experience than the knowledge. When Kimmuriel had led her and Quenthel through the memories they shared in a different way, in a manner that had dispatched the cumulative numbness to crimes and sins that had walked Yvonnel the Eternal down a terrible path, he had inadvertently revealed to Yvonnel the trap of memory without the consideration of perspective and the proper context of the surrounding world.

How was she to truly understand the powers that held her fellow Menzoberranzan drow in thrall if she could not truly understand or appreciate the training, particularly in their upbringing, that had created the warped and vicious perspective?

She had been born with full awareness. She thought of her earliest days alive in this physical form, when she had been suckling at Minolin Fey's breast, when she had been helpless and in the arms of her mother.

Her loving mother?

Had she ever felt the love of her mother?

Yvonnel recalled that her namesake had, but it was a memory so distant that it would take her a tremendous effort to fully recover it in any meaningful way to help her solve the riddles now. And even if she managed it, she wasn't sure that it would prove relevant in this time, for the drow of Menzoberranzan—this Menzoberranzan and not the one of young Yvonnel the Eternal some two millennia before—had been raised in a very different manner.

In this Menzoberranzan, Lady Lolth was ever present, particularly in those earliest hours, days, and tendays of life. Everything good was attributed to her and everything bad was accounted as justified punishment for those who did not truly appreciate and love her.

Love.

That word rang in her head. Was there love in Menzoberranzan, other than the professed adoration of Lolth? Was there joy in Menzoberranzan other than the cruel satisfaction of defeating an enemy?

The closest thing the ancient-young Yvonnel could make of it on a personal level came in the form of a lavender-eyed heretic she had met. She had the body of an adult woman, and couldn't deny the attraction she had felt to Drizzt. It was more than lust, she knew. She had been attracted to several drow over the last couple of years, and to more than one human, as well, including Catti-brie, Drizzt's wife!

But with Drizzt, it was more than physical desire. Much more. Yvonnel wanted to know him, every bit of him. Physically, emotionally, intellectually, Yvonnel wanted to devour him, to celebrate him, his courage and determination and loyalty and . . . all of it. She wanted to make him a better person and didn't doubt for a moment that he would make her a better and more complete drow.

Was that love?

She didn't know, in no small part because in scouring the memories of the adult Yvonnel the Eternal, she couldn't find anything—nothing at all!—to hint at the concept of love.

She knew what was in the eyes of Drizzt and Catti-brie when they looked upon each other, though, and the tenderness when she saw them kissing, and the respect when she heard them arguing. It would have been a very Lolthian thing for her to simply remove Catti-brie from the equation, mercilessly and covertly, to take Drizzt as her own, but the idea had not and could not truly gain traction in Yvonnel's thoughts and heart. She could never do something like that! Not simply because of the sheer immorality of murder, but because how could she possibly claim to love someone if she brought him such pain?

So yes, she admitted to herself, lying on that cushiony bed in her room in House Baenre. Yes, in the lavender eyes of Drizzt Do'Urden, she had discovered love.

And it was a beautiful thing.

And even if she couldn't explore it with him now, and perhaps never might, it was a beautiful thing.

A freeing thing.

A source of joy.

She did not see that in those around her here in Menzoberranzan. Not in the eyes of Velkryst and Quenthel. Not in the eyes of Gromph and Minolin Fey, who had together created her.

Not in the eyes of Minolin Fey when she had held Yvonnel to her breast?

An unexpected burst of emotions rose up within the woman in that moment of terrible revelation, a level of sadness she did not know she possessed. She was curious, too, and confused, and angry, so angry.

She was wearing only a simple silken nightgown, certainly nothing appropriate for a noble of House Baenre to wear in public, but she didn't even grab a robe as she rolled off the bed and stormed for the door, then out into the hallway. She passed several patrolling sentries without a word, ignoring their shocked expressions and how they fell aside and stiffened their backs against the walls, as if trying to melt into the stone to get out of her way.

She lifted her hand to knock on Minolin Fey's door, then changed her mind and threw a spell of opening on the door instead, with such power that the door flew in, swinging hard on its hinges, and banged loudly against the doorstops set in the wall. Across the large room, she saw the curtains of Minolin Fey's canopy bed flutter from the commotion of the woman leaping up in surprise behind them.

In Yvonnel went, and, holding on to her outrage at being so cheated of the most important moments of love anyone might ever know, she threw her emotions into her next spell and took satisfaction in the sheer power of the door slamming closed behind her. And more satisfaction in seeing Minolin Fey so obviously scrambling behind that canopy.

"We are not under attack, you fool!" Yvonnel shouted when she heard the drow woman, her mother, chanting a defensive spell. "It is just me, Yvonnel. Your daughter."

The bed went quiet, then the canopy facing the door pulled away, Minolin Fey peeking out.

She disappeared back behind the curtain, fumbling about, then came forth wrapped in a blanket.

"What do you wish of me, priestess?" Minolin Fey asked, standing before the bed.

"Don't call me that," Yvonnel replied. "And don't fear me. Please, just sit." She motioned at the bed and Minolin Fey backed up a step, pushed the curtain aside, and sat on the edge.

"What would you have me call you?"

"Yvonnel?" she replied, trying to bite back her anger and keep her voice calm here. "Yve? Some other nickname? . . . Daughter?"

Minolin Fey gave her a most confused and plaintive look, one that nearly broke her heart in half.

"Mother," Yvonnel said. "May I call you mother?"

"You sit on the throne beside Matron Mother Quenthel as her equal," said Minolin Fey. "You may call me whatever you—"

"No!" Yvonnel shouted, and she patted her hands in the air and took a deep breath and more quietly repeated, "No." Another deep breath. "I did not come to you from the throne, or to represent the throne, or as someone higher in rank or stature or power or anything else."

"What do you want of me?" Minolin Fey begged.

"The truth," Yvonnel replied before she even realized she was answering. "The truth."

"What truth?"

"Did you love me, Mother?"

Minolin Fey's eyes widened.

"When I was born and you took me into your arms, did you love me?"

When her mother hesitated, Yvonnel felt her eyes tearing up.

"I wanted to," Minolin Fey said. "And I did, but then . . ." She paused, shaking her head, fumbling with her words and, obviously, with her emotions. "I was afraid of you, of what they had done to you. I was afraid of what they would do to me. You were born knowing more of the world than I did! What was I to do for you? What was I to teach you? And in House Baenre, where you were surrounded by the greatest powers of Menzoberranzan, how was I to protect you? Or myself?"

Yvonnel walked over to stand before the seated woman, staring down at her.

"What was I to do for you?" Minolin Fey asked again, her voice barely a whisper.

"Love me," Yvonnel said, just as quietly, and a tear rolled down her cheek.

Minolin Fey half stood, took Yvonnel by the hands, and pulled her down to the bed to sit beside her. "I did!" she said. "I did! I do! My little child . . . I was scared, I admit. You were the daughter of Gromph Baenre, the archmage of Menzoberranzan. You were the living avatar of Lady Lolth, so we were told at the Festival of the Founding only a few years ago when you were still in my womb.

"I only had you as my daughter for a matter of months," Minolin Fey said again, shaking her head. "Not even, for in those earliest times, the Baenres took you from me repeatedly, making me little more than a wetnurse. And when you outgrew me physically with your magic, I was relieved, I admit. But also . . ."

She paused and lifted a hand to stroke the wet cheek of Yvonnel.

"But also, my child, I was angry. Not at you, but at them. I felt robbed of being your mother, of having a daughter."

"Do you even know what that means?" Yvonnel asked, not sharply, not judgmentally.

"I think I do. I love my own mother," Minolin Fey told her. "And she loves me. Not for the power my birth brought to House Fey-Branche, but simply because of our bond—a bond I was too afraid to construct with you."

"Why?"

"Because I knew you wouldn't be mine long enough, that I wouldn't be able to deal with the heartbreak when you were taken from me, either by others or Lolth or by your own desires and the thousands of years of memories living inside you. It . . . it would hurt too much."

"I have not seen the type of love you describe," said Yvonnel. "I see Quenthel with Myrineyl and don't doubt that she cares about her daughter, though perhaps not *for* her daughter. There is a difference."

"Shh," Minolin Fey said. "Take care with your observations here in this house. And she is Matron Mother Quenth—"

"She is Quenthel, my aunt, my peer, my co-heretic," Yvonnel insisted. "I'm not afraid of her. I'm not afraid of any of them. I don't know that they can possibly take from me anything more than I take from myself by being afraid of them."

Minolin Fey stared at her in silence for a long while, then nodded. "Forgive me?"

"There's nothing to forgive," Yvonnel replied. "It was a different Menzoberranzan when I was born unto you. We need it to be a different Menzoberranzan and cannot go back to that."

"I don't want to go back to that."

"Then don't call me priestess. Don't bow to me. Don't lower your gaze from my own."

Minolin Fey thought for a moment, then nodded again.

"You cannot be my mother," Yvonnel said, and the older woman winced. "Not in that way. I was born with this gift—or maybe it's a curse. Who can know? But you can be my friend, and that, I want. I want you to trust me with your very life. I will not let you down. And I want—nay, and I *need* to be able to trust you in the same way."

She stared into her mother's eyes and couldn't miss the hesitance and fear there. She had no doubt that Minolin Fey was wondering if this was some test, some trap.

Yvonnel knew that she couldn't say anything to alleviate those fears, so she just leaned in and wrapped Minolin Fey in a great hug.

She found herself sobbing on her mother's shoulder.

She felt much better when Minolin Fey began sobbing on her shoulder as well.

CHAPTER 4

First Strike

You come with us," Voselly told Dininae. "You have proven your value to me. I would keep you at my side."

Dininae paused and stared at the hulking woman and the three other women surrounding her. They, too, were drow of another time, including her close associate Aleandra, another former member of House Amvas Tol. Perhaps all of these drow were from Voselly's house, for they certainly were all from her era—he knew that just by looking at them. There was something more formidable about them, not just in size but in the way they handled themselves, their posture and the steely set of their eyes. They had all been turned to driders millennia ago, in the earliest days of the city. Dininae wondered if they had been considered large among the population even then, for there weren't many in the city now the size of any of them. Malagdorl Armgo and some of his Armgo associates, perhaps, who were being bred for size and strength.

Voselly had told him that warrior women were commonplace back in her time, before the priesthood of Lolth had almost completely taken over Menzoberranzan's vocations for female drow.

Dininae was a bit intimidated here, but he shrugged that off, thinking that having this group around him probably ensured his safety from the more obvious enemies.

He nodded and fell in with the women. Voselly led them out of the Baenre main hall to the lowest dungeons of the great house. There, Baenre handlers moved them to the front of the line, sending them as the first team into the deep, long tunnel that reached north and down from the Qu'ellarz'orl, the high plateau section of the city upon which many of the ruling houses had been built. They crossed through many secured doorways, and past other doors that opened into corridors to various locations, like Narbondel.

He thought of the towering timeclock as they walked for quite a while. For more than two hours by his estimation, they continued their march, at last coming to the northernmost end of the tunnel and a small circular chamber, where they were greeted by a Baenre contingent led by a tall man in black plate armor wielding a magnificently decorated two-bladed sword.

"Weapon Master Andzrel," Voselly greeted him with a bow.

"You are properly armed and prepared?" the Baenre nobleman asked.

"Always," said Voselly. "And eager."

"Priestess Yvonnel asks that you temper that eagerness with the reminder that you will be fighting fellow drow here," Andzrel said.

Dininae perked up at that, caught by surprise. Why would Yvonnel care?

"The sleeping poison in your quarrels is more potent than normal," Andzrel told them. "Hopefully it will prove sufficient to lay low many of our enemies. The more who can be dealt with nonlethally, the better."

"Are you telling us to be kind?" Voselly asked, and the Baenre weapon master laughed.

"No," he said. "You do what you need to do if the attack comes. Do remember, however, that we all have to live with the consequences of these coming battles."

The former drider nodded. Behind them in the tunnel, Dininae noted the torchlight of the next group approaching.

Andzrel stepped aside and motioned to the door behind him, one of two exiting the chamber. The other was marked with the spider-shaped symbols of the Quarvelsharess, the Fane of the Goddess, the chapel presided over by First Priestess Sos'Umptu Baenre, but this one was blank, and indeed, led into another circular chamber, larger than the first but empty other than a burning brazier and a circle of power inscribed about the middle of the floor. As soon as they all had entered, Andzrel shut the door behind them.

The five milled about, unsure, until Voselly moved forward, daring to breach the enchanted circle. As soon as she had, a magical doorway appeared at the very center of the room, freestanding and seemingly made of shaped fog, glowing with energy.

A man's face appeared in the fog, elongating and shifting on unfelt winds.

"Step through," it told them.

Voselly shrugged and did so, disappearing from sight. The others followed, Dininae going last, and stepping through a connecting magical portal into a room that flooded him with old memories.

"The Do'Urden training gym," he whispered before he could consider the words.

"You know this place?" Voselly asked.

"No, no," Dininae stuttered. "Well, yes, I have heard it described in my days in Menzoberranzan, for this was the arena of a great weapon master, Zaknafein Do'Urden."

"It just looks like any arena," another of the group said. "Every noble house has at least one. I have heard that Barrison Del'Armgo has no less than seven of them."

Dininae realized that he hadn't been very convincing there, and he breathed more easily at the approach of two drow, a man and a woman.

"I am Ravel Xorlarrin Do'Urden," the young man said.

Hearing this stranger use his surname was unsettling to Dininae, but he hid it well.

"Son of Matron Zeerith, elderboy of House Do'Urden," Ravel continued. He certainly looked the part, dressed in lavish purple robes, his *piwafwi* cloak tied with a fine silver chain. "This is my sister, First Priestess Saribel. We have wards and spies set about the streets beyond this compound. You and those coming in behind you will remain here in this arena until needed."

"Then you will be prepared with defensive spells and brought out to ambush points we have determined," Saribel added. "Do you understand?"

"We have been properly informed of our role here," Voselly answered.

Another group of five came through the portal then.

"Spread the word among your warriors of the mighty Blaspheme," Saribel generously said. "We think you will not be waiting long."

With a bow, the siblings turned and left. When they passed through the arena door, a curious Dininae noted another figure out there in the hallway, a hunched and gaunt man leaning on a wizard's staff topped with what appeared to be a hand and wearing robes Dininae surely knew.

The robes of the archmage of Menzoberranzan.

That wasn't Gromph Baenre, though, and it took Dininae a short while to recall the identity of this one.

"Tsabrak Xorlarrin," he whispered. He wouldn't have made that connection had he not been in the house now ruled by that family, even though he had done some training under Tsabrak during his days at the Academy. Dininae, then Dinin Do'Urden, had trained at Melee-Magthere, but that included a rotation in Sorcere, where Tsabrak, even back then, had served as a master. Dininae realized quite pointedly then that he had to hope that Tsabrak, or any of the older Xorlarrins in this house, wouldn't recognize him.

He had been away from Menzoberranzan for a hundred years, but most living in the city were much older than that. Any hints that he was connected to House Do'Urden would easily lead to his unmasking, and nothing good would come of that, he believed. Every misery in Dininae's life had come from his younger brother, and he had been the one to put all of those terrible events in motion by murdering Nalfein, his older brother and the original elderboy of House Do'Urden, to facilitate his own ascension. That action had prevented the sacrifice of the newborn Drizzt.

Then Drizzt had brought shame on House Do'Urden, and then the downfall of House Do'Urden to the very same Baenre family Dininae now served in this second life. His own sister had been the one who had turned Dinin into a drider in a desperate attempt to somehow remove the eternal stain placed upon their house.

And Drizzt's dwarven friend had killed Dinin the drider in battle, completing the circle of misery.

So many conflicting emotions swirled in Dininae's mind as he stood in the training arena of House Do'Urden, strongest among them a sense of great loss. He told himself to blame Drizzt for the whole downward spiral, but there was little conviction in that inner dialogue.

He wanted to blame Vierna. He had been free of the typical Menzoberranzan games, after all, serving Jarlaxle in Bregan D'aerthe. But his sister had intervened and ruined any hope that he would again find a level of peace by sacrificing him to Lolth, turning him into a drider.

Even that seemed hollow to Dininae; he found no conviction in any grudge he might hold toward Vierna. She had been crazed with desperation, like all of them after the heresy of Drizzt. Dininae knew in his heart that he very likely would have done the same to her if the situation had been reversed!

Who, then, should he blame? Matron Malice? Certainly, to some extent.

But it wasn't enough to shield him from the awful truth that in the end, he was responsible for everything that had happened to him.

When the call came for the Blaspheme to move out, the former noble son of House Do'Urden was reminded of that truth with every familiar corridor and room they passed.

He exhaled a breath of sincere relief when the force exited the house and compound and moved out to predetermined positions in a region of tangled stalagmites known as Lolth's Web or along the ridge of the chasm called the Westrift. All of this was done under the cover of magical nondetection spells, even, at one point, with Dininae's team going in a line hand-to-shoulder, all of them invisible. They remained in sight of House Do'Urden's balconies, set against the West Wall, the compound in a clear defensive hunch, with magical lights filling the area before it, wizards and warriors on full display in their patrols.

That was the point, he understood. They had to look ready, but not invulnerable.

The light of Narbondel rose to its brightest cycle, then darkened almost to nothing, more than half a day passing, before the hand signal of a coming force passed along the Blaspheme ranks, strike team to strike team.

Soon after, Voselly pointed out some movement to the other four, a group of drow slipping from shadow to shadow, moving in the direction of House Do'Urden.

Dininae felt an unexpected rage rising within him, an almost primal anger at the thought of someone attacking his home—even though House Do'Urden most certainly was not in any way his place any longer. It didn't matter, not in that moment. Even though he rationally understood the truth of it, he felt like the son of House Do'Urden, fighting for his home.

And in that same moment, Dininae understood who was to blame for the consequences that had led him to this place: the same being that had structured Menzoberranzan society, that had incited a young and ambitious secondboy to murder his older brother.

He was to blame.

And *Lolth* was to blame.

She had brought him to his fall. She had tormented him in the Abyss. She had wrecked everything, for him, for Menzoberranzan, for every drow he had ever known.

He gripped his sword and dagger now, for he had gone back to the weapon combination he had most used in his former existence. He thought of Nalfein, of Drizzt, and mostly of Zaknafein, recalling the many lessons.

He felt the blood squeezing out of his hands, so hard was he clutching those hilts . . .

Hand signals began to repeat down the line, warrior to warrior, as they stood in the stone forest of Lolth's Web. Dininae did his part, too, and focused his attention on the area of interest, soon enough spotting the creeping force of their enemies.

Shadow to shadow they went, but not with too much care, as they were still some way from the front of the Do'Urden compound, which was built right into the West Wall. Clearly these attackers remained confident that the element of surprise was on their side.

The large force moved past, oblivious to the hidden Blaspheme strike teams, and following orders, Voselly and the other leaders let them get ahead, let them get within sight and range of House Do'Urden.

Advance, but quietly. Be at ease, Voselly's hands signed, and that, too, was repeated among all the Blaspheme. *Let House Do'Urden take the first volley and respond.*

Barely had that message been relayed than the first explosions flashed and sounded, lightning and fireballs raining down with sudden fury from the West Wall to the front ranks of the advancing attackers before they even crossed the intersecting avenue known as Blade Street.

For all the fire and fury, though—and there was a lot, as the Xorlarrin family, which now occupied House Do'Urden, was perhaps the strongest magical house of Menzoberranzan, with many practiced wizards—the attackers had come prepared. Lightning splintered into spiderweb arcs as it hit magical shields; fireballs hissed in protest against walls of magical water thrown forth by the attacking priestesses.

It had all been expected.

The attackers responded with fire and lightning of their own, and with volleys of spears and crossbow quarrels, all reaching up at the Do'Urden balconies.

Dininae felt his jaw tighten as he watched his old home take such a concentrated beating. He was glad when Voselly called for the charge, and he was right there beside her in the leading rank.

The eight hundred fighters of the Blaspheme hit the left flank of the attacking drow force in waves, like sheets of rain blown on furious winds. They went through stabbing and slashing, shouldering their enemies to the ground and running on past them, encouraged by cries of "Sweep! Sweep!"

The Blaspheme alone outnumbered the attackers who had come

against House Do'Urden this night, and they fought with the edge of rage pent up through centuries of misery in the Abyss.

Fearlessly, angrily, they plowed through the surprised and out-manned enemies, leaving many squirming on the ground in their wake and sending even more into full flight before them.

Dininae heard the commands being shouted by the enemy priest-esses leading the raid, ordering their charges to stand and fight, only briefly before changing their song and screaming for all to run away.

His sword wasn't even wet with blood, he had only barely stabbed a single attacker, when he spotted Voselly to his right, farther from the wall, moving toward a group of three robed figures in the back ranks of the enemy force.

He ran after her, cutting up the side of a stalagmite mound, then springing away, taking a more direct line than his friend as he tried to catch up.

No, he mouthed when he saw one of those three, clearly a wizard, note the charging woman and lift his hand toward her, releasing a pea of flame.

Dininae felt the wave of heat wash over him even though he was a dozen running strides behind Voselly. The fireball lasted only a moment, the air becoming a roil of biting fiery fury, but when it was gone and Dini-nae blinked his eyes back open, he saw Voselly continuing her charge, her cloak licked with flames, wisps of smoke rising from her singed hair.

She didn't even stumble!

The two drow with the wizard cried out and fell away, but the fellow, apparently confident in the power of his fiery blast, reacted far too slowly.

He did bring his staff swinging across as Voselly came up fast be-fore him, but the skilled ancient warrior went down low and returned with her left hand, her sword only slightly angled as it rose, taking the staff with it. Voselly sprang up right behind it from her crouch, her up-angled short spear catching the wizard in the lower abdomen.

With tremendous strength and momentum, Voselly hoisted the wizard right from the ground, lifting him flailing as the spear slowly slipped into him. She stamped her foot three times, jerking her arm each time, every shock plunging the spear even deeper, reaching it right up through the belly into the heart and lungs.

She had told Dininae that she had once been the weapon master of Menzoberranzan's First House, and he didn't doubt that for a moment now as she straightened her arm before her, that single powerful limb holding the dying wizard up high.

Dininae ran past her, trying to catch up to the two fleeing figures, whom he guessed to be a priest and another wizard, but they were too far ahead and weren't even looking back.

Finally, he skidded to a stop and spun about, and there stood Voselly, Mal'a'voselle Amvas Tol, her trophy, now perfectly still in death, presented high like some battle pennant.

Beyond the woman, the coming wave of Blaspheme warriors surely saw it that way as well, cheering their leader with every running stride.

"THEY CALLED HER MALFOOSH," WIZARD KAITAIN ARMGO told the hulking figure standing beside him. "She was a drider, and one of ancient heritage, it is said. She led them."

The Armgo weapon master, Malagdorl, gave a little growl and reset his grip on his trident.

"Undeniably impressive," Kaitain continued. "They are sweeping through the ranks and will not be slowed."

"Unless she is dead," said Malagdorl.

"Even if," Kaitain replied.

"Let us see," said Malagdorl.

"Weapon Master, I am implored by Matron Mez'Barris to ensure that our ranks here are not lost. House Barrison Del'Armgo does not lead this fight. We . . . you, are here to leave our mark on the victory, not participate in, or fall in, defeat."

"Leave a mark," Malagdorl echoed with a wicked grin. "Whisper to this Malfoosh creature, wizard. Tell her to come and prove herself."

"Matron Mez'Barris will—"

"I will kill you here and now if you disobey me," said the weapon master. "I am here to make *my* mark, to send a message to our enemies, to lift the glory of House Barrison Del'Armgo. Will we lead, Kaitain, or will we cower? This is our moment. Whisper to her, wizard. Bring her to me and let us learn."

HE CAUGHT THE THRUSTING SPEAR IN THE CROOK BETWEEN his off-hand dagger's blade and crosspiece, driving it down hard before him, then reversing suddenly and lifting up and out. His opponent tried to get his second sword in for the strike, but Dininae had the leverage and the speed, his own long sword stabbing underneath the lifting arms.

The drow cried out and tumbled backward.

Dininae didn't know if the wound was mortal, but he didn't rush to finish the fallen man, for the Blaspheme whirlwind was spinning out beyond him, driving their enemies like a panicked herd of rothé.

He scanned about eagerly to locate his fighting partner, then gasped when he found her. Voselly battled at the edge of a small alleyway framed by the pillars of two stalagmite mounds. She faced that alley and so had her back to Dininae as she worked furiously against her opponent.

She went out suddenly to her left, a large black trident stabbing right behind her evasive move, her opponent coming from the shadows, clear to Dininae.

"Uthegentel," he whispered, and the huge man surely looked like that old weapon master, in his splendid black plate mail, trident in one hand, net in the other. This Armgo warrior even had the short white hair, spiked and gelled.

Voselly had barely set her feet up the angled base of the stalagmite when the man caught the trident under his arm, tucking it tightly and securely before turning fast to sweep it across.

Dininae knew he should be running to help his friend, but he was caught by the spectacle, by the memory of the legendary weapon master, and by his fears that poor Voselly was about to have her legs cut out from under her.

If she fell, Dininae wanted nothing to do with this particular enemy.

But Voselly sprang away, up and over the swinging trident and back to the right, to land before the man once more. She stabbed forward with her sword, but her enemy was too skilled, already countering with the net in anticipation before she had even landed from her leap.

The weapons tangled, the sword yanked forward and nearly from her grasp. Her opponent thrust his arm out wide, taking the net and sword with it.

Back came the sweeping trident and Voselly had to let go of her sword and rush backward to get out of reach.

She stumbled, rolled aside, and came back up, spinning her short spear in her hand at her left side, then working it before her, still in a spin, and over to her right hand and side.

Then back again, purely defensively.

Her enemy smiled and shook her sword free to the ground, then took up his long trident in both hands and came on powerfully, stabbing with every step.

Over and under worked the short spear, batting at the longer weapon with all the strength Voselly could muster, strength that had never failed her against any drow opponent.

But this wasn't any drow. And it wasn't the ghost of the man he once knew, whom Dininae thought he recognized.

This was Malagdorl, Dininae realized, weapon master of House Barrison Del'Armgo, heir to the legend that was Uthegentel.

And in terms of sheer physicality, Voselly was not the stronger fighter here.

Malagdorl worked the trident with determination, taking the hits, continuing the stabs, keeping her on her heels, and finally getting her short spear caught in between two trident tines. Just a subtle turn of his wrists locked the spear there, and Malagdorl pressed forward, turning the weapons between them. He threw a head butt and Voselly matched, two skulls cracking together above the trapped weapons. Heads on each other's collars, they pressed and bit and continued to whip their heads at each other, digging in their heels, each trying to find the moment when they could suddenly disengage, create some distance, and come back in for a lethal strike.

Malagdorl drove her back a step, then another, then surprised

Voselly by retreating one step of his own, letting her fall forward once more. He met that reverse by slamming in, then hopped back just far enough to extract and align the trident.

Voselly, too, had her weapon back fully, bringing it to bear.

But they were too close for her to deflect the trident, and her opponent was simply too strong for her to stop its rush.

He had her.

The trident came ahead.

And a blur passed between them, hitting the thrusting long weapon, taking it aside as Dininae ran through.

Malagdorl tried to get his arm up to block as Voselly now rushed in behind that opening, spear jabbing hard.

The weapon master's fast backpedaling and his plate mail saved him from a more serious wound. He staggered farther into the alley, turning his glare over the smaller drow at the right-hand stalagmite.

Dininae caught that look but couldn't begin to match it, or to even hold it, for farther down the alleyway, a robed drow reached out both hands toward him and sent a flashing lightning bolt shooting through the darkness.

Dininae went flying, chips of the stalagmite spraying all about beside him. He was vaguely aware that he was on the ground. He tried to focus his eyes—he saw Malagdorl stumbling back down the alleyway, saw a doorway of light appear there, the wizard, the weapon master, and at least two others going through. They all disappeared before the door vanished with a flash of light.

He lay there, propped on one elbow, staring blankly, his hair dancing wildly, his breath coming in short gasps, his hands gripping for weapons he no longer held.

He felt a hand clamp upon his collar and hoist him easily from the ground, setting him on his feet.

"Why did you do that?" Voselly demanded, her face barely an inch from his and locked in a crazed expression of sheerest outrage. "I had him dead!"

Dininae's mind began to clear and he doubted that she'd "had" anything, but he answered, "I couldn't let you kill him. Not that one."

"Explain!" she demanded.

"Malagdorl Armgo," he said. "That was the weapon master of the Second House, the great rival of House Baenre. They were here watching—if Malagdorl had been killed, House Baenre would find the great houses turning against them. Matron Mother Quenthel would have blamed you!"

She slowly backed away and seemed to calm, and Dininae was very glad his improvised lie had worked. He had no idea if the fallout he had just described was accurate, but he knew that Voselly was wrong here. Had he not intervened, Malagdorl would have defeated her, skewered her, likely lifted her in triumph as she had just done to the earlier opponent.

Even if Voselly had fallen, it wouldn't have changed the outcome here, Dininae knew. The Blaspheme were running on, routing their enemies. Given that truth, Dininae had to take a moment to admit why he had intervened: he didn't want to lose this woman, his new friend, and one he had come to trust and depend upon.

"Come along quickly," Voselly told him, and she started off at a run to the northeast. They caught up to the back ranks of the Blaspheme soon enough as the last of the fighting had begun to settle, the outcome decided.

On they ran in pursuit of the fleeing attackers, around the fingernails of the reaching Westrift and back to the west. They came upon the bulk of the Blaspheme force, stopped and milling in frustration and even confusion, and as Voselly led the way through their ranks, Dininae soon enough discovered why.

Along the road ahead, gigantic animated jade spiders paced, the trailing lines of the retreating drow force running past them to the waiting open doors of a chapel fortress, the Fane of Quarvelsharess.

Soon after, the nobles Saribel and Ravel came upon the Blaspheme and their powerful field commander, standing beside Voselly when a lone figure, robed as a high priestess, strutted to the balcony of the Fane.

"Sos'Umptu Baenre," Dininae heard Saribel whisper to Voselly and her brother. "Sister of Matron Mother Quenthel."

"Sanctuary is found within," Sos'Umptu yelled out to the crowd, her voice clearly amplified by magic. "You cannot pass with ill intent!"

"Now what?" Voselly asked.

"We leave," said Saribel. "We won the day. Our enemies have been stung and scattered, leaving scores lying in their wake, many dead and many more wounded."

"Soon to be dead," Voselly promised.

"No," Saribel declared, surprising her. "Tell your Blaspheme warriors to collect our own dead and wounded, but to take no action against our fallen enemies. All of you return with haste into House Do'Urden. The eyes of many houses are upon us here. They'll not sanction the slaughter of the wounded."

Many more houses than you believe, Dininae thought but did not say.

"Wanton murder bereft of mercy is not the way of Matron Mother Quenthel's Menzoberranzan," Ravel added.

Voselly did as ordered and the Blaspheme force double-timed their way back to the waiting tunnels of House Do'Urden, then inside and through the passageways once more to the arena, where a magical gate waited.

They were down into the underground tunnels soon after, running along at a swift pace back to the south, but not all the way to the Qu'ellarz'orl and House Baenre. For before they even got near Narbondel, they were turned down another secret passage, through a series of heavy doors, magically hidden and warded, and into another long, long tunnel running far to the south and the east, all the way across the city. They came out at the easternmost end of a stalagmite grove known as the Spiderfangs, amid the mushroom groves and farms, with the lake called Donigarten and the Isle of Rothé before them.

There, they were instructed to dig in with trench fortifications, to set perimeters and sentries far and wide.

There, in one bold move, House Baenre seized control of the city's food supply, the extra-Menzoberranzan trade routes and caravans, and thus suddenly and definitively isolated Matron Zhindia Melarn's known ally: House Hunzrin.

CHAPTER 5

Pointed Irreverence

Yvonnel and Minolin Fey entered the House Baenre chapel hand in hand, giggling and playing a game of banging their shoulders together with every step—something Yvonnel purposely increased when she noted the expression on the faces of the mother and daughter who were already in their most hallowed place: Quenthel and Myrineyl.

"You come into this sacred place frivolously?" Matron Mother Quenthel snapped at them, aiming her ire mostly at Minolin Fey, obviously.

"Ah, the reflexive response to centuries of conditioning," Yvonnel answered, laughing, and she jostled Minolin Fey at her side.

Minolin Fey snorted and put her hand over her lips as if trying to hold back a burst of laughter.

Yvonnel winked at her for the performance, for that is exactly what it was.

"Leave us, priestess Minolin Fey," Quenthel demanded.

Minolin Fey looked to Yvonnel.

"No, you stay," Yvonnel told her, then turned to the Matron Mother. "She stays. She is here with me, for a reason."

"Then show respect," Quenthel demanded.

"To whom?"

"To this place. To what it represents, the heart of House Baenre."

"We respect House Baenre by fighting for that which House Baenre has become," said Yvonnel. "Not for what it used to be."

"And you come in here laughing?"

"We won the battle," Yvonnel reminded her. "We swept the attackers of House Do'Urden from the field. We hold impervious strength about Donigarten and the farms."

"It was hardly a decisive win."

"But it was a win. Do you prefer the alternative?"

Quenthel struggled to find a response. She looked to her daughter, who stood with arms crossed over her chest, a scowl chiseled onto her young face.

"Now that's the look I am used to seeing from you, Myrineyl," Yvonnel teased.

Myrineyl dropped her arms to her sides and blinked repeatedly, taken aback and actually stuttering in her shock.

Minolin Fey snorted as she tried futilely to hold back her laugh.

"You would do well to remember where you are," Quenthel growled at her.

"I know exactly where I am . . . sister," Minolin Fey replied.

Quenthel's eyes widened in shock and for a moment, Yvonnel thought she might reach out at Minolin Fey with a powerful spell, a pillar of fire or some mind-wracking assault.

"A few days ago, you called me your sister," Minolin Fey said, not backing down. "Is reciprocation not allowed or acceptable? If not, then what was your comment worth?"

The two at the altar turned to each other with puzzled expressions.

"What game do you play here, Yvonnel?" Quenthel demanded.

"Why do you ask me and not Minolin Fey?"

Quenthel snorted as if the answer were self-evident.

"Then you are blinded by your disrespect," Yvonnel told her, both she and Minolin Fey suddenly dropping their unserious act. "This jaunt into the chapel was Minolin Fey's doing, her idea."

"Good to learn who should be punished," said Myrineyl.

"I told you," Minolin Fey said to Yvonnel.

"Please treat my mother with more respect, both of you," Yvonnel said. She and her sidekick were within a few steps of the other two and the altar then. "She is a valuable member of our effort here, and she is, well, my mother." She finished by turning to Minolin Fey and putting her hand on the woman's hair with a gentle stroke. "She has earned your respect many times over, and with her loyalty to us and her wit keeps House Fey-Branche solidly in our court, whatever odds might stack against us. She also saved the day on the surface with her quick thinking, in telling Zhindia's scouts that her patrol was of Bregan D'aerthe." She smiled and tossed another wink to her mother, then turned back to the other two.

"What was the point of this?" Quenthel asked. "The battle has been joined. The moment is serious and all of our focus must be on how we ensure that we hold strong and bring the Melarni and their allies to heel."

Beside her, Myrineyl recrossed her arms and scowled once more.

"And then what?" Yvonnel asked. "What are we fighting for? Is it just a matter of being rid of Lolth? Is it for justice? Morality?"

"All of that," said Quenthel.

"It's not enough," Yvonnel replied. She looked to Myrineyl. "Smile, beautiful drow. It's not that hard."

"I don't think I've ever seen you smile, Myrineyl," Minolin Fey added. "Not in joy, at least."

"When did you become a fool?" Myrineyl said to her.

Minolin Fey laughed heartily. "Maybe only today," she answered.

"OUR ALLIES WERE ROUTED OUTSIDE OF HOUSE DO'URDEN," declared Matron Zhindia, bursting into Kyrnill's chambers with the handmaiden of Lolth, Eskavidne, at her side. The yochlol's accomplice, Yiccardaria, came in next, with a young and battered, filthy woman dressed in tattered rags chained to her with a spiked collar and tether, which Yiccardaria constantly tugged, drawing little yelps of pain.

Kyrnill couldn't hide her grimace. That was her daughter, Ash'ala, who had betrayed Zhindia and had paid—was paying—a tremendous and terrible price.

"At least fifty are dead or missing, with many likely captured," Zhindia went on. "The Blaspheme fight as if they are still driders. They prove to be undeniably formidable."

Surprisingly to Kyrnill, Zhindia no longer sounded very upset at the news.

"And now House Baenre has used these abominations to secure the eastern reaches," Zhindia said. "I fear that we will soon be eating only magically conjured food."

"That doesn't sound like a favorable position," Kyrnill dared reply. She worked hard to keep her gaze off her daughter, not wanting to show any negative feelings here. Not regret or anger or any hint of sorrow. Ash'ala had betrayed them, and so had been properly punished. And yet . . .

"She is so short-sighted," Yiccardaria teased.

"I don't know how Kyrnill Kenafin was ever promoted to the leadership of a substantial house," Eskavidne agreed.

Kyrnill fought hard to show no reaction. How she wished in that moment, and hardly for the first time, that she had fought for the position of matron in the joining of houses Kenafin and Horlbar into House Melarn a century before.

"It would seem that the Spider Queen chose wisely in elevating Matron Zhindia," said Yiccardaria.

"The Spider Queen always chooses wisely," Kyrnill recited.

"Yes," agreed Zhindia, "and so I, through her guidance, have chosen wisely now. House Baenre has won the opening salvo . . . so they think. But while they have captured less than three score enemies and gained ground that isn't really necessary, we have gained something far greater: their trust."

"Your performance with the freed spirit of Yvonnel was magnificent, dear," Eskavidne congratulated Kyrnill.

"Yes, but I am disappointed," Zhindia admitted.

Kyrnill perked up at that—she had learned the hard way not to take any hints of a threat from this one lightly.

"I have refilled the tub for this poor dirty child," Zhindia elaborated.

Ash'ala fell to her knees at the mere mention of the torture and began making strange, almost animalistic mewling sounds, clawing at her own arms.

"Yes, and now it seems that I have wasted the milk," said Zhindia. "And that will become a precious commodity with the Isle of Rothé under Baenre control."

Her words did little to calm the terrified Ash'ala. She was broken, Kyrnill understood, and she doubted that her broken daughter would ever recover her wits. If she could have struck out then and there and put the poor girl out of her misery, she would have.

"Not to worry," Zhindia said, directing the handmaidens back out of the room and following. "I can conjure something close enough to rothé milk to suffice, I am sure."

She paused at the door and looked back at Kyrnill.

"Be pleased," she said. "The Baenres will err now and suffer for their espionage. We can lose these minor battles many times, but one big win will awaken our greater allies to rally under our banner. Truly, I thought the price would be higher.

"Consider, too, that First Priestess Sos'Umptu Baenre gave sanctuary to the Vandree, Mizzrym, and Melarni fighters in her chapel," she added. "House Baenre will likely soon be at war with itself. How foolish of the Matron Mother and that creature Yvonnel to commit such blasphemy against Lady Lolth. Did they really believe they ever had a chance?"

She walked out, the handmaidens and Ash'ala following, leaving Kyrnill alone.

And truly, the former Matron Kyrnill of House Kenafin had never felt more alone.

"IS THERE A POINT TO THIS FOOLISHNESS?" QUENTHEL DE-manded.

"This foolishness *is* the point," Yvonnel replied. "My mother and I just had a moment together of peace and comfort and happiness to affirm our bond. We took that with us on the way here to speak with you and your daughter, because we think it important. We came here laughing because that, Quenthel, is important. So very important."

"I hope the Blaspheme weren't laughing when they attacked our enemies and drove them aside," said Myrineyl. "Afterward, perhaps."

"Laughter rooted in the pain of others is not the point," Minolin Fey said, drawing confused looks from the two.

"Why did we commit the heresy?" Yvonnel asked rather than answer their eyes' questions.

"To be free of Lolth, who so destroyed the hopes of Menzoberranzan," Quenthel answered.

"And then what? To find again those hopes?"

"Of course."

"Then don't you see what's missing?"

"Why don't you enlighten us," Quenthel said dryly.

"What's missing is what our hope should *be*. When do we laugh in joy and not in superiority over the pains of others?" Yvonnel asked. "When have you, ever?"

Myrineyl shuffled nervously under Yvonnel's gaze.

"When do we play when not in training to fight our enemies?" Yvonnel continued. "When do we take heart in the accomplishments of others when those accomplishments do not reflect upon us, or offer us some gain or advantage?"

"I still do not see your point here," Quenthel admitted. "We have a bloody war staring at us. Are we supposed to be playing games now?"

"But the hope is that we won't always be at war, of course. So, when the war is won, what then? We need to begin considering that. What will Menzoberranzan look like? What will it sound like? Will there be laughter?"

"Don't you think we should win first?"

"No," Yvonnel answered sincerely. "Because when we truly know what we are fighting for, we will fight harder. These answers are— the answers must be—what we are fighting for. Search our common memories, my kindred blessed—or, perhaps, cursed." Quenthel glared at that, but said nothing. "Search the earliest days of Yvonnel the Eternal. I can hardly find them, try though I may. I can hardly recall any days of true freedom, freedom from fear and anxiety, from conniving. A single day when she just played, or laughed, or even got a loving look from someone, anyone, that she returned with equal joy. What have we lost, and for what gain, in our state of perpetual crouch and fear and hunger for power?"

Quenthel didn't answer other than to offer a slight nod of her head.

"Who will rule when Matron Zhindia is thrown down?" Yvonnel asked.

"You or I?" Quenthel asked, seeming caught off guard.

"The Matron Mother!" insisted Myrineyl.

"Why?" Minolin Fey was quick to ask, laying her skepticism out clearly in both tone and expression.

Yvonnel stared at Quenthel through it all, who looked as if she had been slapped, but, encouragingly, only for a moment.

"You speak as a usurper," Myrineyl insisted, her posture turning aggressive.

"No," her mother corrected, reaching out to hold back her daughter. "No, Myrineyl, they are right. They are asking important questions."

"I cannot remember enough of the earliest days to determine the structure," Yvonnel admitted.

"I fear I will find the same haze," Quenthel agreed. "It was so long ago. A different era, when our ancestors were in a very different position."

"I know a little of the societies above," Yvonnel said. "King Bruenor and the dwarves have their way, the lords of Waterdeep, one a bit different. And Jarlaxle's hold on Luskan, different still. The very structure of Menzoberranzan is determined by strength and threat and the edicts of Lolth as expressed by her most powerful matrons. When the Spider Queen is gone, are we really free if the former determinants remain as the basis of power?"

"House Baenre will remain the strongest house," Myrineyl insisted.

"Then only House Baenre will be able to effect the changes we need," Quenthel somberly admitted.

"Find your heart, I advise," Yvonnel told her. "Find your reason for . . . for all of this." She directed Quenthel's gaze to Myrineyl. "Find your daughter, Quenthel. And find her as your daughter."

"Laugh together," Minolin Fey added. She reached out her hand to Myrineyl, who stared at it only for a moment before accepting it.

"We will direct the fight because we must," Yvonnel said. "But we must remember what it is that we are fighting for. Perhaps that starts with respect and caring for all who fight beside us."

"Less station, more . . ." Quenthel started, and seemed to stumble.

"Joy," Yvonnel finished for her. "Just joy. The joy of being alive. We in this city are so forever on edge, agitated and fearful, that . . ." She shook her head. "I sometimes, oftentimes, think that the only people in this city who ever experience simple joy are those in the Braeryn."

"The Stenchstreets?" Myrineyl asked, her face scrunched with disgust.

"That is where Zaknafein and Jarlaxle often hid from the troubles of nobility, or of simply dealing with the constant intrigue of the ruling houses. There, yes, the Stenchstreets, is where they laughed and played. Where they truly *lived*."

Myrineyl shook her head, her expression holding firm.

"When you finally do learn to smile, it will likely crack your face," Minolin Fey said to her.

Myrineyl turned on her mother, the Matron Mother, obviously seeking some support.

But Quenthel was staring hard at Yvonnel, and she hardly looked upset or even disagreeable with Yvonnel's claims.

She glanced back at her daughter, nodded, and smiled.

CHAPTER 6

The Long Game

Great Matron Mez'Barris," Zhindia Melarn said with a low bow. "Accept all of my gratitude to you for agreeing to see me in the midst of this most grand compound."

"Let us see if you still feel that way when we are finished here," Mez'Barris returned in a tone that made it clear that she was not in a particularly generous mood.

"Why would I not?" Zhindia asked. "House Baenre grows more isolated by the hour."

"They have taken Donigarten, and that after chasing your allies from the field."

"Into the Fane of Quarvelsharess, where a Baenre rules, where a Baenre offered sanctuary to those who sought to throw down Matron Mother Quenthel's most powerful and determined ally," Zhindia reminded her.

"The Xorlarrins," Mez'Barris said, almost spitting the name. "Did Matron Zeerith for one moment fear for her safety? Did your attack—"

"It was not my attack," Zhindia sharply interrupted. "And they are now the Do'Urdens, not the Xorlarrins, are they not? Yet another thumb in the eight eyes of Lolth."

The drow flanking the throne of Mez'Barris, including her daughter Taayrul, all gasped at the impertinence of the young and brash matron of a much lesser house. Matron Mez'Barris had gone to war for less insult than that offered by the tone the rude Matron Zhindia had just used with her.

But the matron of the city's Second House did not gasp, did not allow anything more than a momentary flinch to show. "Did the attack," she began, conceding Zhindia's point, "put a single warrior into the Do'Urden compound? Did a single spell penetrate further than the warded balconies of that heretical house?"

"No," Zhindia replied without the slightest hesitation. "It is a difficult target, more so because the force of ultimate heretics, the Blaspheme, as they are called, was lying in wait."

"Hundreds of warriors standing around outside the targeted compound, and no one bothered to notice them?"

"Matron Mez'Barris, I assure you that those who made mistakes will not make them again. But the force that went against House Do'Urden—"

"House Xorlarrin," Mez'Barris corrected. "I do not care what that old witch Zeerith calls herself or her family. Xorlarrin, Q'Xorlarrin, Do'Urden—they are all the same. The destroyed House Do'Urden was never nearly as formidable as Matron Zeerith's wizardly family."

Zhindia bowed again. "We knew the target was a difficult and secure one, and in a defensive crouch with more wizards than any other drow house can put forth. The attackers were prepared to run even as they started their assault, and they knew where to go, and it cannot please Matron Mother Quenthel that her sister, the most devout of the Baenre family, picked a side."

"'We knew'? 'We knew that the target was a difficult and secure one,'" Mez'Barris echoed. "*We* knew. You sit on the Ruling Council. You know the rules that govern Menzoberranzan. My dear Matron Zhindia, are you admitting that you participated in the attack on another noble house?"

"No more than Matron Mez'Barris would admit such a thing," Zhindia replied, bringing more gasps from the Armgo onlookers. "It is widely reported that House Barrison Del'Armgo soldiers were in the region, and indeed, that they engaged."

"Scouts, merely scouts. Including the weapon master, the mighty Malagdorl, who defended an alleyway against a host of Blaspheme until the wizard Kaitain could enact a proper gate to extract our scouts."

"I am glad that your scouts were returned to safety. No doubt the legend of Malagdorl will grow even more impressive."

"He was wounded in the battle," Mez'Barris told her. "Know that I hold you responsible for that, and understand that if he had been killed, House Barrison Del'Armgo would be even now marching for House Melarn."

Zhindia bowed again.

"The attackers lost. They were routed," Mez'Barris stated flatly. "You think the Baenres isolated? My dear Matron Zhindia, in Menzoberranzan, the victors find allies while the losers find extermination."

"It was but a skirmish."

"Do better. Or learn your proper place."

"My proper place with the heretics who stole from Lady Lolth an army of driders?" Zhindia dared retort, an unsubtle reminder that House Barrison Del'Armgo had been in the encampment of House Baenre when that heresy had occurred.

"Who can guess the true will of Lolth?" was all that Mez'Barris bothered to reply. She sat back in her decorated throne and turned to her daughter, taking up a quiet conversation.

It took Zhindia a while to realize that she had been dismissed.

She properly backed away from Mez'Barris, bowing with every other step until she was out of the room.

She could play the game of supplication. She had already promised the Second House that the coming storm would put Mez'Barris in place as Matron Mother of Menzoberranzan, with the condition that House Melarn be elevated to the Second House.

Mez'Barris Armgo had craved the rank of Matron Mother for more than a century, since even before Yvonnel the Eternal had cost Mez'Barris her beloved Uthegentel in a failed raid against King Bruenor's Mithral Hall more than a century before. That hunger and the resentment toward House Baenre had only intensified with the passage of time, particularly of late with the ascent of Quenthel as Matron Mother and the Demon War she had brought to Menzoberranzan.

Yes, Zhindia understood that Mez'Barris was quite hungry for change here. She was glad that Mez'Barris had mentioned Malagdorl, who was Mez'Barris's grandson and her pathetic attempt to replace the lost Uthegentel in both appearance and reputation.

Zhindia meant to fully accommodate all of Matron Mez'Barris's desires, to help House Barrison Del'Armgo obliterate the heretic Baenres, to elevate the standing of Malagdorl, and to get Mez'Barris the title of Matron Mother of Menzoberranzan.

Briefly.

THE FARMLANDS AROUND LAKE DONIGARTEN WERE USU-ally quiet. They were worked by goblin and kobold slaves, fieldhands who had been taught, painfully, to remain silent as they went about their duties. Now, though, the quiet had been disturbed more than a little by the many Blaspheme soldiers digging their entrenchments, constructing spear-lift battlements, and building archer perches. Still, even with the inevitable noises of those works, the hush around Donigarten remained, and seemed even more profound and ominous.

Just a couple hundred yards across the dark waters, the rothé lowed on the island named for them. There, too, the overseers of the herd, the lake, and the surrounding farms moved about along the battlements of the few small towers and single keep built out on the island. These were Hunzrin drow, reputed allies of Matron Zhindia Melarn, and now they were almost fully surrounded by the Blaspheme of House Baenre.

Clearly, they had no idea how to react. Normally they would come out from the Isle of Rothé and demand that any trespassers leave, backed by the standing imprimatur of the Ruling Council.

But these were Baenres, and nobles of the First House walked about those banks, directing the siege.

"Should we fully seal the enemies on their island rock?" Voselly asked Weapon Master Andzrel Baenre, who was directing the operation.

"Leave them a path to the Eastways tunnels, but have scouts count any and all departing or entering," Andzrel ordered. "Let them go, right out of the city, if they so desire. They can find their way back in through other tunnels in other places. The fewer Hunzrins we have out there on the Isle of Rothé, the better for our position."

"You think they'll move against us?"

"Not alone, surely. The Blaspheme under my command could obliterate House Hunzrin itself. This small outpost would not survive an hour if we crossed and attacked, and they know it. They will come and ask our intent, and parley, for what choice have they?"

He motioned toward the grove of towering mushrooms north of their position. "Ravel Xorlarrin Do'Urden will be in there soon with some other Do'Urden wizards, preparing teleportation circles," he explained. "Do not allow any working Blaspheme soldiers to interrupt their important duties."

"To bring in allies if we are attacked?" Voselly asked, for she suspected otherwise.

"Perhaps" was Andzrel's answer. "It is not your concern at this time. Go and direct your forces."

With a bow, Voselly left the Baenre weapon master, who was widely regarded as a superb tactician even if not a top-tier warrior. Beside her went Aleandra.

"That was an unexpectedly ambiguous response," Aleandra told her when they were away from Andzrel.

"We aren't here to fight the Hunzrins, necessarily," Voselly said. "We aren't even here to control the foodstuffs and trade. Is there a house in Menzoberranzan that doesn't have priestesses capable of feeding their ranks? And who is concerned about trading outside the city at this time, when war is sure to erupt?"

"We're here to signal our challenge, then, and perhaps to draw out enemies."

"The Baenres want our enemies to see us and to know that we

aren't afraid of them and that they should be afraid of us," Voselly agreed.

"Then why the Xorlarr—the Do'Urden wizards and their magical circles?"

"Look out there," Voselly told her fellow Amvas Tol warrior. "Menzoberranzan is a forest of rock towers, and one great shadow. Putting the right forces in the right places quickly will determine the winners as much as the quality of the armies will."

"We could do that easily from House Baenre, though, where there is no shortage of wizards and tunnels, as we just did in defending the Do'Urden compound."

"House Baenre does not need us guarding their walls." Voselly was seeing it all more clearly then, and smiling and nodding as she reasoned through it, silently congratulating the Baenre planners. "Out here, we are a true show of force."

"And a target," Aleandra reminded her. "We are the ultimate insult to those who follow Lolth. The perfect place to vent violence and frustration for those wishing to find the Spider Queen's blessing. Didn't we see that very opportunism in the Braeryn a few days ago?"

"We did," said Voselly. "Let them come. Let them all come. Though I doubt any would be that bold."

"Then boredom is our greatest enemy."

Voselly directed Aleandra's attention out to the Isle of Rothé. "Watch carefully. Andzrel will soon cut a deal with those who tend the herd. We'll feast on rothé shanks while our enemies sit in their holes and eat the bread of conjurations. This is no punishment, my old companion. This is our reward. To stretch along the open ground, well fed."

"It won't last long," Aleandra predicted.

"Oh, no, certainly not. My fight in the side alley beyond House Do'Urden was against the weapon master of the Second House, Barrison Del'Armgo, Dininae has told me. Which means it is all connecting.

"The storm is coming, so let us enjoy the peace."

"TAKE HEART," ESKAVIDNE TOLD A SURPRISED KYRNILL KE-nafin Melarn when she unexpectedly burst in upon the priestess in her private quarters.

"Why are you so distressed, child?" the handmaiden asked, closing the door and moving to sit on the bed next to the woman, who had jumped up from a fitful sleep when the door had banged open.

Kyrnill wanted to shrink from the handmaiden, who appeared now, as usual, as a nearly naked and undeniably beautiful drow female. Kyrnill knew the creature's true form, though, that of a lump of animated mud, appearing more like a half-melted candle than anything sentient.

She tried to push that image out of her thoughts now. This was a handmaiden of Lolth, a demon creature before which even the Matron Mother of Menzoberranzan would wisely genuflect.

She closed her eyes and steeled her will when Eskavidne reached up to gently stroke her cheeks and neck.

"Tell me," Eskavidne cooed.

"You startled me, that is all," Kyrnill insisted. "We are at war, after all, and against House Baenre. When I heard the door, I feared . . ."

"Child," said Eskavidne, "the first crossbows have barely fired. House Baenre hasn't even declared. They are looking for other ways than war, I assure you."

"From my earliest days, I was warned of the dangers of crossing House Baenre," Kyrnill admitted.

"Truly?" asked the handmaiden, and she gave a thoughtful "Hmm."

"Matron Mother Baenre, Yvonnel the Eternal, ruled this city beyond the oldest memories of the oldest drow," Kyrnill reminded her. "That house's rule has not been threatened in my lifetime, or in the lifetime of my mother. Oh, indeed, there was grousing and grumbling when the old Matron Mother Baenre failed to take the dwarven city of Mithral Hall, but even then . . ."

"And in the Time of Troubles?"

"Yes, even then, even against House Oblodra," Kyrnill agreed. "Recall what happened to them."

Eskavidne laughed. "Yes, the power of Matron Baenre bared, you think?"

Before Kyrnill could respond, the handmaiden sharply added, "Or the power of Lolth?"

"Lolth, of course! But through the vessel of Matron Mother Yvonnel Baenre."

"And so you were taught, rightfully, to fear her wrath. The dangers of crossing House Baenre. But do you think them worse than the dangers of crossing Lady Lolth?"

"Of course not!"

"Be at ease, child. I am not here to test you or to fight with you." She leaned over and kissed Kyrnill, then huskily whispered, "I come with hints of great promise."

"I . . . I don't understand."

"Who do you think will prevail in this war?"

"Whoever has the blessing of Lolth," Kyrnill recited, for to answer anything else to that question would be considered profane.

"Yes, but there will be casualties even on that side. Many casualties, and truly, in the end, who can say which side will find that needed blessing?"

Kyrnill leaned away from Eskavidne, staring at her curiously.

"And what consequence to she who leads the other side?" the handmaiden added.

It took Kyrnill a long while to digest that, before stuttering back, "What are you hinting?"

"When this is done, however it plays, Menzoberranzan will be a different place. There will be a reordering of things, of houses, of matrons, without doubt. It was Lolth's will that Zhindia Horlbar become the matron of House Melarn when houses Horlbar and Kenafin were joined as one. It was a wise choice."

"Yes, handmaiden."

"Oh, stop that, silly woman," Eskavidne scolded. "It had to be Zhindia, don't you understand? Because she is the most fervent in the ways of the Spider Queen."

"And so she must ascend to become Matron Moth—"

"That's not what I said. Her fervor was needed. Her zealotry, her ambition, her desire, and her fealty were all needed in this time of the great test of Lolth's children. Do you think Lolth could not foresee the heresy of Drizzt Do'Urden? Or the budding independence of Bregan D'aerthe and their iblith-loving leader? Do you know about him, Kyrnill of House Kenafin?"

"I know Jarlaxle, yes. Of course. I ruled a house as matron and every matron knows him. I've dealt with him only rarely, however."

"Do you know his secret?"

She stared at Eskavidne, clueless.

"He is the son of Yvonnel Baenre," said Eskavidne, and Kyrnill feared that her eyes might bulge out of their sockets. "The brother of your current matron mother, the uncle of young and dangerous Yvonnel.

"If you tell anyone this, I will let the maggots eat your daughter wholly, then throw you in the tub atop her bones and feces," Eskavidne warned, and Kyrnill didn't doubt it, but could hardly register it, so shocked was she by that revelation. "Yes, and at the time of Jarlaxle's birth, he became the third son of Matron Mother Yvonnel behind Gromph and Doquaio."

"I do not know of Doquaio."

"That was long before your birth, and he was a male of little importance and reputation," the handmaiden explained. "But he was the secondboy of House Baenre, no small thing. And Jarlaxle, as third, was to be sacrificed, of course, for the ruling house would not dare defy Lolth in that manner. But something happened." She laughed. "The will of Lolth intervened in the form of the matron of House Oblodra, secretly protecting Jarlaxle, redirecting the power of the strike that would have killed him back upon the rather useless secondboy. So much like Drizzt, don't you think?"

Kyrnill shrugged, then shook her head, for she didn't know much about Drizzt Do'Urden. She had heard that he was supposed to be sacrificed, though, except that one of Matron Malice Do'Urden's other sons had been killed that same night in a raid upon another house.

"It doesn't matter," Eskavidne said. "What matters is that all of these extraordinary happenings about you, all this chaos, all of this . . . opportunity, was foreseen. Jarlaxle was a test for the drow, don't you see? For he was given the reins of his own chariot, to climb to places that males should not. And Drizzt is the ultimate test, of course."

"And House Baenre has failed that test," Kyrnill said, but she wanted to ask it more than state it, for she was having a hard time wrapping her head around such a thing. Was it possible that all of this had been predetermined? It seemed ridiculous. Jarlaxle was centuries older than Drizzt Do'Urden, and Drizzt Do'Urden had never been anything more than a minor player in the ways of Menzoberranzan.

Except recently, Kyrnill then realized, when Matron Mother Quenthel and that strange creature Yvonnel—the same two priestesses who had committed the ultimate blasphemy on the surface world in reverting the driders to their drow form—had used Drizzt as Menzoberranzan's spear, channeling power through him and hurling him into the gigantic, monstrous form of the archdemon lord Demogorgon. Drizzt had been the spear used to defeat one of Lolth's most powerful rivals.

And that same matron of House Oblodra, K'yorl Odran, brought back from the Abyss, had been the conduit of that power, directing it from the illithid hive mind and into the physical body of who?

Drizzt!

Kyrnill found it hard to draw breath in that moment. She felt as if the strands of an intricate spiderweb were floating through the air and rejoining before her eyes, becoming a most beautiful and deadly web.

"Do you see, dear?" Eskavidne said. "It all seems so dangerous and wild and out of control, but Lolth merely grins."

"She did all of this," Kyrnill murmured.

"She does *everything*. She is all-powerful, all-seeing. The webs are hers alone to pluck, like the strings of an abyssal lute, to make the song she determines. She needed Zhindia because Zhindia would not bend, would never bend. But when this is done, perhaps there will be a better choice to lead Lolth's children through the chaos. Who can know but Lolth?"

Kyrnill didn't blink—and almost wondered if she would ever blink again!

"Play your part well," Eskavidne told her, whispered to her, and she moved in close again. "The curtain will fall on this present grand symphony, and who will conduct the next?"

She ended with a kiss, long and forceful. She pushed Kyrnill down on the bed and climbed atop her, kissing her, caressing her.

The woman, too overwhelmed to begin to sort out how to react, focused only on keeping the grotesque true form of this yochlol demon out of her thoughts, and did as she was bidden.

DININAE FINALLY TOOK SOME REST, RECLINING AGAINST the trunk of a giant mushroom. His mind whirled with possibility and with fear. Could he survive this war? If not, would he go back before the swirling acrid smoke of Lolth's abyssal home? Would she make of him a drider again, or worse?

Or was he free of her, at long last?

He lay there trying to sort it all out when he noted a form moving toward him, a woman from another time, tall and dark, with wide shoulders and a strong jaw.

"Well met again, young warrior," Aleandra said as she approached.

Dininae gave a little laugh and propped himself up. "Young," he echoed with a snort.

Aleandra dropped down on the moss beside him, letting her short spear fall to her side and unsuccessfully trying to adjust her sheathed sword about a rock protruding from the soft bed. Finally, she gave a great "Hrrr!" and just unbuckled her sword belt and tossed it aside.

"Where is Voselly?" Dininae asked.

"I'll let someone else keep a watchful eye on her for a bit," Aleandra said lightly. "For me, it is time to rest."

"Well understood," Dininae agreed.

"Do you mind if I do so beside you?" Aleandra asked, her politesse surprising the former Do'Urden, who was hardly used to being asked for anything by drow women.

"It's a good spot. The moss is soft and thick," he answered.

She shifted a bit closer, locking eyes with him. "Tell me," she bade him, "have you come to fully appreciate your old body once more?"

"It is good to not have eight legs I need to fold beneath me to rest," he agreed.

"It feels good just to lie down!" Aleandra declared, and Dininae couldn't argue with that.

"If I recall correctly—and it has been centuries, I admit—lots of things feel good in this drow body," she added, shifting even closer. "Pleasures a drider cannot know."

"I think you do recall correctly," he replied, growing weirdly nervous. "But perhaps I, too, have just forgotten the truth of it all."

Aleandra reached over and put her hand gently on his chest. "Would you like to remember together?"

Dininae could feel his heart thumping in his chest. He hadn't even considered such a thing, or rather, he had, but only vaguely, and with Voselly. Now, though, with Aleandra so close, touching him gently, *asking* him instead of demanding from him, he began to feel a stirring.

"No," he said flatly, and looked away.

Aleandra pulled her hand from him and Dininae heard a little gasp. He glanced back after a moment to find her staring at him, seeming truly hurt.

"I will leave you," she said, and started to collect her weapons, but barely had she begun when Dininae grabbed her by the forearm and turned her back to face him.

"I wanted to see," he told her.

"See?"

"If the old rules held with you."

"I am sure I do not begin to understand what you are talking about."

"You asked me."

She looked confused.

"You didn't tell me, didn't demand of me. You asked me," he tried to explain.

"Of course."

"Is that how it was?"

"Again, you confuse me, Dininae."

"In my time, in Menzoberranzan, women, particularly nobly bred women, did not ask a mere man. They told him what he would do to please them, and woe unto him if he didn't grant their every demand."

"Interesting," Aleandra said. "Maybe I would prefer your time." She ended with a laugh, though.

"I would quite enjoy remembering with you," Dininae told her.

He didn't have to tell her twice.

"SURELY SHE DID NOT BELIEVE YOU," YICCARDARIA SAID to Eskavidne, the two alone in the tunnels beneath House Melarn, and in their ugly yochlol forms. Two mounds of goo. "Lolth foresaw all of this? She let the third son of Yvonnel live so that he could play a role these hundreds of years later? I don't remember it well, but what I do recall is that House Baenre lost Lolth's favor for that little switch of sacrifices at the time of Jarlaxle's birth. And by interfering with the ceremony, K'yorl of House Oblodra set herself and her house on the path astray from Lolth with little chance of reconciliation."

"You remember correctly," Eskavidne assured her handmaiden sister.

"But Kyrnill, who was once the matron of a house, believed you?" Yiccardaria grew more incredulous with every word.

"It does not take special intelligence or insight be a matron, of course. Kyrnill Kenafin was never an impressive one. And yes, she believed me, fully so. She thinks this present chaos, this dance, choreographed in centuries past. All of it. A grand marionette play with Lolth as mistress of puppets."

"Were Lolth a puppet mistress, she would sever all the strings and throw the flopping fools into a cyclone, reveling in the chaos," Yiccardaria mused. "The entire notion is preposterous. And now Kyrnill believes that Zhindia may fall, giving her rule of House Melarn—of all Menzoberranzan, perhaps?"

"Dear sister, it is not hard to convince a mortal to believe that which she wants so badly to believe," Eskavidne explained. "It is not hard to suggest deeper reason for mere coincidence, or to create patterns in events unrelated. These mortals yearn for a deeper truth—a hint of such a thing holds a powerful allure. And they seek an orderly multiverse about them, fanatically seeking patterns when none exist, and praying, ever praying, for a controlling figure to parent them."

"And so now Kyrnill Kenafin knows what she knows, and anyone trying to convince her otherwise will be met with a wall of doubt," Yiccardaria reasoned.

"And anger," said Eskavidne. "Great anger. Violent anger. Because what she now believes—nay, what she now *knows* as truth, is what she desperately wants to be truth."

"She will do whatever we tell her to do."

"More importantly, sister, Kyrnill will not do that which we do not want her to do. She will not betray us to Yvonnel Baenre." Eskavidne paused and sighed, a bubbling and truly grumbling sound in her melted-candle form, like an underwater burp from a hill giant. "Truly, sister," she added, "I do not believe that I have ever more enjoyed this game Lolth lets us play with these foolish mortals."

"WHAT DO YOU THINK WILL HAPPEN TO US WHEN THIS IS over?" Aleandra asked Dininae when they were finished, lying side by side under their cloaks deep in the shadows of the mushroom grove. She had quite enjoyed the romp, but expected to enjoy this conversation even more.

"If we live?"

Aleandra giggled. "Yes, if we live. If we die, I hope for oblivion—I think that is the best we can hope for. But it will all be quite beyond our decision."

"I haven't thought much about it," he admitted. "I'm just trying to stay alive." He looked at her with a wicked grin. "More alive now than only a little while ago."

She kissed him. "Do you wish to remain in House Baenre?"

"That would be the safest choice, I suppose, if they win. And I expect they will. Who would ever challenge a soldier of House Baenre when we are done with these Melarni and their allies?"

"I don't want to," Aleandra decided, rolling onto her back and staring up at the mushroom cap high above. "It is too big. There are too many."

"Then where?"

"In an allied house, of course, one with great power and a position of strong defense." She side-eyed him and grinned leadingly. "Perhaps one built within a cavern wall."

"What?" he asked, then it hit him. "House Do'Urden?"

"Why not? They are thick with wizards and priests but thin on foot soldiers, and we have surely proven our worth in that regard."

"I don't know that it will be our choice to make."

"I think it will, to some measure. So, tell me, Dininae."

"Tell you what?"

"You knew that place," Aleandra replied. "Knew of it, at least."

"Of it, yes," he answered, and Aleandra watched as he tried hard to keep his voice steady here and choose his words carefully. "House Do'Urden was ascendant, and dangerous, when I walked the Stench-streets."

"And with a great weapon master," she said overdramatically.

"Truly great," Dininae answered flatly. "I don't know that Zaknafein had an equal."

"He trained you?"

Dininae swallowed hard.

That, too, Aleandra noted. "In the Academy, I mean. He was no doubt a master at Melee-Magthere."

"He was, but no, I never attended the Academy. No sponsor. No house. I did, however, do extensive training with one who had been tutored by Zaknafein Do'Urden. A soldier of House Do'Urden's most elite fighting brigade who had come to live in the Braeryn after the great fall of Matron Malice and House Do'Urden. He was a commander in that brigade, I believe, and a gifted warrior by any standard."

"I see," Aleandra said, and she truly did see. "And tell me, did Dininae ever become as good as this commander of Zaknafein's elite brigade?"

"I killed him," Dininae said. "A fair fight, and I killed him."

"You regret it?"

"No. It . . . it just happened."

"Was that why you were turned into an abomination?"

"No, no, that was . . . no."

"Well, I am glad that you prevailed. And if you fight as well as you . . ." She stopped and grinned lewdly, then said, "I hope we train together often."

She rolled back to her side, up against him, and Dininae looped his arm over her shoulder. Aleandra smiled again when she heard him say, "It is good to be back in this body."

CHAPTER 7

Crouching

To see the force, one need only consider the shadows," Yvonnel told Minolin Fey and Saribel Do'Urden, the three looking out over the farms and mushroom grove from a perch on the north wall. Before them, all the way to the line of stalagmites known as the Spiderfangs, the Blaspheme crouched, this time supported by soldiers of House Baenre and House Fey-Branche. Enough warriors were out there lying in wait for Yvonnel's observation to be only a minor exaggeration.

This time, they weren't going to let their enemies flee. From the results of the first skirmish and the quick retreat of the enemy, it seemed obvious to Yvonnel that Zhindia wasn't intending to let her forces fight a pitched battle this early on. Zhindia's caution, hesitance even, made sense, since a huge defeat with mass casualties might end her hopes of drawing powerful allies openly into her struggle with mighty House Baenre.

Now, though, it seemed as if Zhindia was growing more desperate. With another visit through the psionic power of the illithid, Yvonnel had learned from Kyrnill that House Baenre's siege of Donigarten and the Isle of Rothé was greatly diminishing Zhindia's position with the other ruling houses. This area around the lake was the most open ground of Menzoberranzan, after all, and a force of warriors should not be able to so easily hold this position against the power of priests and wizards.

Yvonnel peered down intently to the southwest, the Braeryn, the Spiderfangs, eager to see the expected movement. According to Kyrnill, Matron Zhindia thought this land held by a force of mere fighters, and so she would fill it with magical destruction, with her own forces sweeping in behind to shatter the siege.

And to shatter the illusion of Baenre dominance.

But Zhindia was deceived, so the Baenres hoped, for those Blaspheme fighter ranks were now quietly thick with Xorlarrin-Do'Urden wizards and Baenre priestesses.

As soon as the fighting began, the Blaspheme would rush along the northern and southern flanks, encircling the attackers, and here in the open, for all of Menzoberranzan to see, Matron Zhindia Melarn's forces would be crushed.

Yvonnel's gaze drifted across the huge cavern to the timeclock of the city. The attack would come when Narbondel's light was halfway back to full, so Kyrnill had claimed.

More than the bottom third of the timeclock glowed already.

It would not be long.

MALAGDORL ARMGO'S TRIDENT SILENCED THE SHRIEKER mushroom after only a single and abbreviated screech came forth. The weapon master turned back to the priestesses who had silenced the area, his scowl promising punishment if he ever figured out which of them had mis-aimed her spell of silence to exclude this one of the fungi sentinels.

Not now, though. Now there was no turning back, no retreat, for the raiders had committed. The Barrison Del'Armgo forces and their allies were already slicing through the outer defenses of this shell of a ruling house.

House Fey-Branche was one of Menzoberranzan's oldest, the family tracing back thousands of years—back, in their telling, beyond even the newly claimed date of the city's founding, as recounted through the memories of Yvonnel the Eternal.

Fey-Branche's Matron Byrtyn Fey, too, was old, her power, like that of her house, considered to be on the wane.

Except, of course, that her eldest daughter, Minolin Fey, was now a Baenre, wife of a former archmage, mother of Yvonnel, who was one of the most powerful figures in Menzoberranzan at this time.

Minolin Fey's good fortune hadn't yet reversed the years of House Fey-Branche's decline, however, and Matron Byrtyn had survived and thrived mostly on alliance and tradition. House Fey-Branche was the Fifth House of Menzoberranzan, but few thought it stronger than several of those ranked behind it, three of which had joined with Barrison Del'Armgo in this most unusual, most unexpected, most devastating raid.

That dangerous reality was greatly exacerbated this night because many of Matron Byrtyn's soldiers were more than halfway across the city, preparing a glorious ambush that they believed would all but end the threat of the wretched Zhindia Melarn.

By the time that single sentry shrieker briefly screeched, most of House Fey-Branche's magical defenses were already dispelled, and two of its outer doors breached.

"COME ON, THEN," AN ANXIOUS YVONNEL MUTTERED. SHE wished that none of this carnage were necessary, but since it was, she wanted it over as quickly as possible. She glanced back at Narbondel, still not quite at half-light.

She started to look away when her attention was seized by a small flicker of light, a blue-white flash that she somehow knew to be a lightning bolt, but one contained inside a structure.

It came from far away, near the timeclock, in the area called the Narbondellyn, and wasn't that curious?

"Lolth be damned," the powerful woman growled as the truth began to dawn on her.

"What?" asked Minolin Fey, who then followed Yvonnel's gaze across the city.

Another light flashed.

"Is that . . . ?"

"House Fey-Branche," Minolin Fey finished, and gasped.

Yvonnel understood exactly what had happened in that terrible moment. She knew then why their enemies had so quickly and efficiently left the battlefield in the ambush outside of House Do'Urden, and why, so conveniently, the Fane of Quarvelsharess had been ready to receive and offer them sanctuary.

"Clever Zhindia," she whispered under her breath. She understood that she had to act quickly and effectively to turn this back around.

Not in time to save House Fey-Branche, though, she realized even before Minolin Fey began shouting orders for the forces to mobilize. No, House Fey-Branche was a weak fortress, more pomp and show and tradition than raw power.

If Matron Zhindia had gone to these lengths to execute this raid, Yvonnel was certain that the power brought against House Fey-Branche had been overwhelming and aggressive.

She glanced at her mother, who was calling down from the wall perch to get the Blaspheme and others up and ready to move, and Yvonnel grimaced, recognizing the horrible truth.

Minolin Fey's mother, Yvonnel's lone surviving grandparent, was very possibly already dead.

MATRON BYRTYN FEY HUSTLED INTO THE MAIN HOUSE chapel, where four of her daughters waited and were fervently praying.

"How was this not anticipated?" she scolded.

Somewhere far below, there came the retort of a blast, likely a lightning bolt, and the entire structure shook violently.

"We were told to participate in the fight across the city by Matron Mother Quenthel," First Priestess Aydiana Fey reminded her. "Our enemies had to know."

"We were betrayed," said priestess Alaghi, Byrtyn's youngest, and perhaps most promising, daughter.

"What have we available?" the matron demanded.

"Less than half our warriors," Aydiana replied. "And with our weapon master and house wizard—almost all of our wizards!—off in the east."

Byrtyn thought of her grandson, Geldrin, who had become one of the most accomplished weapon masters in Menzoberranzan, a classmate and associate—dare she call him a friend?—of Andzrel Baenre. She had been so happy when he had led the Fey-Branche force over to House Baenre, then off to Donigarten the previous day. He would do her family proud in that impending fight, she had believed, and bring more respect to the house—a house that her rivals openly claimed had been given too high a ranking, thus affording Byrtyn too powerful a seat on the Ruling Council.

"Drop all corridors above the first floor," she ordered. "Lock us down up here, and let the light spells fly high and far to let House Baenre know that we are under attack."

No sooner had she finished the thought than some heavy impact slammed against the room's door, turning them all about. The door didn't swing in; it fell over into the room, the jamb falling with it, the rush of air swirling a thick fog that accompanied the broken portal over the threshold. When the fog cleared, Matron Byrtyn stared at a familiar form in the opening, that of Calagher Fey-Branche, her longtime patron and the father of three of her six daughters.

It took Byrtyn a moment to realize that Calagher wasn't standing of his own accord, his legs bowed weirdly, his shoulders slumped, his head lilting to the side.

He came forward suddenly, looking up at her, eyes wide in apparent shock and pain, and pitched facedown on the floor, three equidistant and growing stains of blood on the back of his shirt.

He had been kicked off the barbed tines of a trident, a black trident, one that was both famous and infamous throughout the city.

Malagdorl Armgo stepped into the room, Calagher's blood dripping from the end of his weapon.

Aydiana Fey began waving her arms in the somatic movements of a powerful spell.

"Do you really wish to strike down the favored son of House Barrison Del'Armgo?" came a voice from the foggy darkness behind Malagdorl. A moment later, a woman whose perpetual scowl was well-known to Byrtyn, and to nearly all in Menzoberranzan, walked past Malagdorl.

Aydiana Fey looked to her mother for guidance and Byrtyn gave a quick shake of her head, signaling the first priestess to stop her spellcasting.

"What are you doing here, Matron Miz'ri?" Byrtyn asked the leader of the city's Fourth House, House Mizzrym. "Have you gone mad?"

"We all have our choices to make, Matron Byrtyn. I thought it best to make my own early on." Miz'ri looked to Alaghi, then pointed to Calagher. "He is your father, is he not, child?" she asked. "Go, quickly, and use your Lolth-given powers to save his life."

"You know who you are standing against in this?" Byrtyn asked her peer.

"You know who I am standing *beside*," Miz'ri replied, looking to the hulking weapon master of Barrison Del'Armgo.

"Lady Lolth," she added, as if indicating the city's Second House wasn't convincing enough. "I stand beside Lady Lolth."

"Get out," Byrtyn ordered. "We are as old as any house in Menzoberranzan, sanctioned and sitting upon the Ruling Council for millennia. This is sacrilege."

"Your house has already fallen, old woman," Malagdorl declared. "Just because you are too stupid to realize it does not make it untrue."

Matron Byrtyn stared at him hatefully. Behind her, Aydiana quietly began casting once more, while before her, Alaghi had begun her healing dweomers on the fallen Calagher.

"Stand down your priestesses, Matron Byrtyn," Miz'ri commanded. "Other than the healing I've allowed. The force that has come against you this day would threaten House Baenre itself, I assure you. And they are lurking everywhere in your compound while House Baenre is looking elsewhere. Weapon Master Malagdorl speaks the truth. You are overrun. The battle was over before you entered it—you, too, were looking elsewhere, it would seem."

Byrtyn rolled her tongue about her lips. The Second and Fourth Houses, at least, had come against her, and she didn't doubt that more had joined as well. In Menzoberranzan, the typical assault meant that none could be left alive as witnesses. It was not forbidden for one house to attack another, as long as they didn't get caught.

Yet she was still alive, as were her daughters and Calagher, she realized, when her patron coughed beneath Alaghi's healing hands.

"Matron Zhindia does not blame you for the heresy of your grand-daughter, or the poor choice your daughter made in mating with a foul Baenre," Miz'ri explained. "Your confusion is not unexpected, and is considered reasonable—enough so that perhaps your fate is not yet sealed."

"You speak in clever riddles," Byrtyn scolded.

"I speak about as plainly as the situation now allows," Miz'ri corrected. "We do not wish to obliterate a house as old and, until now, as devoted to the Spider Queen as the family Fey-Branche. We merely wish to . . . take you out of the coming fight. We did so as much for your future as our own."

Matron Byrtyn had been around Miz'ri enough to see the lie for what it was. She didn't think the vicious woman was lying in offering mercy here, but the purpose of this attack was plainly obvious to Byrtyn: Matron Zhindia needed a win to impress her would-be allies, including the two powerful houses standing before her right here in her chapel. With this clever feint and conquest, Matron Zhindia was showing Matron Miz'ri, and more than that, was showing Matron Mez'Barris Armgo, that she, not House Baenre, would prevail.

"Where does this leave us, then?" she asked.

"It leaves you and your daughters as our prisoners, for now. Indeed, this compound will be the prison for all of you, including your wizards and your grandson when they return from Donigarten."

Aydiana and Byrtyn exchanged looks.

"We have the blessing and the eyes of Lolth on our side, Matron Byrtyn," said Miz'ri. "Surely you understand that."

"So, you wish for us to join you in your struggle against House Baenre when it comes?" Aydiana Fey asked.

"No, we merely hope that we do not have to kill you. When we are rid of the Baenres and the Xorlarrins—who dare to take the family name of the great heretics!—and whichever houses are stupid enough to join with them, we wish to restore Menzoberranzan to her rightful glory."

"With Zhindia Melarn as Matron Mother?"

"Matron Mother Mez'Barris," Malagdorl answered gruffly before Miz'ri could.

"It is long past time for a change, particularly after the blasphemy performed by the two Baenre priestesses in the above world. Yes, Matron Byrtyn, including your foolish granddaughter."

"Who was blessed by Lolth's very avatar in the womb," Byrtyn reminded her.

"And yet, Yvonnel chose the wrong path," said Miz'ri. "Such a waste. And now you must choose. We hope we will not have to leave you and all of your remaining daughters dead on the floors of House Fey-Branche. Nor murder Zeknar Fey and his wizards and your treasured grandson when they quite obliviously return to their home."

"Unless they return with the Blaspheme and Baenre armies," Byrtyn said, but Miz'ri just laughed at that.

"We were in so quickly, no one knows, Matron Byrtyn. No lights, no magical calls for help."

She motioned behind her and a line of priestesses walked into the chapel, accompanied by formidable Barrison Del'Armgo warriors and wizards of at least three different houses, including the Second and Fourth.

"Choose," Miz'ri ordered.

Matron Byrtyn looked to her daughters and nodded, then turned back to Miz'ri and held up her hands in surrender.

CHAPTER 8

Counterpunch

The city was quiet.

Minolin Fey stood by her daughter's side on a ledge looking down at the cavern's farm district, at Lake Donigarten and the Isle of Rothé.

"They're not coming, are they?" Saribel remarked, for Narbondel's light was long past halfway up the column.

"I should go to Matron Byrtyn," Minolin Fey said.

"No, you shouldn't," Yvonnel answered immediately. She tapped her fingers against her lips, digesting it all.

She thought back to the fight outside House Do'Urden, replaying all of the reports that had come to her from several different participants, including Saribel. The enemy had been routed, but with surprisingly few casualties. The whole of the attacking band had fled as one when the ambush had hit their left flank, a retreat straight to the Fane of Quarvelsharess and sanctuary.

Yvonnel considered the force assembled below her: fifteen hundred warriors, scores of wizards and priests.

She let her gaze drift to the west and south, to the Narbondellyn, now lighter with the timeclock's glow. To House Fey-Branche, quiet—so quiet that it made her think the flashes she had seen before to be nothing of consequence.

"Matron Byrtyn's reign is likely over," she said to the women standing beside her.

"What do you mean?" Minolin Fey asked. "We must go."

We must . . . Those words alone stuck in Yvonnel's thoughts in that difficult moment. She knew that she had to do something here if her suspicions were correct, if House Fey-Branche had indeed been overrun while Baenre's eyes were turned to this empty place.

But were her suspicions correct?

Was it worth the gamble?

She looked to the timeclock, nearly three-quarters of it glowing now. She looked to the Braeryn, just west of her position, the streets seeming normal with activity for this time of day.

The enemy wasn't coming. Not here. Not now.

Yvonnel swung her gaze back the other way, to Donigarten and the Isle of Rothé. She could see the herds of cattle both on the lake banks and out on the island, along with the hulking and hairy bearlike forms of House Hunzrin's quaggoth slaves.

"You will take the island," Yvonnel told Saribel.

"I thought we were here in siege alone."

"Much has changed."

"Because they did not come?"

"Because they went somewhere else," Yvonnel said.

"Fey-Branche," Minolin Fey whispered, her eyes narrowing in fear and anger.

"How many will you need?" Yvonnel asked Saribel.

"To take it or to hold it?"

"Take it," said Yvonnel. "Kill any that resist, quaggoth, goblinkin, drow. But offer quarter to those who would surrender, particularly the Hunzrins."

"You want me to make prisoners of Hunzrins?" Saribel didn't seem overly enthusiastic about going to war with the city's powerful Eleventh House, one that served the needs of all other houses in many ways.

"Within a few hours, they won't be using that name," Yvonnel promised. "You lead the Do'Urden forces and the Fey-Branche contingent—and make sure that Matron Byrtyn's wizards and particularly her weapon master are kept as safe as possible—and I'll offer six score of Blaspheme soldiers to bolster your ranks. Take the island and hold the position, and make sure that there are no routes, magical or tunnel, to House Hunzrin. If there are, dispel them or secure them."

"We have to go to Fey-Branche!" Minolin Fey insisted as Yvonnel's plan became clear.

"In time," said Yvonnel. "It is not enough to return to the previous state. Matron Zhindia pays for this." She turned to Saribel. "I will whisper in your mind when we are ready in the Eastmyr. You will begin the battle. Go, quickly, organize your force."

Saribel turned a wary eye on Minolin Fey, who shifted nervously.

"You're igniting the kindling of war," Minolin Fey said.

"It's already begun," Yvonnel replied, and she tried hard to keep her doubts out of her mind. "House Fey-Branche has been taken."

"We cannot know that," Saribel said. "If you're wrong . . ."

"Go, quickly," Yvonnel repeated.

"I should speak with Matron Zeerith."

"There is no time." Yvonnel walked to the ledge and started down the stairs. "Our moment is now and only now. And yes, if I am wrong, then there will be consequences, no doubt." She looked directly at her mother. "I do not think I'm wrong."

"I feel it, too," Minolin Fey admitted.

"Be bold, sisters," Yvonnel said. "Now is our moment. Only now, immediately now."

"KILL AS FEW AS NECESSARY," YVONNEL INSTRUCTED HER warrior hundreds as they neared their target in the Eastmyr. "Incapacitate, overwhelm, kill only when you must." She gave a wry smile and added, "And know that this mercy and this attack will anger Lolth even more."

Voselly and the other Blaspheme commanders nodded at that

last part, she was glad to see. They wanted a fight, were hungry for blood after centuries of torment, but beyond any other consideration, they wanted to pay back Lolth. And Yvonnel did not want a blood-bath here, in any case, both because of her own aversion to such mass slaughter and because there remained within her a sliver of a doubt.

She might be wrong. She didn't know for certain that House Fey-Branche had fallen. It was a gut feeling supported by little evidence. And if she was wrong, then the more dead Hunzrins, the harder this error would be to unwind.

"We want to scare them," Yvonnel told the wizards and priests. "We want them to see the force arrayed against them, to know they cannot win. Whisper to them to surrender. Put them to sleep, confuse them with fog and darkness."

"You want it quiet," one wizard reasoned.

"No, I want it loud enough to shake the doors of every house in Menzoberranzan. I just don't want unnecessary deaths."

"All deaths in war are necessary."

"That," she said, "is where you are wrong."

Wrong about so much.

Every shadow in the streets about House Hunzrin was soon filled with soldiers.

Yvonnel waited.

"Flashes to the east," Minolin Fey told her.

A moment later, a magical whisper entered Yvonnel's mind. *The quaggoths are melting before us, falling to the ground and begging for mercy.*

Very soon after, another message, *The Isle of Rothé is ours. We are in pursuit of the surviving Hunzrins in the tunnel that runs under Donigarten toward the Eastmyr.*

"They're running for home," Yvonnel mentioned to those around her. "Give them no home to run to."

A few moments later, all of the faerie fires within the House Hunzrin compound went dark, magical blackness blotting the place from sight, and to the walls went the Blaspheme and Baenre soldiers, up and over, hand crossbows loaded.

Now the strike teams worked in concert with selected wizards and priests. The globes of darkness went away one at a time, and whenever one revealed a surprised Hunzrin, or a goblinkin or white-furred quaggoth slave, those enemies were met with a hail of poisoned quarrels. Many of the drow, of course, resisted those sleep poisons—powerful houses trained to build such resistance in their fighters—but few of those soldiers who did not fall into slumber stayed around to fight.

Yvonnel and Minolin Fey ran to the Hunzrin main entrance, Yvonnel signaling to the Baenre wizards to open it.

A barrage of lightning bolts did exactly that, blowing the gates from their hinges.

The sounds of battle surrounded them, though Yvonnel was heartened by the lack of volume in what seemed to be more individual fights and no larger-scale, pitched battles.

Voselly and her strike team awaited them, having taken the front door, and Yvonnel herself led the way in, directing troops left and right through various rooms and corridors as she marched toward the large double doors at the end of the long hallway. She threw spells before her to defeat glyphs and wards, to expose invisible enemies, to create light so bright that it stung drow eyes, to create magical forces that blew open every hatch, even doors sealed with enchantments, which could not resist the sheer overwhelming power of Yvonnel.

House Hunzrin boasted two hundred soldiers and nearly ten times that number of slaves, a total nearly equal to the force that had come against them. But, as was always the case, many of those slaves and drow were not within the compound but out in the farmlands and on the Isle of Rothé. And many were not even in the city, for House Hunzrin's primary source of power and wealth was in extra-Menzoberranzan trading. The three score Hunzrins and two hundred slaves within the house this night had no chance, for goblins and kobolds and even the powerful quaggoths were no match for the Blaspheme and surely no match for the Baenres, whose ranks were thick with powerful wizards and priestesses and whose soldiers wore the finest armor and wielded weapons to a one greater than those even a Hunzrin noble might hold. The Hunzrins hadn't the magic, they hadn't the weapons, they hadn't the gear to even slow the march of drow coming over the walls from every angle.

Even at full strength, Hunzrin, like all but perhaps one or two of the city houses, could not stand for long against an assault from House Baenre, and shorter still with the Blaspheme involved.

And shorter still when Yvonnel Baenre, the most powerful drow in Menzoberranzan at that time, led the attack.

FIRST PRIESTESS CHARRI BURST INTO HER MOTHER'S AUDI-ence chamber to find Matron Shakti huddled with Patron Barag and some others.

"They've breached the main halls!" she told them.

"They've breached everywhere," said elderboy Xeva Hunzrin, who served as house wizard.

"What madness is this?" Charri said. "Who would dare?"

"The Baenres," Matron Shakti told her, and she gasped in fear. "Baenres and their filthy Blaspheme allies. Come, we must flee to the tunnels."

A commotion in the hall behind Charri turned them all, and in through the doors stumbled a bloody Weapon Master Keptus Hunzrin.

"They are destroying our forces fleeing Donigarten," he cried.

"Fleeing Donigarten?" Shakti asked incredulously.

"The Isle of Rothé has fallen," Keptus said. "The Do'Urdens and their wizards."

"Seal the floor," Shakti ordered her weapon master, and to Xeva, she added, "Prepare a gate to Lolth's Web and House Melarn."

He nodded and Keptus rushed back into the hall—almost. For just as he crossed the threshold of the audience chamber, four metal plates appeared in the air above him, and, as if on invisible hinges, swung down at him on all sides, slamming together edge to edge, forming what looked like a coffin about him.

It bounced into the air just a bit, then dropped back down on its end and slowly tipped. All watched in hushed shock, until the silence was shattered when the coffin crashed upon the floor.

Into the room walked Yvonnel Baenre.

"Be reasonable, Matron Shakti," she said. Minolin Fey, Andzrel

Baenre, Voselly, and other Blaspheme warriors spread out inside the room all about her.

"You *dare?*" Shakti retorted.

"We didn't start the fight, Matron, and you know it," Yvonnel said in tones so controlled and confident that her words conveyed a most awful threat. "Take them, all of them," she instructed her forces. "Take their weapons, take their spell components, and if any speak out of turn, perhaps to cast, take their tongue."

"The city will come against you!" Shakti warned.

In response, Yvonnel held her finger up over her pursed lips. "We can discuss it later, Matron Shakti, and when we do, I would greatly prefer that you are able to respond with more than grunts."

Voselly walked over and yanked Shakti out of her chair with frightening ease, and when Xeva Hunzrin began to intervene, reaching for a wand, she hit him in the face with a backhand that landed him on the floor, writhing and groaning.

Before he could regain his wits, Dininae's sword was tip-to-tip with his nose.

"That one comes with me," Yvonnel told Andzrel as she pointed to Charri. "I have always found you to be a reasonable one, priestess. Don't disappoint me now."

"A good win," Andzrel said to no one in particular.

"A good start only," Yvonnel told him. "March the Hunzrin slaves and all their common drow to House Baenre. Leave only the nobles here, with just enough guards to kill them quickly and flee if a counterattack ensues."

"And you?"

"And us," she answered. "This wasn't much of a fight. Are you ready for another?"

"This same day?"

"We go to visit an ally, openly, and with weapons bared," Yvonnel told him.

"House Fey-Branche," Minolin Fey agreed.

Yvonnel turned to Shakti, who stood impertinently at the end of Voselly's short spear.

"If your dear friend has murdered my grandmother, then expect that House Hunzrin will cease to exist," Yvonnel said.

"My friend?" Shakti dared argue. "House Hunzrin—"

"Shut up," Yvonnel demanded, and she motioned to Voselly, who prodded the matron. "You try to walk so fine a line, smiling both left and right, Matron Shakti, but I see you for what you are."

Yvonnel subtly used her magic then, making her stare so intense as to seem beyond mortal, making those in the room see her as if she had somehow grown, powerful and terrible, and even the lighting all about her seemed to change, highlighting her alone. Her white hair blew on unfelt breezes and she lifted from the floor, arms outstretched, presenting herself in that one moment as almost godlike—so much so that even Voselly, who had served at the abyssal altar of cruel Lady Lolth for millennia, had her jaw hanging open.

The moment passed.

"Come, First Priestess," Yvonnel said to Charri. "You will be my emissary to House Fey-Branche. The enemies of House Baenre will leave Matron Byrtyn's abode or they will die, to a one."

"Fey-Branche?"

"I've already told you: don't play the fool," Yvonnel warned. "We know." She knew that she was taking a great risk here, for they certainly did not know any such thing. Still, she was confident enough in her hunch to take this risk and conquer a well-known and valuable, powerful house and so she had to play it out to its logical conclusion, after all.

The concerned expressions that flickered across Charri's and Shakti's faces provided more confirmation to Yvonnel that her guess had been correct.

"There are powerful houses involved in that conquest," Shakti admitted.

"We are powerful houses, too. Please tell me that Malagdorl Armgo is there," Yvonnel replied in a most wicked tone. Matron Shakti blinked repeatedly at that.

"Tell me, Matron, do you think his pride or his wisdom will prevail?" Yvonnel teased. "Will he be wise enough to retreat from his illegitimate attack, or will he horribly perish?" She turned about, directing all eyes to the metal coffin lying by the door, and she ended the debate and deflated the Hunzrin arguments once and for all.

"Weapon masters fall so easily."

CHAPTER 9

Consequence

Charri Hunzrin had no escort and so felt completely vulnerable as she walked to the hastily repaired gates of House Fey-Branche—gates now guarded by soldiers of other houses.

She breathed a bit easier when she was recognized and orders were called out to let her in, and quickly. Once inside, she was hustled to the house chapel, where sat Matron Miz'ri Mizzrym and her allies, while Byrtyn Fey and her daughters stood chained and guarded at the side of the room.

"They are coming, Matron," Charri said as soon as she was formally announced.

"They?"

"A force from House Baenre and her allies. One great enough to sweep this house clean before Narbondel goes dark again, and before your families could possibly arrive in any numbers to help." She turned to look at Malagdorl as she finished, making the point that even House Barrison Del'Armgo, perhaps the only house whose presence here could more balance the coming fight, could not hope to intervene in time.

"House Hunzrin has fallen to them already," Charri continued. "As has Donigarten. They struck with purpose and full force as soon as House Fey-Branche fell."

"Hunzrin? Hunzrin isn't even here, other than you," Matron Miz'ri protested.

"I'm aware," she said bitterly. "They *knew*, somehow. And they swept in like a river's flood. An overwhelming force. They were all the way to the chapel before Matron Shakti even knew that we were under attack, like a mirror of your own attack on Fey-Branche. This is the first time the power of Baenre has been unleashed in Menzoberranzan against another house in decades. Since the fall of Oblodra? They are everything we feared, and more. High Priestess Yvonnel Baenre sent me to you now, to warn all here to be gone before they arrive. They were merciful to House Hunzrin. Not many Hunzrins are dead, I believe, even among the house's many slaves. Yvonnel told me that such will not be the case when they come here. Any found here who are not Fey-Branche will be put to the sword, or worse." She paused and looked at each in the room. "Or much worse."

"Let them come," said Malagdorl. "We will kill them as they cross the walls."

"Enough, Weapon Master," Miz'ri demanded, locking Charri in a stare. "What of the Blaspheme?" she asked.

"You will see for yourself if you do not flee this place," Charri warned. "I tell you again, they overran the Isle of Rothé and all of Donigarten, then swept through House Hunzrin, and I believe that it all began after your victory here. How long have you been in here, Matron Miz'ri? A few hours? That alone was enough for Yvonnel Baenre to strike."

"Go out in the hall," Miz'ri told Charri, and the matron motioned for some guards and a priestess to go and guard over her. "And close the door," she ordered.

"WE ARE LOSING OUR ELEMENT OF SURPRISE," ANDZREL Baenre told Yvonnel. The force was making its deliberate but slow way toward House Fey-Branche, using magical silence in many places and spells of invisibility. Still, none there entertained any notions that they were traveling wholly undetected, as they were passing many houses that were well guarded even against such protective enchantments.

"Give them time to leave," Yvonnel replied. "Better for us, better for Matron Byrtyn and the rest of House Fey-Branche if we do not have to kill them all in that compound."

"If Matron Byrtyn is even still alive," Andzrel said, and Minolin Fey sucked in her breath.

"If that is the case, we are still better off in simply repelling them," said Yvonnel. "There will be a council after this long and deadly night. Many will be brought to account for their deeds, and the slaying of a matron, one of the Ruling Council no less, is among the highest crimes a house can commit."

"I think she's still alive," Minolin Fey said. "Let me try to contact—"

"No," Yvonnel flatly replied. "We will know her fate soon enough. I am as impatient as you, but we must allow it to play out."

Voselly and Aleandra came rushing back to them.

"House Fey-Branche is quiet," Voselly reported. "And now surrounded."

"Filter Baenres among your forces, ones who will recognize many of those who flee," Yvonnel instructed. "I wish an accounting of every house that went against Matron Byrtyn this night."

The two Blaspheme warriors bowed and rushed away.

"You'll find half the ruling houses among the ranks of the attackers, I do not doubt," Minolin Fey warned.

Yvonnel didn't disagree and remained quite unsure of her actions here, for she knew well that she had taken a great risk—indeed, more than one great risk, since she had come to believe that Matron Zhindia or her allies had attacked House Fey-Branche.

She was near enough now to House Fey-Branche, near enough to Charri Hunzrin, to begin to get some clarity on the situation, however. She closed her eyes and began a spell.

DON'T CLOSE IT ALL THE WAY, CHARRI HUNZRIN SIGNALED to the guard at the chapel door. When he scowled at her and gripped the doorknob, she hastily added, *I have seen the approaching force. All of our lives might depend upon what they do in that room.*

The guard looked to another Mizzrym soldier, who was clearly torn, which Charri understood, because she was, after all, asking them to disobey their matron's command. Still, the guard shut the door lightly, enough so to allow Charri to move near it and hear the arguments within.

She wasn't surprised to hear Malagdorl raising his voice above the others.

"They were defeated! There must be a price," he said.

"She is a matron; you are a weapon master," Matron Miz'ri replied.

Charri mumbled a curse under her breath. Malagdorl wanted to kill Matron Byrtyn Fey-Branche. She wasn't surprised, but knew that such a move would be the end of any chance of peace in Menzoberranzan. Would her own mother be executed in response? Would House Baenre immediately go to war with House Barrison Del'Armgo? Such a conflict would spread throughout the city in short order, inflicting thousands of deaths, she believed.

She took a deep breath and focused again on the conversation beyond the doors, or tried to, for then she heard a different conversation, a different kind of conversation.

They will leave now or die, Yvonnel Baenre's magical whisper imparted to Charri Hunzrin. *Now. Or die.*

"Open the door and announce me at once," Charri instructed the guard.

He hesitated and looked to the other soldier.

"Now, our enemies are almost upon us," she insisted. "If you hesitate, we are all most assuredly doomed. Now!"

The Mizzrym soldier went to the door, knocked once, and pulled it open. "First Priestess Charri Hunzrin insists on immediate audience," he said to the startled and angry expression worn by Matron Miz'ri. "She insists," he reiterated, putting it all on Charri as she pushed by him fearlessly.

"Now," she told Miz'ri. "We must depart now. Our enemies are all about us. Yvonnel Baenre just whispered in my mind. We leave now or we fight. There is no third choice."

Miz'ri looked to some of the others.

Malagdorl growled and vowed to impale Yvonnel Baenre and hold her up high in the air so all could witness her dying moments.

"Matron Miz'ri, I am leaving," Charri declared. "I humbly suggest you do the same."

She bowed, turned, and moved for the door with all speed.

The guards at the door turned to accompany her, but Miz'ri motioned for them instead to stop her. She sat there for just a moment, considering Charri's returning scowl, so thick with fear, and her desperate retreat, seeing in those hurried footsteps a true measure of the power Charri had just watched overrun House Hunzrin. Hunzrin, ranked eleventh, was not a ruling house, but it was more powerful than at least two of those ruling eight—including the very house she sat in now—and was thick with many slaves that included an army of formidable quaggoths.

All that power . . . and she watched a terrified Charri Hunzrin attempt to run away.

So suddenly, Matron Zhindia's power seemed much hollower to Miz'ri Mizzrym. Was Zhindia really a shield to stand behind with the power of House Baenre bared?

"We go," she decided.

"No, we fight," said Malagdorl.

"Who is 'we'? Where is House Barrison Del'Armgo, Weapon Master?" Miz'ri asked him with a sneer.

"Malagdorl, no," said the wizard Kaitain. "This is not a fight Matron Mez'Barris would wish. I will create the portal and we—all of House Barrison Del'Armgo—will depart at once."

Malagdorl obviously wanted a fight. Because he was a stupid man who thought only with his sword. He narrowed his eyes and squeezed his hand about his trident. Miz'ri almost sighed with the frustration of his shortsightedness.

"Matron Mez'Barris would not be pleased to find her dear Malagdorl is prisoner of the Baenres," Miz'ri scolded him. "You would steal from her any hopes she has in doing battle with Matron Mother Quenthel, for she would not risk the likelihood of a drider named Malagdorl fighting against her."

That took a bit of the puff out of the weapon master's chest.

"Take the noble priestesses," Miz'ri ordered her soldiers.

"There will be consequences for your treachery!" Matron Byrtyn yelled at her.

"You take *her*," Miz'ri told Malagdorl, and his scowl lessened even more as he looked at Miz'ri with surprise, and turned into a grin as he swiveled his head to stare at Matron Byrtyn. "Get to your house with all speed and give her to Matron Mez'Barris as my gift, to do with as she thinks best . . . or worst."

Malagdorl was more than happy to oblige. He roughly grabbed Matron Byrtyn by the arm and tugged her forward, or tried to, for the surprisingly strong woman managed to pull free. She had just started to protest when Malagdorl's left hook caught her in the jaw, throwing her to the floor. The powerful and brutish warrior pushed aside her daughters, warning them back with his trident, and went to the fallen woman, grabbing her by the collar of her gown and hoisting her with ease up into the air, flipping her over one shoulder. Carrying her like a sack, he motioned for Kaitain to open the gate.

Charri Hunzrin continued to stare hard at Matron Miz'ri, her eyes making it clear to the matron what she thought of another matron being handled so roughly by a mere male.

She softened a moment later, in response to Miz'ri's nod, the matron telling her that she, too, was appalled by such a sight.

These were the unwinding strands, Charri feared, that would doom any alliance against powerful House Baenre.

Miz'ri discovered she agreed, as soon as the dozen Armgos passed through the gate and were gone.

"That one is so determined to hold the reputation of Uthegentel, he forgets his place too often," Miz'ri admitted openly in the room. "I will explain to Matron Mez'Barris that such treatment of a matron, any matron, particularly one of an old and noble house, is not acceptable."

Charri noticed that she aimed her last remarks at the Fey-Branche daughters, and that, too, bothered the Hunzrin priestess. Matron Miz'ri was attempting a bit of diplomacy and mitigation in a house she had just overrun.

Did she really believe that the Fey-Branches would ever forget or forgive?

In that moment, Charri Hunzrin understood that there would be no turning back here. They would pick their sides and they would win or they would lose everything.

They would live today. But Menzoberranzan would not heal.

PART 2

COLD, HARD TRUTHS

If everything is one, is one lonely?

The question sounds ridiculous, and yet it has haunted me in re-cent days, since the very notion of this unexpected paradox came into my thoughts. The beauty of transcendence, so I came to believe in my short experience with it, was the oneness—with everything, with every stone and tree and living creature and empty space and star. It was a vast ex-amination of complete consciousness and understanding, a higher level of thought and of being, no doubt. That was the comfort and the joy. New experiences and understanding lying open before me, settled in a multi-verse of supreme contentment and harmony.

But if I become one with those who went before, if our conscious-ness and understanding, our thoughts and our feelings, are fully shared, and at such a level of intimacy that the word "shared" comes nowhere near to properly explaining the joining, does that also imply a solitary existence? All-consuming, omnipresent, and omniscient . . . but therefore alone?

That would be heaven and that would be hell.

So no, I say and I hope. Oneness and appreciation that we are all starstuff should not, and I hope do not, completely replace some piece of individuality.

In a paradoxical and wholly unexpected way, viewing the multiverse through the sense of transcendent oneness has led me to a place of truer empathy and appreciation for those with whom I disagree. Arguing, debating, the very experience of having your "truths" challenged, is the flavor of life and the key ingredient of growth. To lean toward perfecting oneself is the challenge, to be better with each passing experience, to climb the proverbial mountain on trails smooth and paths difficult is to feel that forward and upward movement and so experience the sense of satisfaction and accomplishment.

Is that lost in omnipresence?

Is omniscience so perfect and complete that such feelings are no longer needed?

I cannot know and will not know (or perhaps know not at all) until this mortal being is no more, and that inescapable truth put in me a disinterest, or more accurately, a distance, from the tribulations of the material, mortal world. A revelation that should be naught but beauteous instead instilled a melancholy.

I see the simple joys still. My smiles are not strained when I look upon Brie, or Catti-brie, or any of my friends, but my interest surely is.

Or was.

For that melancholy, I see clearly now, has been paid for by the detriment of those I love.

That cannot stand.

And now I see, too, that for all the beauty of transcending this mortal coil and all of its limitations, what I lost in that short journey is not subtle and not without regret.

Because I want to argue. I want to be challenged. I want to disagree.

And most of all, I want to come to understand the perspective of the other person—the separate and distinct individual, carrying the weight of their own experiences and trials and joys and needs, with whom I am at such odds.

The cost of transcendence goes even deeper than that, I now see. Perhaps "loneliness" is the wrong word for a state of omniscience, or more clearly, it describes only a part of the loss.

For in this journey toward the state, there is hope, and through the trials, there is accomplishment, and even the scars of failure have value as signposts toward betterment.

I lived alone for many years, relying only on myself. That changed when I met Mooshie, and shifted even more completely when I first climbed the slopes of Kelvin's Cairn in Icewind Dale and discovered myself as a willing member of a group, of a family.

They rely on me, and that feels wonderful.

I rely on them, and know I can, and that feels better still.

Together we are stronger. Together we are better, sharing joys, dividing grief and pain.

We are bonded, yet we remain distinct. We argue—oh, how we argue!—and we grow. We fear for each other in battle, and remain glad that we are all in it together.

Even before we ventured north, Grandmaster Kane could have simply shed his physical body and remained within me, joining my thoughts, sharing my flesh, guiding me and strengthening me, offering all without question and without any room for disagreement, since we two would understand— would perfectly understand—every thought and command.

But Kane didn't do that, and he wouldn't, and there need be no explanation offered as to why. For we both knew and know the joy of individuality.

When I was gone from this existence and Brother Afafrenfere came after me to tell me of Brie, to whisper to me that my time here was not completed, he and I remained distinct beings.

Even within that omniscience and omnipresence of transcendence, we remained distinct.

I pray that detail does not blur to nothingness in whatever truly comes next after this life journey is ended.

I need my companions.

I need to be needed by my companions.

This is my greatest joy.

—Drizzt Do'Urden

CHAPTER 10

A Crashing Dose of Reality

Azzudonna tried to compose herself, but the world had gone so suddenly crazy that she wasn't even sure what that might mean. She collected her thoughts, focusing on the present moment, the seemingly dangerous situation, so that she could fully realize and react to this unexpected reality before her.

Namely that she was in a room, a bedroom, facing an open door and a human woman she did not know. Sunlight streamed in through a window to her left—sunlight! And that's where her confusion—her questioning of reality—came in. Because Quista Canzay had passed and night had fallen.

So how could there be sunlight?

It was another trick of Catti-brie's cat—it had to be. But to what end? For Guenhwyvar was gone from her side, becoming insubstantial mist and floating away to nothingness, abandoning her in this strange place—perhaps in this different time?—without any explanation or grounding at all.

The human woman standing in the open doorway before her held her hands up, as if trying to appear unthreatening, and kept speaking, but in a language Azzudonna could not begin to decipher—although it was certainly the same tongue she had occasionally heard used by the four travelers who had come to Callidae.

The aevendrow realized only then that she wasn't holding her spear. Fearing that she had dropped it back in the glacial ice hallway when she had been slammed from behind by Guenhwyvar, she started to glance around nervously. But her attention was abruptly diverted as an older man, another human, came up behind the woman who was still talking to her.

Reflexively, Azzudonna's hand went to the hilt of her white-ice sword, which was sheathed at her right hip, and when she glanced down at the weapon, she saw, too, her spear! She hadn't dropped it back at the glacier, but here, in this room. Wherever this room might be.

The human woman pumped her hands at Azzudonna and pleaded with her, and she recognized that the woman was trying to implore her to remain calm. Behind her, though, the man in the hallway began subtly waggling his fingers.

A spell!

The aevendrow warrior dropped fast and scooped up the short spear. She came right back up, the weapon spinning end over end before her, then rolled across to her right, and then back and out to her left. She ended the flourish with the weapon leveled in both hands, its magical blue-white ice tip pointing menacingly at the woman.

Azzudonna jabbed it forward, coming up well short, trying to force the woman back out into the hall, buying some room and some time as she searched desperately for an escape route. She didn't want to kill, but wanted to make it clear she could if she needed to.

The man in the hall extended his hand, index finger pointing at Azzudonna, then stopped the movement short and jabbed it at her from afar.

Azzudonna cried out, expecting a bolt of energy or some other attack. She threw herself to the left, out of line with the open doorway and out of sight of the man. She kept going, leaping upon the bed, running across it and springing for the wall or, more particularly, for the room's side door, which opened onto a balcony. At least that's what it seemed, from what she had noticed through the nearby window.

She crashed into the door, tried to push and tried to pull, but no, it was locked. Expecting some magical attack to slam her again at any moment, Azzudonna didn't slow, rolling along the wall past the door toward the back of the room, coming up before the window.

"No, we are not enemies!" the woman cried amid the crash of shattering glass, with Azzudonna thrashing her spear all about to clear the way. She went through and was out on the balcony, to the rail, which she caught with one hand and rolled right over, throwing her spear to stick in the snowy ground some dozen feet below.

She dropped, landed in a roll, and retrieved her spear, already starting away before it even occurred to her that the woman's last words weren't gibberish, and that, perhaps, she had understood some of them, at least.

No matter, though. She could sort out that mystery later. She was outside an enormous house of amazing design—if it was even a design at all, rather than a hodgepodge of a dozen different towers and wings and dormered windows and roofs angled every which way. Smoke rose from a host of chimneys, winding gray lines dancing in the wintry wind. She was up on a high hill with few trees on this side. To her left and down the hill, she saw other buildings, a small town, while straight ahead loomed a forest.

She didn't hesitate. She needed to be away, to find someplace to settle and sort this all out, to come back to these people, perhaps, but on her own terms.

"No, no! Who are you?" she heard the woman yelling behind her, having come out on the balcony.

She put her head down and sprinted down the slope.

"Beware!" the human woman warned. "Take care! Hold up! Oh . . . stop!"

The terrified Azzudonna didn't stop or slow, until she did, abruptly, brutally, painfully, smashing into an unseen and unyielding wall. Her spear hit it first, her face second, the weapon going up and across so that when she fully slammed in, its barbed side drove hard and deep into her left shoulder.

But she barely felt it, caught fully in the white flash of shock and pain in her nose, her face, her head. She bounced back. She tried to keep her footing, but all the world had gone soft and uneven, and she didn't know which way was up.

She felt a hot burn in her shoulder.

She felt the warm blood in her mouth.

She felt the cold against her and somewhere deep in her mind understood that she was lying in the snow.

Then she couldn't see. She couldn't think. She couldn't feel . . . anything.

"GET A CLERIC!" PENELOPE HARPELL YELLED TO THOSE coming down the hill. A couple of the Harpells rushing down the snowy hillside skidded to stops, talking and jostling for just a moment before two ran off toward the village of Longsaddle below the Ivy Mansion, with three others scrambling and slipping back up the hill toward the great house.

"There's none in the house or the town who'll be fixing these wounds," said Dowell, Penelope's husband, as he rolled the wounded drow over onto her back and pressed the area about the embedded spear, trying to stem the bleeding.

Looking at the sheer amount of blood coloring the snow nearby, Penelope feared that he was right.

A magical door appeared right beside the three then, startling Penelope and Dowell for just a moment, until old Kipper Harpell stepped forth, bearing a healing kit. He handed it to Penelope, who began fishing through it for some bandages and salves.

"This won't be enough," she told Kipper.

"Get her comfortable," Kipper, the oldest member of the Harpells, replied. "Enough to get her in the house. The cold will kill her with these wounds and so much blood already spilled. Let's fix what we can, and then worry about the rest."

"We need a priest," Dowell insisted. "We need a powerful priest."

"As I said," Kipper replied.

Penelope glanced up as she handed the bandages to her husband, and noticed the ghostly imprint of the drow woman's face on the invisible fence that surrounded the Ivy Mansion. The Harpells were not unused to picking up dead birds that had flown into the barrier, but now with this tragedy, perhaps the debate over adding some greater opacity to the fence would take on greater urgency.

"Go to the teleport gates," she told Kipper. "Travel Gauntlgrym and see what priests King Bruenor can send."

The old man nodded and began waggling his fingers and chanting the arcane words of a spell to create a new dimension door to get him back up into the house.

"Then to Luskan with all speed," Penelope decided. "Find the priestess Dab'nay and bring her. This must be one of Jarlaxle's associates."

"She didn't act like any member of Bregan D'aerthe," Kipper replied. "I mean, they know of us. An assassin, perhaps, sent from Menzoberranzan to be rid of Jarlaxle?"

"Or Zaknafein, more likely," Penelope reasoned. She shook the notion out of her head, though—it just didn't seem correct to her. This one was well armed and could have attacked her back at the house, after all.

Behind her, Kipper was "hmm"-ing repeatedly.

"Go!" Penelope bade him.

Kipper startled, then nodded and stepped through the gate, disappearing instantly.

"Can we get the spear out?" Penelope asked Dowell.

"Only if we want her to bleed to death right here," he answered. "It's in deep and it's hooked tight with those barbs."

"What *is* it?" Penelope asked, for she had never seen such a weapon, the long and large spearhead etched with beautiful and intricate designs and fashioned of some material she did not recognize.

"I don't know," Dowell admitted. "It doesn't feel like metal, but . . . I just don't know."

Penelope reached over and touched the exposed part of the broad spear tip. It had a little sting to it, a sensation of coldness. "Ice?" she asked. "Can we melt it out of her?"

"How can it be?" Dowell asked, and he shrugged, having no answers. "How could a weapon made of ice have such strength and resilience? And if it is, I doubt it would melt so easily."

Penelope angled her hands so as to not strike the fallen woman with her spell, and blasted forth fingers of magical fire that shot out beyond the woman and across the snow, melting some, lifting a slight burst of steam into the sky.

She felt the spear tip when she was finished, seeking wetness, searching for some malformation. But there was none. Her spell had done nothing to the weapon.

"No ice that I know," she said.

She took the offered end of a long bandage and wrapped it under the embedded weapon, then under the fallen drow's shoulder and up the back, where Dowell tightly tied it off. Other Harpells reached them then, with one man pulling off his large cloak and setting it out on the ground as a litter. Carefully, the group got the drow onto it and hoisted her, then began the climb to the Ivy Mansion.

"We shouldn't have dismissed Kipper so soon," Penelope lamented, for that one always had minor teleportation spells at the ready, and they could have walked the poor woman through a dimension door instead of bouncing and staggering up the hill with her.

Almost as if Penelope had summoned him, a doorway appeared in the air right beside the group, Kipper poking his head through.

"Come along, quickly," he told them, then, as he disappeared back into the Ivy Mansion on the other end of the magical tunnel, he called to them. "I'm away to Gauntlgrym!"

"I GOT IT OUT, BUT I'M NOT KNOWIN' WHAT I GOT," PRIESTess Copetta of Gauntlgrym announced, coming out of the room where they had put the wounded drow.

Copetta handed the spear to Penelope in two parts. "Had to break the shaft—no easy task, that—to be able to angle them nasty barbs and pull the durn thing out without tearing the poor girl's shoulder to shreds. Now, if ye'll be excusing me poor tired self, I've spent all me spells and need a good long sleep. The drow priestess Dab'nay's taken over with her magic, and more priests'll come through from Gauntl-grym, to be sure, but not to be sure that we'll be needin' 'em."

"Our visitor is going to be okay, then?" Dowell asked.

Copetta shrugged. "She woke up, maybe. But not for long, and she wasn't hearin' us or seein' us, from what me own eyes could tell. Back to her sleep she went, so I came out to yerselves to let Dab'nay finish her healing spells. A good night's sleep and might be that she'll be up and around."

"Now we just have to figure out what she's all about," Penelope remarked. "And what happened to Catti-brie and our friends."

"What's this to do wi' Princess Catti-brie?" Copetta asked. "Ye think this girl here's one o' Jarlaxle's lasses, then? Ye think she went north with Jarlaxle's band?"

Penelope shook her head. "Maybe nothing," she answered. "Maybe everything."

THE WORLD BEGAN TO BRIGHTEN AROUND HER, LIKE THE sunrise of Conception Verdant.

But no, that couldn't be right.

The brightening was coming from inside, Azzudonna realized. Her eyes, her senses, her mind, reawakening from a deep darkness. She tried to remember what had happened.

Where was she?

She recalled running down a hill.

Then a bright flash, then . . . this.

Had she been hit by a powerful magical evocation?

Her face ached. Her shoulder ached. She tried to shift to change the angle of her arm and only then realized that she couldn't lift her arms—or her wrists, at least.

Am I bound?

Her vision came into focus. She was in a room full of strange furniture and design. Even her bed and bedding were foreign to her, of fabric and construction she did not know. There was no window in the room at all—why would anyone build a bedroom without a window?

That thought reminded her more clearly of when she had arrived at the place. She thought of the window she had broken through, and the balcony beyond. The house on the hill.

She was lying on her back, propped up by pillows, and dressed in a simple light-colored smock instead of the magnificent sealskin, silk, and hagfish mucus of her traveling outfit. She craned her neck to confirm that her wrists were tightly bound to the bed frame, and realized only then that her ankles were similarly tied. She twisted and pulled, to no avail.

A voice startled her. She turned her head to the side to see a woman, a drow woman with short silver-white hair. Her shining red eyes and plump red lips stood out dramatically against her dark gray skin, which showed just a blush of pink under her exquisite high and angled cheekbones.

She spoke again, her tone soothing, but Azzudonna couldn't understand a word of it. She shook her head, but the woman merely repeated her words in that unknown language.

"I do not understand," Azzudonna stated.

The woman appeared confused. She paused and scrunched up her face.

"You do not speak the Common tongue of the surface races?" the woman asked her in Drow—not quite the same as the language used by the aevendrow, but surely understandable, particularly since Azzudonna had heard the same from Jarlaxle and Zaknafein.

Azzudonna shook her head. "No."

"Very well," she replied. "I am Dab'nay. Once, I was Dab'nay Tr'arach of Menzoberranzan, but now I am just Dab'nay. What house do you hail from?"

"House?"

"Your noble house? Or are you from the Stenchstreets?"

Azzudonna realized from her interrogator's sly gaze that her face had scrunched up in confusion, and that, likely, was giving some things away here. She swallowed hard and sighed and didn't reply.

"Who are you and where are you from?"

The second part of that question stopped Azzudonna cold before she blurted her name, an unsubtle reminder of what was at stake here. For all of her life she, like the others born and raised in Callidae, had been trained to avoid such questions, the consequences of which could end the very existence of their beloved city.

"You are not among enemies," Dab'nay added when Azzudonna hesitated and even looked away.

In response, Azzudonna flexed her arms against the ties and stared sternly at Dab'nay.

"Could it be different?" Dab'nay asked, her voice thick with incredulity. "I have just healed some of your wounds, and will do so again when I am not so weary."

"After I was struck down?"

"Struck down?" Dab'nay repeated, and she gave a little chuckle. "You ran face-first into an invisible wall of force!"

"Where am I? What is this place?"

"Who are you? And where are you from?" Dab'nay shot back.

Azzudonna looked away, but Dab'nay came up to her and stood towering over her until she finally looked back to match the priestess's stare.

"We are not your enemies—yet," Dab'nay said, her voice low and even. "But understand me well here. You have come to us uninvited, by surprise, brought here by Guenhwyvar, the animal companion of a woman beloved in this place. What is your name? Is that too much to ask of one who appears in our midst in such a manner?"

Still she was wary. But the hint of a hope proved all too much, and finally, she said, "Azzudonna."

"Your name is Azzudonna?"

She nodded.

"Of what house?"

Azzudonna shook her head.

"That was Guenhwyvar who brought you to the Ivy Mansion, to Catti-brie's own room."

Azzudonna shrugged noncommittally, causing pain to course through her left shoulder.

"How did you get here?" Dab'nay asked more pointedly. "We know the panther brought you, but from where? Why?"

"I don't know," she answered, not untruthfully.

Dab'nay sighed. "Well, I will leave it to others to speak with you more directly, but I warn you, Azzudonna, we have four friends, dear friends, people we love, missing somewhere in the north, and we will get our answers. If you are worthy of our friendship, or even of not being our enemy, you will help us understand."

"I know less than you think. I do not even know where I am."

"The Ivy Mansion," the priestess said without hesitation.

Azzudonna shrugged and shook her head.

"The home of the Harpells in the town of Longsaddle."

"None of those names mean anything to me."

"Icewind Dale? Luskan?"

She shook her head.

"Menzoberranzan?"

"I *have* heard of Menzoberranzan, but I know not where it is."

"You are drow, but you do not know of Menzoberranzan?" Dab'nay asked. "I find that hard to believe."

Azzudonna replied with her favorite answer: a shrug.

There came a soft knock on the door and it opened slowly, revealing the woman Azzudonna had first seen when she had come through the travel tunnel beside the panther. Behind her were a couple of men, including the one who had pointed a spell at her.

Dab'nay walked over to the newcomers and motioned them back out of the room, saying something in the other language. Azzudonna recognized the end of the short sentence, though, and so she could guess easily enough that the drow priestess had merely informed them of her stated identity.

Dab'nay went out behind them, leaving Azzudonna alone.

She tried her ties again, struggling futilely. Her every instinct forced her to consider an escape.

But how? And to where?

The fact that the first attempt had ended disastrously also weighed on her.

She thought of Dab'nay's words. The Ivy Mansion in Longsaddle? The names meant nothing to her.

She pressed more forcefully against her ties anyway, more out of frustration than out of any expectations that doing so would gain her anything. Even if she escaped the bindings, would that do anything more than anger her captors?

"Captors?" she quietly asked.

These were the friends of Catti-brie and Entreri, of Jarlaxle and Zaknafein. They were good people, she had to believe, and so perhaps "captors" was not the right word—at least, not for long.

She hoped that to be the case.

But then what? The enormity of the situation was beginning to wash over the poor, lost aevendrow. Even if she was right in her hopes that this Dab'nay and the others would not harm her, even if they would not keep her chained or otherwise imprisoned, then what?

Her life as she knew it was over.

She couldn't possibly begin to find her way back to Callidae. She certainly couldn't ask these strangers to help guide her!

For a hopeful instant, the image of Guenhwyvar flashed in her thoughts—perhaps these people could somehow summon the panther and get the cat to take Azzudonna back to where she had been abducted.

Just an instant, though, and the hope left her shaking her head again at her foolishness. For even in that instance, she would be betraying her kin, would be violating the most important and sacred oath of all who called Callidae home.

No, her life as she had known it was over, likely forever, but almost certainly for many, many years, at the least.

Azzudonna lay back, lifted her head, and slammed it down on the pillows several times in frustration.

Get it all out, she told herself. *Smash your anger and frustration into this pillow here and now and be done with it.*

She had to come to terms with the reality presented to her. The quicker, the better.

If she was to find happiness again, hope again, life itself again, it would be in this new reality.

She thought of Galathae and Emilian, Vessi and Ilina and all the others.

"Biancorso," she whispered, a great bittersweet name at that time.

Biancorso had been the focus of her life. Her years were spent in training for the great test called cazzcalci.

The joy of her life, cazzcalci!

The joys of her life, her friends!

The joy of her life, Callidae!

Her lovers!

And Zaknafein, too, a man for whom she had felt something even more . . . even Zaknafein was lost to her.

And he was probably dead. No, if she was being honest with herself, almost certainly dead.

She felt the tears running down her cheeks. The weight of loss would not be easily denied, she realized, as much as she tried to stifle the sobs.

"HER NAME IS AZZUDONNA," DAB'NAY REPEATED TO PE-nelope and the others out in the hallway. "She won't tell me where she's from. She won't tell me how she got here. To be honest, I'm not sure she really knows how she got here."

"You are sure she's not of Bregan D'aerthe?"

"She's not, and more than that, I believe that she is not from Menzoberranzan. Her accent, her dialect, even many of the words she uses . . ." Dab'nay shook her head. "I do not know where she's from, and don't believe that she even knows how she got here."

"That cannot stand," Penelope answered. "The more I replay it in my head, the more I am positive that it was Guenhwyvar I saw beside her. Our friends are in trouble, I am sure, and she might be the only one who can lead us to them."

"You cannot be *sure*," Dab'nay said.

"I *feel* certain," Penelope countered.

"King Bruenor'll be here soon enough," said Copetta, and her words sounded very much like a threat.

"We've got to keep trying," Penelope said, and she looked directly at Copetta when she answered, "Gently."

"I don't think she's an enemy," Dab'nay agreed.

"Then what's she hidin'?" grumbled the dwarf. "Are we to learn there's another city akin to yer own Menzoberranzan? What war's coming, then?"

"You don't know any of that, and I don't know that she's hiding anything at all at this point," Dab'nay replied.

"She's crying," said Dowell Harpell, who was standing by the door, his ear against it.

Dab'nay led the way, Penelope close behind. She knocked again and pushed open the door, catching Azzudonna in the last shake of her head—a physical and mental shrug, both she and Penelope understood, as the stranger's expression shifted to one of steady determination.

Penelope began to cast a spell, but stopped short when Azzudonna's eyes went wide with obvious trepidation.

"Tell her it's another spell so that we can speak to each other," Penelope instructed Dab'nay, who translated.

Azzudonna spent a long while just staring at Penelope, and the Harpell wizard understood she was sizing her up, trying to figure out if she could trust Penelope or not. After a while, she shook her head brusquely and spoke in Drow to Dab'nay.

"She has nothing to say at this time and wants to know where she is," Dab'nay translated.

Penelope considered casting her spell anyway, and perhaps following it with some other, more intrusive and less hospitable ones so they could understand each other and get some answers. She backed away, though, for Azzudonna seemed truly a pitiful sight at that time, slight and gaunt and obviously weakened from the brutal wound—and probably more than a bit dizzy from the smash she had taken on her head.

"Just ask her about Catti-brie," Penelope told Dab'nay. "And why she was with Guenhwyvar."

"Are you sure that was Guenhwyvar?" Dab'nay asked. Penelope's immediately reaction was incredulity, but as she considered the question, she had to admit that she had only heard the growl of a large feline and seen a panther form melting into mist and then nothingness, as was typical of a dismissed Guen.

Was she really growing more certain, or was she merely doing a better job of convincing herself?

Was Guenhwyvar unique?

"Just ask her," Penelope decided, and Dab'nay did.

Azzudonna gave only a slight tell of recognition in response, her eyes widening just a bit and her mouth opening as if to finally answer. But for some reason, that was as far as it got, and the woman just shrugged—then winced profoundly from the effort of lifting her shoulder—and turned her head to the side, looking away from her hosts.

Dab'nay asked again, more insistently, but Azzudonna just shook her head and didn't even look back at the other two women.

Dab'nay reached for her, but Penelope grabbed her arm and held her back.

"She's scared," Penelope said. "Just tell her that she cannot leave, that her room is well guarded, but that she is safe here and should relax and heal."

Dab'nay sighed. "She knows a lot more," she quietly replied to Penelope. "It's not just Catti-brie up there, missing. If that really was Guen who brought her here, our friends likely have a problem. Your fears are well grounded and surely shared."

"I'm aware. And so we'll get our answers," Penelope promised. "Just let her rest a bit and clear her thoughts. She'll see we're not going to harm her, and hopefully learn to trust us."

Dab'nay was clearly skeptical. But she relayed the reassurances to Azzudonna, and the group left the mysterious drow alone—but left the room's door open after setting a trio of guards to stand watch just outside.

"Captors," Azzudonna whispered.

CHAPTER 11

Quiet and Cold, Like Death

From the beginning of his current dilemma, Jarlaxle had decided that he had to ignore the pressing fears regarding his friends. Repeatedly, he reminded himself that they were either already dead or, more likely—more hopefully—encased in the same icy stasis they had found with those who had come in here before them. Over and over again, he replayed the image of the aevendrow woman and the orc they had freed from these same mounds, still alive after months in the icy cocoon. Pitiful both, but alive.

His friends were alive. Over and over again, he told himself that, trying to force himself to believe it.

But he just could not know. What he did know, without doubt, was that time was his only ally here, that patience alone could save him in this place of terrible monsters. With his magical boots, he was warm enough to survive, at least. With his pouch of holding, he had plenty of food and comfortable bedding.

But the dark solitude was playing on him, and his little cubby at the bottom of his magical hole was beginning to smell foul.

"I shall have to speak to Gromph about fashioning a commode of holding," he whispered, and the sound of his own voice startled him. He realized they were his first words in many hours—in a couple of days, likely.

This was a battle of his very sensibilities, then, and one he was already losing! Here in the dark and the cold and the sheer emptiness of his existence, it wasn't just about food and drink and warmth, oh no. His sustenance went far beyond those basic physical needs, and it wasn't being met.

He had to take the chance that the chamber above had cleared. He had to get out of there now.

He pulled his bedroll from his pouch, rolled it into a thick cylinder, then got onto his knees, placing them on the cushion. A snap of his right wrist brought a magical dagger into his hand.

He took a deep breath and reached his other hand out to the pole that supported the umbrella. He wasn't sure if he should bring it down now—would he be inviting a chunk of ice to drop upon him and crush him?

He tried to play it out in his thoughts even as he began searching for another way. Perhaps he could dig a tunnel out from under the umbrella, then go upward beyond the lip of the device.

Jarlaxle shook his head, determined not to overthink it. Even that rational moment flittered and flew away, overwhelmed by a sense of foreboding and sheer terror that continued to mount within him. For he was growing frantic to be out of that place—desperate, even, for the walls were now closing in on him, he was sure!—and so he squeezed the release of the magic, retracting the pole and the fan immediately.

The only thing that fell upon him was his hat.

He laughed. He didn't know why, but he couldn't stop himself.

He picked up the wide-brimmed chapeau and noted that the magical feather was growing back, though his magical bird wasn't nearly available to him as of yet. He started to put the hat on his head, but paused and studied the nub of the regrowing feather more closely. It was not an exact process—the giant bird had sometimes become usable merely a day after fighting for him, while other times, it had taken four full days to recharge the summoning dweomer. He was fairly sure that he had been in this hole at least a day, however.

Now what?

Should he make some light? Wouldn't it shine through the ice block above him, which he was certain was also a small pillar standing in the room? A light would invite attention from any monsters in that chamber, surely, as would any sound.

Again, he silently berated himself for overthinking his situation.

He berated himself for berating himself. The voices in his head were arguing, and they were getting him nowhere.

He needed to be out of there. Nothing else mattered!

Up shot the drow's hand, the magical dagger biting into the hard ice above, though not nearly as deeply as he had hoped.

A flick of his left wrist brought a dagger into that hand, too, and the drow began stabbing and picking and shaving at the ice, flakes and small chips and chunks dropping all about him. He stayed at his work for a long while, finally cutting enough to break off a piece of ice as large as a head, which pleased him until he realized that he was still kneeling, the icy ceiling still too low for him to stand in his hollow.

He knew that the magical hole was fully ten feet deep, and guessed, too, that the magical tornado that had tried to engulf him had left this pillar of ice substantially higher than the floor of the cavern.

Which meant, for all his efforts, he had barely made a dent.

Some time later, Jarlaxle slumped back down to the floor. It took him considerable effort to clear his bedroll and reset it so he could rest.

He tried to empty his thoughts and develop a strategy for getting out of this place. Perhaps he could brace one of these daggers, set it into the ice, then transform it into a sword! Mere ice would top the magic, and so the growth would cut into the block deeply.

A moment of elation was replaced by the drow sucking in his breath in fear. To this point, the one block of ice of any size at all that he had dislodged had crashed down hard to the floor, skimming and nicking his hip and knee on its descent.

"Careful," he whispered, realizing that he could easily inadvertently break off too large a chunk and bury himself here. "Patience."

So he lay back down, determined not to act rashly. A short nap and a quick bit of food had Jarlaxle back at his work, shaving and chipping, picking out small bits, and by the time he stopped that second round of effort—and after a lengthy, *necessary* rest—he had dug out a cylindrical shaft. For the first time in many hours or days—he could not tell—Jarlaxle stood fully upright, his head and shoulders, sans his hat, which was too wide for the shaft, fully within the ice chimney.

And he stood there for a long while, forcing satisfaction, focusing his mind on the task ahead. Now he was beginning to understand the consistency and the stubbornness of the ice tomb. Now he was formulating some ideas of how he might possibly bring down larger pieces, upon which he could set his bedroll, upon which he could reach higher as he continued his dig.

Now he was a little less frantic, and a lot more focused.

In his next effort, hours later, Jarlaxle got his hand up high into the ice chimney and worked his blade horizontally, back toward the wall of his magical hole. The result was both heartening and terrifying, for when he got there, the tip of his blade striking the magical wall, huge chunks of ice tumbled down around him, banging against his legs and nearly tripping him up at one point. He watched as the ice crashed below.

If he had fallen, one of those blocks would have landed on his back or head.

It was a long while before he was digging again, for he had to build a floor with these fallen ice chunks and set all of his belongings out upon it. In a bit of cleverness that Jarlaxle prided himself on, he found a way to angle and reset his umbrella to give him some cover and protection as he went farther. He also began marking the ice wall at the side of his hollow so he could measure his progress.

Jarlaxle didn't know how many hours, or days, had passed when he finally went sideways with his digging efforts, poking an opening in the ice stalagmite just above the floor of the cavern.

The rush of air overwhelmed him. He slumped back down to his bedroll, which was now set on the ice fully halfway above the magical floor of the hole, and found himself shaking in relief and drawing in the new air as if it were some delicious, flavor-filled scent from a far-off land.

He climbed back up to his feet soon after and peered out the small hole he had made. It wasn't fully dark out there, but he saw no movement. He followed the light, a green glow, and could see the edge of the same somewhat-translucent circle in the far wall, like the giant colored windows he had seen in great cathedrals built by humans. He grew convinced that this was the same portal the giant slaad had shattered to call in the wrath of the freezing wind. It had been repaired, or had regrown, and now it was whole, letting in the glow of the Merry Dancers of the polar night sky.

Jarlaxle held his breath as he recalled that godlike creature, who had shrugged off a party of powerful veteran adventurers as if they were children, who had summoned the northern wind, the northern ice, and defeated them in mere moments.

Now the window of ice was back, like a trap reset.

Jarlaxle produced a magical ear horn, set it in place, and put his ear to the hole. He waited there unmoving for a long, long while.

He heard nothing but the moaning of the wind as it blew through the vast cavern.

Slowly and deliberately, Jarlaxle worked his sword about the small tunnel out of the ice stalagmite, widening it. He paused repeatedly to peer through, to listen carefully, then went back to his work, shaving the sides of his frozen tomb.

Eventually he'd had enough. He poked and worked the tip of his dagger into the ice, then flexed and gripped, elongating the blade, setting the hilt against the floor and using the magical growth from dagger to sword to crack deeply into the ice.

The much-enlarged weapon blasted through, upward and out. A large chunk of ice broke free and tumbled down outside the stalagmite, crashing to the chamber floor.

Jarlaxle held his breath, fearing that such a racket had cost him dearly here.

But the room remained quiet.

Just the cold wind, blowing through, groaning.

Jarlaxle climbed back down from the lip, collecting his belongings, then setting himself and releasing the umbrella.

As soon as he did the ice in the hole shifted, part of it tumbling away, but Jarlaxle managed to stay above it and get back to the hole he'd been digging.

Now he worked more furiously, chipping and cracking at the tunnel's edges, breaking it open, finally, so that he could crawl through.

He slowly came up to his knees outside the ice mound, and remained there, glancing around, getting his bearings. He noted the tunnel through which they had entered the cavern. He noted the mounds holding Doum'wielle and the others who had fallen months before. He saw the orc and the aevendrow he and his friends had freed, slumped over and encased in ice once more.

"Are you still alive?" he whispered under his breath, to that orc, to that aevendrow, and to his friends.

And there was Entreri, caught low and angled weirdly, having lost the steed beneath him in his descent to the floor, the magic of the fiery nightmare dismissed as its master fell away to unconsciousness.

And there stood Catti-brie, upright, a ghost in the pillar of ice. Beyond her, to the side, a slight sparkle caught Jarlaxle's eye.

Zaknafein's sword.

Jarlaxle looked to his own tomb. He wanted his portable hole. Could he dismiss it? Would doing so crack the base of the pillar and bring it all crashing down?

He probably wouldn't even be able to retrieve the small cloth in that event, at least not without making far too much of a commotion. He spotted something else as he considered the action, and reached for the item, his obsidian steed figurine, but found it encased in ice where it had fallen to the ground.

Where to begin?

Zak's sword, he decided, and he crawled across, past his mound, past Catti-brie in her tomb, to Zaknafein. A plan began to form as he moved near the sword, the creation that had been forged by Catti-brie, two weapons combined: a blade of light and Zak's fiery whip with its extra-dimensional reach. The weapon was only partly encased, its fire and residual heat having melted the solidifying ice about it before the blade had disappeared back into the magical hilt. To his relief, Jarlaxle realized that he could extract that decorated hilt rather easily.

Then what?

He went to work on the ice, considering his options, replaying the fight and those tactics that had, and had not, worked.

His nightmare, he realized almost immediately. Both he and Entreri had put the hellsteeds to devastating use against the enemies and the stalagmite mounds.

"Hang on, my friend," he whispered to Zak when he at last freed the blade, and he rushed back the other way, sliding down beside his trapped figurine.

Up went the hilt, Jarlaxle bringing forth the magical blade in all its brilliant glory and flame. The shock of the sudden light in the dark cavern surprised him and stung his eyes, but he couldn't stop now, he knew, for he was fully committed. Down came the blade of light, its radiance and fire destroying the ice about the figurine. He pulled the obsidian steed free and leaped up, spinning about, seeking enemies—and seeing them rising up all about him. Ice golems encasing the dead forms of aevendrow and orcs and kurit dwarves and Ulutiun humans.

The n'divi! An army of n'divi.

And he saw the shimmering about the floor, like sheets of water flowing over the ice, and knew that the cante, the uninhabited, were coming for him from every direction. Coming to make of him an n'divi.

He looked to the fiercely glowing sword. "Well, we tried," he muttered.

"WE GO ALL THE WAY TO THE CITY THIS DAY," GALATHAE announced to her expedition. "The weather will hold, the Merry Dancers are bright. We push through."

The arktos vorax teams dug into the snow at the call of their masters, the sleds gliding swiftly across the ice pack. Galathae and Ilina shared one of the sleds, and had barely spoken through the first days of the retreat.

They exchanged glances often, though, and each understood the pain of the other.

"Azzudonna," Galathae said simply when they broke to give the vorax teams a rest. The paladin shook her head.

"It's not your fault," Ilina replied. "And we still do not even know what really happened to her."

"We know that she is gone. They are all gone."

"They knew what they were getting into," Ilina argued, but fully for Galathae's sake, since she, too, felt the profound sting of loss, and not just for Azzudonna. She was surprised at how close she had become with Catti-brie in the weeks she had known the human woman. Their faiths were not so different, both centered in deities that exalted the natural world and the harmony of the cycle of life and death.

"Azzudonna didn't believe that she was getting into anything more than we were," Galathae reminded her.

"And she didn't. That could have been any of us in the hallway, attacked by . . . whatever it was."

"I think it was the panther."

"The panther was an ally," said Ilina. "Let us tell all to the Temporal Convocation, that they can direct the diviners to try to find her, or what happened to her. Is it possible that our visitors escaped with magic and found a way to take Azzudonna with them in their flight?"

"The Temporal Convocation will not be pleased to hear that," Galathae replied. "What might it mean for Callidae if our four visitors have escaped both the slaadi and our own spells of forgetfulness, and with proof of their claims?"

Ilina considered it for a long while, then answered, "I hope they escaped. All of them." She considered her own statement for a moment, then nodded her head. "I trust them."

"Even Jarlaxle?" Galathae teased, wearing a smile for the first time since they had left the caverns.

"Especially Jarlaxle," Ilina replied. "He likes secrets, that one."

Galathae leaned in and kissed Ilina on the cheek.

"We will keep hope," Ilina remarked.

"I would like to do more than hope," said Galathae. "I would like to lead an army back to that cave and settle this once and for all time.

I've had more than enough of the slaadi and their giant servants and their ice golem creations."

The sleds were moving again soon after, and for Ilina and Galathae, the hopeful mood could not hold.

Azzudonna was lost to them.

Catti-brie and the other three visitors were lost to them.

That was the reality they had to face, whatever their hopes.

JARLAXLE DROPPED THE FIGURINE AND CALLED FORTH HIS hellsteed. With a great leap, he was upon it almost as soon as it appeared, and he wasted no time in putting the nightmare mount into motion.

To stand still was to be caught. To be caught was to be destroyed.

His flaming sword became a whip, and he cracked it out to the side at once, its fiery tip biting into an n'divi, slicing through the ice encasing the aevendrow with ease. As he turned away, he thumped the butt of the whip against the hellsteed's flank, and the mount responded with a kick that shattered the stumbling and wounded n'divi and sent it flying away.

"Entreri!" Jarlaxle called, as much to himself as to his friend, who of course could not hear him. He urged his hellsteed in that direction, thinking that Entreri should be the first he freed, for Entreri, too, had a hellsteed out and ready, and perhaps the two of them could get their friends up on their mounts behind them and be swiftly away.

But now the floor was spraying with every pounding hoof as cante swarmed in. Before he had even completed the reasoning, the recollection of those two—aevendrow and orc—that had been freed of their ice tombs came to him with crystal clarity. A frustrated Jarlaxle veered to the side and galloped away from the stalagmites and his trapped companions.

Those two they had freed had been alive, though battered and clearly dazed. After months encased in the ice, they were still alive!

Those encased as n'divi, captured and possessed by the cante, were dead, undead.

If he freed any of his friends at this time, the cante would take them before they even fully regained their sensibilities.

Thus, to free his friends at this time would be to doom them.

He hated what he was going to do, even as he knew he had to do it. Jarlaxle raced his hellsteed about the area, whip cracking whenever an n'divi came near, the cante splashing beneath the fiery hellsteed hooves. As long as he kept moving . . .

That's what he wanted to see now. Could the hellsteed stay free of the cante's frozen bite? He was trying to formulate plans, trying to figure out how to be safely away, trying to figure out what he needed to return.

Because nothing would stop him from coming back for his friends.

Another n'divi went spinning down from a thunderous crack of that magical whip. Another was blown apart by a kick of the hellsteed, and two more fell trampled by the powerful demonic beast.

Perhaps more important, considering the relative danger they posed, the multitude of swirling cante splashed to bits, unable to gain a hold on the hellsteed, its fiery hooves melting their icy grip before they could attach.

Worried before, Jarlaxle was now beginning to think he could win here, could actually clear the room and free not only his friends but also Doum'wielle and all the others encased in the icy stalagmite mounds.

On one wide turn, though, he looked across the way to the large ice ramp from the higher shelf that ran the length of the back of the room, a ledge dotted with tunnels.

N'divi poured forth from those tunnels, running to the ramp and throwing themselves down in a slide. An endless line, it seemed, and then, worse, larger forms appeared. Giants and slaadi.

Back to the original plan.

Jarlaxle leaned over the neck of his mount and drove it forward with all speed toward the exit tunnel. He was glad of those fiery hooves when he cut a sharp corner on the ice floor, for he didn't go skidding sidelong into the wall.

He had to stay low the whole way, the ceiling just above him.

The ceiling.

Were there cante flowing along the ice *above* him?

The whip became a fiery sword, and Jarlaxle lifted it up before and above him, scraping the ceiling as the nightmare charged on.

He struck a cante. At first he was elated, but then the monster dropped onto the head of the nightmare.

Jarlaxle cried out, thinking he was doomed.

But the hellsteed snorted fire and thrashed its head about, and as the stubborn cante began to freeze and grasp on, Jarlaxle laid the flat of the fiery sword against it, against the side of the hellsteed's head.

Melted by the flames, the cante finally fell free.

Unbothered by fire, the hellsteed galloped along.

Jarlaxle passed the side room where he and his friends had first encountered these strange and dangerous golems, or monsters, or necromantic creations, or whatever they were—such distinctions could be sorted later! He went into the tunnel where they had left their Callidaean escorts, the exit to the glacial rift visible before him.

"Go, go, go!" he urged the hellsteed. So close—

A huge form stepped before the tunnel, blocking the exit. A frost giant. But no . . . an n'divi.

A frost giant n'divi!

A monster before him. Monsters pursuing him.

Nowhere else to go.

So Jarlaxle drove his mount harder. He began to scream and kept screaming, leveling the sword before him.

Don't think, he said to himself. "Don't slow!" he ordered, and the fearless hellsteed didn't. Closer they came, into the face of an undead horror, toward the slightly lesser danger, and then rider and mount were crashing into the giant n'divi full speed and head on.

Knocked nearly senseless, Jarlaxle felt himself flying. He had lost his grip on the hellsteed's thick mane, but he stubbornly, desperately, kept his other hand tight about the hilt of the magical sword.

He hit the ground, snow and ice, in a bouncing roll, and came to a hard and sudden stop against a shelf of ice and stone many strides from the tunnel, almost all the way across the glacial rift.

He wanted to lie back and collect himself, but he knew he had no time. He shook the dizziness from his head and focused back the way he had come.

The n'divi giant stood back up, the ice encasing it showing multiple cracks. Up, too, came the nightmare, immediately lifting its front hooves to pound against the frozen behemoth.

Every reflex in Jarlaxle, mental and physical, told him to run, and he even rolled up to his knees facing the outlet of the glacial rift, the ice pack beyond it shimmering under the light of the Merry Dancers and the polar night practically beckoning him.

He turned back before he even gained his feet, though, for Jarlaxle knew that he could not run—literally. Without his mount, he'd be dead.

If he lost that hellsteed, he'd lose everything.

A heavy swing of the n'divi giant sent the nightmare spinning to the side. The undead monster stalked in pursuit.

Jarlaxle growled and sprinted back to intercept. He took up the sword hilt in both hands, threw himself into a kneeling slide, and crashed into the back of the n'divi's thick leg. He bounced back, the n'divi continuing as if it hadn't even noticed the impact.

"Here I am!" Jarlaxle growled, and across came the flaming blade, both hands driving it, the drow turning fast to throw all of his weight into the strike.

The hot blade cracked through the ice and slammed the calf of the giant. It cut, but not deeply, and ricocheted off the frozen limb, and no blood came forth.

But the n'divi giant lurched, clearly stung, and began to swing about.

Jarlaxle hopped up and ran for all his life. His sword became a whip, and he slid down again, turning as he went and coming back to his feet facing the pursuing monster.

Zak, give me help, he silently implored, for no one could wield a whip like Zaknafein. He had no doubt that with this whip in his hands, Zak could take the eyes from the charging giant in two snaps.

Jarlaxle brought his whip arm straight up above him, pointing to the sky. He rolled his arm down before him, then up behind and over until his arm lined up with the head of his enemy. When he snapped his wrist he sent the bullwhip reaching forward and up, cracking right in the giant n'divi's face. Jarlaxle reached deeply into the whip, demanding everything of its magic, cutting a tear to the Plane of Fire.

The whip shattered the ice covering the giant's nose and cheeks, and the dripping tear brought elemental fire against that frozen flesh.

The giant staggered, allowing Jarlaxle to run out to the side, and allowing the nightmare to rush up beside it, pivot, and double-kick the giant right in the hip, knocking it sideways and to the ground.

Jarlaxle cracked the whip into it repeatedly as it tried to stand, and drew out a wand and blasted the giant in the smoking face with a lightning bolt.

In came the hellsteed, spinning and bucking before the rising titan, kicking the face so hard that all the encasing ice flew away from the snapping head.

The n'divi fell prone. Jarlaxle moved as if to finish it, but looked to the tunnel opening across the way, where more of the smaller monsters were now coming forth.

Not now, he thought.

He called to his mount and pulled himself up, hitting a full gallop almost immediately.

Out of the rift he fled, turning a sharp right and charging along the towering walls of this unnatural glacier known as Qadeej, speeding to put as much distance as possible between him and the pursuit. Only many strides later did he realize that there was no pursuit.

Yet he didn't slow. He had to get to Callidae. The only chance his friends had, he realized, was for him to convince the aevendrow to come forth with overwhelming force.

How he wished he had his magical whistle, that he could call to Kimmuriel and have the psionicist bring him back to the south to rally King Bruenor and Bregan D'aerthe.

But he couldn't get to them.

The fate of his friends was in the hands of the Temporal Convocation, the mona Valrissa, and the folk of Callidae.

"I will be back," he whispered into the cold.

CHAPTER 12

Yelping at the Moon

A storm is coming," the young monk said to Drizzt one night on the back porch of the Monastery of the Yellow Rose.

Drizzt looked up reflexively to see a nearly full moon high above, but with lines of clouds streaming by on swift winds. The stars twinkled. High-pitched baying sounded in the distance.

"You hear them?" the monk asked, and Drizzt turned to regard him.

Short and slight, he looked as if his robes were three sizes too large. His dirty toes stuck out from under the front folds of the dark brown garment that had gathered up about his sandals—Drizzt noted that one of the shoes had a broken tie that had been repaired with a vine of some sort. The monk had a pleasant face with just a hint of a mustache, and unkempt brown hair parted in the middle and brushed forward to frame his thin cheeks like a cowl.

"Coyotes," Drizzt said.

The monk shook his head, drawing a curious look from Drizzt. The night darkened as a cloud passed before the moon.

"They do sound like coyotes, I admit," the monk said. "I used to make the same mistake."

Drizzt arched an eyebrow.

"They do that on purpose," the monk explained. "Listen more carefully, not to the baying but to the quieter noises in between yelps."

"Is that really your name?" Drizzt asked, his change of subject clearly surprising the young man.

"My name?"

"Brother Tadpole?"

"You know of me! I am honored."

The moonlight streamed down brightly again and the baying resumed. Drizzt did as advised and paid attention to the quiet interludes. A wide smile spread and he nodded, recognizing the yipping and yelping.

"Gnolls," he said.

"Yes," said Tadpole. "Yes, gnolls, and yes, that is the name they gave me when I was a child, abandoned at the front door of the monastery."

Drizzt studied the man and saw no celebration of victimhood there, no desire for sympathy, no indication at all that his earliest experiences had left any scars. In fact, Tadpole seemed perfectly content. If he felt that he was lacking a family, he certainly showed no outward sign. Drizzt could certainly understand that—the monks of the Monastery of the Yellow Rose seemed as much of a family to each other as the Companions of the Hall did to him.

"They're very active this night," said Tadpole, stepping past Drizzt to lean on the porch railing. "They get like this when autumn grows long, announcing the cusp of winter."

He nodded out to the north, pointing up at the flying lines of clouds. "And the days grow short as the north wind grows stronger. It will be a big storm, I expect."

"How does Brother Tadpole know so much about gnolls?"

"Because I'm outside most of the time and the Galenas are thick with them," he answered. "How does the great Drizzt Do'Urden know of Brother Tadpole?"

Drizzt smiled at the superlative Tadpole had used before his name. "The great Drizzt Do'Urden," he echoed quietly, ending with a chuckle. "Brother Afafrenfere spoke of you."

"Master Afafrenfere," Tadpole corrected.

"He always desired the title of brother," Drizzt said.

Tadpole shrugged and nodded. "I miss him. Where you there when he died?"

The straightforward question struck Drizzt sideways and bounced around in his mind, taking him back to those moments when Afafrenfere had come after him in the early beginnings of glorious transcendence. Afafrenfere had sacrificed himself to serve as a conduit to bring Drizzt back to the living material world. "Somewhat," he answered, because he didn't know what else to say. How could he possibly begin to explain the sensations he had known in that remarkable time?

"A reminder that we must live with the days we are given," Tadpole quietly remarked. "What of his friend, the dwarf?"

"Athrogate?"

"No," Tadpole said, and even in the moonlight, Drizzt could see that he was blushing.

"Ambergris," Drizzt said. "Amber Gristle O'Maul of the Adbar O'Mauls."

"She kissed me," Tadpole said, clearly embarrassed. "I was very young. She was my first kiss."

Drizzt replied with a smile but slowly shook his head, deflating the young man.

"She died a hero," Drizzt told him.

"Too many heroes die," said Tadpole.

"Many would disagree," Drizzt quietly replied, drawing a confused look from the monk. Drizzt just laughed in response, not wanting to go down that philosophical rabbit hole. Through decades of experience, Drizzt had come to learn that many living people would remain underestimated and unappreciated for their sacrifices and efforts by critics who yipped like gnolls under a late autumn moon.

Until their deaths, of course, at which point, the people of action and consequence would often be lionized and elevated to near-godlike status—something, of course, that those who took up the mantle could never live up to.

Until they were dead.

Would that be his own fate, he wondered, and he chuckled at the silliness of that thought, for to his way of thinking, Drizzt had been given more credit than he deserved, and better friends, who understood the truth more than the "legend," than anyone deserved.

His smile didn't last, and his gaze went reflexively to the north. Catti-brie was appreciated, surely, and when she met her end, all the dwarves of Gauntlgrym and Mithral Hall, Adbar and Felbarr and Icewind Dale, all the halflings of Bleeding Vines, the whole of Longsaddle and the Harpells, and much of Luskan would be truly crushed at the tremendous loss to them all!

But what of Jarlaxle? Who truly understood that there was so much more to the rogue than his self-serving connivances?

What of Zaknafein? Drizzt appreciated the depth of the man's sacrifice, but not many now alive had any idea of the things he had done in his days in Menzoberranzan.

And what of Artemis Entreri? His reputation was surely known far and wide, but that was mostly the reputation of a man who no longer existed, the exploits of a perfect killer, and hardly the measure of the man he had become!

It would be up to Drizzt . . .

The drow sucked in his breath and nearly fell over! How could he allow his thoughts to wander such a dark and morbid course?

He knew how, and that was the problem.

He was so terribly worried.

"ARE YOU SURE THAT WE HAVE TO DO THIS?" MISTRESS OF Winter Savahn asked.

"Kimmuriel has contacted me," Grandmaster Kane replied. "There may be trouble afoot."

"But you haven't told Drizzt."

"There is really nothing to tell at this point. We have taken him as our responsibility, you would agree?"

Savahn looked at him curiously.

"He is in the middle of his training," Kane explained. "Training which I and the Order offered him. Is there a more vulnerable position than that? Drizzt is a great warrior, of course, but he has not yet learned to perfectly fuse the two disciplines he now carries. He is close, but not quite ready. We're going to make him ready." He nodded out toward the back porch, where Tadpole and Drizzt were looking out to the east, listening to the gnolls yelping at the moon.

"Brother Tadpole is playing his role well," Kane said.

"It seems a bit dishonest," Savahn noted.

"It is. And more than a bit. But would you prefer that I tell him the truth of our play here? For then he would go rushing back to whatever trouble awaits, and I tell you without hesitation that he is not ready."

Savahn considered it for a few moments, then shook her head. She had seen this situation before, and had heard about it from Kane regarding some legendary heroes of the Bloodstone Lands, the Grandmaster of Flowers' associates from long, long ago. Witnessing his feats, more than one had desired to learn more of the ways of the monk. The style of fighting and movement was different, though. Very different. It could complement the training a warrior had known before, or it could contradict it—and the latter at the most inopportune moments.

"It is as simple as the way one draws breath," Kane explained. "A warrior puffs out his chest and draws in his belly, all air inhaled to make him appear larger and more imposing. We understand the value of a softer belly, of breathing into our joints, of using breath to fuel the muscles instead of some birdlike display of power."

Savahn considered that for just a moment before replying with a laugh.

"There is a difference of approach, and it manifests itself into a difference of action," said Kane. "You have heard of this creature they call the Hunter?"

Savahn stared at the old monk for just a moment. "Do you mean this inner fire that simmers within our guest?"

Kane nodded.

"I have heard that Drizzt goes to a place of pure function, of primal rage. I have not witnessed it . . ."

"I have. Only once, when I was with Brother Afafrenfere, in his thoughts and soul during the War of the Silver Marches. It is quite impressive, do not doubt. Almost animal-like, his every move instinctive or reactive, his every strike powerful and precise."

"It sounds impressive."

"Oh, it is, depending on the enemy at hand."

"Because he does not think, not truly?" Savahn asked.

"Exactly. How do you believe you would fare against such a primal, feral even, killer?"

Savahn considered it for just a moment, before stating quite confidently, "Drizzt, this Hunter creature, would be killed."

"Why?" Kane asked.

"Because I would use his ferocity against him, to tire him out."

The Grandmaster of Flowers nodded. "We should move more quickly. I sense that there is urgency in this one's path. Fortunately, Drizzt is a quick study."

SAVAHN LED THE WAY UP THE MOUNTAIN TRAIL THE NEXT day, the north wind buffeting her and the drow ranger walking behind her. She rounded a corner, coming to a small plateau, north-facing and fully exposed to the winter elements.

"This is part of your training?" Drizzt asked through the howling wind when he came up beside her.

"Was," she corrected. "It was a major requirement of my ascension to my current rank."

"Mistress of Winter," said Drizzt.

Savahn nodded and smiled. "And as such, the winter cannot defeat me."

"I'm not sure what that means."

"Take off your cloak," she instructed.

Drizzt, who had just tightened the cloak about him, looked at her skeptically.

She held out her hand.

With a shrug, the drow removed the garment and handed it over. He gave a great shake, steeling himself against the freezing wind, and it was indeed already biting him hard.

"Sit," Savahn told him. "And give me your boots and socks."

"And your gloves," Savahn added when he had done so. "Sit straight-backed and cross-legged, your hands on your knees, as you do in meditation."

He did so, but before he closed his eyes, he noticed that his toes were already showing signs of the cold, the skin color and texture changing.

"Go to a quiet place," Savahn instructed. "Trust that the wind cannot hurt you."

Drizzt's wince revealed his doubts, but he tried, and managed to fall into a meditative state.

Only for a short while, though. It wasn't long before he couldn't ignore the icy bite. He grimaced and opened his eyes, glancing again to see redness forming on his toes and fingers.

"It hurts?" Savahn asked.

"Numb," said Drizzt.

"Your physical body is surviving by sacrificing your toes and fingers," she explained. "The blood is staying close to areas more vital. Your heart and torso. Don't let it."

It occurred to Drizzt that the woman's teeth were not even chattering here, which gave him hope that she knew what she was talking about.

"Overrule your instincts," Savahn instructed. "Drive the blood back to your hands and feet. Look inside. You are in command here, consciously."

Drizzt pictured the blood flowing through him as if it were a series of mountain streams cascading through the foothills. He used the same techniques Grandmaster Kane had taught him for performing minor healing on himself.

He felt some relief—not complete, certainly, but enough to make him glance again and take heart that some of the natural color had returned to his extremities.

"Good, good," Savahn told him. She reached down and grabbed his foot in her hand, and Drizzt nearly jumped at the warmth of her grasp! It wasn't just because of the contrast. Savahn's hand was *hot,* so much so that he looked over at her, expecting that she might be running her fingers over a candle or some other heat source.

But no.

She dropped his boots, gloves, and socks, instructing him to bundle up, and when he was back in his cloak and standing, Savahn shocked him by stripping down to only her light undershirt. She raised her arms out to the sides and accepted the buffeting of the freezing wind.

"Keep doing what I told you," she said to Drizzt. "Make yourself warm, my friend, as if a summer day were shining down upon you."

Drizzt went back into a meditative posture and visualized those mountain streams.

His teeth stopped chattering. He felt the warmth flowing through his hands and feet.

After a while, he opened his eyes and saw that Savahn was still standing there, almost naked in the face of the merciless northern wind.

Finally, she lowered her arms and turned to regard him, then began to dress.

"Your turn," she said. "Just as I did."

Drizzt complied and lifted his arms.

In the end, he didn't last nearly as long as Savahn had, but she was a master, and he still just a student. As they began their trek back down the mountain trail, he understood that he had been given a tremendous gift.

Night was falling when they neared the monastery again, the full moon peeking over the eastern horizon.

Somewhere in the night, a wolf howled. Then the gnolls began again, in force, yelping and yipping.

"They are fast becoming a problem that we must address," Savahn told Drizzt.

"The storm nears, so I was told."

"It will be snowing by evenfall tomorrow, which means I should follow these yelping demonic beasts to their lair, no doubt a cave, this very night. It seems as if there are more of them every year around this time."

"So the monastery has taken it upon themselves to battle the gnolls?"

"Not battle the gnolls; *protect* those the gnolls would attack. If we don't, the villages on the eastern slopes in Damara will pay a heavy price for our inaction," Savahn explained. "The gnolls prey upon towns huddled against the winter blow, their intended victims clustered together and with nowhere to run."

Drizzt couldn't disagree with that assessment, particularly after the carnage that had recently occurred in Luskan during the Demon War, with a diabolical army comprised mostly of gnolls.

"I'll come with you," he said.

"Indeed, you will. Grandmaster Kane claims that you are an excellent tracker." She stopped on the trail ahead of Drizzt and turned to look back at him, a wicked smile spreading. "Why wait?"

"Now?"

"Are your fingers and feet properly warmed, Drizzt Do'Urden?" she asked. "Are you up for a fight?"

Drizzt smiled wickedly, too.

FROM A BLUFF NOT FAR AWAY, GRANDMASTER KANE watched Savahn and Drizzt change course, turning down a trail heading east, in the general direction of the yelping gnolls.

He, too, started on his way, moving silently and with great speed to overtake the pair, hoping to arrive at the gnoll cave before Drizzt and Savahn found their way to it. He kept putting his hand on the sack he carried, which held one of Brother Tadpole's sandals and the young man's shredded and bloody robe.

After a short while, he spotted the pair moving along below him, on a hillside splotched with snow and dotted with large rocks.

He picked up his pace, speeding for the cave, a place he knew well. He circled around the entrance—set against a natural stone wall and guarded by only a single gnoll—and came to a perch behind a tree high above the guard.

Kane knew that he had to move quickly here.

He jumped down the thirty feet to land in a low crouch right beside the surprised monster.

The gnoll nearly jumped out of its boots. It turned and swung its polearm about, but Kane sprang up from that crouch, rising high and tucking his legs above the sweeping weapon. He could have kicked out and finished the gnoll, but he didn't just need it dead.

He needed it noisy.

He landed easily, left hand grasping the polearm staff before the gnoll could reverse its cut. His right hand shot forward and up, fingers tucked, palm forward, catching the nearly seven-foot beast under the front of its thick hyena-like snout.

The gnoll yelped in pain and let go of the polearm with its left hand, reaching, clawing, for Kane.

The Grandmaster of Flowers was already gone, though, tugging out with his left and darting under the gnoll's right arm. He gave a sudden twist with his grasping left hand, nearly taking the weapon from the brute—and he could have done that if he had wanted. Instead, though, Kane continued with a spin, moving right behind the gnoll, trailing a low circle kick that buckled the demonic creature's knees, followed by a left-hooking kidney punch that brought a louder and more emphatic cry.

One that its yelping comrades would surely hear.

As the gnoll staggered forward a few steps, Kane turned and rushed into the cave, which he knew to be a shallow foyer to the gnoll complex, with several tunnels moving deeper into the mountain.

The gnoll appeared before the door, howling now, full-throated, and taking up the chase.

Responding calls came from the tunnels, and from outside, Kane noted with a grin.

The Grandmaster of Flowers moved down into the darkness.

DRIZZT KEPT ICINGDEATH SHEATHED, FOR THE BLADE was glowing icy blue in the freezing night air, and he and Savahn certainly didn't need that or any other light with the bright moon rising.

The two easily found the bare hillock where the gnolls had been yowling, and knew it to be the correct location by the scramble of footprints all about the patches of snow and the areas of dirt.

The gnolls were gone, and had left in a hurry, and so were easy to track.

Drizzt and Savahn barely made a sound as they raced along, gracefully leaping fallen logs and navigating boulder tumbles. They came to a narrow tree line before a steep incline and pressed to the far edge, glancing up the rise to a cave opening, where a pair of gnolls milled about.

"Straight in?" Drizzt whispered to his companion.

"Right through them," Savahn agreed.

Drizzt was already running up the hill, his scimitars still in their sheaths.

The gnolls saw him and cried out—he wasn't trying to hide—and lifted bows. One arrow flew wide; the second drove right for Drizzt's chest. His hands crossed before him in perfect timing, flipping the missile around right before it struck. He caught it there and flicked his arm forward, launching it back at the archer!

The gnoll yelped in surprise, then in pain, as the arrow stabbed.

Right behind it came Drizzt.

Scimitars appeared in his hands, Vidrinath's glassteel blade sparkling in blue, Icingdeath glowing blue-white. He went in hard, his right hand stabbing at the gnoll as it tried to pull the arrow from its shoulder, his left hand flicking out to the side to take the next arrow from its set on the other gnoll's bow.

Savahn seemed to fly up the last expanse of the rise, soaring in with a brutal double kick on that unfortunate archer, sending it tumbling backward into the darkness of the cave opening.

With his focus now fully on the wounded gnoll, Drizzt bore in, rolling his blades up high and out, over and over again, cutting apart the longbow as the gnoll tried to defend. The bow paused his assault just long enough for the gnoll to set its feet and even draw its sword, before Drizzt snapped both blades up high at it again, forcing a parry.

But it was just a feint, just a distraction when the gnoll began to feel comfortable enough to settle in its crouch, for that was the position Drizzt wanted it in when he dropped down low, then came up in a spin, leaping forward and burying a circle kick right into the gnoll's chest. It slammed back against the rock edge of the cave opening, its breath blasting out with a sound that was half yelp and half grunt.

Up went Vidrinath horizontally, sealing the gnoll's sword up high, and in went Icingdeath below it, creasing the creature's chest.

Drizzt ran away, into the cave. He went right past Savahn, whose open hands were drumming the life out of the other gnoll, every strike just ahead of its attempted block, or just behind, just far enough so that the blocking arm had moved up too high.

Her speed and precision made Drizzt want to cast aside his blades and fight as she did. But no, for four gnolls were coming fast to meet the intrusion, three firing bows.

An arrow flew past to the left of Drizzt, speeding for Savahn, but the drow cut it out of the air with Vidrinath. A second and third flew for Drizzt, but Icingdeath took the leading shot harmlessly out of the air, and Drizzt went down in a forward roll so that the third flew harmlessly above him.

He came up, still in a run, not far from the group. A large gnoll stepped past the archers, sword and shield ready, while the others drew their blades.

Drizzt came in straight for the largest, until he didn't, cutting suddenly and sharply to the right, leaping up to the wall and running along it for three strides, then back down to the floor just past the gnoll with the shield and straight for the one right behind it, who turned, trying to bring its sword in line.

Vidrinath smacked hard against that blade, launching it from the gnoll's hand back at the turning gnoll, who got its shield up just in time to deflect the impromptu missile.

Even as Drizzt's left hand executed the powerful block, his right stabbed forward, plunging through the gnoll's attempt to block with its hand and into the demonic beast's side. Barely had it fallen back when Drizzt stopped fast and abruptly spun, meeting the stabbing sword of the next in line with a barrage of parries that had the gnoll grasping its sword in both hands in a desperate attempt to hold on to it.

A shield rush came at the drow from the left, but he was suddenly prone on the floor as the gnoll barreled past, tripping over him and flying headlong deeper into the cave.

And Drizzt was up again before the gnoll standing in front of him even realized what had happened. It was actually turning its head to follow the stumble and fall of its companion before it realized that the drow was still there, right there, then moving beside it, Icingdeath coming up under its snout, up through its throat, and into its brain.

Drizzt let go of that stuck sword as he moved past to the third in line and fell into a sudden basic parry routine, up high, down low, up high, down low, the gnoll stabbing high, then low, with the thrusts being pushed left and right by Vidrinath.

"Are you bored yet?" Savahn called from a short distance away.

She wasn't joining in, merely watching and, seemingly, enjoying the show.

Up went Vidrinath, up and out to push the gnoll's sword wide to its right. A subtle twist put Vidrinath's glassteel edge over the gnoll's sword, Drizzt forcing it back in and down, where he kept rolling his scimitar, now back up and out again with great force, throwing the sword from the gnoll's hand and back up the tunnel at Savahn.

She caught it.

Drizzt punched the gnoll with a right cross, his shoulders rotating with tremendous power to extend his reach and snap the gnoll's head back violently. Up into the air went Vidrinath as a straight left jab followed, driving the gnoll back several steps. Drizzt chased its fall, keeping just ahead of the first gnoll, stumbling toward him, grasping its torn side.

A second right followed that, this time with fingers stiffly extended, aimed perfectly for the staggering gnoll's throat.

Its shriek came out as a gout of blood, spewing from its torn throat and not its mouth.

Drizzt barreled forward, driving the dying gnoll back and to the ground. He stomped right on its chest and sprang off at the wall just beyond it, laid out backward as he went, absorbing the impact with his bending legs, then sprang back off the way he had come, flipping and twisting to land a flying kick right between the surprise-widened eyes of the pursuer.

His kick broke the gnoll's snout cleanly, sending it scrambling away, shrieking in pain and slapping at its shattered upper jaw.

Drizzt fell flat to the floor, grabbed Vidrinath, and leaped right back up, spinning and charging across the tunnel to meet the remaining enemy, who was coming back cautiously, shield leading.

Drizzt veered just enough to grab Icingdeath, which was sticking straight up from the throat where he had planted it, the gnoll lying flat on its back.

"Thank you for holding that," he said to the dead beast, yanking it free.

He charged for the gnoll with the shield. It angled the blocker for him, turning slightly, sword resting on top of the round buckler.

A flicker to the right surprised Drizzt, but surprised the gnoll more, for the sword, thrown like a spear, took it right in the ear.

It fell in a lump.

Drizzt stopped and straightened, looking back just in time to see Savahn snap the neck of the broken-snouted gnoll.

"I wasn't about to let you have all the fun," she explained with a shrug.

"You think it's over?" Drizzt asked, and as if to accentuate his point, there came some baying from far down the tunnel.

Drizzt was about to move toward that sound when he noted something just to the side. He leaped over and lifted a shredded robe with his scimitar, noting the blood covering it, then noting with more interest and surprise a single sandal with a broken tie that had been repaired with a piece of vine.

"Those are—" Savahn noted.

"Brother Tadpole's," Drizzt finished, his thoughts spinning as he tried to figure out how that was possible. Tadpole had been back at the monastery, taking care of . . .

There came another sound from deep down the tunnel, an unexpected sound, the cry of a human baby, and one Drizzt was sure that he recognized.

Any thought of this being grim duty shattered. This was personal now.

With only the glow of Icingdeath and Vidrinath showing him the way, Drizzt charged headlong down the tunnel.

SAVAHN WATCHED HIM GO FOR A MOMENT. THIS WAS THE Hunter, as they had wanted. All joy was gone from Drizzt now, replaced by that primal killing machine.

She didn't like the image. Not from Drizzt, who she knew could be so much more than a feral instrument of destruction.

But Savahn just sighed and gave chase.

Distasteful as it was, she knew that this was necessary, and not just to be rid of the demonic gnolls.

CHAPTER 13

A Disciplined Mind

Azzudonna lay awake for a long while, trying to figure out where she might begin, or what she could even say. She replayed again her flight from the room in this very house, the sudden and wild sequence that had led to her injury. She had come to believe fully that these were not her enemies here—and she understood, too, that the spell the older man had cast upon her was no explosive evocation but a spell of comprehending languages. Even as she had fled the house, the human woman had pleaded with her and warned her to stop—not because she didn't want Azzudonna to get away, as the aevendrow had initially believed (before she had even realized the implications of her understanding the woman!), but because she was trying to warn Azzudonna about the invisible, unyielding barrier.

They could have left her to die. They could kill her now, easily. They could torture her—perhaps they would when she continued to refuse to answer their questions!

But Azzudonna didn't really believe that. These were friends of Catti-brie and the others, clearly. Those four who had come to Callidae would not torture a prisoner. She was sure of that. She knew the hearts of the visitors, of Zaknafein most especially. Indeed, only now in the midst of the profound loss had Azzudonna realized that she had fallen in love with Zaknafein—how she longed to be with him again, to lie beside him on quiet winter nights, to fight beside him in cazzcalci.

And these were his friends. These were her only link to him. Perhaps *back* to him.

She wanted to answer their understandable questions. She wanted to tell them everything. She wanted to beg them to help her go back and learn what had happened to Catti-brie, Jarlaxle, Artemis Entreri, and—most of all—Zaknafein.

She wouldn't do that, though, no matter how much she desired it. Azzudonna knew the rules of her city and knew her responsibility. She couldn't tell these people what they wanted to know without risking the secrecy of Callidae. She was in the south, of course, she understood now. And that meant that she was among populations many times larger than those of her beloved homeland—which could not stand against any intrusion from these more populous and powerful kingdoms.

As the aevendrow were not going to let the four newcomers leave Callidae with their memories intact, so did Azzudonna have to live in the same manner of ignorance feigned.

Which meant she needed to concoct a story, of a long imprisonment at the hands of evil slaadi in a place she did not know and could not find. Catti-brie and the others had been killed in a battle, she would tell them, and she alone had escaped, though she wasn't even sure of how she might have done that. Yes, she'd tell them that a great cat had tackled her and taken her flying through the planes of existence to this place, wherever it might be—they'd already seen the panther, so there was no point in denying that. More, though, she would not say.

She played the story over and over in her head, looking for leaks in the roof and walls she would construct. After a few moments she dismissed the notion of the slaadi as the killers of their missing friends, for that might create a tangent that would evoke great action on the part of the southerners. Did she really want to be the cause of sending an army charging to the north? Even when she had pared the story to an acceptable enclosure, the confused and hopeless aevendrow real-ized that she could not maintain the lie here—any lie! She thought of Galathae and the inquisitors. They could detect lies easily. Should she expect anything less from these people? This was a sophisticated soci-ety, rich in magic, if Catti-brie and Jarlaxle had been any indication.

No lies, then. Rather, she'd rely on half-truths and obfuscation—things that she could stick to easily without betraying her oaths. She could only hope that would get her through this without fully alienat-ing them all.

But . . . then what?

Then she'd have to simply live here, or in some other community in the south, and let the long years flow past until she could find some way, somehow, to get back to Callidae.

"They are Zaknafein's friends," she whispered to herself, needing to hear the confirmation that these were not cruel and evil enemies. She could live here. She could sacrifice her desires to return home for the sake of her people.

No one from Callidae would be expected to do less than that.

"OBVIOUSLY SHE KNOWS MORE THAN SHE'S TELLING US," Copetta said to Penelope and Dowell later on. "I hope you're planning to keep her well guarded."

"Our visitor isn't going anywhere," Penelope assured the Gauntl-grym priestess.

"We'll get our answers." Dowell nodded in agreement.

"Sooner than you believe," came Kipper's voice from out in the hall, and the old wizard entered with a pair of unexpected guests.

"Where is she?" Gromph Baenre asked, pushing right past Kipper.

Penelope realized that the great wizard already knew the answer to his question, since the mere asking had brought the answer to her mind, and likely to the minds of Dowell and Dab'nay as well.

Which meant that Kimmuriel had heard their thoughts clearly, as he and the other drow were already moving toward their guest's room.

And that meant, too, that these two psionicists were indeed going to get some answers, whether this Azzudonna person decided to supply them or not.

THERE CAME NO KNOCK THIS TIME, JUST THE DOOR SWING-ing open, startling Azzudonna and Dab'nay, who was completing the healing on the wounded aevendrow.

In strode two drow men, grim-faced and menacing. Behind them came Penelope, her expression one that spoke of sympathy.

Azzudonna didn't like the look of that. She studied the two strange men, one broad and imposing in fabulous robes and wearing a more frightening scowl, the other small and slight, dressed simply and clad in an expression that seemed wholly unreadable.

Dab'nay bowed slightly and hurried off to the side and out of the room, motioning for the three to follow her.

The more formidable drow seemed not to like that, even snorted in derision at the request.

"I would see you now," Dab'nay insisted, and Penelope even grabbed the clearly impatient man by the arm.

With an exaggerated sigh that screamed, *Oh, if I must*, the man followed.

The last one leaving, the small man, cast a stern glance at Az-zudonna and shut the door.

Azzudonna's mind spun with possibilities, none of them good. She reminded herself of her duty here, repeatedly. She told herself that these were friends of Catti-brie and the others, trying to settle her nerves, but she understood that the discussion now was about to get more serious and more insistent, and likely, judging by the robes of the larger drow, more magical in nature.

She took a deep breath. She had trained all of her life for this possibility—had trained earnestly, even though it had always seemed a remote possibility, because it was simply a matter that important to her people.

She once again tried to find her limits here, on the things she could reveal and on those she must not.

Unbidden, tears welled in her eyes when she thought of all the things she could not tell them about. Things like cazzcalci and the miracle that had saved her new friend, the one she would be abandoning for the good of Callidae. *Perte miye Zaknafein,* she silently mouthed.

It occurred to her that these people around her could save him, perhaps. They could save the man she had come to care for so deeply in so short a time. Dare she say it, the man she had come to love?

But just as quickly, she told herself in no uncertain terms that it was not an option. Because she was Azzudonna.

Azzudonna of Callidae.

Callidae was her home, and its safety was paramount. She would give her life before she would give up the secret of the city hidden in the belly of Qadeej, and so, too, would she give up the life of Zaknafein.

It would not be easy, Azzudonna knew. The power in these southerners was not something she'd encountered. But she was strong, too, and so she quietly mouthed her mantra, finding the place of her resilience and training.

"SHE SPEAKS DROW," DAB'NAY TOLD THE TRIO OUT IN THE hallway, "but not Common, and her dialect is nothing I've heard before."

"Did she tell you anything about our friends?" Kimmuriel asked.

Dab'nay shook her head. "Her name is Azzudonna. That is all she revealed."

"That's all she revealed to *you*," Gromph Baenre said ominously, and he pushed through the door again.

Penelope Harpell moved to follow, but Kimmuriel held her back.

"Let us begin the questioning."

"She's still weak," Dab'nay warned.

"That will make it easier."

"Don't hurt her," Penelope ordered. "She's terrified."

"And maybe killed our friends?" said Dab'nay.

"She could have stabbed me with that curious spear, but she did not," Penelope reminded her.

"She won't be hurt," Kimmuriel assured the leader of the Ivy Mansion. "But neither will she hide her knowledge from us."

He followed Gromph into the room and closed the door behind him.

"You are Azzudonna?" he heard Gromph asking the woman, but in the Common tongue.

She looked at him curiously, then said, "Azzudonna."

"Azzudonna of?" Gromph asked, now using Drow.

"I am Azzudonna," she replied.

Gromph looked at Kimmuriel, cueing him.

The psionicist focused on her intently, sending his mind's eye into her, seeking her every notion, every flashing image, every idea, every intent.

Gromph hit Azzudonna with a barrage of questions about her home, about their friends, about how she got Guenhwyvar—and was that even Guenhwyvar?

Gromph listened with his ears.

Kimmuriel listened more intimately.

THE QUESTIONS CAME AT HER RAPID-FIRE, ONE AFTER AN-other before poor Azzudonna could begin to answer, or even begin to decide whether or not to answer.

The man mentioned Guenhwyvar and she immediately pictured the panther, recalling the first time Catti-brie had introduced her to the beautiful creature.

He was on to another question before she could even deny that knowledge, though, then on to another.

Azzudonna caught on. She had been trained. She had been warned.

She looked inside and focused all of her mental power on the intruder she believed to be in her thoughts, and as soon as she believed that she had sensed an "other" within, she followed her training and pictured one simple thing: the summer sun shining on the flat ice cap.

The whiteness. A blinding, unrelenting whiteness.

KIMMURIEL TRIED TO SEE THROUGH IT, TRIED TO LISTEN
around it. But there was not a whisper of sound. Just the light, all-encompassing, unrelenting. He couldn't even hear Gromph's questions anymore. Had she died?

Had this strange drow taken him with her into the realm of Death?

The psionicist pulled his mind back to his own form, snapping his eyes shut tight to fend off the waves of dizziness that followed him.

Now he heard Gromph again. "Tell me of Jarlaxle! Where are you from? How did you get here?"

Kimmuriel lifted his arm out toward his companion, patting his hand in the air and shaking his head to convey to Gromph to stop.

"She cannot hear you," Kimmuriel managed to gasp. Slowly he opened his eyes and faced his puzzled partner.

"She isn't in there, or rather, she is, but so far in there that your words and my thoughts cannot penetrate."

"How is that possible?" Gromph asked.

"She has trained against us," Kimmuriel told him.

"She is a psionicist?"

Kimmuriel thought on that for a moment, then answered, "No. No, I doubt that. She has been trained against magical spells of mind-reading, I would guess, but the defense is the same, and it is as strong in this one as in any person I have encountered who is not illithid."

"In any?" Gromph asked doubtfully.

"Maybe not Drizzt with his new training."

"In any?" the perturbed archmage repeated.

Kimmuriel looked him directly in the eye. "Yes. Even you. We're not going to get our answers in this manner—at least, not in this manner alone."

"What are you suggesting?"

Kimmuriel looked at the woman and shook his head. "I don't know."

He moved to the door and Gromph followed him out of the room, Dab'nay passing them to return to her healing of Azzudonna.

Penelope and Copetta were out in the hall waiting for the two men.

"What have you learned?" Penelope asked when they walked over.

"Very little," Kimmuriel replied. "It was Guenhwyvar, I am now sure, and I saw an image in her mind of a strange place I do not know, and of Catti-brie, smiling while this very same drow lying in your room comfortably patted the panther."

"That's good, then," said Copetta. "Might mean that she's not an enemy."

"Even if she's not, even if she's a friend, why and how is she here? Why would Guenhwyvar leave Catti-brie's side with this one if Catti-brie wasn't in dire trouble, or even dead?"

"Careful in sayin' that," Copetta said. "King Bruenor's on his way with her other friends and that's not something he's wishin' to hear."

"No more than I want to say it," Gromph said. "But it doesn't change my question."

"Drizzt would know more about the panther," Penelope remarked. "He should be here."

"He's at the Monastery of the Yellow Rose," Kimmuriel said. "It's quite a journey, so let us see what we can learn before we send for him."

"And how are we to do that?" asked a dour Gromph.

"I have already alerted Grandmaster Kane that we might need to retrieve Drizzt," Kimmuriel replied. "Stay with her and keep her safe," he instructed Penelope. "She speaks Drow fluently, but with a curious accent that I cannot place."

"I'll stay with her," Copetta volunteered. "She's needin' more o' me spells and I got one ready so we can understand each other." The dwarf winked and grinned, then moved into the room.

With a nod to the two drow, Penelope followed her.

"You think they're all dead," Gromph said to Kimmuriel when they were alone.

"We cannot know that."

"You're as bad as that priestess. Surely we can *think* it. Why is she here? How is she here? She doesn't have the onyx figurine that summons the cat. You haven't heard a call from Jarlaxle on that whistle he wears? Not one?"

"None. But perhaps I can reverse the dweomer and contact him."

"Or perhaps we can try harder to garner some information from this Azzudonna creature."

"Torture her?" Kimmuriel said with a dismissive laugh.

"It can be very effective."

"Effective at ruining every alliance you've forged. *You*, I say, for I'll have no part in any such thing."

"You have changed, my friend."

"That is my hope. But even if I hadn't, I don't think you'll get much from torture."

Kimmuriel nodded respectfully then and left his friend, heading for one of the many small private rooms in the vast Ivy Mansion.

Gromph stood there in the hallway for a long while, watching Kimmuriel depart and staring at the empty corridors after the psionicist had gone, his focus turned inward and hardly noticing the scene before him until Kipper Harpell rounded the corner.

"Where can I rest and study, old wizard?" Gromph asked.

"Old? From what I am told, you're five times my age, at least," Kipper answered with a grin.

"But I'm not old," said Gromph.

That brought a laugh from Kipper. "Come, I'll show you to my private library. It's nothing to rival the ones at the Hosttower, of course, but you'll find some interesting tomes there, and some exquisitely comfortable chairs that I've crafted with my own magic."

Gromph glanced to the door blocking Azzudonna's room. He could hear the three women chatting within. He held up a finger to Kipper, begging a moment, and moved to the door, putting his ear up against it.

"So, a dwarf?" he heard Azzudonna say, but in the common surface language. The priestess's spell had worked.

"A dwarf, aye. Ye never seen a dwarf?"

"I have, but not any who look like you."

"That a good thing, or a bad?" Copetta asked lightheartedly.

"Oh, good, of course," Azzudonna replied. "It makes you quite interesting."

Good indeed, Gromph thought. They were putting the stranger

at ease, taking her off her guard. Perhaps she'd be less stubborn in her resistance . . .

"Are we going?" Kipper asked, stealing the thought before Gromph could fully realize it.

The archmage nodded and followed.

KIMMURIEL CLOSED THE CURTAINS, DARKENING THE room as much as possible. He pushed aside the small desk and sat cross-legged in the center of the floor.

He closed his eyes and fell deeply within himself, then extracted his sentience from his physical body, stepping out of himself.

Unbound from the pull of the world and its physical barriers, he floated up through the ceiling and the ceilings above that, and through the roof, up, up, up into the air.

Night had fallen and the stars were out, but they didn't hold Kimmuriel's attention at all, such was his focus. He looked down to the world below, and still he forced himself higher, widening the horizons.

His thoughts blocked out all distractions: the chimney smoke drifting skyward, the lights of Longsaddle, the lights of Luskan, and even the few fires burning in Icewind Dale, far to the north. Everything went away—everything, until he was in utter blackness.

With only a single tiny exception.

Kimmuriel had gone to great lengths to produce the magical whistle he had attuned to Jarlaxle. Given their relationship and the constant threats of a surface world they still did not fully understand, he thought it worth the effort. The whistle was designed for Jarlaxle to contact him, a single, simple, and quiet note that would reach outside the physical reality and then back in again to his ear alone. What Jarlaxle didn't know was that Kimmuriel could use that beacon even when the rogue did not activate it.

He focused on it now, completely, utterly, with the singular concentration that only one who had trained for so long in the illithid hive mind could achieve.

A sole, distant pinprick of light appeared to him. He had no idea of the direction or distance, for he was not "seeing" it by any physical means.

He was simply sensing its magic.

His disembodied threads flew fast for the dot of light, speeding along, thinking he would find Jarlaxle.

But no, it wasn't the mercenary at all holding the item, and the thoughts Kimmuriel sensed came from a source foreign to him. A drow, he understood, sensing the identity of his host, and one alerted to the intrusion, one terrified and already trying to expel him.

Kimmuriel held on just long enough to see through the drow's eyes, a flash, an image: a crypt, or some deep substructure of a large building, he thought, with low archways glowing pale in meager candlelight, but still clearly enough for him to notice the same types of etchings decorating them as those he had noted on the strange spear Penelope had shown him, one carried by Azzudonna.

Coffers, scroll tubes, boxes, and chests of all shapes and sizes lined the many shelves cut into the pale walls.

At Kimmuriel's mental demand, the terrified drow—Kimmuriel got the feeling that it was a young man—looked down at his own hands, at his clothing and boots.

Yes, a drow, and one wearing clothes similar to those of Azzudonna—

The intruding psionicist was expelled then, suddenly and without recourse.

He didn't resist, and instead blinked open his own eyes in the darkened room in the Ivy Mansion.

There were more of them. Many more, he sensed, for the young man he had briefly possessed had thought of a great council chamber.

And they had Jarlaxle's whistle.

And they probably had the onyx figurine of Guenhwyvar—for perhaps that was how they had accessed the magic to send Azzudonna on her journey.

Where was Jarlaxle, though? Catti-brie?

Where were his friends?

What fate had they found in the far north of Faerun?

Kimmuriel feared that he already knew the answer.

CHAPTER 14

Friendship, Magic, Hope, Fear, and Terror

A nd thus we have returned, our duty complete," Galathae finished. She placed her hands flat together before her sternum and bowed her head in respect to the mona and the gallery of the Temporal Convocation.

The elected representatives had all gathered in the Siglig immediately upon receiving word of the return of the group that had accompanied the strangers to the dangerous caverns below the frost giant fortress. The appointed leaders of that expedition, Galathae, Ilina, Emilian, and Azzudonna, had been summoned before they had even exited the tunnel bringing them into the northernmost borough of Callidae, at Mona Valrissa Zhamboule's personal invitation, though of course only three of them had been able to answer that call.

The chamber remained utterly silent for a long while after Galathae had finished. The paladin did not take her seat between Emilian and Ilina on the blue-ice chairs set before the gallery.

Finally, Mona Valrissa rose and walked to the raised dais at the center-front of the curving, semicircular gallery. She paused there and looked around at all the representatives. The people of Callidae were not strangers to tragedy, of course, but this one seemed to sting them all particularly hard.

Because they all knew, and had known, this was how it would end. Mona Valrissa knew.

Galathae knew.

Emilian and Ilina knew.

Alviss, the inugaakalikurit dwarf, who had been on that expedition and who had followed Galathae, Emilian, and Ilina back to the Siglig so that he could take his seat in the Temporal Convocation as a representative of the borough of B'shett, knew, and had known.

They shouldn't have gone to that place of tragedy again, however compelling the story, however heartrending the desires, of the four strangers.

Galathae knew it most of all. She had led the previous trek to those caverns, a half year earlier, to the greatest tragedy Callidae had known for many decades, since the glacier had reclaimed the borough of Cattisola. Caught up in the excitement of what was already whispered about in the whole of Callidae as the "Miracle of Cazzcalci," the curing of the stranger named Zaknafein of the chaos phage by the sheer emotional prayer of the Callidaeans, and in the promise of these remarkable visitors, had she worked hard enough to dissuade them from going?

Shouldn't the journey have simply been forbidden, for the sake of Callidae and the sake of the four doomed visitors?

"Holy Galathae, you were instructed not to accompany them into the chambers," Mona Valrissa said, breaking the silence, which had continued beyond the called-for moment of respect for the five who were lost and become more a breathless expression of shock and confusion.

"We did not," the paladin answered. "We only traveled a short way into the entry tunnel so that we could determine the fate of our visitors when they entered the complex proper."

"But you did not learn of it."

"No," Galathae confirmed. "We did not go in deep enough to truly determine what had happened. I thought it too dangerous and made the decision to leave. And we did, with all expediency, except for Azzudonna, who paused . . . too long."

"And we do not even know what happened to her," Mona Valrissa reminded them all. "You think it the panther companion of Catti-brie that took her from us?"

"I do," Galathae answered, and turned back to her two seated companions. She grimaced, pained, when she noted the fourth chair, empty. The chair the council had set out for Azzudonna, expecting her along with the other expedition leaders.

"I saw it only briefly and from afar," Ilina answered. "But yes, I do believe it was the panther."

Emilian nodded. "Agreed."

"And when she was gone?"

"We fled," Galathae said, as she had explained in the presentation. "It pains me to say it as it pained me to order it. But this convocation was explicit: we were not to engage within the caverns.

"We moved to the end of the rift beyond the cavern and waited," the paladin continued. "I know not how long exactly, but an hour at the least. The four who came to visit us did not emerge from that tunnel in any timely manner. The room where their friend, our friend, Doum'wielle had been lost in that earlier tragedy was barely a few hundred strides within the complex. Had they been able, I am certain they would have sent word back to us, at least to inform us of their progress."

"So, are we to presume they are dead?" Mona Valrissa asked. "Captured?"

Galathae sighed, shrugged, and reluctantly nodded, and all in the room seemed to sigh with her.

Except, perhaps, for Mona Valrissa. "Or did they escape?" she added. "And did they send the panther companion to take one of you as their prisoner?"

The sighs became gasps and fearful gazes turned to friends, as if sharing the dark implications of what Mona Valrissa had just asked would somehow diminish the shock.

"No," Galathae stated flatly, and loudly, stealing the moment and pulling the convocation back from the edge of its collective nerves.

"If they had escaped, they would have come to us. I would never have agreed to take them from the city if I did not trust them. We knew better. We understood them. They were as they presented, through trial and time."

"I agree," said Mona Valrissa. "But we must at least consider all possibilities."

"Over the length of the journey back to Callidae, I kept glancing over my shoulder," Galathae said. "Not for pursuit by our enemies, but in my fleeting hope that I would find our five lost friends rushing to catch up to us, perhaps even accompanied by some of those who were lost in the time of Conception Verdant. I say 'fleeting hope' only because anything is possible, but in truth, it was a fancy without any reason or justification. We knew what they would face in those caverns. I only wish now that I had been even more insistent to them that they did not go."

Mona Valrissa nodded, but Galathae understood it to be a polite concession without conviction. For Valrissa knew as Galathae knew: the four southerners would not have been deterred in their quest to find their lost friend, and in the end, the Callidaeans had no ethical right to deny them.

Still, everyone in that room mourned their loss, as they mourned the loss of Azzudonna.

"We will sing this night beneath the Merry Dancers," Mona Valrissa declared. "All of Callidae will gather and say goodbye. And we will wake up tomorrow and go back to our work, our ways, our lives."

She paused and looked around, and Galathae understood that Mona Valrissa was checking to see if any others wished to be heard. The mona ended by looking to the three witnesses, who all nodded confirmation that they had nothing to add.

"This is the way of Callidae," Mona Valrissa called out, the traditional closing of the Temporal Convocation.

Galathae turned to her two friends as they prepared to leave.

"We knew it could happen," Emilian reminded her. "That it likely *would* happen."

"It doesn't make this easier to take."

"No," Emilian said quietly.

"Let us hope that Azzudonna, at least, managed to get out of there, and if she did, that she finds a good life wherever she was taken," said Ilina.

"We will sing for her tonight," said Galathae. "And for Zaknafein and Jarlaxle, Artemis Entreri and Catti-brie."

"This is the way of Callidae," Ilina said.

The three shared a hug.

"AM I AN EVIL PERSON BECAUSE THERE IS A PART OF ME that hopes the five who did not return were all killed?" Mona Valrissa asked Alviss later on, the two sharing a meal at a Mona Chess tavern.

"I've had the same thoughts, lady," Alviss admitted. "Ye know me love for Azzudonna, of course, even if I blame her for beating B'shett two games ago! And, aye, I became very fond of the human woman, Catti-brie. But Alviss'd be a liar and Alviss isn't a liar, if I denied that I share yer fears here. If they escaped us, on purpose or by the situation, they did so without going through the ritual. They know where we are. They know who we are."

"They know our defenses," Mona Valrissa said. "And our vulnerabilities."

"Do you wish we'd done things differently?"

Mona Valrissa sat back in her chair, took a long swallow of her drink, and replayed the last tendays. "We should have stopped them from their hopeless quest," she decided. "At least until they went through the ritual and so would not find their way back to Callidae. We should have done that and had the Burnooks alone drive them to the north, to the last rift, and there leave them with a map to the caverns and their lost friend."

"Why didn't ye?" Alviss asked.

Mona Valrissa shrugged and shook her head. "Because I believed them and believed in them. After what happened with Zaknafein at cazzcalci . . ."

"Not a night any of us'll e'er forget, lady," the dwarf said.

"I trusted them," Mona Valrissa said.

"We all did. But do ye still?"

"Do you?"

"Aye," Alviss said. "I fear they're dead in the cavern, or if they got away, me guess is that they'll be coming back and not with an army."

"And Azzudonna?"

The dwarf shrugged. "Who's to know?"

Mona Valrissa shared a resigned nod with Alviss, then held up her glass.

The dwarf raised his as well.

"To Azzudonna of Biancorso," Mona Valrissa toasted.

Alviss clinked her glass, then called out loudly, "To Azzudonna!"

All conversations in the tavern hall stopped, all eyes turned to the two, and every glass was raised, a hearty cheer from the score of people in the common room to their lost hero.

Mona Valrissa smiled appreciatively at Alviss. She had needed that.

"Watch this, lady," Alviss said with a wink, and he lifted his glass again and shouted, *"Perte miye Zaknafein!"*

The common room exploded in a great and enthusiastic echo of that sentiment.

Mona Valrissa took a deep breath to steady herself. It had been a remarkable few tendays, an emotional roll of budding friendship and powerful magic that led to hope, and now to fear and even terror.

"I'm trustin' them," Alviss was saying, but Mona Valrissa wasn't really listening. She was replaying every decision, every move, reminding herself that these four strangers had previously led them to an important victory in a nearby cave complex against a hatchery of enemies that would have done harm to Callidae.

Perhaps she had indeed owed them this chance to find their lost friend. Perhaps, in just this one instance, whatever the outcome, taking the risk had been simply the right thing to do.

JARLAXLE CAME TO THE LAST RIFT ALONG THE SIDE OF the Qadeej Glacier before Callidae, the one where he and the expedition had climbed out of the tunnel and met up with the Burnook orc clan. He thought to go over the short wall and back into the tunnels leading into the city, but changed his mind and flew his hellsteed all the way up to the top of the glacier instead. The winds buffeted them dangerously, but Jarlaxle and his demon mount fought through it and got up on top of the ice pack.

The Merry Dancers were bright, the stars shining, too, and soon after, running along the glacial roof, Jarlaxle noted the great fissures ahead, the holes that marked the boroughs of Callidae. He sorted them easily as he neared, and made his way back to Scellobel, the borough with which he was most familiar.

Those down in the city who noted his final approach looked on with shock and even trepidation, indeed, for down the great prow of rock that divided the borough came a drow half riding, half floating a steed with flaming hooves puffing hot smoke from its nostrils.

Jarlaxle dismissed the mount as soon as he set down on the base level of the city, and ran along the main boulevard to the inn called Ibilsitato.

He took a moment to collect himself, to straighten his clothes and adjust his great hat just right, before going through the door, and by that time, more than a few onlookers were coming up behind him, curious.

He was barely two strides inside when all conversation in the nearly full room abruptly stopped, all eyes turning his way.

"It's you!" said an aevendrow man with a tray of food, whom Jarlaxle recognized.

"It *is* me. Good Billibi," he greeted, sweeping his hat off in a low bow. "Couldn't you say that correctly to anyone?"

"But . . . but . . ." the man stammered, and Jarlaxle flashed his irresistible smile.

"Jarlaxle!" cried another, the woman Aida'Umptu, who was called Ayeeda. She came running across the common room. "It's you!"

"Don't," said Billibi, right as Jarlaxle began to repeat his quip.

"The others? Azzudonna?" Ayeeda said breathlessly, rushing up and crashing into Jarlaxle with a great hug.

Jarlaxle's smile disappeared. He wore a curious expression for just a moment, and mouthed *Azzudonna?* He let that curious comment go, though, with a determined shake of his head.

"I need to speak to the congress. To Mona Valrissa."

"We just did," said yet another voice, and the three turned to see Galathae, Ilina, Emilian, and Vessi entering the inn.

Jarlaxle breathed easier at the sight, though he noted that Azzudonna wasn't among this group, as was usually the case, and he thought of Ayeeda's question. Yet when he looked back to her, he offered a warm smile. "Your generosity—nay, the mere thought of your generosity—sustained me all the way back to Callidae," he told the gentle and friendly woman. "You filled my pouch with persimmons and cheese and lovely wine. It touched me, and reminded me when I sat alone in the darkness of why I needed to survive."

"Where are the others?" Galathae insisted, coming over.

The warmth left, both in his smile and his soul. "My friends are lost, encased in ice."

"N'divi," Ilina murmured.

"No," said Jarlaxle. "They weren't taken by the cante and doomed as n'divi. It was something different. A great wind."

"To the same effect," said Galathae, and Jarlaxle remembered that she had seen this before. And yet, there were some revelations she hadn't seen.

"No!" he told her. "Not the same. We broke a couple of your lost companions free, but they were taken again. But they were alive! Not undead like the n'divi, but alive—just suspended in the ice. We have to get back there, all of us. As great a force as Callidae can muster."

He noted that while they all initially showed intrigue and a bit of excitement, only Vessi among the four friends maintained a hopeful expression.

"Your friends were powerful," Galathae replied. "How much progress did you make in there? How long were you in that cavern, Jarlaxle?"

"Briefly," he admitted. "We were overwhelmed, caught by surprise. But now I know what to expect. If we bring the proper forces—"

"The Temporal Convocation will never agree to such an expedition," Galathae cut him short. "Nor should they."

"You've got a dozen friends, at least, frozen in ice pillars in that room. Of course we must go back!"

"Of course, you think that. In a way, I do, too. But we survive because we can defend ourselves—*here*," she explained. "Even that, though, would be difficult if you were all so easily beaten. To go there would be to invite whatever attacked you back, and put us all in peril. What *did* you find in the room? Slaadi? Giants? Cante and n'divi?"

He nodded, not adding anything about the being he believed to be Ygorl, the actual Ygorl, who was the Lord of Entropy, a veritable god among the slaadi. Such a revelation wasn't about to make the leaders of Callidae more eager to go anywhere near that place.

"The cante and the n'divi cannot come here," Galathae continued. Jarlaxle noticed that the others, Ilina particularly, kept wanting to say something. The priestess was perfectly agitated, but she didn't interrupt Galathae. "Not with the warmth of the River Callidae filling our boroughs," said Galathae. "If we go north with a force as you suggest, and lose, they will come south with great power—more than enough strength to overwhelm our advantages. Our war with them is a skirmish, a border war, fought on the ice pack and in the tunnels beyond our boroughs. Callidae can survive such a war."

"So can your enemies."

Galathae shrugged. "Then at least *we* survive."

"Where is Azzudonna?" Ilina blurted.

Jarlaxle winced at this second reference to the woman. He looked at Ilina curiously. "She was with you."

"She was taken from us," said Ilina. "By Guenhwyvar."

Jarlaxle's expression revealed his surprise. "Guenhwyvar?"

"Yes," said Ilina.

"We believe it was the cat," Galathae added. "Nay, we are certain. It happened quickly. Azzudonna was run down from behind and then was gone into insubstantial mist along with her feline attacker."

"It looked very much like Guenhwyvar," Ilina said.

"I don't see how that's possible," Jarlaxle said. "Guenhwyvar would not have attacked Azzudonna—the two were friends. Also, Catti-brie was among the first to fall, and she did not summon in the panther to the fight. I was trapped in a hole, but not frozen. And I could hear, and all the room was quiet."

"That cat was not there when you escaped?" asked Ilina. "Azzudonna was not there? Not encased as were the others, even?"

Jarlaxle shook his head and shrugged. "I cannot . . . when I managed to get out of the hole, I was accosted immediately by cante and n'divi. I barely escaped, and that only because of my summoned steed. I didn't get a chance to take a close look at much. I know nothing of Azzudonna's fate—I thought she would be with you until this moment. Nor do I know anything of Guenhwyvar—except that Catti-brie did not bring her forth in the chamber when we were set upon."

Galathae looked to Vessi. "Run back to Mona Chess and tell Mona Valrissa to reconvene the congress."

With a nod, Vessi was gone.

"Do you need some food or rest?" Galathae asked Jarlaxle.

"No food," he said, and he reached out and pulled Ayeeda back to him and kissed her on the cheek. "And no rest. Our friends cannot wait."

He could tell from Galathae's expression that she expected their friends to be waiting for eternity, but the paladin merely nodded and led the way out of Ibilsitato.

KAPFAAL SHIFTED ABOUT IN THE DEEP, TIGHT HOLE AND angled her shoulders to better line up her next pick strike. The small and slender dwarf had a feeling that she was near her goal, and not just from the perspiration on her face. Her kurit sensibilities, honed by years of working the blue-ice tunnels, told her that there was some sort of hollow not far below.

Out on the ice, the best miners—and Kapfaal was at the top of that short list—had to get as near as possible to the too-warm ice sitting too near the unfrozen polar ocean in order to find the best compressed blue ice. They often dug without their boots on so that the soles of their feet would tell them when to stop.

Kapfaal had been wearing her boots when she had begun her descent in the entry of what had once been the borough of Cattisola. Initially, she had been digging through tough ground here, not ice, after all, and had cleared plenty of sharp rocks, particularly early on. These last couple of days, however, some hundred feet down, the dwarf had abandoned the boots.

Now, whether it was her feet, or her dwarven sensibilities in general, or the sound of her pick whenever she struck, she believed she was getting close to . . . something.

She struck a rock hard, the blow upending one side of the fairly flat stone. She reached down and tried to work it free, and when that didn't work, she hooked her pick head under the side and braced it against a rock on the wall of the narrow shaft. She pulled her guide rope down just a bit more so that she could get some leverage here, then bent low, braced, and heaved.

The rock turned almost upright, but then suddenly fell away, taking Kapfaal's pick with it as the bottom fell out of the shaft. A rush of heat washed up over the dwarf and down she dropped to the end of her rope, and then farther as the sudden shock forced those bracing the rope forward. She slid down a dozen feet, leaving her hanging in an open room from the chest down.

A huge room, and a hot one—she wiggled her toes and waggled her feet with the sudden discomfort.

Kapfaal quickly pulled off her headband and the magically glowing gemstone it held, and twisted and bent to lower her face into that room, holding the gem out before her to try to get a glimpse.

The hot air took her breath away, and when she sucked it in, it stung her throat and lungs.

She heard Mattaval the aevendrow calling down to see if she was all right, but she ignored the woman and tried to hold on just a bit longer, noting the sparkles of reflection coming back at her from far below.

But she could take the heat no longer. She threw the headband to better illuminate all that was in the area, and lost her breath again, this time from sheer shock at the spectacular sight beneath her!

"By the gods," she whispered, or tried to, for she had no breath to blow forth to carry the words.

She couldn't stay, not another moment.

She straightened again, getting her face out of that hellish room, grabbed up at her rope and at the second rope that held the bucket, and tugged herself with all her considerable strength, trying to climb.

"THEY ARE ALIVE!" JARLAXLE PLEADED WITH THE GATHERing at the Siglig. "I've told you everything."

"Yes, including how easily you and your powerful friends were defeated," Mona Valrissa reminded him.

"For all of your warnings, we didn't really know what to expect. And there simply weren't enough of us. Give me a host of aevendrow, wizards and priests, and we'll crash through that room and be quickly away."

"Crash through with fireballs?"

"They were most effective of the spells, yes."

"And thus we will awaken Qadeej, as you did."

"It wasn't Qadeej," Jarlaxle insisted. "It was . . ." He paused, reminding himself to be vague here, to not reveal the name of Ygorl. "It was a large slaad."

"Who called to Qadeej," Mona Valrissa replied. "I'm sorry, my friend, for your loss and for ours, but we cannot take such a risk as you ask."

"But they're alive!"

"They *were* alive," Mona Valrissa corrected. "You cannot know if that is still the case. Perhaps your attack—and more than that, your escape from that ice tomb—has convinced the slaadi that their prisoners are not as secure as they had believed. You may have inadvertently doomed all of those you left behind in your fighting retreat from that room."

Jarlaxle started to reply, but the words caught in his throat. He wanted to deny them, of course, but he knew that indeed she might be right.

"We cannot take that risk, Jarlaxle," the mona said solemnly.

"Then send me home, now," the rogue replied. "I will bring forth such an army that this land has never seen. Grim-faced dwarves and hosts of drow. A cadre of wizards beyond—"

He stopped when he saw the shocked expressions coming back at him from all in the gallery, heads shaking, jaws hanging open. For one of the very few times in all of his long life, Jarlaxle immediately regretted his words.

"Please," he begged. "Just send me home, and you have my word that I will expend all energy and expense in finding Azzudonna, and my word that I will not divulge anything of this place."

"We cannot, I fear," Mona Valrissa replied. "Not now. How would you even get home, wandering the northern ways? And when we do send you home, you will go without knowledge of this place, or of what happened in that cave."

"Blur my memories of Callidae alone!"

"It does not work like that. In the spring, after Conception Verdant, we will put you on the path to your home if you still so desire. But without any memory of your time here."

"Now. I cannot stay longer. Send me home."

"To your death? You would not survive the winter winds. No magic that we could provide would sustain you long enough to get far from this place."

Jarlaxle's thoughts spun. He couldn't let it end like this!

"Give me back my whistle!" he pleaded. "I can get home with that whistle. Do with me what you must to protect Callidae and put me far from here, but with that item Jarlaxle will bother you no more."

"You'll not even remember what happened to your friends," Mona Valrissa told him.

Jarlaxle shrugged. "And so, what? Am I simply supposed to stay here then, pretending nothing has happened? No, I cannot stay. Not now. Not after all of this."

Mona Valrissa looked around at the congress, her questioning stare being met with many nodding heads.

"Not another tenday," Jarlaxle said.

"Very well, Jarlaxle."

"Even if I left with my memories, I would not tell them," Jarlaxle assured them.

"I believe you. Most in here believe you. But that is not enough, and we will not risk our secret, even for a friend such as you. Say your farewells to those you must. You will be taken to the cazzcalci rink soon for the ritual. And again, from all here and all in the city, we are glad that you and your companions found your way to us. The loss of Azzudonna is painful, but we are used to such risks and such losses. And the loss of Catti-brie and Artemis Entreri and Zaknafein pains us as it pains you. This is the price of living, Jarlaxle, the risk of boldness and the cost of loyalty. You and your friends will not be forgotten in Callidae, and not only because of the magic on that night of Quista Canzay, no. You touched many hearts here, all of you."

"We would never have taken you to the caverns, or even allowed you to try, were that not true," Galathae added. "Though in retrospect, I wish we had forbidden that foolhardy attempt."

"So do I," Jarlaxle said. "Though I wouldn't have ever forgiven you if you had."

MATTAVAL TUGGED HARD ON THE ROPE, DIGGING HER heels, which had been set with cleats, powerfully into the ice.

"Help, help!" the drow woman called, and a large orok rushed over to grab the taut line and stabilize it.

They heard coughing from far down the shaft, then "Pull me up!" in a gasping, distant voice.

The drow and the orc set themselves firmly and began walking away from the hole, straining. Others rushed over to take up the lengths and help drag Kapfaal upward.

"I'm okay!" the dwarf called from below soon after.

While the others steadied and set the rope, Mattaval rushed back to the lip of the dig and peered in. She looked at the amount of rope they had pulled from the hole and was surprised that she could not see Kapfaal's light.

"Are you there?" she called down.

"Where else would a dwarf be?" Kapfaal called back. "I lost me light. Dropped it, and oh, but girl, ye won't believe what I seen."

"Why's your face all red?" Rigfen the orc asked.

"What did you see?" asked Mattaval.

"It's hot," Kapfaal replied. "Kill-ye-to-death hot. Big cave, full o' crystals."

"Like Jarlaxle told us," said Rigfen in wonder.

CHAPTER 15

Discordant

H
e felt his heart pounding and his teeth grinding.

The image wouldn't leave him: Tadpole's sandal.

Tadpole's bloody and shredded robes!

Drizzt was reacting too fast to even think about it, his feet working past the rocks and ledges of the uneven tunnel with speed and precision beyond his conscious ability to keep up. He was falling into a different state of being, something far more lethal.

The baby cried out again, somewhere far below.

Drizzt tried to just let go, to just become the Hunter. With his magical anklets, he had no choice. He had to let go or his thoughts would slow his reactions.

But he couldn't, because the Hunter did not align with his training here at the monastery, where calm consciousness and mindfulness carried the day, even in times of desperation.

Around a sharp curve in the tunnel he went, leaping up on the wall, full speed.

He clipped his foot on a jag hidden by shadow and came down to the floor in a stumble, fighting hard every step not to pitch headlong to the floor.

But then he had to just let himself crash down, for coming around the other side of the bend was a trio of gnolls, launching javelins at him.

More good fortune than skill had Drizzt skidding down painfully under the trajectory of those missiles. He scraped his arms and hands and face, and lost Vidrinath in the tumble, but didn't slow, letting himself roll and spin, taking the beating on the uneven floor and sharp jags. His body reacted as he had trained it, turning and twisting, legs coming in close, feet going under him, and he scrambled up in a dead run for his enemies, the gnolls only a dozen strides ahead.

A dozen strides, more than half of which the Hunter didn't take. Barely three steps along, the trained monk launched himself into the air, denying the Hunter's scramble and calling instead upon his ki, the magic of life force. He brought forth the power of his connection between thought and muscle, lifting him and making him soar.

He turned a complete circuit in that great leap gracefully, in full control, then came out of the turn with a suddenness that shocked the middle gnoll, and with enough control to get his foot past its feebly blocking sword.

Tadpole's sandal . . .

In the midst of battle, Drizzt let go, let himself fall fully into that state of primal rage.

The Hunter's heel smashed against the gnoll's snout, launching the beast down the tunnel.

At the same time, Icingdeath went out to the right in a vicious sweep, up and under, taking out that gnoll's shield arm as it tried to slam the drow as his momentum carried him past.

The Hunter skidded to slow, leaped up to the left against the wall, and sprang away in a twisting flip that had him charging back up the corridor at the two. Closing fast, he turned aside a thrust spear with a backhand, rolling Icingdeath and stabbing ahead to drive that gnoll away another step. He went forward as the gnoll to his left now attempted a half-hearted swing with its sword, stumbling and spewing blood from its nearly severed arm.

The Hunter kicked the wounded and unbalanced brute on the side of the knee, cracking bone, sending the gnoll stumbling even more. It came almost as an afterthought to the furious drow warrior, whose focus remained squarely on the threatening spear wielder.

The baby cried out.

The Hunter battled the composure of his monk training.

He was fighting now with only one scimitar, but alone against him, the gnoll had no chance. It thrust the spear and had it batted aside, then again as the drow pressed forward.

The gnoll lowered its shoulder and shield-rushed, but the very beginning of the move gave the plan away to the instinctual warrior, and he easily sidestepped, then kicked the gnoll's trailing foot as it overbalanced past him, so that the gnoll kicked itself in the back of the ankle and pitched to the floor.

It recovered quickly and started to rise, almost quickly enough to prevent Icingdeath from stabbing through its spine.

Almost.

Savahn was in sight then, so the Hunter turned and raced down the tunnel, leaving the limping, bleeding, and fast-fading gnoll here, and the unconscious one lying farther down the tunnel—was it even alive?—for her.

The Hunter ran.

With the immediate heat of battle relieved, Brother Drizzt ran with it.

The two fought for control.

The Hunter demanded immediacy and fury, a wild anger coursing through in a need for action, for enemies, for kills. Drizzt kept trying to remind himself of his training, picturing snips of his slow-muscle-memory movements to hold balance and feel every muscle.

Another gnoll appeared, coming fast toward the sounds of battle. Drizzt decided to take it down with a subtle drop and sweep, then just run past and continue on his desperate quest.

The Hunter had hit it a dozen times, bashing with the pommel, slashing and stabbing with the scimitar, head-butting, driving stiffened fingers into its exposed throat when that head-butt rocked the hyena-like head backward, before Drizzt even realized that his instincts weren't listening to his plans.

He had reduced the gnoll to a bloody pulp, but he had lost time, something that stung him acutely when he heard another cry from the toddler, his beloved baby, he knew, and this one clearly revealing pain and fear.

Around another bend, the Hunter came into a short descending tunnel bathed in bluish light under a ceiling crawling with glow worms. At the far end loomed a chest-high barrier of rocks, capped with a large log.

Gnolls popped up behind that construction, lifting bows and spears.

The Hunter didn't slow.

His arm and scimitar worked frantically, slapping aside missiles. He cut left and threw himself back to the right in a sidelong roll, springing up from it with another flip over to bring his feet against the right-hand wall. And springing again from there, down to the floor and rolling back to his feet and speeding ahead.

Another javelin came at him, but the Hunter's left arm slapped it aside with a backhand. Another arrow sped for his face, but Icingdeath came up at the very last moment to tick the barbed head, redirecting it just enough to scratch the side of the Hunter's scalp.

He went down low as he approached the barricade, but came up high suddenly, not slowing, diving right over to fly into the tunnel behind the line of gnolls. He landed in a headlong tumble, rolling and turning and coming right back at the enemies.

He felt the sting as an arrow got through, jabbing hard against his mithral shirt.

He bore in, slashing and stabbing, leaping into a circle kick that caught a gnoll in the chest and sent it flying aside. He landed in a low crouch beneath a sweeping short spear, then sprang up behind that cut, scimitar going out wide to stab a gnoll charging in from the side, left palm coming up under the snout of the spear-wielder—and with such force that it lifted the three-hundred-pound gnoll right up and over the barricade.

But more bore in, clubs, swords, and spears leading.

Up he jumped, kicking out powerfully to either side. He landed and sprang again, spinning this time to send his scimitar in a wide circle cut, pushing back his enemies.

A gnoll went flying away, then another, and the Hunter didn't even register any attacks on them.

One near to him had its face creased by Icingdeath, its life ending with a strange yelp and gasp. The Hunter pushed right over it, extracting the scimitar with a forward thrust that took the next in line in the chest.

The Hunter tugged the curved blade back in and turned—but too late, he only then realized, as a club came in for his head, a strike he could neither block nor dodge.

He was sure that he was dead. The Hunter flew away in the realization that he, Drizzt, wouldn't win here, and so wouldn't get near to rescuing his beautiful, wonderful Brie.

He had failed, and he understood in that darkest instant that the discordant internal argument, instinct against reason, monk calm against primal rage, had cost him everything.

CHAPTER 16

Tricks and Trust

Penelope Harpell greeted the guests from Gauntlgrym when they came through the fiery portal into the Ivy Mansion. King Bruenor led the way, pushing through the door out of the basement chamber, dressed in full battle gear, with his one-horned helm and his magical expanding shield, which was now wound tightly into a small buckler. He had his battleaxe, too, strapped diagonally across his back with its many-notched head showing over his shoulder.

Beside him, one step back, came Thibbledorf Pwent, and it was clear to Penelope why Bruenor had brought this one. In his ridged armor with that enormous head spike and clawed punching gauntlets, Pwent appeared like the stuff of nightmares to any who did not know him. He had been cured of vampirism, so Penelope had been told, but when he sneered as he came through the door, it seemed to the wizard that he had somehow managed to keep the fangs.

Next came Regis Topolino, dressed in finery with his blue beret, white shirt, and black vest, a brilliant rapier on one hip, three-bladed dirk on the other, and a hand crossbow of magnificent design hanging on a chain at his chest, under the folds of his exceptional traveling cloak.

"The mustache quite becomes you, master Regis," she greeted him.

He twirled one end of the large growth and bowed gracefully.

Last in the line came Wulfgar, the giant barbarian, wrapped in his wolf-fur cloak and carrying that most mighty of weapons, the warhammer Aegis-fang, which had been crafted by King Bruenor himself in another age.

Despite the gravity of the situation, Penelope gave the giant man a wink, bringing a smile and a mutual understanding that both were hoping they might share a bed during his stay.

"Where is she?" Bruenor demanded gruffly.

"Resting," Penelope answered. "The poor lass is quite disoriented, and took a heavy blow when she ran headlong into our wall."

"You need to paint butterflies on that invisible barrier," Regis said, but if he was hoping to lighten the mood, Bruenor's responding scowl stole that possibility away.

"'The poor lass'?" the dwarf king echoed incredulously. "Where's me girl, Penelope?"

"I don't know."

"This poor lass, as ye're calling her, came in with the cat, I been told."

Penelope nodded. "I think it was Guenhwyvar, yes, though I cannot be sure. Azzudonna—that is her name—doesn't have the figurine—"

"But she had the cat?"

Penelope shrugged. "She doesn't have the figurine and didn't have it when she came to us, we are sure. How she might have brought Guenhwyvar, or been brought with Guenhwyvar . . ."

"She doesn't need it," Regis interjected. "Not always, at least. There have been a couple of occasions when Guenhwyvar has taken one or another of us away to the Astral Plane of her own accord. Usually to rescue . . ." His voice trailed off and he swallowed hard as the implications came clear to them all.

"What'd she tell ye?" Bruenor asked, following as Penelope led the way through the massive mansion.

"Not much, I'm sorry to say. She is terribly afraid. I don't think her an enemy, but she's far from trusting us."

Bruenor stopped short, putting his hands on his hips.

"She knows where me girl is," he said. "If she ain't for tellin', then aye, she's an enemy o' meself. And she won't much be liking that, is me solemn promise to ye."

"Me king!" Pwent growled at his side.

"Take me to her," Bruenor demanded. "Straightaway."

"Bruenor, she needs some time," Penelope said. "We're trying to gain her trust."

"Time? What time's me girl got, then?"

"I don't know."

"Aye, ye don't. Take me to this drow lassie and I'll get her tongue wagging, don't ye doubt."

Penelope knew that she was walking a very fine line here. This was her place, her domain, not Bruenor's, but the dwarf was among the most powerful people in the north. Penelope loved and respected King Bruenor and thought him fair and kind, but she also understood well his fatherly protectiveness of Catti-brie and all the others he considered his family.

It was not wise to cross King Bruenor Battlehammer on matters of family and friends.

"Archmage Gromph is with her now," Penelope informed them. "He is using the mind magic taught to him by Kimmuriel to try to find some hints of events she will not readily divulge. Kimmuriel has already spent some time with her, and will again when he returns. He has gone to Luskan to search some books and charts in the library of the Hosttower. We expect him back at any time."

They moved down a long interior hallway on the mansion's third floor that ended at a door. As soon as their destination became obvious, Bruenor pushed ahead.

"Let me go in and speak with Gromph," Penelope begged.

"I can talk for meself," Bruenor replied.

"King Bruenor!" Penelope said sharply, and the dwarf wheeled about.

"She won't even understand you, or you her," Penelope explained. "She speaks Drow, only Drow, as far as we can tell, and in a dialect that makes it difficult—"

"I know enough o' that tongue to get by," the dwarf assured her, and started again for the door.

"Even the drow have trouble understanding her!" Penelope declared. "At least let me get priestess Dab'nay or Copetta or some other, to prepare another spell of language comprehension so that there will be no misunderstanding between you two."

Bruenor didn't slow.

"Gromph will be angry," Penelope warned.

"Gromph can kiss me hairy bum." Bruenor shoved through the door, nearly hitting Dab'nay in the face as she was moving to exit the room.

"Found her." Bruenor harrumphed, looking back at a sighing Penelope. The dwarf pushed past the startled drow priestess, Pwent and Regis close behind.

Dab'nay held up her hands in confusion, offered a nod to acknowledge Wulfgar, and went back into the room, closing the door behind her.

"You've learned nothing from her?" Wulfgar asked when he and Penelope were alone.

"Very little," Penelope replied. "Kimmuriel tried his mind tricks on her, but he came away convinced that Azzudonna was trained to defeat such intrusions. She's young for a drow, but a seasoned veteran, I am sure."

"And she doesn't even know how she got here?"

"Of that particular detail, I am also fairly certain that she is telling the truth. But it was Guenhwyvar. I keep wanting to believe that it was not, but when I allow my hopes to lead me in that direction, I know in my heart that I'm lying to comfort myself."

Wulfgar sighed, kissed Penelope on the forehead, then started for the doorway.

"And there's more," Penelope unexpectedly continued, and Wulfgar skidded to an abrupt halt and turned back with a curious expression.

"Kimmuriel tried to contact Jarlaxle," Penelope explained. "He believes that he found that magical whistle that Jarlaxle carries, which he explained to me as their connecting beacon. But when he followed its magic, he discovered that the whistle was held by another drow, one dressed similarly to Azzudonna."

"Dressed similarly?"

Penelope opened a magically concealed doorway on the side wall of the corridor and led the barbarian inside a small chamber where Azzudonna's belongings had been placed, her clothing hanging on a rack. She cast a magical light spell, pulled Wulfgar in behind her, and shut the door.

"Sealskin," the man from Icewind Dale said as soon as he moved near the black pants. "This is clothing to protect from the cold winds."

"Which is supposedly the very type of place where Gromph deposited our four friends."

Wulfgar wore a grim expression. "One wouldn't wear this in a deep Underdark cavern."

"And that broken spear and sword are fashioned mostly of ice," Penelope told him, pointing to the weapons set against the side wall. "Copetta had a difficult time in breaking the spear to extract it from Azzudonna's wound . . ."

Wulfgar looked at her with surprise at mention of the wound.

"Forget that wound. For now, suffice it to say that it was difficult to break the spear, and thus far, has been difficult for Copetta to use her magic to repair it."

"Okay." He took a deep breath. "So what does this mean? That she's not from the same place Drizzt is from. And she is from wherever Catti-brie went."

"That's what I'm thinking."

"Then, what: There are drow living up north?" Wulfgar reasoned. "On the surface?"

"So it would seem."

Wulfgar considered it all for a moment. "Take care how you present this to Bruenor," he warned. "He'll sail the armies of Gauntlgrym, Mithral Hall, Adbar, and Felbarr on ice floes across the Sea of Moving Ice to get to anyone he believes to be holding Catti-brie against her will."

Penelope didn't argue the point. Then again, she had no intention of floating any of this by the king until she had more information.

As she'd noted: you don't get between Bruenor and his family.

BRUENOR CRASHED INTO THE ROOM, DRAWING STARTLED looks from Gromph and the drow woman who was sitting up on a bed.

"Get out," Gromph ordered.

"Where's me girl?" Bruenor demanded of the stranger. "Ye tell me now or I'm not putting me fist up yer nose!"

"I won't kill her for ye, me king!" Pwent growled threateningly.

"What?" Regis asked behind them, for the words from the two fiery dwarves certainly didn't match their ferocious tone and threats.

Gromph sighed.

"'Tis good knowin' meself's among friends," Azzudonna said, shaking her head.

It took Bruenor longer to realize what he and Pwent had actually said than it did for him to realize that this drow was speaking perfect Common, and with a dwarven dialect!

"Thought she only spoke Drow," Bruenor said.

"I cast a new spell of tongues upon her so that we could converse," Dab'nay explained.

"And a second spell to fill the room with truthfulness," Regis realized.

Bruenor paused, and sensed it then. He wanted to come in with roars and threats, but the zone of truth was preventing him from actually speaking those hollow threats.

"You cannot lie in this room, foolish dwarf," Gromph told Bruenor. "Your bluff was revealed even as you blustered it."

"Which might prove all the better," said Regis, and he pushed past the dwarves to stand before Azzudonna. "You know now that we're not really enemies, and not all that scary." He glanced at Thibbledorf Pwent. "Well, that one can be," he admitted.

"If my hosts had wanted me dead, I'd be dead," Azzudonna calmly replied. "I am Azzudonna."

"Of?" Regis asked.

The woman didn't answer, other than to chuckle at the feeble attempt.

"Well met, good lady. I am Regis Topolino of Bleeding Vines. This is King Bruenor Battlehammer of Gauntlgrym, and his shield dwarf, Thibbledorf Pwent."

"Get the Pwent?" Pwent asked her, puffing out his chest, punching his hand into his palm, then lifting it to flick a finger against his enormous head spike. " 'Cause ye're tellin' us about me king's girl or ye're *not* going to get the Pwent!"

"Explain the spell of veracity to the battleraging fool, please," Gromph said to Bruenor. "He's confusing enough when he thinks he knows what he's saying."

"King Bruenor is the father of Catti-brie," Regis told Azzudonna, and her momentary expression of surprise revealed to the halfling that she knew that Catti-brie was no dwarf, and so, that she knew Catti-brie. "Anything you can tell us of our lost friend would be most appreciated."

"I'm sure she is terrified by your threat to not torture her," Gromph dryly remarked.

Azzudonna just looked at Regis, showing some sympathy, and shrugged.

"Please, she's me girl," Bruenor said, stepping forward. "And ain't no lie when I'm telling ye that I'd march armies across the world to save her."

"I'm sorry that she's missing," said Azzudonna.

"But ye know her? And ye know something about why she's missing?"

The woman looked away.

"I won't torture ye, but that don't mean I won't punch yer pretty face," Bruenor warned.

"Ah, he thinks you're pretty, Azzudonna," said Gromph.

"Ye ain't helpin', wizard."

"Ain't tryin' to, dwarf," Gromph shot back. "We've been at this for hours, and you storm in here as if we're all to bow down before you. Treat me like a subject, King Bruenor, and you'll understand the life of a newt." He pointed his finger upward, indicating the room, reminding of the spell. "And that is no lie."

"None of you are helping," Dab'nay said.

"Let me speak with her alone," Regis said, turning about. "And release the spells—not the language spell, but any others compelling behavior. Please."

As he finished, he cleverly revealed a particular ruby pendant about his neck, one Bruenor knew from long ago, and one Regis had only recently recovered as a gift from Jarlaxle in exchange for some cheating in a gambling game and a wild adventure on the high seas.

"Ye let me king speak!" Pwent said, but Bruenor held him back.

"Aye, Rumblebelly," Bruenor said. "Yerself should speak with the girl. None loved me Catti-brie more than Regis, and ye've the right . . . attitude for interrogatin'."

"I've had quite enough of this nonsense anyway," Gromph announced, standing up dramatically. He turned a glare on Azzudonna. "I am not bound by the codes of these others," he warned. "You will tell me what I need to know, I promise you."

The threat was honest.

Regis watched as Dab'nay reached out and put her hand on Azzudonna's shoulder. The two locked stares and nodded in mutual support.

Gromph left the room, Dab'nay following after dispelling her zone of truth and casting a second spell of language comprehension on Azzudonna to refresh the duration.

"Please, elf," Bruenor said to Azzudonna. "Catti-brie's me little girl. I canno' be losing her. If ye're knowin' anything, anything . . . please, elf."

He turned and pulled Pwent out of the room, shutting the door.

Regis took the chair Dab'nay had been sitting in.

"I'll tell you all about us and you'll understand," he explained to Azzudonna. "We're not your enemies—at least, I hope not."

THE GATHERING IN ONE OF THE IVY MANSION'S LARGE common rooms was somber. Penelope, Kipper, and several other Harpells were there, along with the few drow from Luskan who had come back with Kimmuriel and Bruenor's contingent. They discussed their options and their information, all of which seemed very limited at that point, particularly when the psionicist stated without reservation that the only way he had any chance of getting information from this stranger would be to mentally tear it out of her.

"With her training, she might not survive such an intrusion," he explained to the group. "And even if she did, it would scar her for the rest of her existence. There is little that one can inflict upon a person that would prove to be more of a violation."

"Why should we care about her?" said Gromph.

"Well, ye can take the drow from Menzoberranzan, but ye canno' take the Menzoberranzan out o' the drow," muttered Bruenor.

"This is *your* missing daughter, or so you keep saying," Gromph shot back at him.

"Aye, she's me girl, and me girl'd not e'er forgive me if I tortured this one so, as I'd not e'er forgive meself."

"She wants to tell us something," Penelope said.

"She does," Dab'nay agreed.

"She won't even admit that it was Guenhwyvar that brought her to us, and it is clear that it was," Gromph reminded them. "What a coincidence would it be for some other astral panther to exist and just coincidentally drop a strange woman into Catti-brie's room."

"Clearly Azzudonna knows a lot more than she's revealing, but it's paining her," Penelope explained. "I see it plainly on her face. We'll wear her down, but more effectively with trust than with threats."

"More effectively or quicker?" Bruenor asked, reminding them that time might not be on their side here.

"More effectively?" Gromph muttered, staring coldly at Kimmuriel. The archmage snorted and added, "Only if the threats are idle."

Bruenor glared at him.

"You would be amazed at what people will tell you with the proper . . . prompting."

Bruenor glared harder.

"So, what are our next moves?" Wulfgar put in before the conversation could go off in that dangerous direction. "Where did you land our lost companions with your magical gate those months ago?" he asked Gromph.

"In the north."

"That doesn't narrow it down."

"On a hillside in the snow," the archmage replied. "They wanted to go where Doum'wielle Armgo went. I don't know where that fool was thrown, so I opened a gate on the side of a mountain, some mountain. In the north."

"That doesn't—" Wulfgar started.

"Concern you," Gromph shouted back. "Jarlaxle knew the limitations when the gate was opened. He knew that I had no real idea of what we were looking at, or where we were looking, other than somewhere in the far north. He knew that. Zaknafein knew that. Artemis Entreri knew that. And Catti-brie knew that. They stepped through without any prompting from me. So not another word from you on this matter. I told Jarlaxle he was a fool for doing this. I told them all that. Did you?"

"Seems yer favorite word is 'fool,'" said Bruenor.

"My least favorite," Gromph shot back at him. "But the one most often appropriate, to my great distress."

"So, what are our next moves?" Wulfgar repeated loudly.

"I have something to tell you," Dab'nay quietly interjected.

All gazes fell over her, more for her tone than the words.

"Jarlaxle swore me to secrecy, but now I must tell," she began. "When we went to speak with the Moonwood elves, we traveled to Silverymoon to inquire about some rumors that Jarlaxle had uncovered. Jarlaxle spoke with an old elf, an ancient elf, named Freewindle, who dreamed of a city of drow in the north."

"Dreamed?" Kimmuriel asked.

"Maybe a dream, maybe an addled memory from long ago. Maybe a combination of the two. It wasn't really anything definitive, but this rumor, that conversation with the confused elf in Silverymoon, was a large part of why Jarlaxle wanted to go to the north. It wasn't just Doum'wielle—and certainly not to somehow cure the sword Khazid'hea of its demonic influence. He thought that perhaps . . ." She paused and shook her head.

"It seems that Jarlaxle and this old elf in Silverymoon might have been correct," Penelope said.

"So, are our friends dead? Captured? Living in the north?" Wulfgar said.

"That is what we need to determine," said Gromph.

"Aye," Bruenor agreed. "And if the first or second, then we're needin' an army."

"BUT WHERE?" REGIS PRESSED, GIVING A SUBTLE LITTLE turn of his shoulders to keep the magic ruby spinning. "You know that you want to tell me."

"I think . . ." Again Azzudonna stopped short.

"You must trust me," said Regis.

"Is that why you try to mesmerize me with trickster magic?" Azzudonna answered. She put on a sour expression as she stared at the ruby, obviously catching on to its charm.

Regis sighed and tucked the gem away. "What would you have me do? What would you do if it was your friends who were lost and I was obviously hiding something?"

"Probably worse to you than you—any of you—have done to me," Azzudonna admitted.

"Then you understand my pain, so tell me."

Azzudonna stared ahead, but chewed her lip as if she was considering something, at least.

"Where are they?"

"I do not know."

Regis looked at her doubtfully.

"Go and get the priestess. Bring forth the zone of truth again if you doubt me."

"But you know them?" Regis asked. "You admit that?"

Azzudonna hesitated and started to look away, but her struggle was plain to see.

"I met them many tendays ago," she admitted. "I helped them. We became great friends. Zaknafein . . ."

She stopped there and swallowed hard, and Regis was amazed to see moisture lining her pretty purple eyes.

"What about Zak?"

Azzudonna shook her head, seemed unable to reply at that moment.

"Tell me," Regis begged. "Something. Anything!"

"They are lost to you," Azzudonna said. "They went to a place they should not have—I begged them not to go. But they were stubborn, and claimed the duty of loyalty."

"Loyalty? Doum'wielle?" Regis reasoned.

"She was lost many months ago," Azzudonna said.

Regis nodded, then his eyes widened indeed! Doum'wielle had been lost several years before, so even if his friends had spoken of the woman to Azzudonna, her answer would have only made sense if she had known Doum'wielle as well.

"They are lost and will not be found. That's all I can tell you."

"Dead?"

Azzudonna fixed him with a determined stare. "Dead if they were lucky. Undead if not. Mourn them and bury them in your thoughts, and let them recede into joyful memories."

"If we do that, how are we to get you back home?"

"There is no home. There is nothing, no place to go. I am here now. This is my life, however you and your friends determine I may live it."

Regis stared at her earnestly. "It doesn't have to—"

"It does," Azzudonna answered.

"WE HAVE TO TELL DRIZZT," SAID PENELOPE.

"Tell him what?" Gromph grumbled. "What do we know?"

"We know that . . ." Penelope started to argue back, but she stopped and looked to the door, and all the others followed her lead when Regis walked into the room.

He had his beret in his hand and reached up to scratch at his curly brown locks. He sniffled, the moisture on his cherubic cheeks glistening in the firelight.

Bruenor hopped up from his chair. "What d'ye know, Rumblebelly?"

"I believe her," the halfling replied in a tiny voice.

"And?" the dwarf demanded.

"That was Guen who brought her here," he answered. "And I think our friends are forever lost to us."

Bruenor growled; Pwent cried out.

"And I don't believe—nay, I am certain!—that their fall had anything to do with Azzudonna. She's not an enemy."

"But she's still hiding something," said Wulfgar.

"After hearing of Jarlaxle's trip to Silverymoon, I think we know what that might be," Kimmuriel reminded him.

"Go back to Grandmaster Kane, and to Drizzt and bid him to come home," Penelope told Kimmuriel, who nodded.

"And to Silverymoon," Bruenor declared. "I'm wantin' to speak to this elf named Freewindle."

That sparked a discussion, shouts flying back and forth from every direction.

"Let us argue in the morning," Penelope said above the din, and the room quieted. "It is late. We are all exhausted. Let us go and rest and see what thoughts and ideas the dawn brings."

"Yer gemstone worked on her, did it?" Bruenor asked Regis.

He shook his head. "She saw it for what it was. She told me more than I expected, but little really, and I don't know if trying to get her to divulge more will do any of us any good."

"Again, the morning light will clear many heads," said Penelope. "Perhaps Azzudonna's among them."

"I wouldn't count on it," Gromph muttered.

CHAPTER 17

Memories

J arlaxle sat on the edge of his bed, rubbing the reverie from his eyes. He was weary, worn out, defeated—emotions that he had little experience with, surely.

He knew what was going to happen this day. He knew that it had to happen.

And he understood clearly that the inevitable side effect of the coming ritual might well forever doom his three traveling companions.

Had he lost dear Catti-brie, his friend, the more-than-worthy partner of Drizzt Do'Urden, the woman who had served as an avatar of a goddess to help deny Lady Lolth's plans for Drizzt in no uncertain terms? What a terrible loss to the world!

Had he lost Entreri, whom he loved as a brother, a man with whom he had shared the road for many decades? Why, once Jarlaxle had crowned Entreri as the king of Vaasa, which of course had in no short order landed Artemis Entreri in the jails of King Gareth Dragonsbane!

Jarlaxle laughed when he thought of those many days he and his dour friend had spent in the Bloodstone Lands. What a grand adventure that had been!

Had he lost Zaknafein again? His oldest friend, his most trusted associate in days of old, and now again in the present times? Had he watched dear Zak come back from the precipice of death in the throes of the chaos phage only to lose him so brutally soon after?

Jarlaxle had brought them all up here. They had trusted him and come willingly. He had pulled them with half-truths and grand promises, tempting carrots that they might make the world better. And now they were gone, frozen in time and in place—a fate and a place Jarlaxle wouldn't even remember when the aevendrow were done with him this day.

At least, Jarlaxle *hoped* that they were still there, frozen and undisturbed. In that event, there would be some chance to rectify this. He had to pray that his own escape hadn't prodded the slaadi to make sure no others got away.

He considered the three again, and reminded himself that he would retain those older memories, of course, even if the new ones were taken from him up on the cazzcalci rink in this practiced ritual of the aevendrow.

Jarlaxle nodded. He pulled up his left leg and set his ankle over the top of his right thigh, then snapped his magical bracer to bring a dagger into his hand. He considered his words carefully, feeling the needlelike point of the weapon with the top of his index finger, using the sharp pain as a focus to sharpen his thinking.

He didn't have much room.

A call from outside his door told him it was time to go.

He didn't have much time.

Using the dagger, Jarlaxle scratched *ILH-DAL-AUT* on the bottom of his left foot. Barely had he finished when his room's door began to open, so he stuffed his foot into the boot that was standing next to his bed, not even trying to otherwise stem the bleeding. He looked up to see Ilina and Galathae, who stared back, and more particularly, who looked to the dagger on the bed beside him.

Jarlaxle scooped it up and tucked it into a belt strap on his boot.

"Just getting ready," he answered their stares. "I am allowed to carry weapons with me, I presume."

"Of course," Galathae answered.

"You have my whistle?"

"You will get it back," Galathae said.

"If you gave it to me now, I could make sure that it's working," Jarlaxle told her. "I mean, before you leave me out in the wilderness to die."

Galathae chuckled at the irrepressible rogue, but Ilina took him much more seriously.

"Why don't you just stay?" she asked, her voice even and sincere. "We've got so much to offer to you here in Callidae, and there is so much more we wish to learn from you, so many stories left for you to tell."

"I do enjoy recounting such great adventures, but I have left behind many beloved friends," Jarlaxle said somberly. "As my lost friends have left behind many beloved friends, who will want answers."

"Answers you won't be able to give them," Galathae said—rather sharply, Jarlaxle thought. "And that chasm in your mind will forever torment you, and your remaining friends."

"I know," he answered with a sigh. "But I have to go back and be there for those I have lost and for those who are waiting. I owe them that . . . I guess." He paused and shook his head. "Does that make sense?"

"It does," Galathae admitted. "The return of Jarlaxle would raise many questions, but it would likely offer some closure to them all, at least. Come along now. We have many powerful priests anticipating our arrival. They have busy lives and it would not do to keep them waiting."

Jarlaxle pulled on his second boot, collected his traveling cloak, and stood up. When he lifted his great hat from the bed, he grimaced, remembering that his prized portable hole was no longer hidden within.

At least the diatryma feather was fully regrown and ready for use.

ILINA KEPT HER FOCUS ON GALATHAE, WHO WAS CENTER-
ing the circle beside Jarlaxle, as the thirty priests slowly walked to
their left. The rink was bright, very bright, for every priest, as well as
Galathae, had cast a magical light spell onto the red pom-pom atop
the black biretta they wore.

Now the gathering of priests represented the summer sun, circling
and never setting, showering their radiance and magical dweomers
toward the target, Galathae, who magically, divinely, changed the
timbre of that barrage of spells and redirected it into the true target,
Jarlaxle. Galathae was the key here—she had to fashion the magic
like a cutting blade to excise the victim's most recent experiences and
memories. It was not an exact art, certainly. Some targeted memories
would survive, often cloudy and hidden in a swirl of doubt, and other
memories, more distant, more personal, might inadvertently be lost.

But this was the price that must be paid by any visitor choosing
to leave Callidae after any stay, no matter how short. It would take
decades, at least, to train someone against simple spells and desires to
properly protect the necessary secret. This ritual was the only alternative to imprisonment or even execution.

The ceremony went on for hours, though Jarlaxle's eyes glazed in
a manner of complete detachment with the first infusion of the collective, disorienting magic. He was no more than the pure receptor
here, his willpower clenched tightly within a cocoon of light so that
he could not hope to resist.

The ceremony pained Ilina more than she had expected. She had
done this before on three occasions, but this was the first time she had
developed such a powerful bond with one who had wandered into Callidae. She hated having to do this to Jarlaxle, hated even more the loss
of the other three visitors, almost to the level of the pain of loss she felt
for Azzudonna, who had been her friend for years.

She felt the tears on her cheeks as she continued her casting and
her slow walk, and she even snorted aloud, nearly interrupting her
spell, as the circle came fully around and she approached the spot
where she and the others would come back to where they had begun,
would end their walk and end the ritual.

JARLAXLE CAME AWAKE WITH A START AND JUMPED UP
from his bedroll, eyes darting about, head snapping left and right. The
drow turned all around, trying to figure out where he was.

And where his friends might be.

Why was it nighttime? What had happened to the brilliant sunshine on the white snowcap?

Yes, the snow.

He had avoided the avalanche.

The avalanche!

The snow was deep everywhere outside the sheltered overhang,
but as he pushed his way out, Jarlaxle only grew more confused, for he
wasn't on the mountainside where they had been chased down by the
wave of powdery snow. He was in a valley surrounded by mountains,
but none near enough for such an avalanche to come anywhere near
this place.

He tried to sort through it. Catti-brie had gone over the ridge, but
no, not the one now forming the overhang above him. Entreri, too,
had plummeted over the edge, but Jarlaxle had leaped and floated,
above the rolling wave of snow.

"Zak?" he whispered, for hadn't the weapon master, too, escaped?
He thought that maybe Zak had floated up, but he couldn't be certain.

No, it had to be Zak, he realized. Someone had brought him here.
It had to be Zak. Something, a rock likely, must have bounced up from
the ridge and struck him, knocking him senseless.

Zaknafein had saved him.

"Zaknafein?" he said a bit louder, though he didn't dare yell. He
moved out from under the overhang, his gaze searching all about.

He shook his head in confusion, then looked back to where he had
awakened, searching for a clue, any clue.

He realized that the only tracks here were the ones he had just
made in leaving the small sheltered campsite. He bent and felt the
snow and grew even more confused. He was no expert, but the top
layer was crusted over a bit, making him think that this snow lying
about him was not new-fallen.

But where were the other tracks? Where were the footprints of

Zak, or whoever had brought him here? Or even his own tracks, if he had wandered here in a daze?

"How long have I been asleep?" he asked the quiet night.

Jarlaxle moved out farther, then climbed the overhang to get a wider view.

Nothing. Just jagged and rocky mountains and piled snow. A few scraggly tree skeletons dotted the area, casting swaying shadows under the dancing greenish lights above. The night was perfectly quiet other than the moan of a slight breeze, and the only movement was of the shadows and those waving lights up above.

Waving and dancing, he thought, and he mouthed, *Merry Dancers*, then stopped, surprised and confused, thinking for just a moment that he might have heard that phrase before.

Somewhere.

Jarlaxle brought a hand to his head in frustration, rubbing from his bald pate to his chin.

His hand was back on his hip before he even registered that his great hat and eyepatch were missing!

He rushed down and around, through the snow and back into the hollow and his bedroll. He took a deep and steadying breath indeed when he found his prized items. He pulled the eyepatch on immediately and looked around, thinking he might see things more clearly, wondering if he had been deceived by some illusionary magic.

But no, everything remained the same as before.

Jarlaxle went for his hat, then paused, thinking it might be wise for him to set up a more secure extradimensional shelter while he tried to sort through the mystery.

He dismissed that even as he reached inside the hat's chimney—Zaknafein had to be coming back for him, right?

Before he reversed his motion, though, he noted that something else was missing, for the underside of his hat's top did not have a separate piece of soft cloth set into it. Jarlaxle went at the chapeau furiously, but no—his portable hole wasn't there.

"Zak has it," he told himself, and he growled in greater frustration still as he tried to remember.

He pictured the cloth in his hand and himself standing before a great mound of piled, not windblown, snow—but it was a fleeting image. Perhaps a conjuration of his imagination. Perhaps a memory. Perhaps a hope.

"Where in the Nine Hells is Zak?" Jarlaxle whispered. "Where am I?"

He plopped down into a cross-legged position on the bedroll, took a complete inventory, then sighed and waited.

And waited.

Hours passed. Thanks to his boots, he wasn't too cold, at least.

More hours passed with no sign of Zak or anyone else. Jarlaxle went out several times, climbing back up, even going off a bit to a higher crag of stone, straining his eyes, trying to find something, anything.

More hours passed. Where was predawn light?

Then more. Where was the dawn?

He didn't understand. None of this made sense.

He paced about. He waited. Eventually, he got hungry and searched about his enchanted belt pouch for some food.

What he brought forth confused him. It felt like a piece of dried fruit, but he couldn't quite place it. He brought it to his nose and sniffed. Yes, tangy . . . he knew what it was, but he couldn't quite remember the name. And he had never seen one sliced and dried like this before.

In the same pouch with it was a block of some strange-smelling cheese. Strong, but not offensive. He took a bite of it.

Interesting, he thought.

Next, a bite of the fruit, and then, on a whim, a bite of both together.

It was truly delicious, and more than that, the sublime taste sent Jarlaxle's thoughts swirling. He had tasted this combination before. Somewhere.

But where? And how had these foods gotten into his pouch?

As much as he felt it was important to know, he felt an equal compulsion to not pursue the question. He had more important things to deal with. Where were his friends, Catti-brie and Entreri? Had they survived the fall and the snow tumbling over the ledge upon them?

He waited.

He paced.

The sun didn't come up.

Jarlaxle was a creature of information, and this indecipherable situation was driving him mad.

He felt about in his pouch, producing his obsidian steed, but he just held it there and didn't summon it. Where would he go?

Some time later, perhaps a day, perhaps more, and still with no sign of the dawn, Jarlaxle did call the hellsteed, and rode it far and wide, even trying to ascend the side of a mountain to gain a better vantage point—an attempt cut short by a powerful buffeting wind that tossed him and his mount far afield.

He did get many wider views of the area, none of which showed him any more landmarks than the hollow where he had awakened.

"Zak, where in the Nine Hells are you?" he called, loudly this time, after another rest, another meal, and several more hours of empty tedium.

Torn and troubled, one thought alone came very clear to him: he couldn't stay.

But, again: Where was he supposed to go?

CHAPTER 18

Sum of the Parts

T he club stopped its descent.

Simply stopped, as if it had struck a stone wall.

Drizzt looked up to see a wrinkled and tanned human hand below it, angled between the spikes, holding the club steady, perfectly steady. No wiggle, no movement at all.

The drow glanced forward to the attacking gnoll's face, so full of shock and outrage. It held that look when the stiffened fingers of a second hand shot forward to strike the beast in the throat, and then retracted, taking the front of the gnoll's windpipe with it. It held that look as it fell away, dead, to the ground.

The silence that followed struck the Hunter so profoundly that the feral alter ego slipped aside and let Drizzt consider the scene with a clear head. He glanced about.

They were all dead. The gnolls were all dead. Even the ones he hadn't gotten to yet.

Grandmaster Kane stood beside him.

Savahn came rolling over the barricade to the other side of him, handing him Vidrinath.

"You fight against yourself," Kane told him.

The shock of the moment wore away and Drizzt called to the Hunter within and leaped ahead to charge down the tunnel—or tried to, but a simple arm bar from Kane held him in place as if he, like the descending club, had hit a stone wall. Full of anger and confusion, he glared at the old Grandmaster of Flowers.

"You would have just met your end had I not intervened," Kane told him.

Drizzt tried to deny that, but he knew he would be simply lying to himself and so he didn't speak the thought aloud.

"I must go," he said instead. "We must go! Now!"

Kane shook his head. "You must find your balance. There are many more gnolls below. The internal battle you wage will get you killed, to no one's gain."

"They have Brie!"

Kane shook his head. "You will do her no good lying dead on a stone floor in a dark cave."

Drizzt swallowed hard and kept staring.

"This other being within you that you brought forth in your outrage," Kane said. "You have spoken to me of him before. This warrior you allow yourself to become, this Hunter, is a reactionary fighter, instincts moving too fast for consideration. Reactionary, only that."

"Effective," Drizzt countered, and he pressed against the arm bar.

"No," Kane replied, shaking his head. "Once, perhaps, but no more."

"I don't have time for this!" Drizzt growled through gritted teeth.

"You *must* have time for this," Kane countered. "So hear me first and hear me well. Your training with us is a design of anticipation, not reaction. The Hunter is purely reactive. Which therefore negates all your training with us . . . unless you step back. You cannot do both unless you understand both. Your instinct toward action will lead you to a place of disaster when your longer and more considered fighting form is trying to take you to a favorable place. What just happened here with these gnolls was no aberration, and nothing I didn't anticipate and expect. As the Hunter, you would have won here. As a master monk,

you would have won here. As both, however, you will fail, repeatedly—
well, repeatedly if you survive repeatedly, which you won't."

"I don't have time for a lecture!" Drizzt decided, and he pushed
past the arm, turning back only because Kane's fist clenched his
shoulder.

"Let me go with you."

"I have been begging you to—"

"No, within you. Let me in. I will help you find the balance."

"Just come beside me! My daughter—"

He stopped when he felt Kane let go of his hand and grab at his
mind instead. The physical form of Kane crumpled before him, slumping down into a cross-legged position, Savahn moving right beside to
support and defend.

Drizzt opened his mind and let the spirit of Kane flow into him.
He had seen this before, with Brother Afafrenfere. Kane had come to
the Silver Marches in the mind of Afafrenfere for that great war, and
the brother had become a much greater being in that short time, both
physically and spiritually.

I will help you achieve balance, Kane telepathically imparted.

Drizzt nodded to Savahn, who stood guard over the empty vessel of Grandmaster Kane's body, then he ran off down the tunnel,
speeding along, sidestepping stones, leaping up on the wall when going
around a bend. He sensed an uneasiness in Kane, but he didn't pause
to explore or communicate that explicitly.

More gnolls showed, charging the other way, firing bows and yelping as soon as they noted the intruder.

A duck, a twist, a backhand slap with Vidrinath, and all three
missiles went harmlessly wide or high.

Drizzt blazed ahead, closing ground faster than the gnolls expected,
clearly, for one hadn't even drawn its sword, and another hadn't fastened its shield when he arrived.

The Hunter would have had all three dead in short order, but
Drizzt didn't fall into that state. As Kane had indicated that he was
physically out of balance, so too was he mentally conflicted now, with
the Grandmaster's spirit within him. He almost felt as if he were back

at the Academy, trying to fight correctly under the watchful eyes of the drow masters.

He worked his scimitars beautifully, of course, though not with the viciousness so often exhibited by the Hunter. He disarmed the one gnoll that seemed ready for him with a block by Vidrinath, followed by hooking Icingdeath under both blades and pulling it back hard. As the sword fell away, the gnoll shield-rushed, barreling into him—almost.

For Drizzt fell back, knees bending fully to bring him right to the floor so that the gnoll tumbled over him. Both of his scimitars went up under the bottom of the gnoll's shield, and as the demonic creature fell over, those blades slid deep into its belly. The gnoll screeched in pain and tried to bite, but Drizzt snapped his arms upward, lifting it too high, holding it in place by the crosspieces of the scimitars, which were now flush against its skin.

Drizzt felt the influx of ki, his life energy coming forth in a powerful movement that flipped the gnoll over him to the floor, extracted both of his blades as the torn creature flew free, and sent him right back up to his feet.

The other two gnolls rushing to charge in on the seemingly defenseless drow opened their maws—not to bite, but in abject shock.

One just turned and fled. The other didn't even close its mouth until the fourth stab of Drizzt's blades. Its tongue lolled out as its guts spilled to the floor.

Drizzt rushed past it.

His desperation to get to Brie banged against a stubborn demand that he stop.

I cannot let it flee, he imparted to Kane, and he forced his feet to move.

You are unbalanced! he heard in his thoughts. *Your feet are too fast for your hands.*

That surprising claim did bring Drizzt to a halt.

The bracers you wear as anklets, Kane told him.

They speed me.

Then run, Drizzt Do'Urden, Kane agreed.

And he did. And he came to a level tunnel, ending at a downward stairway that led to a near-circular natural cavern below. The flee-ing gnoll was ahead on the stairs, yelping and growling in its strange language, and Drizzt easily deciphered the words, or at least their meaning, for in that room below, several more gnolls danced about a smoldering firepit.

Brie! Drizzt thought, looking at that dying fire. He didn't know why that horrible image came to him, but it did, and was followed by Kane calling upon him to fully let go, to give in to the rage.

The Hunter didn't run down the stairs.

He flew.

The Hunter leaped long and far through the air, a bound expanded by rage and by ki, a blend of the primal and the spiritual, landing with great balance right behind the fleeing gnoll, falling into a deep crouch to absorb the weight of the impact even as he sent Icingdeath slashing across to take the gnoll's legs out from under it.

His sensibilities were almost blinded by rage and fear, but his body was not. In he went, running over the falling gnoll and springing far and high. He landed in a run before the nearest gnolls, diving into a roll between them, then coming up and springing backward and up in a somersault above their thrusting spears. He hadn't even touched down when his scimitars flashed out to either side.

Spears fell as the gnolls grasped their torn throats.

The Hunter couldn't, and so didn't, hesitate, flashing ahead sud-denly into a half dozen gnolls forming a defensive line, too close for them to effectively throw their spears.

Vidrinath swept out wide to the left to turn aside a thrusting weapon, pushing it into a second one, the tangle stealing any angle for the third gnoll on that side to come directly in at him.

Straight ahead, Icingdeath stabbed hard against a gnoll's shield, the tip driving through to sting the creature. It wasn't a deep or mortal hit, but the Hunter felt the sudden vibration in his blade, a release of ki flowing through him, through the weapon, into the gnoll. The mon-ster stiffened and straightened and fell back a step, its eyes suddenly wide and unblinking.

Out went Icingdeath to the side, to deflect a pair of thrusting spears similarly to Vidrinath's parries, and the Hunter followed that sweep, moving to the right quickly.

Now Vidrinath stabbed at the gnoll Icingdeath had struck, and the stunned creature had little defense.

The Hunter stopped as the two to his right bore in, one of those to the left coming in hard as well, another rounding behind it to find its way to the seemingly trapped drow.

Spears came in at him, front, back, and both sides, and cleverly, at different heights.

But none as high as the Hunter, who sprang straight up with amazing agility and strength, lifting, lifting.

But also anticipating, thinking ahead, understanding what was coming next instead of waiting for it to happen and then just being too fast, precise, and vicious for his enemies.

His feet kicked out to either side with tremendous power and accuracy. Vidrinath stabbed ahead, and a reverse grip on Icingdeath sent it stabbing out behind.

When Drizzt landed, turning as he fell to face back the way he had come, only a single gnoll remained upright, and that one wanted no part of him.

It threw its spear, turned, and fled.

Brother Drizzt dropped his blades, caught the spear and turned it about in one fluid motion, and sent it flying off to impale the gnoll at the base of its skull.

The Hunter dropped back down, gathering his blades, then skittering about like a frantic crab, stabbing, slashing, bashing at the fallen gnolls, every strike spraying blood.

Some many attacks later, Drizzt returned to full consciousness, and he screamed in pain, such pain, the image of Brie on that smoldering fire stuck in his mind, driving his fury and his weapons.

She isn't there, came Kane's insidious, telepathic call, over and over again until it finally registered.

Drizzt's swirling thoughts demanded a clarification, but he felt Kane leave him then, abruptly.

He hopped all about, looking to the fire, seeing no signs that a child had been burned there. No bones, no bits of smoldering clothing. He looked to the walls of the circular cave, seeking an exit—there had to be more to the caverns!

But no.

He came all the way around, noting the approach of Savahn and Kane, both running hard to join him.

"She isn't there," Kane called to him.

"She isn't here at all," Savahn added.

"But Brother Tadpole!"

"Is at the monastery in new robes and sandals," Savahn replied.

"But I heard her!"

"You heard me," Kane replied. "I did not wish to do that to you, but I sensed a problem here, an unbalance between the fighter you were and the monk you've become. The two combined should be greater than the whole, but that was not the case, Drizzt Do'Urden, at least not on those occasions when you gave in to this other and darker emotion within you."

"How could you?" Drizzt asked him breathlessly, and he wanted to lash out physically at Kane in that awful moment.

"Because I knew that I was right, and I know that the lives of your wife and your friends might depend upon this correction—a correction I could only make when I better understood the conflict within you."

"What are you talking about?"

"Kimmuriel came to me," Kane explained. "There are indications of trouble in the north. You will be leaving soon. You need to be ready. Now I see that you are almost there."

Drizzt stood there dumbfounded, not knowing how he was supposed to respond at this point as he tried to digest all that had just occurred.

"Almost there," Kane said again, and he pointed at Drizzt's anklets. "They are bracers," he said. "For your wrists."

"I was too unbalanced when I tried that many years ago," Drizzt explained. "The enemy I took them from did use them as bracers, but it didn't work for me. My hands already moved too quickly."

"Because your feet could not adjust to proper balance," Kane explained. "You are wise enough now in the ways of the Order to correct that. And you are simpler faster afoot. The bracers offer you only minor advantage as anklets, but on your wrists, you will find that the balance is far closer now."

"That's it? You took me through all of this to tell me to put the bracers back on my wrists?"

"You know better than that, Drizzt Do'Urden. Brother Drizzt Do'Urden."

Drizzt didn't need that last clue, for he was already looking deep inside, replaying the last battle. He thought of the ki flowing through his weapon to stun a gnoll. He replayed the fight as if from afar, his leap that sent out a devastating attack in all four directions. The Hunter had executed double kicks before, but never like this, arms and legs working independently yet in perfect harmony, in simultaneous attack.

And yes, that was it, Drizzt understood.

Harmony.

A blending of styles, warrior and monk. The two becoming one, the one greater than the sum of the two.

"Brie is unhurt?" he asked.

"She is at the monastery in the care of Brother Tadpole," Savahn replied.

"I could not evoke your true rage without her mimicked cry," Kane told him.

Drizzt winced, still more than a little angry at that deception and the pain it had brought to him.

But he understood now. He looked down at his bloody scimitars, wiped them on the gnoll at his feet, and slid them away, then looked Grandmaster Kane in the eye and nodded, accepting the price of the critical lesson.

CHAPTER 19

A Missing Length of Rope

I thought you were going to get Drizzt," Penelope said when she saw Kimmuriel walking the halls of the Ivy Mansion the next morning.

"I am."

"I thought you were going yesterday."

"There are many side streets," Kimmuriel replied. "King Bruenor wishes to speak with the elf, Freewindle, from Silverymoon. Do I bring him here or bring Bruenor there? Or would it be better to keep Bruenor here and allow those of . . . less intensity to visit the old and addled elf? We are trying to sort it all out. Is the halfling with Azzudonna again?"

"He is, or was, at least," Penelope answered. "I think Wulfgar is with them as well. Wulfgar knows the north better than anyone, although I think Gromph threw our friends beyond the regions we typical think of as the north."

"You are not pleased with the archmage."

"I find it irresponsible to teleport a group of people to an unknown destination. Wouldn't you agree?" Penelope asked him.

"They had ways to come back almost instantly, or to be retrieved."

"And yet, here we are," said Penelope.

"We do not know where we are. Azzudonna says they are lost to us. Somewhere. Somehow. That is all we know."

"Yet you haven't gone to retrieve Drizzt."

"Does it matter?" Kimmuriel said. "What do you expect him to do? Run to the north? The next moves are my own and those of Gromph. If we can find a way to better search for our missing companions, we will act."

"Really?" Her sharp tone stuck his forthcoming words in his throat. "You know something and you're holding back," she accused.

"I cannot get through Azzudonna's mental discipline," Kimmuriel admitted. "Nor can Gromph or any spells any of you will place upon her or in the room about her. Her willpower is impressive."

"But?"

"If I took her to the hive mind, all she knows would be revealed," he said. "Everything she has ever known, every thought she has ever had, would be revealed."

"And you don't want to do that," Penelope reasoned.

"You cannot begin to comprehend the level of intrusion," Kimmuriel told her. "Her deepest secrets, deepest fantasies, darkest acts, would be laid bare, torn from her against her will. It would be perhaps the greatest violation any being could suffer."

Penelope turned her head a bit and studied the psionicist with a side-eyed gaze, a smile curling on her lips as if she was catching on to something in Kimmuriel's tone. "How do you know this?"

Kimmuriel chuckled.

"You?"

"I am Oblodran," he answered. "And we were trained to accept the intrusions of the hive mind as the door to our greatness. Yet these centuries later, the first time my mind was scoured still haunts me. I try to forget about their intrusions, but they are with me often, and usually without warning. A smell, a notion, an action, something I see or hear—anything at all can bring me back to that experience. It tries me and chases me in my nightmares—and again, I submitted to it willingly! For Azzudonna, this act, forced upon her against her will, would utterly break her. Irrecoverably, I am sure."

"Yet you survived it," Penelope said after mouthing the beginnings of several remarks, apparently filtering that one supportive notion out of the plethora of thoughts from the no-doubt surprising revelation Kimmuriel had just offered.

Even Kimmuriel found himself surprised at how open he had been with Penelope.

"It is one thing to be tortured and violated when you believe you are doing it for personal, even noble, purposes," Kimmuriel somberly explained. "It is quite another thing to be tortured and violated for the gain of the torturers."

"So you won't subject her to the hive mind?" Penelope asked, and she didn't hide the fact that she was quite in agreement with such a course.

Except his response wasn't what she expected. "I did not say that," Kimmuriel answered coldly, putting her back on her heels. "Let us play this out as we can, for now. If any Harpells have the magical abilities or insights to either locate the missing four or perhaps to coax better answers from this stubborn woman, then please do."

"The spells for such mental intrusions are not nearly as powerful as your mind magic, but you know that."

"She is stubborn," a frustrated Kimmuriel remarked.

"Trained," Penelope corrected. "And terrified. Regis is taking the correct approach with Azzudonna. He is making of her a friend, and trying to show her that we are not her enemies and can be trusted."

"Ah, yes, the clever halfling," Kimmuriel said with atypical drama in his voice. "Do tell me if he finds anything other than vague references that cannot be confirmed or investigated."

He shook his head and continued on his way, but had barely gone two steps before Penelope called after him and stopped him short.

"Why, Kimmuriel," she said, "are you grieving? You are full of surprises this day. I would never have expected such a state from you, surely."

He only glanced back briefly at her, not wanting to show any more than he already, apparently, had. He started on his way again, now considering her observation.

He couldn't deny it.

The loss of Jarlaxle and the others, which seemed more likely than not, was hitting him harder than any loss he had ever known. He had been more outraged at the fall of House Oblodra those many decades before, but even with that catastrophe, even with the loss of his mother and family, he had not felt like this.

For now, for the first time in his centuries of life, Kimmuriel Oblodra realized a profound sense of sadness, a level of grief that wouldn't even allow him to plot or scheme around it, whether to find some manner of revenge or to better protect himself from any repercussions.

None of that even seemed to matter at this time.

He was just sad. Nakedly so.

"I CANNOT SIMPLY BOUNCE AROUND FROM LOCATION TO location," Gromph told a frustrated Bruenor.

"Ye can't take me to Silverymoon?"

"I'm not *going* to Silverymoon."

"Th' elf's there! Freewindle, or whate'er. We should be talking to him."

"And if I choose to speak with him, I shall," said the archmage. "I do not need your company."

"Ye take me to speak with him, or I'm talkin' with the girl," Bruenor warned. "And I'm tellin' ye that me patience with that one's wearing thinner than a halfling's try at a beard."

Regis walked into the room then, Wulfgar beside him. Bruenor met the gazes of both, and Regis shook his head.

"Azzudonna wasn't in much of a talking mood," Regis explained. "I think she feels like she probably told me too much yesterday in simply admitting that she knew our friends."

Bruenor growled and cursed under his breath, then looked to Wulfgar, who nodded.

"We got to get to Silverymoon, and get Kimmuriel to go and get

Drizzt," Bruenor decided. "We'll go through the gates to Mithral Hall and ride from there."

"And then whatever will you do, dwarf?" Gromph asked.

"And then ye'll send us to the north to get our friends," Bruenor replied. "Our friends, me own and yer own. Or will that be askin' too much of ye?"

"The north?" Gromph echoed. "Where in the north?"

"Same place ye sent the four!"

"Winter," Wulfgar put in, and Bruenor and Gromph turned to him.

"It's winter," he said. "Icewind Dale will kill you quickly in winter without shelter, and it likely gets worse the farther north you go."

"We got this thing called magic . . ." Bruenor answered him, turning to Gromph as he did.

"They've been gone for months," Gromph reminded the dwarf king.

"Ye got a better idea?" Bruenor shouted at him.

"I always have better ideas than you, dwarf."

"Ideas that bring what results, eh?"

Gromph and Bruenor glared at each other, holding the stares for many heartbeats.

The others in the room understood—these were two of the most powerful people in the world.

And now, they seemed so very impotent.

OUTSIDE THE DOOR IN THE HALLWAY, KIMMURIEL LIS-tened carefully, shaking his head. He thought of the hive mind again, but he truly didn't want to go anywhere near that option with this woman. He hadn't lied to Penelope: he had no doubts that taking Az-zudonna there would completely shatter her.

"No," he heard the frustrated Gromph admit. "I have no better idea. No idea of where they might have gone, no idea of what happened to them, and no idea of what we're even supposed to be looking for. I do not even know where I sent them, and I was certain that

Catti-brie would simply recall them in short order with her magic, or that Jarlaxle would call to Kimmuriel through that magical whistle to guide us as we went to retrieve them."

The resignation in Gromph's voice was easy to recognize, and that pressed hard on Kimmuriel.

"Silverymoon first, then," he heard a determined King Bruenor decide. "We'll go and tell Penelope, then be off to Gauntlgrym, and right through there after talking with me queens. We'll dine in Mithral Hall this night, and lunch in Silverymoon tomorrow."

"Me king!" said Thibbledorf Pwent.

"Good enough, then," Regis agreed.

Kimmuriel heard it all and was ready to go into the room and argue.

But then he heard something else.

It started deep in the back of his mind, like a distant bell chiming. But it continued, and it grew, a single, constant note, and not a bell.

A whistle.

Kimmuriel quickly moved away from the door and into a closet at the side of the corridor, closing the door behind him, shutting out all external distractions.

He fell within himself, farther from this place, chasing the beam of the whistle's note as surely as if it were the light of a candle in an otherwise lightless cavern.

He didn't send his mind flying for the source tentatively, though he surely expected to find some other drow waiting for him on the other end—perhaps a mage or a priest from whatever community had been home to Azzudonna and now somehow had possession of that most unique item.

There was some possibility of danger here, he knew for sure, but he had to go. He had to try, for his friends and for Azzudonna.

His heart soared when he approached and recognized the drow blowing the note. He fell deeper into the image and the sound, contrasting reality about it, stepping through the attuned music to a wind-cleared stone under an overhang beneath a swirling green sky in a land deep with snow.

Stepping beside Jarlaxle.

"Ah, good, you heard my call," Jarlaxle said, clapping Kimmuriel on the shoulder. "I'm sorry for calling you so soon, but you have to help me find the others."

Kimmuriel started to respond to the first part of that last sentence, but held back. "Where?" he asked, looking curiously at the strangely disheveled drow. A great chill blew right through Kimmuriel, aching his bones, and he knew he couldn't remain in this place for long.

"I don't know," Jarlaxle admitted. "Under the snow, I think. An avalanche on the mountain buried them. I shouldn't have waited so long to call, but I can't . . ." He stopped and looked around, shaking his head. "I have no idea where they are or where I am. We landed on a snowy mountainside, but which one? Catti-brie and Entreri were caught in the avalanche, but I escaped. Zak, too, I think. But I don't . . . he must have been the one who brought me here."

"When was this? How long ago?"

"From the start."

"What start?" Kimmuriel's teeth were already chattering.

"A day or two ago," Jarlaxle replied. "When we first came through Gromph's gate. I've lost track of the time, because there is no dawn. Why is there no dawn?"

Kimmuriel stared at him blankly, trying to make sense of the reply. "Jarlaxle, you've been gone from us for months."

Jarlaxle started saying something else about the avalanche, but stopped and turned a perplexed look on his friend.

"What do you mean?"

"Exactly what I said."

Jarlaxle shook his head.

"A drow came to us, a woman," Kimmuriel told him. "We think Guenhwyvar brought her to the Ivy Mansion, to Catti-brie's own room. But she's told us little."

"What are you talking about? Catti-brie has Guenhwyvar."

"Perhaps. But Azzudonna is with Penelope and the others, and Penelope believes it was Guenhwyvar who brought her there."

"Azzudonna?"

"You . . . do not . . . know her?" Kimmuriel asked, gasping. He was shaking more violently by the word, his breath coming in painful bursts, his lungs already aching from the cold.

"What games . . ." Jarlaxle started to ask, but he stopped and turned a sly eye on Kimmuriel, studying him through the true-seeing magic of the eyepatch.

"It is me, as you called," Kimmuriel said, catching on, and knowing full well what that eyepatch could show.

"You do not believe me," Kimmuriel stated a moment later, when the obvious doubt didn't leave Jarlaxle's face.

"I don't know what I believe. I've been here a couple of days, no more." Kimmuriel shook his head.

Jarlaxle narrowed his one visible eye, but then shook his head as if in surrender. Kimmuriel knew what the eyepatch was showing him. The was no illusion standing before him, and no deception. Jarlaxle held up his hands helplessly. "It would seem that I don't know very much about anything," the rogue helplessly declared.

JARLAXLE'S RETURN TO THE IVY MANSION WAS MET WITH more confusion than celebration. Before any of the others could even begin to question the rogue, Kimmuriel hustled him away, demanding an audience with Azzudonna.

"He don't go nowhere till he's tellin' me about me girl!" Bruenor roared above the conversation.

Kimmuriel noted the expressions of agreement from the others and could see that Bruenor was growing hotter and hotter. Almost physically, too, it seemed, for the dwarf's face was as red as his hair, and his bottom lip was looking more and more chewed.

Considering the loyalty of this one, ferocious, even vicious, Kimmuriel understood it all very well.

"You come with me, King Bruenor," he offered. "I have a task that you will serve better than all others."

"Aye, and him, and him," Bruenor replied, pointing out Regis and Wulfgar. "And ye get yerself to Drizzt, ye durned elf, as soon as we're through here. We ain't for sittin' and twiddlin' when one o' the five's missing!"

"The five?" Kimmuriel asked.

"The Companions of the Hall," Jarlaxle answered, and he nodded at Bruenor.

The rest of the gathering followed the group down the corridor to Azzudonna's room.

Pay attention to Azzudonna's face more than Jarlaxle's, Bruenor, Regis, and Wulfgar all heard in their thoughts from Kimmuriel.

"You three go in first," Kimmuriel told them. "And move to the side so she gets a clear view when Jarlaxle and I enter the room a moment later."

"What is this all about?" Jarlaxle asked. "Who is she and what is it that she needs a clear view of?"

"You," said Kimmuriel. "You watch her face when she sees you and you'll better understand, I think."

He pulled Jarlaxle to the side of the hallway, out of Azzudonna's line of sight, and sent Bruenor, Regis, and Wulfgar on their way. "Close the door," he told them.

"If you understood how angry I'm growing, you'd be more forthcoming," Jarlaxle warned as those three moved into the room.

"There is something very wrong here," Kimmuriel replied. "And here," he added, tapping Jarlaxle's head. "You've lost months, my friend, and I have a feeling that if we don't get those memories back, the three companions you took with you on your journey to the north are forever lost to us. And perhaps much more is lost as well," he finished, looking to the door.

"Come."

Kimmuriel went in first, offering a quick nod to Bruenor and the others, who were lined up against the wall to his left. "I brought you something I think will be of interest," he told Azzudonna, and he stepped aside, allowing Jarlaxle entry.

For all her discipline, for all her training, Azzudonna could not suppress her initial response, her eyes going saucer-wide with obvious shock.

"By Moradin's beard and Dumathoin's hairy bum, ye durned drow girl! Ye start tellin' me what I need to know or ye're to be a notch on me—"

"Bruenor!" Regis scolded.

"You know me," Jarlaxle said, and was clearly surprised and confused by that observation.

Kimmuriel hushed him and turned to Azzudonna. "Who is this?" he asked.

The woman looked trapped, glancing all about nervously. "Jarlaxle," she said.

"How could I have forgotten meeting one as enchanting as you?" Jarlaxle asked, but no one was paying him any heed.

"You told me they were dead, or undead," Regis said. "He's not either!"

"I thought . . ." Azzudonna stopped and shook her head, looking very confused and more than a little crestfallen.

Kimmuriel was in her mind then, superficially, and he understood that the expression on her face was an honest reflection of that which was in her heart and soul.

"You need to tell us where they are," Regis prompted.

"I cannot. I know not," she replied, then twitched, then turned an angry glare at Kimmuriel.

"You mean that you *will* not," Kimmuriel corrected.

"I'm not sure—how can I be? But yes, I will not!"

"Oh, but ye will," snarled Bruenor, and he stepped forward—or tried to, until Wulfgar put his arm out to bar him.

"Just ask him," Azzudonna said, indicating Jarlaxle. "Why do you . . ." She stopped there and seemed confused for just a moment, as if working through something.

Then she smiled and gave a little chuckle and nod.

"Jarlaxle is alive, so the others might be," Regis said to her. "Would you really not tell us what you know and thus let them die?"

"If only it was that easy," Azzudonna replied.

"Make it easy," growled Bruenor.

"Come," Kimmuriel told his friends. "We are done here for now."

"I'm going to stay a bit," said Regis, but no sooner had he an-nounced that than another voice sounded from the open door.

"No," Penelope ordered. "All of you, out. I'll sit with our guest."

The emphasis she put on that last word was only strengthened by the stern look she gave to Bruenor when she uttered the reminder.

"WHY'RE YE WAITING? WE GOT TO GET UP THERE!" BRUE-nor told Kimmuriel when the psionicist joined him, Wulfgar, Regis, Pwent, Dab'nay, and Gromph in a sitting room a short while later, returning to them, notably, without Jarlaxle.

"I could get you to where I found Jarlaxle right now, if that is your goal," Kimmuriel answered. "There was nothing around, and no guid-ance on where to go from there."

"How hard did ye look?"

"I couldn't stay, and neither could you."

"Because it was cold," Wulfgar reminded him.

"That doesn't begin to describe it," Kimmuriel dryly replied.

The barbarian nodded. "That explains Azzudonna's clothing. Had you worn it when you went for Jarlaxle, you would have been more comfortable."

"There was nothing there, anywhere to be seen," Kimmuriel re-iterated. "Great mountains of rock and stone, all covered by white, all shrouded in darkness. It would take years to properly search that remote land."

"Which is why Jarlaxle was put there when he called out to you," said Gromph.

"What're ye knowing?" Bruenor demanded.

"Whoever it was that took Jarlaxle's memory put him far afield," Gromph replied.

"Leavin' him to die?"

"They likely knew that he had the whistle to contact me," said Kimmuriel, and that brought curious looks from all around. "I would guess that they probably gave it back to him, else he would have used it sooner."

"Who is this 'they'?" asked Wulfgar.

"That's the question, isn't it?"

"And Azzudonna's got the answers," said Bruenor.

"And Jarlaxle's got the answers," Regis quickly added. "Or had them, at least."

"Why ain't ye doin' yer tricks on him, then?" Bruenor demanded of the psionicist.

"Because he's resting. He needs to."

"Bah! Rumblebelly, get yer gem and go pay him a visit, eh?"

"It won't do any good," Kimmuriel assured the dwarf. "That ruby coaxes truth in the same way too many potent drinks might, but Jarlaxle's inability to answer has nothing to do with any reluctance on his part."

The room's door opened then and Penelope came in beside Jarlaxle, who was wearing only one boot and holding the other in his hand, a perplexed look on his face.

"What?" Bruenor asked.

Jarlaxle moved to the middle of the group, sat on the arm of a chair, and lifted his bare foot for all to see the three notations in dried blood: *ILH-DAL-AUT* carved into his sole.

"Ilhdalaut?" Regis asked.

"What in the Nine Hells?"

"Is that a name your captors gave you?" asked Regis. "Or just scars from torture?"

"I think I did it," said Jarlaxle, his voice as unsteady as any of them had ever heard from him.

"It's not an old wound," Wulfgar noted.

"A day to two at most," Penelope agreed.

"But what does it mean?" Regis asked.

"Ilh? *Ilharess*, matron?" Gromph asked. "*Ilharn*, patron? Were you made into someone's patron?"

"No," said Dab'nay, coming forward. She dropped to her knees before Jarlaxle and took his foot in her hands to better view the clearly recent cuts. "*Ilhar*, possibly." She paused, mouthing many iterations, then smiled and nodded and announced, "*Ilhar, delharil, autna.*"

"Could be," Gromph admitted.

"Mother, daughter, granddaughter," Regis translated. "But what could it mean?"

"It is a common saying at the prayers," said Dab'nay. "The continuity of drow matriarchy, the demand of Lolth."

"Jarlaxle's praying to Lolth now?" Bruenor asked with a snort.

"Yvonnel, Quenthel, Yvonnel," said Gromph, staring at Kimmuriel.

"What's that mean?" asked Bruenor.

"What do those three have in common besides the familial bonds noted on the foot?" asked Gromph.

"Memories," Jarlaxle answered, and he, too, looked to Kimmuriel, who had been instrumental in helping Quenthel and the younger Yvonnel sort through the memories they had been given of Yvonnel the Eternal.

Dab'nay moved aside as Kimmuriel took her place, easing Jarlaxle into the chair.

"Give us some privacy," he told the others.

"I ain't going nowhere," said Bruenor. "Not now."

Kimmuriel looked at him but wasn't about to argue, particularly since none of the others seemed to be moving for the exit, either. "Just be silent." He focused on Jarlaxle. "Let me in."

"Please do," Jarlaxle replied, and he raised his magical eyepatch.

Kimmuriel closed his eyes and lifted his hand to place his fingers lightly on Jarlaxle's forehead. In mere heartbeats, Kimmuriel's consciousness was within Jarlaxle's mind, seeing his every thought, searching his memories.

Soon, whether those in the room around the two mentally joined drow were loud or quiet became wholly irrelevant, as Jarlaxle and Kimmuriel were completely turned inward—inward on Jarlaxle's thoughts. To Kimmuriel, the folds and synapses of Jarlaxle's brain became as a collection of various-shaped building blocks that he could fit and refit along multiple paths. He could visually separate all of Jarlaxle's more recent memories, those from the time he had awakened under the overhang where Kimmuriel had found him, from those more distant, such as the avalanche Jarlaxle had referred to on several occasions.

Kimmuriel saw that avalanche clearly. He felt himself sliding along an ice depression down the side of a snow-covered mountain. He heard and felt the thunder of rushing snow closing in from behind. He watched Catti-brie far ahead, going over a ledge, then watched Entreri slide to a similar fate.

He thought of, exactly as Jarlaxle had thought of, the easy escape: enacting levitation as he went up over that ledge.

Kimmuriel felt himself floating. He saw Zaknafein rising beside him, and watched in horror, as Jarlaxle had watched in horror, as the great wave of snow, tons of white powder, broke over that ledge, falling atop Entreri and Catti-brie, burying them where they lay.

The unfolding events went from bright white, blinding white, sun on snow, to the night sky with the aurora, under a ledge—not nearly the same ledge where Catti-brie and Entreri had fallen—waking up on a windblown shelf of rock, surrounded by deep snows in a mountain valley.

Furiously, Kimmuriel backtracked, looking for some image, some flash of recollection, between the two events.

But no. Every time he tried to follow any trail backward from that ledge, he collided into the memory of the avalanche burying his friends.

Kimmuriel broke the connection and fell back from Jarlaxle, blinking repeatedly in confusion. He wasn't sure how long he had been exploring within the maze of Jarlaxle's mind, but he did gather from the location and expressions of the others in the room that he had been "gone" from them for some time.

"Do ye know it now, elf?" Bruenor asked Jarlaxle.

Kimmuriel turned back to stare at Jarlaxle, who sat there blinking, as much at a loss as before. "It didn't work," Jarlaxle said, or asked, or something in between, looking from Bruenor to Kimmuriel repeatedly.

"Do you know?" Jarlaxle asked Kimmuriel a few moments later. "Tell me what happened to me."

Kimmuriel spent a long while replaying the events he had uncovered, trying to make some sense of it all, and more than that, trying to figure out how he might convey both the realities and the limitations of what he had seen. He rose from his chair and looked around at the others in the room, all of them staring at him intensely, desperate for some answers. How to explain it? "Think of memory as a long rope," he told them after a long pause. "That is very simplistic, because everything you see, everything you hear, everything you feel, creates side pathways, side lengths of rope that tie to previous experiences or imaginings. But for this explanation, I ask you to think of memory, even your own memories, as a single line of rope, lengthening with every moment of every day."

"Very well," Dab'nay prompted for all of the anxious and puzzled onlookers.

"Whatever was done to Jarlaxle is unlike anything I have ever encountered," Kimmuriel explained. "It is not like the typical memory tricks, the spells of forgetfulness a priest or wizard or even an illithid might employ. It is more as if someone cut out a piece of Jarlaxle's memory, took a length right out of his rope, then stitched the beginning and end points together, seamlessly, perfectly, aligning his memory to two points of reality separated by months of time."

"Well, we know that," said Bruenor. "That's why yerself's doing this."

"No, you don't *know* that, good dwarf," said Kimmuriel. "You could not have known that, for I have never seen anything remotely akin to this. Jarlaxle and the others landed through Gromph's portal on the side of a mountain blanketed in white, deep in the snow. They were caught quite by surprise by how very cold it was—Catti-brie and Entreri were freezing." He looked to Jarlaxle, who shrugged, then nodded.

"Zak mentioned that it was like sitting in the mouth of a white dragon," Jarlaxle added. "And indeed, it was, until he put on his boots, which, like mine, protected him from the cold. Catti-brie had spells to shield herself and Entreri, and I gave them magical rings to continue the protection when her enchantments expired."

"It was very slow going in the deep snows, and the mountain started to tremble," Kimmuriel put in. "Catti-brie knew it was getting very dangerous, so she used her magic to bring forth a ball of flame, and used that to create an icy slide to get them off the mountain."

"But not in time," Jarlaxle said, sucking in his breath as he finished, as those terrible last moments crystallized in his thoughts. "She slid down, then we followed, but the avalanche chased us. Catti-brie went over the ridge, Entreri too . . ."

"And Jarlaxle escaped, as did Zaknafein, with drow levitation," Kimmuriel added. "The sliding snow went over that same ledge to bury the two humans."

Bruenor cried out, and Kimmuriel stopped.

"Then what?" Wulfgar demanded, jumping up from his seat.

"Then Jarlaxle was in the place where I found him, far from that spot in both distance and time."

"But what happened?" the huge man demanded angrily.

"That is the length of the memory rope that was removed," Kimmuriel said. "From that moment floating in the air beside Zaknafein, their two friends buried in snow below them, to the moment he awakened in the place where I found him."

"Me girl's gone?" Bruenor asked, his voice weaker than anything Kimmuriel had ever heard from the blustery dwarf. He seemed to melt in his chair as he said it, his entire body crestfallen, limp, shrinking, his eyes hollow and empty.

"We don't know that!" Jarlaxle said.

"Yerself's knowin' it, elf!" Pwent shouted. "Think!"

"I'll use my pendant on you," Regis offered.

"Stop!" Kimmuriel told them, and when everyone quieted, he continued. "Jarlaxle can't fight his way through whatever it was that was done to his mind. There's nothing there. The length was removed. The enchanted ruby will do nothing. None of Dab'nay's spells or Gromph's spells will affect this complete of a mind wipe. In his memories, Jarlaxle simply did not exist for the months between the moments we just recounted to you."

"Then me girl's gone," Bruenor said again.

"There has to be a way," Gromph argued. "There is always a way!"

Kimmuriel locked eyes with Penelope then, and understood that the woman was thinking the same terrible thought as he. She wasn't speaking, but her expression was pleading with him:

Take Azzudonna to the hive mind.

PART 3

INESCAPABLE

As I pause and consider the recent revelations about the founding of Menzoberranzan, I am struck by the deeper notion that perception shapes morality as much as does objective truth. On the one hand, this offends that in me which demands reason and fact, but on the other, for all of my complaints, I find this observation undeniable.

I do not know—I cannot know—which version of Menzoberranzan is real, the one taught to me at the Academy, the one of Lolth saving her children some four millennia past, or the one revealed by the memories of Yvonnel, which count the city as only half that age, and claim its founding was based in the highest demands of egalitarian fairness—indeed, even the belief that I hold that when the collective consciousness and conscientiousness guide policy and direction, that world becomes more just and fair.

I cannot know which version was true, and it startles me to realize that there really is no way for me to even verify the age of the oldest buildings and artifacts of the city of my birth, or whether the stalagmites and stalactites were hollowed by the drow who settled there or by a culture previous to them.

I cannot know! And that is the inescapable "truth" of history: that it is, in the end, a story, and one that could well change with new information.

Still, hearing of the events that played out on the field outside of Gauntlgrym, of the magical web that stole the curse from the tormented driders, and more importantly, the source of that web, has brought me great hope, for I know which version I wish to be true, and therefore choose to believe. And thus, which story I will use as I go, because the tale of Yvonnel points to that which I know in my heart to be true.

It was Lolth's doing. It was always foul Lolth.

But what, then, of those who went along with her in the earliest days, her disciples and matrons? I cannot believe that they were only there for the power and riches Lolth offered them, because, were that the case, the Spider Queen's hold would not have endured these many centuries. No, they believed her lies, I am sure. They believed in her way and guidance, and so believed themselves in the right, particularly since believing that they were in the right brought them that which they desired.

None is more dangerous than a villain who thinks she's noble, and none is more convinced or convincing than a converted disciple. No chance to proselytize will be missed, no sermon given in flat tones, no hint of doubt ever revealed.

Menzoberranzan is a small place in the grander scheme of Faerun. The cavern isn't ten miles across in any direction, and there really aren't nearby cities or trusted cultures, or any source where the drow within that cavern can garner the information, the truth, that will guide their day-to-day actions. And so it is easy for a few select minions of the Spider Queen—in this case, the matrons and powerful priestesses—to well control the story taught to every drow.

Some know better, of course. Kimmuriel's family found their truths at the hive of the illithids, and a wizard of Gromph's power can wander the very planes of existence to find answers. But most of Menzoberranzan's drow do not have such resources, and so, typically, that which they believe is that which they are taught.

They just know what they know. I doubt that I am the only one whose conscience demanded a questioning of those accepted truths. Indeed, I know I am not the only one, but I doubt that even those few others I know of—Zaknafein, Kimmuriel, Jarlaxle, Dab'nay—are rare exceptions. But again, I must remind myself, Menzoberranzan is not a large place. Nor was Ched Nasad or the other few drow cities of the Underdark. And in those places, such heretical thoughts are dangerous and bear with them the most dire consequences imaginable. So even though many don't speak out, I am certain that I am not the only drow who felt completely alone and helpless in my heretical notions.

There is a profound difference between the dupers and the duped. Lolth, of course, is the queen of deceit, but her handmaidens are no less culpable. And those drow who went along with—who still go along with—her demands for reasons self-aggrandizing or enriching are no better. These are the dupers, and "evil" is the only word I can use for them.

How many of the rest are the duped, I wonder? How many believe in the cause of Lolth because they have fallen under that spell, likely since birth, and so believe in the nobility of their ways? Is it evil to kill a human, an elf, a dwarf, if you truly believe that such peoples are enemies, mortal and irredeemable enemies, who will kill any and all whom you love if you stay your blade?

Had I killed Artemis Entreri in one of our earliest encounters, had I pursued him until I found the means to finish him, would that have been an evil act? If I believed that he would wantonly murder innocents if I didn't finish the deed, would I have been evil for killing him, or would it be more damaging and, aye, evil if I let him live and so doomed other innocent people to death?

When you are a drow in Menzoberranzan and fall under the spell of Lolth, everyone who is not drow is thought to be that dangerous version of Artemis Entreri that I feared would prove true.

This is the challenge in the coming struggles for the heart and soul of Menzoberranzan, to separate the dupers from the duped, and to convince the duped that the truth is not what they have been taught, and that there is a better way, a gentler way, a more prosperous and moral way.

No easy task, that. In many cases, when a person is convinced of a truth, no amount of evidence will be enough to dissuade them, and I have found, to my horror, that the very act of presenting contrary evidence often pushes that person deeper into their beliefs!

Yes, this is the challenge, and in the coming struggles, we will either convince them or we will kill them, or they will kill us.

I am sure that Lady Lolth will enjoy the spectacle either way.

Until it is over, I say, for the side of truth will win, and then Lolth will no longer be welcome in the hearts of the drow.

That is my vow.

—Drizzt Do'Urden

CHAPTER 20

Off the Maps of History

I t is not Matron Zhindia," First Priestess Taayrul Armgo told her mother and matron, Mez'Barris.

The tall matron of the Second House seemed taller still as she glared down from her dais and throne at Taayrul. "I told Matron Zhindia to come here, explicitly. Do not tell me that she sent that sniveling Kyrnill Kenafin here in her stead."

"No, Matron, it is not a priestess at all," Taayrul explained. She turned back to the chamber door and nodded to the sentry there, who opened it.

In walked a pair of beautiful drow women, tall and strong, wearing little clothing, and striding with a confidence that could not be missed or dismissed by any in the center of power of this great house, including Matron Mez'Barris.

As they neared, Mez'Barris recognized one of them, and her scowl softened. This was no insult by Zhindia sending an inferior to speak for her.

"Eskavidne," Mez'Barris greeted her with respect.

"Ah, you remember me, great Matron Mez'Barris," the handmaiden replied. "And recognize me in this lesser form. I am honored."

"I had hoped to speak with Matron Zhindia," the matron replied. "It would seem that she miscalculated a bit in her desire for aggression."

"In what way?" asked the other handmaiden, Yiccardaria.

"She held House Fey-Branche for but a few hours, and lost House Hunzrin for the effort," said Mez'Barris.

"Yes, she did not anticipate that the Baenres would realize the attack on House Fey-Branche so quickly, but no matter," said Eskavidne. "She brought the Baenres out of their hole, that they would reveal their power."

"And now almost every house in the city is huddled in fear of that power," Mez'Barris said, drawing a surprising chuckle from both handmaidens.

"Only because Matron Zhindia did not come forth fully against them, nor did House Barrison Del'Armgo," Yiccardaria was quick to answer.

"Did you expect me to empty my compound to fight Yvonnel and the Blaspheme on ground of their choosing?"

"Oh no, Matron, that would have been a terrible choice," said Eskavidne. "And better that it played out to this result. Now, if we are clever, we can better judge the commitment of those onlookers about the city. Which houses will openly side with Baenre? Which matrons will protest the attack on House Hunzrin at the meeting of the Ruling Council that you will convene?"

"That I will convene?"

"Yes. Matron Mother Quenthel will be eager to hear your position on these dramatic events—a position that you will couch very ambiguously in that council meeting. Measure the reactions of the others, led by the poles of Matron Mother Quenthel and Matron Zhindia. Measure most carefully the words of Sos'Umptu Baenre."

"And that is only half the information we will now garner," Yiccardaria added. "Thousands of Menzoberranzan's people are not affiliated with major houses, and almost half of those, with no house whatsoever. We are learning now how these events will play among many of them, particularly the hundreds who live in the Braeryn."

"We expect the downtrodden to see hope in House Baenre's blasphemy and continuing heresy," Eskavidne explained. "They are the losers in the ordering of Lady Lolth's Menzoberranzan, after all, and so the most vulnerable to the Matron Mother's self-serving promises of change."

"That will be a problem, then," Mez'Barris replied. "The Baenres already have a great army. Two great armies now that the Blaspheme have run to their side. And from everything I can tell, these former driders are fanatical in their hatred of the Spider Queen."

"They will learn better," Yiccardaria put in, but Mez'Barris just kept talking.

"And Matron Mother Quenthel has a formidable collection of wizards with House Xorlarrin—who now so sacrilegiously call themselves House Do'Urden—in full support. They should be dropped into the Clawrift!"

"It has been done before," purred Eskavidne.

"If the houseless rogues of the Stenchstreets flock to Baenre's cause, our position will prove weak indeed," Mez'Barris finished.

"Most of them are houseless rogues because they are weak-minded," Eskavidne explained. "They will be reminded of that which they seek to overturn. Matron Zhindia is not here now because she is hard at work following our directions to create a major gate to the Abyss. She will bring forth demons to take up the fight in the coming days, both to remind the weaker houses and the houseless drow of their proper loyalties and to keep the pressure on the Baenres."

"In the meanwhile, what we need from you is patience," Yiccardaria added. "We want you to speak with Matron Miz'ri often, to make sure that she is properly handling the Fey-Branche children, while we, with your agreement, will remind Matron Byrtyn of her loyalties. Beyond that, keep your compound at full preparation, but quietly."

Mez'Barris sat back and considered that for a few moments before asking, "When should I demand a council convened?"

"Wait a couple of days," Eskavidne answered. "Let us better measure Menzoberranzan. Let the demons fight for us among the Stenchstreets and let us see how the Baenres respond. If they do nothing, their lie of some community based not on the will of Lolth will be exposed. If they come out to fight, they will be taxed, and perhaps will learn that the fears of some of their eager Blaspheme warriors outweigh their hatred for our beloved goddess."

"Show us to Matron Byrtyn," Yiccardaria commanded. "And Matron Mez'Barris, be wise here. Keep your vicious weapon master close at hand and out of trouble. I can assure you that Matron Byrtyn's daughter, and particularly her granddaughter, are quite prepared to repay Malagdorl for his rough handling of Matron Byrtyn."

To the side of the throne, Malagdorl issued a low and simmering growl.

Both handmaidens laughed at that.

"Perhaps your pride will lead you to victory over Minolin Fey Baenre, Weapon Master," Yiccardaria told the brutish warrior. "But be warned: Yvonnel will do things to you that you cannot begin to comprehend, and they won't be pleasurable."

The warning was aimed at Malagdorl, perhaps, but Mez'Barris heard it keenly. In all of the calculations going through her head as to her proper next moves, as to whether she could indeed put together an alliance formidable enough to finally be rid of House Baenre's hold on the title of First House, the one thing that made Mez'Barris's reveries restless was this strange creature that had been born to Menzoberranzan only a few years before but now stood as an adult drow woman hinting at powers beyond expectation.

To hear the handmaiden so clearly warn Malagdorl not to face Yvonnel served as a stark and grim reminder.

"AND WILL MATRON BYRTYN ATTEND THIS COUNCIL?" Quenthel asked the courier from House Barrison Del'Armgo.

"Yes, Matron Mother. So much has happened. Matron Mez'Barris feels it necessary—"

"And where is Matron Byrtyn?"

"Matron Mother?"

"Where is she? Where is the matron of House Fey-Branche?"

The courier stammered for a few moments, then just shook her head helplessly.

"You go back to Matron Mez'Barris and tell her that, yes, the Ruling Council will convene in two days," Quenthel commanded. "And tell her that if Matron Byrtyn Fey is not there, the council will be aborted. And if Matron Byrtyn Fey is injured, if she has been mistreated, then the council will be no more than a declaration of war, and Matron Mez'Barris will feel the full wrath of House Baenre and our allies."

The courier nodded repeatedly, stupidly.

"Go!" Quenthel shouted in her face, and she nearly fell over herself trying to get out of the audience chamber.

"That was rather forceful," Yvonnel said when the woman was gone.

"Too much so?"

Yvonnel snorted. "Minolin Fey here would have returned only the courier's head as an answer. That would have been too much."

"I agree with your approach, Matron Mother," Myrineyl interjected. "And applaud your great wisdom."

"Quit sniveling," Quenthel said to her, but she ended with a wink to tell her daughter that she appreciated the support.

"Matron Mez'Barris knows war is coming unless she breaks cleanly with House Melarn," Minolin Fey said. "Perhaps this council will afford her that opportunity. Her house was only barely involved in the attack on House Fey-Branche, so she can deflect the blame more fully to Matron Miz'ri, who led the attack."

"She won't do that unless she is certain that she cannot win," Quenthel replied. "Mez'Barris is imposing and sly, but she is also hungry. She knows that this is her last, best chance. If Lolth is with her, she can claim the title of Matron Mother of Menzoberranzan, she believes, and that is something she has coveted since before she became the leader of Barrison Del'Armgo."

"Then where does it go?" Minolin Fey asked.

"We are off any maps that I know of," admitted Yvonnel. "Three house wars in a single night, one house fully conquered, another conquered, then surrendered, but without the safe return of the noble family immediately after. Even when I search the memories of Yvonnel the Eternal, this is an unprecedented level of chaos."

"Lolth must be pleased," Minolin Fey said dryly, but all in that room knew that her words were no joke.

"The city is quiet, the hush of a predator," Quenthel said. "Too quiet. I fear that we should have pressed on from House Fey-Branche."

"To House Mizzrym?" asked Minolin Fey.

"Melarn," Quenthel answered. "Straight to Zhindia and her zealots." She looked at Matron Shakti Hunzrin and Charri, who stood quietly off to the side. "And I assure you all that when we go to visit Zhindia Melarn, we will not be as merciful as we were with House Hunzrin."

Matron Shakti moved as if to speak, but held back and lowered her gaze to the floor.

"You wish to know of your fate," Quenthel said.

"Yes, Matron Mother," the prisoner matron quietly responded.

"You are living it," said Yvonnel. "Take heart, Matron, for this coming war will engulf the entire city with the exception of but one house."

Shakti looked up, and she and Charri glanced from Baenre to Baenre.

"You and your family and all the drow of House Hunzrin are out of the fight," Quenthel explained. "Though you will likely lose many of your goblinkin and quaggoths, as they will fight for House Baenre, or they will be put to the sword. But you are out of it and in no danger. And if our enemies win, no doubt you will find great prosperity for House Hunzrin in the aftermath."

"And if House Baenre wins?"

"When," Minolin Fey corrected.

"Then you and I will have much to talk about," Quenthel said. She motioned to the guards. "Take them to their chambers. There, you will be watched closely, my Hunzrin guests. And I do hope that you understand the limits of our mercy. If you try to escape, if any of you cast a single spell, if any of you pray to Lolth within the walls of House Baenre, you will very much regret it."

When they were gone, the four Baenre priestesses were alone in the audience chamber.

"Do we wait for the Ruling Council to convene?" Minolin Fey asked. "No doubt Matron Zhindia is plotting."

"In a previous day, I would bring in a horde of demons and send them to dance in the streets before Houses Melarn and Mizzrym and Barrison Del'Armgo," said Quenthel.

"I doubt we will ever go down that road again," Yvonnel said.

"Let us pray we do not."

Quenthel then directed the discussion to the coming Ruling Council and the roles that she and Matron Zeerith would play. Of greatest concern to Quenthel was the sabotage that Sos'Umptu might attempt, and for the first time, she truly regretted giving the woman that ninth seat . . . and letting her keep it. After the fight at House Do'Urden, particularly with her belief now that the retreat had been orchestrated long before the actual battle, she understood more clearly which side her sister would come down on. She had hoped to keep Sos'Umptu out of the war, but that was not to be, she now recognized.

"Sos'Umptu claimed neutrality in offering sanctuary to the attackers of House Do'Urden," Quenthel told the others. "But I know my dear sister so very well. Her world is Lolth and Lolth alone. She has no ambition beyond her faith. Such a waste of a life."

"Perhaps we should pay her a visit in the Fane of Quarvelsharess, then, and before the council is convened," Yvonnel offered.

"I was thinking the same."

"But I fear the repercussions of that," Yvonnel admitted. "To attack a matron and her house is one thing, particularly when it is done in retaliation. To attack the Fane could be seen in the streets as nearly as great a blasphemy as the web we wove to steal the driders."

"Perhaps we should visit her simply as concerned family, then," Quenthel said. "To reassure her."

"When this is done and we have won the city and shaken off the Spider Queen, what will Matron Mother Quenthel do to the Fane?" Myrineyl asked.

Quenthel looked at her daughter curiously, surprised by the question and the questioner.

"You will flatten it, or you will convert it," Myrineyl answered her own question. "Perhaps convert it to worship another goddess, perhaps make it simply a place of meditation, as we have done with the Baenre chapel. You cannot allow such a center of devotion to the Spider Queen to survive the war."

"You see?" Quenthel said to Yvonnel. "Now you understand why I let this clever one into our conversations."

"Clever, yes," said Myrineyl. "And so is Sos'Umptu."

Quenthel conceded the point and abandoned her plan to go to Sos'Umptu with a nod, unable to refute it.

"But I don't like this quiet," Quenthel said after a moment of silence. "Zhindia Melarn isn't waiting for the council. She is stung, and badly, and knows that her needed allies are one fewer now. If Matron Mez'Barris loses more faith in Zhindia, her chances to defeat us are ended."

"Unless she can find another army," said Yvonnel. "Lolth gave her retrievers and driders before. Lolth gave her a demon army up on the surface, as well."

"And Zhindia squandered all," said Quenthel.

"Yes, but if Lolth thinks Zhindia is her only means to hold on to Menzoberranzan . . ." Yvonnel said, letting the grim thought hang between them.

Sure enough, later that same day came word that a cauldron of chasme demons was flying about the high stalactites of Menzoberranzan, while other demonic creatures stalked the streets of the Braeryn, terrorizing the houseless rogues.

Strike teams of Blaspheme slipped through the tunnels out of House Baenre soon after, heading for a fight in the Stenchstreets.

"THEY'RE VROCKS," VOSELLY TOLD HER TEAM OF THIRTY, including Dininae and Aleandra. "Seven of them, with at least two score manes and other lesser demons in support."

"There are a half dozen chasmes watching over them from on high," another Blaspheme warrior reported. "I wish we had more wizards."

Voselly shook her head at that. "No, these are brute-force demons resistant to spells and best dealt with by the sword."

"We all know them well," Aleandra reminded the strike team. "How many centuries have we spent beside them, fighting them?"

The other warriors all nodded at that.

Voselly sent ten of her best spear throwers to the rooftops of this ramshackle lane in the Braeryn. She then divided her remaining force in half, separating speed from strength. "You lead your squad," she instructed Dininae. "Your focus will be on the manes and only the manes. Strike only in passing at any vrocks who come against you, for the manes outnumber you by more than four to one. My squad will take down the vrocks while you keep the lesser fiends at bay."

"You want us to keep the manes rushing about, whittling their ranks," Dininae confirmed.

"As the vrocks and chasmes fall, you'll find reinforcements," Voselly replied.

"We'll have the manes ripped apart before you get there," Dininae challenged her, and the two shared wicked smiles.

"I should be with Dininae's group," Aleandra surprised Voselly by requesting, for she had always been close to the other Amvas Tol warrior. "I've always liked killing manes. You know that." She winked at Voselly. "And I've always been much quicker than you."

"And I've always been the stronger," Voselly reminded. "Very well." She swapped Aleandra out with another of Dininae's warriors. "You take the lead, then, of that squad."

"No, no," Aleandra deferred, looking to Dininae. "He leads. I'm happy to follow. Let us see if we have another fine tactician among our ranks here."

The three groups broke immediately, the spear throwers scrambling up to the available roofs, Dininae leading his team around the back of the nearest building and down the narrow alleyway to get nearer the demon force, and Voselly and her warriors holding their ground, ready to leap out and meet the vrocks who fronted the demon force right there in the lane before them.

Screams began to mount down the street as the demon horde neared their position, and several drow came running past the alleyway where Voselly and her group hunkered.

They're more interested in terrorizing than murdering, Voselly's fingers told her fellows. *Matron Zhindia is making a statement here in the hopes of keeping the houseless rogues afraid of joining with House Baenre.*

For the most part, that held true, but these were demons, after all, and more than a few drow were being pulled out of their homes, or the alleyways they called home, and torn apart, and while a large group rushed out of a tavern, fleeing every which way, the screams inside made it clear that not all had gotten out.

Voselly gripped her short spear and sword. The scene unfolding was angering her more than she had expected.

In that moment, the ancient drow from another time came to understand that more than her hatred of Lolth was driving her.

For in her dismissal of the Spider Queen, she was finding something else, something more important, and something that had been buried since before she had been turned into a drider: her own sense of right and wrong.

DININAE'S GROUP CROUCHED SILENTLY IN THE SHADOWS of an alleyway as the vrocks rambled past on the street, the shambling forms of manes, the zombielike least demons, trying to keep up.

Voselly engages first, Dininae's fingers flashed, the order echoed among the squad.

That was not to be the case, however, for before all ten Blaspheme had even nodded in agreement, a woman turned the corner of the alley, running and shouting frantically, a vrock in close pursuit.

Dininae leaped from concealment as soon as the woman passed him, his sword and dagger coming up in a fast cross, forcing the vrock's arms out wide and driving the surprised demon back on its heels, or its hallux, or whatever one might call the back of a demon vrock's bird-like foot.

He hoped to get his blades back in close quickly that he could strike before the vrock recovered, but the demon had another weapon ready. Its head snapped forward, pecking at Dininae's head with its huge and powerful beak.

Dininae had no choice but to fall backward. He kept his feet planted, widespread and even, and bent at his knees, falling straight back, arching slightly at his waist so his backside would absorb the impact. He thought to bounce right back up, but held and blinked as a spear, Aleandra's spear, stabbed above him, hitting the vrock right in the chest.

The demon shrieked and fell back, and at the same moment, Dininae felt a foot hook under his shoulder. With Aleandra's boost, he was upright fast, leaping forward.

At the sound of the fighting, manes turned into the alley, and Dininae's allies rushed past his fight to intercept.

Aleandra's spear was still stuck in the vrock's chest, so Dininae used it to his advantage. His sword snapped out as a distraction, but he followed the strike with a punch, slamming the hilt of his dagger into the butt of the spear.

The vrock shrieked and staggered, and Dininae wasted no time in moving forward, flipping his weapons to the opposite hands and going in just to the right of the vibrating spear shaft. He stabbed his sword upward just before the vrock's shoulder, and when the demon's left arm swept up to block, Dininae rolled under it, but kept his sword arm before it as he turned, locking his arm and blade between that arm and the vrock's neck. That was the least of the demon's problems, though, for as he turned around the demon's back, Dininae flipped his dagger into a reverse grip and came in stabbing, repeatedly, his fine Baenre blade plunging into the vrock's shoulder blades and the back of its neck.

He had the creature fully tied up, using his speed to keep ahead of it as it tried to turn to face him.

It didn't get far, anyway, for Aleandra grabbed her spear and jabbed it, twisted it, then roughly tore it out.

The vrock shrieked, or tried to, for no sooner had it opened its great beak than Aleandra's spear came straight into its mouth with such force that the tip exploded out of the back of the demon's head.

Dininae extracted himself quickly and threw himself into a leaping turn, landing right before a manes and cutting the nuisance apart before he had fully brought his feet flat on the ground.

He glanced once at Aleandra, to offer his thanks and to make sure she was in control, and she answered him by yanking the spear back and to the side with such power that she sent the vrock into a flip against the alley's wall. Down it went to the ground, slumping into death and already smoking as its material form melted back into the Abyss.

Before that happened, though, the vicious Aleandra calmly leaped over, planted her foot on the dying demon's neck, and ripped out her spear.

She went with Dininae side by side out of the alleyway and into the manes, the two cutting down the least demons with abandon and calling out their kill number with every falling monster.

The whole squad became a ball of murder, wading through, tearing the humanoid, zombielike demons apart.

"Down!" Dininae yelled a short while later, before the group had worked their way to join with Voselly's squad.

The skilled Blaspheme warriors heeded that call, dropping low, lifting their eyes high, and noting the diving chasme demon, a monster that looked like a giant fly with a bulbous and bloated humanoid face.

The chasme swept in low, scoring no hits, and began to climb out the back of the alleyway. Barely had it risen above the nearest rooftop when a barbed spear flew out, trailing a chain.

The chasme couldn't slow before that length of chain played out, and the shocking jolt of the secured chain sent it tumbling down to the street.

Where Dininae and Aleandra fell over it and battered it to pieces.

The fight was over in mere moments, the demon force cut apart, and, following the orders given them by Yvonnel, Voselly led her strike team swiftly across the city, all the way to the West Wall and House Do'Urden, where they would serve Matron Zeerith in securing the compound.

CHAPTER 21

Lifeline

I need more demons," Matron Zhindia insisted to the two hand-maidens. Word had come from the Braeryn that many of the summoned monsters had been rather rudely sent home, their material forms destroyed. "Greater demons."

"Demons who can summon other demons?" Eskavidne asked.

"Yes!"

"Many of them are banished, my dear Matron Zhindia," Yiccardaria reminded her. "Remember that hundreds were destroyed and thus banished for a century from the Material Plane in *your* war on the surface, and hundreds more, including Demogorgon himself, in the fighting here in the streets of Menzoberranzan only short years ago. You should understand that few remain who wish to jump into this battle forth and suffer the same fate. Demons prefer to come and go often, and for less ambitious reasons."

"I am fighting for the very power of Lady Lolth here in Menzoberranzan!" the matron snapped.

"A fight that first and foremost involves drow against drow," said Eskavidne.

"Open your gates to the lower planes as you will," Yiccardaria said. "I can tell you that the greatest fiends who will answer your call are of the same power as vrocks, perhaps a few glabrezus."

"Yes, sister, glabrezus always enjoys a fight," Eskavidne agreed.

"But there aren't many of them who can come forth at this time, their numbers so greatly depleted by the two events I have already referenced. Enough to inflict some pain, nothing more. But dear Matron Zhindia, your task is not merely to inflict pain. Demons may wound your enemies, but they will not convince your skeptics."

"My skeptics?" Zhindia replied with a rude and insulting snort. "Lolth's skeptics, you mean, and that number has no doubt climbed precipitously since the counterattack by House Baenre. Fey-Branche was lost to us before most in the city even knew we had taken it, and House Hunzrin was among my most important allies."

"They were two hundred out of twenty thousand drow," Yiccardaria scolded. "And Shakti Hunzrin did not sit on the Ruling Council."

"Their tendrils outside the city—" Matron Zhindia began.

"This fight is *inside* the city," Eskavidne joined in, her tone equally critical. "You do not seem to properly understand that. Lady Lolth will not grant you retrievers or a drider or another full army of demons in this struggle. This is not a war of brute force but one of ideas. A war between the weakness of whatever false truth House Baenre now embraces against the glory and power of the Spider Queen and all that she has done to bring Menzoberranzan to such heights of power and security over the centuries. Who dares come against the City of Spiders, Matron Zhindia? And who within dares challenge Lolth's supreme rule? What happened to House Oblodra when they tried to take advantage in the Time of Troubles? What happened to the assassins of the Jaezred Chaulssin when they overstepped in the Silence of Lolth? That was a test, and the drow passed it, and so have thrived again."

"Matron Mother Quenthel's reign was saved by Lolth only a few years ago, and by those same gifted memories of Yvonnel the Eternal the ungrateful Quenthel Baenre now twists to deny the goddess," Yic-cardaria added. "The memories told her that demons were the way to solidify her hold on power after the first disaster in Gauntlgrym, when Bruenor's dwarves chased Matron Zeerith Xorlarrin out. Lolth granted Matron Mother Quenthel those demons. Yet look how she repays the glorious Spider Queen!"

"The whole of the city participated in the fall of Demogorgon," Zhindia dared to remind the two handmaidens.

"Indeed, and that, too, shined the brightest light of Lolth upon Matron Mother Quenthel and Yvonnel, who facilitated Demogorgon's destruction," Eskavidne countered. "Enough of this banter, for the point is all moot now. We are in this place and from this place we must emerge. You are the chosen leader, Matron Zhindia, so find your way. You were given great gifts, retrievers and driders, and you failed. Do not fail again."

"Your choice is me or Matron Mother Quenthel," Zhindia shot back, but there was an unmistakable quaver in her voice. "And she will not have you! She will not have Lolth!"

"Then win," Eskavidne finished. "Win their hearts to Lolth, win this fight against Baenre, and win your rightful place on the Ruling Council."

The two handmaidens turned to each other and giggled—strangely, Zhindia thought—then turned on their heels and walked out of the audience chamber.

Zhindia slumped back on her throne, chin in hand, nervously rubbing, talking to herself, trying not to think of the potential consequences of failure, trying to find an elusive answer.

What could she do?

DININAE SWAYED BACK AND FORTH, DOWN LOW IN A DEEP crouch, sword in his left hand and out before him, dagger back behind his hip.

Voselly started toward him, then stopped, but he didn't flinch, didn't change his posture at all.

She did it again, then a third time, and on the fourth start, she leaped.

But Dininae was ready, moving forward and to his right as she came on. His dagger jabbed ahead, forcing a parry from her sword and an attempted dodge back to her right—but not quick enough to avoid the thrust of Dininae's sword, the practice blade cracking hard into her ribs.

Her reply came in the form of a downward stab of her short spear, and she connected slightly on the smaller drow's head as he threw himself backward and to the floor, rolling over and coming back to his feet.

"I still would have had you!" the woman said, declaring herself the winner.

"And you would have a hole in your chest, perhaps to your heart," Dininae replied. He blinked his left eye slowly and stretched his neck, trying to fully recover his senses. She hadn't hit him hard—by her standards, at least. But this one was so very strong. "If you tire of House Baenre, I expect that Matron Mez'Barris would welcome you as a weapon master," he chided.

"So, I would be wounded, but you would be dead," Voselly growled at him.

"Is that how you wish to wander the battlefields?"

To the side of the Do'Urden training arena, Aleandra laughed.

"How did you know I was coming forward on the fourth feint?" Voselly asked.

"The bend of your left knee," Dininae answered.

Voselly looked to Aleandra, who merely shrugged.

"Come, let us go again," Voselly said.

Dininae shook his head. "Enough. If enemies come against House Do'Urden this day, we'll all be too weary to properly defend the place."

Voselly huffed and dropped the practice weapons to the arena floor. She moved to the side of the room, where Aleandra tossed her a towel, and after a quick rub-down, she shed her practice padding and dressed in her more normal attire: a blousy red shirt, knee-length skirt, and brown rothé-leather boots. Dininae and Aleandra also cleaned up and dressed, and the three left the Do'Urden training arena soon after, navigating the halls toward their assigned barracks. At one intersection, though, Dininae turned left as the other two crossed straight ahead.

"Where are you going?" Voselly asked.

"I'm hungry," Dininae replied. "You wore me out and my stomach is growling."

Voselly and Aleandra glanced at each other and followed.

They wound their way through the House Do'Urden substructure, Voselly and Dininae chatting easily, Dininae leading the way, and soon enough smelled the delicious aroma of rothé ribs smoking.

They entered the compound's lower common room soon after, to find other Blaspheme in there. One wall was lined with trays piled with various foods and racks of bottles of water and wine.

The three of them had been in this room only once before, when the wizard Ravel had shown the strike teams their accommodations for their stay. On that occasion, they had entered from a door on the other side of the large common room, one going to a corridor and a flight of stairs back up to the cavern ground level of the compound.

It occurred to Aleandra then that Dininae had found his way here far too easily. She would have had to go back up to that first level, navigate her way across, then come down those stairs beyond the opposite door. Dininae had been with her and Voselly the entire few hours since they had come into House Do'Urden. They hadn't walked these tunnels between the arena and the lower common room at all in that time, or in their short stay here before the ambush a few days prior.

Dininae knew his way around too well.

The trio spent a long time in the common room, engaging in conversations as more and more of the Blaspheme strike teams found their way into House Do'Urden after battling demons in the Stench-streets.

They cheered their victories and toasted their fallen. Of the three hundred former driders Quenthel had sent forth to repel the demons and then continue along to bolster House Do'Urden, nearly a dozen would never arrive, and more than three score more had to be carried into the Do'Urden compound to be tended by the priests.

By all measures, though, the campaign had been a success, with hundreds of demons destroyed, and the mood of the gathering was one of victory and pride. The Do'Urdens were treating it that way, clearly, sending down food and drink and nothing but good wishes for their new allies. At one point, Matron Zeerith herself came into the common room to give her personal thanks for the great warriors.

In the spirit of victory, Aleandra wasn't surprised when Voselly and Dininae decided to take their leave, together, for a more private celebration.

"If your play is as good as your sparring, I expect Dininae to have a few tricks for you," Aleandra teased as they rose to depart. "And I know that Voselly will overwhelm you, Dininae. She'll learn from you, and adapt, and you'll wind up on your back."

He shrugged and smiled and didn't seem very upset by the forecast.

When they were gone, Aleandra considered finding a playmate of her own, but dismissed the notion just as quickly. Her mind was in other places, her thoughts spinning along a path of curiosity regarding Dininae's familiarity with this place, and along a parallel course of trepidation. Where had the soul of the fallen Blaspheme gone this day, she wondered?

To Lolth? To be returned to abomination and punished doubly for their attempted escape from her eternal torment?

She wasn't the only one having such thoughts, she realized as the flame of the party began to lower, many leaving, others passing out where they sat. Aleandra made her way around those still upright and talking, listening particularly to those conversations pertinent to her fears.

Rumors were already circulating of Blaspheme being captured and returned to their eight-legged former selves. Others expressed concern—Aleandra had heard this since the fields on the surface— that the magic which had ended the torment and returned them to drow form was a test for them and nothing more, a final trial to see if they could be redeemed in the eyes of the Spider Queen.

"They never went to the Braeryn," she heard one man say of a pair of members now reported as missing from one of the strike teams. "They came straight across to the West Wall, but not to House Do'Urden."

"Where, then?" another asked, leaning forward and clearly engaged.

The first looked around at the small group, making sure that all were attentive, before answering, "The Fane of Quarvelsharess."

That brought gasps, and Aleandra did well to suppress her own.

"They offered themselves back to Lolth," the speaker continued.

"They are driders once more?" another woman asked, horrified.

"No! Don't you see? They passed Lolth's test. They are forgiven. They'll not be returned to the Curse of Abomination, here or in the afterlife at Lolth's side."

Some arguing ensued, and Aleandra wandered away from the group. Her own thoughts conflicted with these troubling possibilities, and nothing being said in the budding debate was going to help her sort them.

She continued across the room, thinking to leave and find a quiet spot where she might rest, but she was met at the door—indeed, crashed into—by a woman coming in.

"Priestess Saribel," she said. "My apologies. I did not see you."

"No need to apologize," the young priestess replied. "But surely you got the best of the collision. You are quite formidable . . ." She ended the sentence with a rise of tone, prompting an introduction.

"I am from the earliest days," Aleandra told her. "Aleandra Amvas Tol."

"Ah yes, I saw you with Mal'a'voselle. I have heard that more women were warriors back then."

Aleandra nodded. "Priestesses were rare, as were wizards. Menzoberranzan's earliest defenses were mostly built upon the sword."

"Someday I would like to sit with you and learn all about it," Saribel said. "Of the houses and the city's structure. All of it."

"You are Xorlarrin?" Aleandra asked.

"Do'Urden now, but yes, I was . . . am."

"I did not know your house. I was gone before it was founded. Of all the houses I have heard of in Menzoberranzan, the only two whose names I recognize are Baenre and Fey-Branche."

"Houses come and go, so it seems," the priestess said somberly.

"What of this house? Are there any Do'Urdens among the ranks of the Xorlarrins who claimed the name?"

"No, it was fully eradicated years ago," said Saribel. "Well, except for the two heretics, Drizzt and Zaknafein, who live on the surface. Now it is mostly former Xorlarrins, although we have brought others formally into the new family Do'Urden, as our own ranks were thinned in a battle not long ago. Perhaps you will become a Do'Urden when the fighting settles about the city. Matron Mother Quenthel owes a great debt to Matron Zeerith, and a contingent of great warriors of yesteryear would be a fine show of gratitude."

"But no Do'Urdens are still alive in here? In the city?"

"No." Saribel cocked an eyebrow and tilted her head suspiciously. "Why do you ask?"

"I find it fascinating," came Aleandra's quick response. "Considering such things among the living drow and recent history of the city allows my mind reprieve from the memories of abomination, and from the fears of coming fights and consequences of losing."

Saribel nodded and put on a sympathetic and understanding expression. She even reached up and patted Aleandra on the shoulder.

"I would like to learn so much more about this new Menzoberranzan," Aleandra said. "This house. Can you tell me their story?"

"Parts, but not much," Saribel answered. "Other than the heretic . . . although with the return of Zaknafein to the ranks of the living, I expect that it would be more accurate to speak of the heretics. Other than Drizzt, and now Zaknafein, I know of no Do'Urdens. They were obliterated before my birth. Well, there are stories of Matron Malice and her insatiable lust, but that is more entertainment than information."

Aleandra nodded and smiled.

"Perhaps someday when these troubles are past, I can arrange for you to speak with Matron Zeerith," Saribel offered. "Or better, with Yvonnel."

"Yvonnel Baenre?"

"Yes, she holds the memories of every era of Menzoberranzan and would know all about the rise and fall of House Do'Urden. Her namesake, from whom she garnered those memories, dealt directly with Matron Malice on more than one occasion, I have heard. And this young Yvonnel has spent many days beside Drizzt, both here in the fight with Demogorgon and up on the surface after that great victory."

"Why would she speak with one as lowly as me?" Aleandra sincerely asked.

"She is not a matron. And she certainly doesn't carry herself like one. Not at all. I think she would enjoy hearing your tales as well. When the troubles have passed and we are victorious, when the city settles into whatever new reality the Baenres plan for us, I will speak with her on your behalf, Aleandra of House Amvas Tol."

"My gratitude, priestess," the warrior woman said, bowing. "You are too generous."

Saribel smiled and stepped by her into the room, and Aleandra started out, but stopped when Saribel called to her.

"There is a small library in one of the anterooms of the house chapel," she said, as if she had just recalled the thought. "There remain many volumes from the days of House Do'Urden before its rebirth. There might even be one that was penned by Matron Malice herself."

"Am I allowed . . ."

"Of course," said Saribel. "Come, I will show you there."

"But your business here?"

"Just hunger," said Saribel. "I will guide you quickly enough and come back for my feast."

ALEANDRA WENT TO THE DO'URDEN CHAPEL ONLY THAT one time, for she found her answers quite easily in a book of notes written by a priestess, a daughter of the noble family.

Information was power, she knew, and more than that, in this instance, it might mean survival.

She rejoined her companions and strike team the next morning and went about her days, training, eating, and learning. She listened to every rumor, and listened far more than she talked. She didn't press Dininae at all on his apparent knowledge of the place, because she didn't need to. Not anymore.

They were sent out from House Do'Urden several times over the next few days, now three strike teams at a time, to finish the cleansing of Matron Zhindia's summoned demons, whose numbers fast dwindled.

There had been a meeting of the Ruling Council, which Matron Zeerith had attended. But it had come to no resolution, and indeed had been adjourned quite early and, from the whispers coming back through Saribel, had nearly come to blows between Matron Mother Quenthel and Sos'Umptu Baenre.

Now, a tenday later, the city was quiet, too quiet. There were some skirmishes being reported in seemingly random locations, from the Qu'ellarz'orl to the banks of Lake Donigarten, from the Stenchstreets to Lolth's Web, wherein lay House Melarn. Mostly, the battling came from proxy fights, various slave groups taking the brunt of the damage, but there had been at least two more confirmed skirmishes between small drow groups.

"They don't like it," Voselly told the gathering of the Blaspheme in House Do'Urden after returning from an audience with Matron Zeerith and the Do'Urden nobles. "Their patience runs thin. They fear that Matron Zhindia is plotting, perhaps secretly summoning demons and hoarding them away somewhere until she has sufficient numbers to use that diabolical force to lead an assault on the Baenre compound—or more likely, an attack on us here in House Do'Urden. We need to be alert and to uncover the shadows of Melarn."

"We're going back out," one of the team remarked.

"Smaller groups and shorter patrols, but yes," Voselly confirmed. "Our allies occupying House Hunzrin will patrol the Eastmyr, the Braeryn, and all the way to Donigarten. House Baenre watches the Qu'ellarz'orl, of course. Bolstered House Fey-Branche patrols the central reaches of the city, and we are tasked with the North Rim and the West Wall, all the way from Tier Breche to Lolth's Web, and even into the Westways beyond the city proper."

"We patrol about House Melarn, then," Dininae quietly mentioned to Aleandra, who nodded and replied, "And the Fane."

"Each strike team will rotate three shifts, three groups into their assigned areas," Voselly ordered. "Our hosts will provide a guide who knows well each route. If you find enemies, fight or flee back to House Do'Urden. On your decision, not your guide's, while out in the field. We are out there more to keep a watch and to learn what we may, but if there is an opportunity to sting the enemy, or to take some captives perhaps, do what the Blaspheme does best."

"Victory!" someone yelled, and the near three hundred warriors took up the cry.

They began their patrols soon after, Voselly taking the lead of the first group from her strike team, assigned to the areas around the Fane of Quarvelsharess. When they returned from their uneventful patrol, Aleandra led the second patrol into that same area, which was considered the most important by Matron Zeerith.

It made sense. If Matron Zhindia was hoarding demons or opening greater gates to the lower planes, then what better place than the great chapel that translated precisely to "the shrine of the goddess"?

Aleandra handed off the scouting duty to the third group, led by Dininae, upon her return. And so it went.

Another tenday passed. There had been a skirmish near Lolth's Web with some Melarni drow, to no real conclusion. A greater fight had broken out near Tier Breche when a large group of kobold and goblin slaves had surrounded a Blaspheme patrol. Things had looked troubling for the ten drow until Tsabrak Xorlarrin Do'Urden and some masters had come out from Sorcere and filled the alleyways and cubbies all about the drow patrol with noxious gases, obliterating the creatures, killing most and sending the rest running. Neither fight had seemed a premeditated ambush, though, more likely an unwitting intersection of opposing forces.

"Do not get lulled into complacency!" Voselly warned the Blaspheme forces every morning, but that warning was easier to hear than to follow as the days dragged on.

Aleandra led her team around to the north of the fingernails of the chasm called the Westrift one night. They moved quickly and carefully past the long and narrow compound of House Duskryn, the city's Ninth House and one that had shown no indication of alliance to either of the warring factions. Still, caution was necessary, they had been instructed. House Duskryn should have been elevated to the eighth position, and all preparations had been made to that effect, but the return of House Xorlarrin, given new life as House Do'Urden, had pushed Matron Berni'th Duskryn out of her coveted seat before she had ever taken it.

Thus, while Duskryn hadn't formed any alliance that any knew of, they were a formidable house with a sizable army, and it was reasonable to think they might hold some particularly bad feelings toward House Do'Urden—and thus House Baenre—at that time.

The patrol moved away from Duskryn to the north. Soon, the decorated entry awnings to the tunnels of the Fane of Quarvelsharess were in sight. All was quiet. They lingered for only a short while, noting no movement along the many balconies of Sos'Umptu's shrine, then reversed and marched back for the fingers.

Aleandra first recognized trouble when she spotted the point drow of the march dropping fast to his knees and ducking back around a corner. She flipped her hands out to either side, telling her eight associates to spread out for cover, and not a moment too soon.

For barely twenty strides before her, the point drow lifted his hands to signal, and instead began jerking erratically.

Hand-crossbow quarrels!

Down! Down! Form up in threes! Aleandra's fingers began flashing to her squad, and she herself ducked quickly, only barely avoiding a quarrel that would have struck her right in the face. She crawled behind some stacked barrels and tried to pick out her point drow.

But he was down, probably fast asleep from the poison.

"Where are you?" she whispered at her unseen enemies, and when she saw them, she wished she hadn't asked.

A score of drow came charging around the building where her point man had fallen, including a wizard who lit up the area with a lightning bolt, shattering a fence not far from Aleandra and launching two of her squad from their hiding spot.

Aleandra leaped up and called for a full formation, and only then realized that the rooftops, too, were thick with enemies. Quarrels clicked off the cobblestones and cavern floor about her. One struck her in the chest, but her armor repelled it. Another stuck into her arm. She felt the poison immediately and ripped the dart out, and could only hope she could resist its lullaby allure.

The Duskryns, she believed—and her fear was confirmed when a second lightning bolt came forth, this one from the south, from the wall of the House Duskryn compound. It hit a Blaspheme warrior squarely, sending her writhing and jolting uncontrollably to the ground.

They couldn't win.

"Run!" Aleandra shouted. "To the shadows!"

She took her own advice and retreated back toward the Fane, initially thinking to turn north and run along the north wall in the hopes of linking with the patrols up there. It was a desperate hope, she knew, for her enemies were likely already moving straight north to cut off that route.

Aleandra changed her mind when she saw another of her squad run out behind her, straight for the Fane.

"Sanctuary?" Aleandra whispered to herself, trying to sort out the possibilities here.

She had no choice.

Into the tunnel she went, scrambling past side rooms where priestesses prayed and called out in alarm.

One door was as good as another, so she believed—until she crashed through one to find herself stumbling into the main chapel of the Fane of Quarvelsharess, to be greeted by a host of priestesses and guards and scrambling jade spiders.

She skidded to a stop, dropped sword and short spear, and held up her hands. "Sanctuary!" Aleandra declared.

The room went very quiet.

A slight laugh drew Aleandra's eyes to a decorated drow.

Sos'Umptu Baenre.

CHAPTER 22

Broken

A jade spider, a huge and deadly construct, stood beside Sos'Umptu, seeming anxious for the kill as it crouched and rose, crouched and rose on its eight legs. It loomed over another of the Blaspheme, who was lying prone on his back, arms up to defend—which seemed rather pathetic, since the jade spider's mandibles could so easily snap right through those skinny drow limbs.

"Sanctuary?" Aleandra repeated, this time plaintively.

"You expect to come into this place of Lolth and be granted mercy and sanctuary?" Sos'Umptu Baenre asked as if the whole notion were preposterous.

"You granted sanctuary to those who attacked House Do'Urden," Aleandra said.

Sos'Umptu laughed. "I did no such thing. It is not in my power to offer such a judgment."

"Sanctuary is the absence of judgment. Is that not the whole purpose?"

The powerful Baenre laughed again, mocking Aleandra.

"You say you offered no sanctuary to the attackers, yet they came in here and the pursuing forces were not allowed through your gates."

"'The absence of judgment,'" Sos'Umptu echoed, obviously feigning deep consideration as she looked around at her fellow Fane priestesses. "Would that not be neutrality? Do you really believe that this place is neutral in the battles going on in the cavern beyond? When Lady Lolth herself is under siege?"

Aleandra swallowed hard and regretted dropping her weapons. She wondered if she might grab them up and at least kill one of these priestesses before they took her down.

"We are *central* to that struggle," Sos'Umptu stated. "I did not grant sanctuary to those attacking House Do'Urden, for that is the judgment of Lolth herself. No, we here at the Fane offered them shelter from those who attacked them. And we would have fought beside them against the forces of those who deny Lady Lolth if they hadn't fled back to House Do'Urden.

"The idea of the Blaspheme coming in here asking for sanctuary? It's preposterous. You should be groveling for forgiveness, though I doubt you'll find any. You should be on your knees begging for a quick and merciful death, but even that would not really be merciful, of course, since you would then be relegated back to the Abyss, where you would answer to Lolth. The Spider Queen is generous to those who properly serve and worship her, but not so much to those who defy her."

To the side, the jade spider was urged away from the fallen Blaspheme warrior, who was quickly collected and held fast by a pair of priestesses. Aleandra didn't know what to think here or what she could possibly do. She reflexively glanced down at her dropped weapons again.

"Do it," Sos'Umptu teased. "It will ensure that my prayer to Lolth will be answered. For you see, I have prayed to be granted the power to cast abomination on those who escaped their eternal sentence."

Aleandra froze at that. Over to the side, her fellow Blaspheme warrior whimpered at the mere mention of such power. To become a drider again was the worst torture she could imagine. Every day, every movement, was pain. No thought independent of the eternal shackles—a mere notion of turning against any drow loyal to Lolth would send wracking agony through a drider. There was no free will, no beauty, no hope, no cessation of the mental anguish and torment. It was a curse that did not lessen with time, a curse against which neither the mind nor the body could numb itself.

She just couldn't do it.

A hard shove to her back sent her stumbling forward, and with sickening dread she realized she might not have that choice. She caught herself after a few steps and managed to glance back, to see a spectral hand floating in the air where she had been standing. A pair of priestesses ran up to flank it and retrieved her weapons from the floor.

She turned back to find Sos'Umptu glaring at her.

"Why aren't you kneeling?"

Aleandra fell to her knees. "Please, mercy."

"I already told you you'd find no such thing here. Fetch Matron Zhindia," Sos'Umptu ordered a priestess. "She will enact the Curse of Abomination on him." She indicated the other Blaspheme. "This woman, I save for my own spell."

Aleandra's body failed her at that moment. She felt herself sinking into the floor and only caught her tumble with her outstretched arms at the last moment, then vomited on the floor between her own hands.

She heard Sos'Umptu Baenre laughing at her.

She couldn't do this.

She had to find a way out.

Her head snapped up, her eyes meeting those of the powerful priestess.

She lifted her hand, her thoughts spinning, seeking a way, any way, to avoid her fate. Her fingers flashed her desperate play before she even considered the words.

I have information!

SHE STUMBLED ALONG, HOODED, CHAINED, AND BATTERED, her body feeling as if it were on fire from the venomous bites of the living serpents on Sos'Umptu's five-headed scourge. She wanted to fall down, but had learned from bitter experience on this march that doing so would only get her back ripped open more by the snakes.

Hands grabbed her by the shoulders and forced her to stop. A sash was tied tightly about her waist, and Aleandra found herself rising suddenly from the floor, being hoisted high into the air. She had suspected, and now she knew: she was being taken to House Melarn, which was up in the high cavern ceiling in the tangle called Lolth's Web, built within the stalactites and connected with platforms of thick webbing reminiscent of the fallen drow city of Ched Nasad.

Aleandra was grabbed roughly and pulled to one of the platforms. Finally, her hood was yanked off and she was pushed along toward a door on the side of a large hanging spear of stone. It opened as she approached, and as soon as she crossed the threshold, her feet were kicked out from under her. With her hands tightly bound behind her back, she landed hard, but barely was she down when strong hands grabbed her by the hair and dragged her along, with other drow beside her, prodding her with the sharp tips of javelins.

They pulled her right up a staircase, then along a dark tunnel— she believed she was above the cavern ceiling then, but she couldn't be certain.

The next door brought them into a chapel, the House Melarn chapel. Aleandra had seen Matron Zhindia before, up on the surface when she had been part of Zhindia's army, when she had been a drider, and yes, this was Matron Zhindia standing before her now as her handlers yanked her into a kneeling position.

"This is the one?" Zhindia asked.

"Aleandra of a very ancient house whose name has long been erased," answered Sos'Umptu from behind the kneeling prisoner.

Aleandra didn't dare glance back at her tormentor. She kept her head bowed, staring at the floor, considering her move here. She felt terrible, emotionally even more than physically. How could she do this?

But how could she not?

They were going to make her a drider again! They were going to make her betray those who had broken the curse in any event.

And she knew, to her profound horror, that death would not alleviate the punishment. She would be right back in the Abyss, serving demons.

"Look at me," Matron Zhindia ordered.

Aleandra lifted her gaze.

"Who do you serve?"

"Lady Lolth," Aleandra said.

She felt the fangs of one of Sos'Umptu's snakes sink into her neck, felt the agony as the serpent held its bite and let its venom drip into her.

"Who?" Sos'Umptu asked from behind.

"Lady Lolth," Aleandra said through her grimace.

"Who did you serve?" Matron Zhindia asked when the serpent was done. "And don't you dare mention the goddess."

"I . . . we all, did not know what we were supposed to do," the poor woman blurted. "We thought ourselves redeemed and so believed that our redeemers were acting with the blessing of—"

"Don't you dare," Zhindia warned.

Aleandra abandoned that course.

"We did not know what—"

"I asked not about *we*, I asked about *you*!" Zhindia screamed, coming forward and lifting her own scourge.

"Look up at me!" the matron roared when Aleandra reflexively dropped her gaze.

"I did not know what to do, so I followed the commands of the person I believed to be the Matron Mother of Menzoberranzan," Aleandra blurted.

"Now, was that so difficult?" Zhindia teased. "Who do you serve now?"

Aleandra started to answer, but bit it back in the face of the restriction Zhindia had put upon her.

"You are not worthy to speak her name," Zhindia said. "But I am told that you wish to begin your journey back to worthiness."

"I do, Matron."

"What do you know? Why has Mistress Sos'Umptu brought you

here instead of putting the Curse of Abomination on you back in the Fane?"

Aleandra paused at that moment of truth. She wanted to leap up and charge at Zhindia, force the beatings, revel in the beatings, and the venom and all the pain these vile creatures could exact upon her.

But not the return of her drider existence. All the rest she could accept, but not that.

Not that.

"There was one who marched beside me these tendays," she said. "He was prized by my cousin of House Amvas Tol for his fighting skill and techniques that were not available to us when Menzoberranzan was young. He claimed to be a houseless rogue before he was given to the Curse of Abomination, but that was not true. His training was too detailed. I knew that he had gone to the Academy, at least, but also that he had been tutored by a weapon master."

"Why do I care?" Zhindia prompted, her patience obviously short, though not as much so as that of the hungry serpents that writhed upon her scourge.

"I discovered his true identity," Aleandra said. "When all of us were sent to serve as soldiers in the house of Matron Zeerith, my companion was back in his home."

That brought a confused look for only a moment before Matron Zhindia's eyes went wide.

"He calls himself Dininae, but that was not his name before the curse," Aleandra said. "He was Dinin Do'Urden, the elderboy of House Do'Urden, the older brother of the heretic Drizzt."

Zhindia stood there, jaw slack, for a long while before finally demanding, "How do you know this?"

"He knew the house, all the ways and tunnels. There were other clues, and when I got into the chapel of House Do'Urden, I found the writings of his sister, priestess Vierna. It was she who cursed him into a drider."

"Is this true?" Zhindia asked, looking past Aleandra to Sos'Umptu.

"Dinin Do'Urden was cursed to abomination by Vierna, yes," Sos'Umptu confirmed. "I remember it quite well. If I recall correctly, he was later killed in a fight with Drizzt's friend King Bruenor."

"And thus sent to Lolth," Zhindia said. "And stolen from Lolth by the traitors."

"It would be quite a statement, don't you think?" Sos'Umptu asked.

"To let the whole city see the power of Lolth take back that which was stolen from her?" Zhindia replied. "Yes, it would indeed remind Matron Mez'Barris and all the others of the true power of Menzoberranzan, and of that which they risk."

THE EXCITEMENT OF THE DISASTROUS ENCOUNTER, WITH two Blaspheme dead, five others missing and presumed to be in the clutches of Sos'Umptu, only gradually quieted as the days rolled past in House Do'Urden. Even as the leaders at last plotted their retribution upon House Duskryn, there came from Matron Berni'th an apology and a return of two of the missing Blaspheme.

"We did not know," the wizard Havel Duskryn explained to Matron Zeerith after delivering the captives. "We thought we were being surveilled, and had information that House Baenre, that you, would move against us, though Matron Berni'th is determined to remain neutral in this fight."

"Neutral? There will be no neutrality," Matron Zeerith sharply replied. "Your Matron Berni'th remains outraged that I have been placed back on the Ruling Council, that her seat was stolen from her."

"I cannot disavow that," Havel answered. "And will not try. Matron Berni'th believes our house more worthy than others among the selected eight, but she knows that such is not hers to decide, and knows quite well that House Do'Urden, now comprised of House Xorlarrin and with powerful additions, is not among those less deserving. Matron Berni'th will sit on the Ruling Council soon enough, Matron Zeerith. We both know that."

He smiled and looked Zeerith right in the eye, then cryptically added, "Because House Duskryn will choose its side or no side carefully."

"Is this return of your prisoners choosing?"

Havel Duskryn stiffened and stood taller, but did not answer.

Zeerith gave a little laugh.

"None of House Duskryn will come against your patrols again," Havel promised. "This is my word and that of Matron Berni'th."

"There are still three of my soldiers unaccounted for."

"They went into the Fane of Quarvelsharess. As far as we know, there they remain."

Zeerith looked over at Archmage Tsabrak. "Go to House Baenre and inform Matron Mother Quenthel."

The archmage bowed and departed.

"You will not strike out at my patrols?" Zeerith asked.

"No. House Duskryn is now settled behind our walls, awaiting clarification."

"From Lolth? From Matron Berni'th's prayers?"

"From everything," Havel replied. "We are not a ruling house and so we seek clarification from the Ruling Council."

"And if it splits, as it most certainly will? What then, Havel Duskryn?"

"It is not my decision. I am but a lowly male."

"Get out of my house," Zeerith told him. "And I warn you, and so warn Matron Berni'th: An attack on the Blaspheme, or on any of House Do'Urden, is an attack on House Baenre. Do not doubt that the Matron Mother is ready to teach you the same lesson House Hunzrin so painfully learned."

TRUE TO THEIR WORD, HOUSE DUSKRYN WAS NOT IN-volved in the next incident, though it occurred not far from their walls.

It turned out House Melarn did not need Duskryn's help.

Five Blaspheme were killed in that ambush, and one was very deliberately taken prisoner.

How pleased was Matron Zhindia Melarn when Dinin Do'Urden was delivered to her dungeon, awaiting the Curse of Abomination. She could not use Kyrnill's misinformation any longer, but this coming demonstration would be a stronger play by far.

PART 4

A JOURNEY OF HEROES

Considering the question of the boundaries and relationship between that which is internal and that which is external in training with the monks has been truly enlightening to me.

The world is external to us, of course. It is all around us, populated by people and animals and creatures who have free will and desires different from our own. Lightning will strike a tall tree in the forest whether or not I hear the shock or see the flash. The world turns around us when we are gone, and so of course it is external to us.

Yet, not completely.

Our perception shapes that which we see and hear and feel. The world is as it is, but as it is will not always, not even often, be the same thing to two different people. And that which you hear about the world around you also shapes your perception.

I watch the sunrise. It holds great meaning for me, not just because of its external beauty but because it reminds me of the deprivation of Menzoberranzan and the Underdark. Watching the sun climb above the horizon is to me a replaying of my own ascent to the world of daylight.

Not everyone will feel this way about the sunrise, and so this external event is also an internal event. The world around us shapes us and we shape the world around us.

That may seem like a small thing, but because of the monks, because of Kane most of all, I have come to better appreciate the gravity of that simple and seemingly obvious notion. For oftentimes that external shaping is debilitating or restricting. And other times, it can lead to false meaning—you can quite truly lose yourself within the moment of philosophical introspection, to the point where you have lost touch with the other things, and more importantly with the other people, around you. The inability to recognize the very different perception another might find from what you consider to be a shared event will lead to confusion and often conflict.

Also, standing deep in expectations for that which is around you can be akin to wallowing in an intellectual puddle of mud.

When I allowed Grandmaster Kane's spirit into my mind and body in the gnoll cave, he saw something quite obvious that I had completely missed, because I was standing deep in such mud. When I first acquired Dantrag Baenre's bracers, I found them confusing and detrimental. My mind could not keep up with my hand movements when I put them on, and worse, my feet could not keep up with my weapon movements, throwing me out of balance.

But I am not that young warrior any longer.

With my training beside Grandmaster Kane, with the brothers and sisters of the Order of St. Sollars, I have greatly increased my foot speed. Understanding the harmony of hips and legs—no, not just understanding, but sensing every connection between them—has greatly increased my ability to run and jump and turn quickly, to say nothing of the added fluidity and the simply physical power afforded by a proper understanding of the life force, ki.

I wear my bracers as bracers now, clamped about my wrists, and the movements of my arms, my scimitars, are matched and paced by the turns and steps. Two strikes become three, and no balance is lost.

Kane saw it immediately when he was within my form as we did battle—he most likely saw it from without well before that. Regardless, I believe that without his slightly different viewing prism, I never would have found this simple adjustment.

More importantly, Kane's temporary presence within me has helped me find the harmony between two distinct fighting styles, warrior and monk. He showed me the balance intimately, and with his skill and understanding, I saw and felt the true harmony, though I believe I still have some way to go before I can find that balance on my own. But now I know where to go. Before, I would fluctuate back and forth between the two styles as the situation presented—leaping like a monk, rolling my blades in warrior routines, striking with ki from afar or catching arrows like a monk, parrying and riposting like a warrior.

Now the disciplines are more united within me, a blend of styles that will, when perfected, provide me with more options, more tools, and more choices, both conscious and instinctive, in any situation.

In terms of battle, my internal adjustments and perceptions have changed the world around me. I see a tunnel, a hill, a riverbank, a parapet in a different way now as I calculate my best course of action and shape the battlefield to my advantage.

Now, too, I see the sunrise differently. I still view my own journey in its ascent above the horizon, still see the sheer beauty of the splayed colors, but now, after transcending my mortal form, I see, too, the distance of the celestial bodies, the great voids between them, the starstuff they represent, of which I am a part.

The sunrise is more beautiful to me now.

And I am more formidable.

—Drizzt Do'Urden

CHAPTER 23

Rewriting Memories

Y ou have no idea how maddening this is," Jarlaxle told Kimmuriel when the two were alone later on. "Was I dead for those missing months? Is this a resurrection, akin to what Zak experienced?"

"No, Azzudonna knows you," Kimmuriel replied. "The recognition on her face was unmistakable. If you had died soon after arriving there, how could that be?"

"Maybe she was the one who brought me back."

"No, she knows you, and knows our three missing friends," Kimmuriel insisted. "She told Regis as much, or at least hinted at it strongly. I do not think she was merely following the halfling's lead and feeding him information to satisfy his probing. She knows you and was shocked to see you walking into the room."

"I caught that."

"Shocked to see you *alive*," Kimmuriel clarified. "She told Regis that you and the others were lost. She was relieved, too, that her belief was proven wrong in your case. I recognized this on her face clearly."

"So, again, maybe I had been dead."

Kimmuriel shook his head. "From where your memory ended and where it began again hints at no such thing."

"Maybe something killed me in the air while I was looking down at the snow piled on my friends. Something hit me by surprise and snuffed out my life, then and there."

Kimmuriel remained very clearly flustered. "It is possible, but I don't think that's correct." He looked at Jarlaxle very seriously and re-iterated, "She *knew* about the others, including Catti-brie and Entreri. It seems less likely to me that you were killed in that first day than . . ."

"That they were not," Jarlaxle reasoned.

Kimmuriel nodded.

"Regis is with Azzudonna now," Jarlaxle said. "Perhaps he will bring us more information."

"I wouldn't hope. A hint, maybe, nothing more. She is disciplined and well trained. The only way we're getting more information from her would be for me to subject her to the intrusions of the hive mind. No discipline or magic can resist that—the illithids can retrace every side connection to work around such discipline and mental defense. We are all loath to do that, for the violation to Azzudonna would prove tremendous and lasting, perhaps forever debilitating. But the temptation is growing, I warn."

"The violation," Jarlaxle echoed, nodding his head.

"An incredible violation."

Jarlaxle looked up suddenly. "Then take *me* to the illithids."

Kimmuriel started as if he had been slapped. Looking horrified, he began shaking his head.

"You just said that no magic can resist the hive mind," Jarlaxle argued. "If I wasn't dead, then my memory has been altered by magic, yes? I want to know what I can't remember, desperately so, and the lives of Zak, Entreri, and Catti-brie may well depend upon it."

"I hesitate to take Azzudonna, this woman I barely know and know not at all as a friend, and you expect me to subject you to the intrusion of the hive mind?"

"Why, Kimmuriel, did you just admit that you love me?" Jarlaxle teased, but the psionicist was having none of it.

"To find that which is missing, the illithids would have to go to your deepest secrets and rebuild every pathway and connection, memory to memory. If it even worked. You thrive on secrecy and you would have none—none!—from them."

"I care little about the mind flayers," Jarlaxle countered. "I would never try to bargain with those things, and have no illusions that I could ever trick one of them in any case. Nor am I afraid that the illithids, of all creatures, would try to blackmail me—for to whom would they offer such information? Who would trust them? No one trusts them! Even *you* aren't sure if the conception of Menzoberranzan they presented to you and Quenthel and Yvonnel was the full truth of it."

Kimmuriel was still shaking his head, his voice going very somber. "Such an intrusion has consequences far beyond the rational and logical. It is a violation of the deepest and most personal secrets. They will know your every thought, your every fear."

"The price is not too high," Jarlaxle told him.

"They will know that which scares you."

Jarlaxle shrugged. "I'd tell them that myself, if it meant having this memory back."

"That which arouses you," Kimmuriel continued.

"Then be afraid for them!" Jarlaxle replied, and it wasn't clear, even to Jarlaxle, if he was kidding or not.

But Kimmuriel was not amused. "No, do not minimize the potential trauma of this. We each have thoughts too deep to share. Every one of us. Every living, reasoning being has secrets only unto themselves. Things they think, thoughts that flitter unexpectedly, things that please or arouse or frighten, vicious thoughts that would mark them as horrible and evil if spoken aloud. It is what makes us individuals. What makes you *you*."

"You have a cynical view of people, my friend."

"No, I have an honest understanding of people. Everyone has wicked thoughts, flickering notions of aberrant or evil behavior. Most would never act upon them, of course, but even the best wonder at such things—perhaps an inner dialogue of personal gain after the tragic loss of a loved one, or the relief that one for whom you were caring, one whom you dearly loved, has finally passed on and ended your burdens. Or a parent not loving a child, or thinking they do not, even briefly. Or a consideration of cruel murder of an enemy. Or unusual, perhaps vicious, perhaps simply embarrassing sexual desires."

"Guilty," Jarlaxle admitted, and he held up his hands as if he didn't see the problem here. "If we all have them, then why fear them?"

"Because none admit them, and doing so would be a mark of shame."

"You've often called me shameless."

"You keep making light of something that is not, Jarlaxle. To have that part of our innermost selves revealed to another is no joking matter and is, I know from personal experience, everything to fear."

"Isn't this what Kimmuriel does to others all the time?"

"No," he said firmly. "Not like this. Not as I am describing to you. The only chance you have of recovering those lost days would be to rebuild your memories, every connection, which would mean having the illithid collective begin at the beginning of Jarlaxle and follow every second, every line, every web, every moment of sense and thought. It is a violation beyond anything that can be done to you physically, I assure you."

"You're serious?"

"I have never been more serious."

Jarlaxle rested back in his comfortable chair, looked away, and considered the information honestly. After a long while, he turned to Kimmuriel. "Is there anyone in the world for whom you would take an arrow?"

Kimmuriel looked at him curiously.

"If an arrow were flying for my heart, would Kimmuriel throw himself into mortal danger to try to intercept it?"

"I would place a kinetic barrier—"

"Stop it!" Jarlaxle demanded. "You know what I mean here. Is there anyone, myself or anyone else, Kimmuriel would sacrifice himself to save? Yes, my friend, reach into those deepest and darkest corners of your complicated mind and please answer honestly. Don't try to impress me here, don't flatter me, or fear my response—"

"Yes," Kimmuriel interrupted.

"Yes?"

"Yes. Few, of course, but yes."

"For the good of the world or your feelings toward that person?"

"Either or both. The answer is yes."

"Then take me to the hive mind, right now," Jarlaxle told him. "The worst that can happen to me there is my death, and that is worth the price of the truth regarding our three lost friends."

"That is not the worst that could happen."

"Yes, it is, for if something happens that is clearly worse, Kimmuriel will kill me, on his word."

Kimmuriel stared at Jarlaxle for a long, long while.

"Are you sure?"

Jarlaxle didn't blink.

"I won't participate in this scouring of Jarlaxle, out of respect to you," Kimmuriel told him. "The illithids will see all, but I will not, and I will ensure that they never inform me."

Jarlaxle's expression turned to one of puzzlement.

"I wouldn't do that to you," Kimmuriel explained. "You share with me that which you choose to share with me, as I do with you. As we all do with each other. I have broken that mutual agreement of civilization in the past under extreme circumstances. Many times. But I prefer to pick my battles more carefully now, and to wage none of them on people I consider my friends."

"Or even upon innocents?" Jarlaxle slyly asked.

It was Kimmuriel's turn to wear a confused expression.

"You really do not want to take Azzudonna to the hive mind," Jarlaxle said bluntly.

Kimmuriel considered that surprising train of thought for just a few moments, then nodded.

KIMMURIEL HAD NEVER SEEN AN ILLITHID LOOKING shaken before, and while he wasn't even sure that such was what he was now witnessing—how might one truly judge an expression on a face full of tentacles, after all?—he couldn't be rid of the feeling that the one standing before him was truly unnerved when it exited the main chamber of the hive mind to discuss the ritual the collective had just completed on Jarlaxle.

"I always knew that we should be careful around that one," the illithid remarked in its bubbling, watery voice.

Kimmuriel stared at the mind flayer carefully, trying to place it. It wasn't true that all illithids looked alike, of course, and Kimmuriel was familiar enough with the hive mind to pick out many individuals on first glance. This one, however, he did not believe he had ever met before, though the creature was surely acting toward him with familiarity.

What he did recognize, however, was that this creature had just told a bit of a joke, which was something illithids rarely, if ever, did.

"You do not recognize me, Kimmuriel of Bregan D'aerthe? Of course not, for I was not in this form when last we parted ways."

"What form were you in?" Kimmuriel asked hesitantly, fearing the answer. Was this a member of his destroyed family, perhaps a disjointed consciousness of a dead drow psionicist that had somehow found its way into the corporeal form of a mind flayer?

The response came as a series of images telepathically offered to Kimmuriel: a long-lost rival . . . an ancient red dragon . . . a three-sided lamp . . . the legendary Crystal Shard . . . a dracolich . . .

"Yharaskrik," Kimmuriel breathed.

"Three became one," the illithid continued aloud. "The Ghost King, we were called."

"Three," Kimmuriel agreed. "Crenshinibon, Hephaestus, and Yharaskrik."

"But I was expelled and doomed," Yharaskrik said, and in his mind, Kimmuriel felt the illithid's gratitude.

For Kimmuriel had saved the disembodied spirit of Yharaskrik in that long-ago time, giving the spirit refuge in the Astral Plane, where it could survive without its corporeal form.

"Amazing," Kimmuriel murmured.

"Indeed. I am rarely here at the hive mind, but when I heard the subject of this ritual they had planned, I felt a need to join in. For now, as you can see, I have found good fortune in the death of another's consciousness, but the preservation of its physical body. I was welcomed back, but continue my study on the Astral Plane. The telepathic emanations of the hive mind have shown me that whenever Kimmuriel Oblodra visited of late, interesting events have transpired. This moment was no exception."

"Amazing," Kimmuriel said again.

"It is a small multiverse after all, my old companion," Yharaskrik said. "And the winding of paths is forever unpredictable. As with you and as with Jarlaxle. Old enemies have become friends, it would seem."

"You disapprove?"

The illithid's face tentacles waggled, a signal typical of surprise.

"Your pardon," Kimmuriel said, realizing the foolishness of his question, for why would an illithid approve or disapprove of anything that didn't involve the hive mind?

"Jarlaxle has survived the intrusion?" Kimmuriel asked.

"Surprisingly well, but then, even the hive mind is rarely not surprised by that one. He does not abide by expectations."

"Or customs."

In his mind, Kimmuriel heard Yharaskrik's unspoken thought, *He fornicates with dragons!*

"Jarlaxle sees his entire existence as something to be enjoyed and explored," Kimmuriel said. "And did you not just admit to a former relationship with a great wyrm that would be no less intimate? Where three became one?"

"Jarlaxle is . . . interesting," said Yharaskrik instead of answering.

"Unnerving," Kimmuriel corrected.

Yharaskrik's thoughts flickered in Kimmuriel's mind.

Disturbing . . .

Kimmuriel snickered as he imagined Jarlaxle's proud reaction if he ever told him about this particular conversation. "As I said, this is his way of muddling through," Kimmuriel reiterated. "And so, he viewed the ritual as yet another adventure, one where his shamelessness would carry him to victory."

Yharaskrik gave a mental nod of agreement.

"You have recovered his memories?"

"Take him home, Kimmuriel. He is piquing the interest of too many now, and I fear his antics might lead them into situations that will confuse the entire collective!"

Another joke? An exclamation spoken aloud and with passion?

Kimmuriel had been desperately worried about subjecting his dearest friend to the intrusions of the mind flayers. Perhaps he should have been more worried about subjecting the illithids to the sensibilities of Jarlaxle.

JARLAXLE WALKED INTO AZZUDONNA'S ROOM ALONE AND closed the door behind him.

He met her gaze, the two measuring each other for a long while.

"*Perte miye Zaknafein*," Jarlaxle said.

Azzudonna did well to not react. After a moment, she shrugged and shook her head.

"I remember it," Jarlaxle told her. "I remember all of it, all of Callidae. The fight in the wine barrel when we discovered the chaos phage infecting Zak's shoulder. Scellobel and the other boroughs. The Temporal Convocation in the Siglig. The journey along and within Qadeej.

"My memory has been fully restored."

Azzudonna lay quiet on her bed, staring at him.

"On my word, I won't betray you or your people," Jarlaxle promised.

She didn't blink.

"But we are going back for my friends—for *our* friends," he said, indicating her as well, "for there are many of Callidae encased in the icy mounds in that room in the cavern below the giant fortress. Whether you join us in that fight is up to you, but either way, we will take you back to the north and provide you with passage to your home."

Azzudonna was clearly fighting hard to not react.

"You didn't betray the aevendrow, nor will I," Jarlaxle told her, and he nodded and left. He paused outside the door and listened for a bit.

Azzudonna was sobbing softly.

He hoped it was in happiness.

He hustled along the hallways and met Kimmuriel outside the audience chamber, where Kimmuriel had bade Penelope to assemble all the principal players.

"What did she say?" Kimmuriel asked him.

"She didn't have to say anything." Jarlaxle took a deep breath. "What might she tell me that I do not already know?"

"Her reaction to your revelations," said Kimmuriel.

Jarlaxle blew a heavy sigh. "I told her that I wouldn't betray her people," he replied. "I haven't, have I?"

"What do you mean?"

"To the hive mind," Jarlaxle explained. "By allowing them to reconstruct my memories, I gave those memories to them, did I not? I hadn't even considered such a possibility when I agreed to go there—how could I, when I didn't remember why I didn't remember? But now, given that truth, have I betrayed the aevendrow to the illithids?"

"No," Kimmuriel answered simply. "There is nothing on Toril they do not already know—nothing as substantial as a city of nearly fifty thousand, mostly drow, certainly. They knew of Callidae."

"Then why didn't Kimmuriel know of it?"

"Because I never asked them, or looked. And even if I had, the world is a big place, my friend. Just because the knowledge is out there, floating in the memories of the hive mind, does not mean that I or any of the illithids would ever find it."

"Then I *did* betray them, because now it is in their collective consciousness."

"No." Kimmuriel seemed very confident, Jarlaxle noted, and that helped him relax here a bit. "If the illithids cared, they would have found Callidae all on their own—the knowledge was already there. They did not care. They *do* not care. They will remember much of their exploration of the mind of Jarlaxle, I expect, but none of it will have anything to do with Callidae."

Jarlaxle nodded, sighed, then nodded again. He shook his body head to foot, a sudden convulsion as if throwing off any negative energy or feelings. "Let's get this over with," he decided, and he barged through the door, striding with confidence and determination.

"I think they're alive," he told the gathering. "And I know where to find them. Are you up for a fight, King Bruenor?"

"Me girl?"

Jarlaxle nodded.

"Me king!" cried Pwent.

"Let's go," Regis said.

"I'll bring the armies of Gauntlgrym, Mithral Hall, Adbar, and Felbarr!" Bruenor promised.

"No," Jarlaxle told him.

"No?" he said, incredulous.

"No. That would not be wise. And it would not work. We go with a small troupe, carefully selected."

"If ye're thinkin' to leave me behind, ye might be thinkin' again," Bruenor said.

"Gauntlgrym will be so quick to let their king walk out on such a dangerous journey?" Kimmuriel asked.

"I'll be back afore any who question me'll wake up from me fist up the side o' their heads," Bruenor promised.

"Then let's go," Regis said again.

"It won't be that easy," Kimmuriel replied, his expression clearly doubting that he had considered the diminutive halfling for the journey. "If we hope to be fast and efficient, we cannot be taking many up there, so we have to pick our war party wisely."

"And though we must keep our own numbers small, we will find a formidable enemy awaiting us," Jarlaxle added.

"If me girl's there, then Rumblebelly's going," Bruenor declared. "Wulfgar, too, and Drizzt, o' course."

"I will go and retrieve Drizzt," Kimmuriel promised, but Jarlaxle held up his hand.

"No," he said. "I have a better idea. We'll get Drizzt, but we will speak later."

"Me king?" Pwent asked, hopping nervously from foot to foot.

"Pwent's coming," Bruenor told Jarlaxle.

"No," Jarlaxle replied, and to the growling Pwent, he added, "You're really not suited to the type of enemies we will face up there. Nor is Regis, I fear."

"Rumblebelly's coming," Bruenor said again.

"Him or Pwent?" asked Jarlaxle. "We cannot carry both."

Bruenor looked to Regis, who scowled, then to Pwent, who looked down at the floor and sighed.

"Rumblebelly's coming," Bruenor decided. "And what of Athrogate? Ye planning on bringing him along?"

"Again, we've limited room, good Bruenor," Jarlaxle explained. "The Companions of the Hall can join in, of course. As for the remainder of the troupe, while I understand the fierce loyalty of your bodyguards to you, and yours to them, there are others who will prove essential if we are to succeed." He ended by leading Bruenor's gaze over to Dab'nay and Gromph. "We'll need a priestess. And an archmage would be an invaluable addition."

Gromph responded with a doubting look.

You will wish to come, Kimmuriel telepathically imparted to Gromph. *There is something grand that you must see.*

"Azzudonna is coming as well," Jarlaxle explained.

"That's nine," Regis said.

"Eleven," Jarlaxle replied, but he wouldn't elaborate on the unnamed two. "And we'll need to do something about the cold. Rings or spells or—"

"I am well used to the cold," Wulfgar interjected. "As are Bruenor and Regis."

"Not like this," Jarlaxle told them. "You've seen Azzudonna's clothing; we haven't that kind of gear, so we'll need magic, or you'll be dead before we get near to our lost friends."

"There are no more such items at the Hosttower," Gromph said.

"I gave you four, and you returned with only the boots you now wear."

"Me king! Me king!" Pwent yelped, hopping all about excitedly.

"I said you can't go," said Bruenor. "No more of it from ye."

"But me king!" Pwent said, shaking his head.

"I have spells that will offer limited protection," Dab'nay said into that distraction. "But we'd need to be very quick."

"They wouldn't be enough," Jarlaxle replied.

"Me king! Me king!"

"What?" Bruenor relented.

"Pikel, me king. Pikel!"

"Pikel Bouldershoulder?" Jarlaxle asked.

"Of course," Regis agreed. "Pikel has spells that could protect the whole group from the breath of a white dragon. His repertoire includes the druid spells of old, lost to the world in the Spellplague and the Sundering."

"A dozen members?" Jarlaxle asked Kimmuriel and Gromph.

"We can manage that number," Kimmuriel replied.

"Then with Pikel, we won't be needin' her," Pwent said, pointing to Dab'nay. "Take me, me king!"

"We will need Dab'nay," Jarlaxle insisted. "I'm sorry, Pwent, but if any of our friends slip toward death as we free them, Pikel might revive them as a hamster or some other critter, but Dab'nay can save them. Would you be comfortable with the result if we do as you so badly and rightfully desire, but it costs the life of Zaknafein? Or Catti-brie?"

The dwarf looked crestfallen but said nothing.

"That's our group, then. Fourteen returning if we are successful," Jarlaxle said, causing some alarm as the friends registered that a dozen and three did not add up to fourteen. Before they could question, though, Jarlaxle explained that Azzudonna would not be coming back to the south with them.

Kimmuriel looked to Gromph, who nodded.

"To Gauntlgrym to get your gear," Jarlaxle told Bruenor. "We will meet outside the Hosttower in Luskan at dawn in three days and will likely be fighting within a day of our departure, possibly before noon."

He paused as soon as the last word passed his lips and gave a little chuckle.

"What?" Bruenor and Regis asked together.

"Noon," Jarlaxle said, shaking his head. "There is no noon. Not there."

"What're ye babblin' about, ye damned elf?" Bruenor demanded.

"You will see, King Bruenor. You will see."

WHEN AZZUDONNA HAD DRESSED, HER FANTASTIC CLOTH-ing returned to her along with her weapons, the troupe said their farewells to Penelope and seven went through the portal back to Gauntlgrym, Jarlaxle and Kimmuriel remaining behind for the time being.

"You'll bring Catti-brie back to us?" Penelope asked the drow rogue.

"I believe we will, yes, good lady," Jarlaxle said.

"What else do you know, Jarlaxle?" she asked. "There is more, much more. I can tell."

"I'll not disagree with you, and will not lie to you," Jarlaxle told her. "But neither is it my place to tell you. We're going for Catti-brie, Zak, and Artemis Entreri. That is all that matters to anyone here."

Penelope nodded. "It would be good if we knew where to come and help you, if that became necessary," she said.

"If the group I am assembling cannot do this, then none other should try," Jarlaxle replied. "Now, may we borrow a quiet room for a short while? Kimmuriel and I have to reach out across the world to Grandmaster Kane . . ." He paused abruptly and snapped a look to Kimmuriel. "*Verve zithd?*"

Kimmuriel looked startled for just a moment, trying to figure out why Jarlaxle had just asked about the common reference to thirteen as a "baker's dozen," or *verve zithd,* as it was called in Menzoberranzan.

Jarlaxle smiled wickedly.

Kimmuriel shrugged and nodded.

"What just happened?" Penelope asked.

"Probably nothing," said Jarlaxle. "And nothing to concern your-self about."

"Who are the mysterious two you mentioned earlier?" Penelope asked. "Can you tell me that, at least?"

"You know them," Jarlaxle said, and winked.

Penelope started to respond, but stopped, her expression showing her figuring it out. "Come," she said, and led them to the quiet room.

CHAPTER 24

A Baker's Dozen

A cold wind blew past him, throwing Drizzt's heavy cloak out wide and tossing Andahar's white mane wildly as Drizzt tried to strap his heavy pack on the unicorn's broad back. The drow looked to the gathering dark clouds in the north and sighed, hoping he might get ahead of the brewing blizzard. If he got caught by the first real snowstorm up here in the mountains, he wouldn't easily traverse the trails to the lower lands.

"I thought Grandmaster Kane asked you to await his return?" Savahn asked, moving out from the monastery's northern door to join him.

"He also said he might not return until noon," Drizzt answered, and nodded his chin to the dark clouds in the north.

"That is only a few hours. Would you deny the Grandmaster his request over three hours?"

"He asked me to wait, yes, but the storm is collecting early, it seems, and I simply haven't the time to delay. If I don't get ahead of it, how many days will I lose?"

"Perhaps your friends will magically come for you," Savahn offered.

"Grandmaster Kane told me that they wouldn't."

"Surely this storm is not surprising to Kane, who has lived in these mountains for the entirety of his long life. He knows the weather patterns, and the signs. He would not have asked you to wait if he thought doing so would cause you or your quest any harm."

Drizzt paused and spent a while mulling that. It was hard to disagree. Grandmaster Kane was as true an ally as he had ever known. The man wanted nothing more out of his later life than to serve, whether as guardian, as teacher, or as friend.

"Brie is awake and taking her breakfast with Brother Tadpole," Savahn said, half turning back toward the monastery in invitation.

Drizzt couldn't deny the temptation. Spending the morning in play with his daughter was among the greatest joys he had ever known.

But then he thought of her mother, and of Kane's words the previous night.

"He asked you to stay," Savahn stated flatly.

"I haven't the time. I must be away with all speed, to Citadel Adbar and then through the tunnels and portal to Gauntlgrym."

"He asked you to *stay*," Savahn said even more insistently.

"I . . ." Drizzt started, but he stopped, caught by the unrelenting and uncompromising glare of the accomplished and powerful woman— one who would likely someday soon become the second-ranking monk of this monastery.

"Hasn't he earned at least this much from you, Drizzt Do'Urden?" Savahn asked. "Your journey will take many days, but Grandmaster Kane asks for a few hours."

"Not so many days. Andahar does not tire and neither will I."

"Even more reason this one morning won't make that much of a difference, yes? Grandmaster Kane promised that he would return to you by noon. Have you ever known him to break a promise?"

In response, Drizzt looked back to the gathering clouds in the north.

"Trust me: Grandmaster Kane sees the storm better than you do," said Savahn. "Unless you think he is trying to trick you into getting caught here when the winter snows come deep, he would not let you become trapped."

Drizzt considered it, gave a sigh, and began unstrapping the bag from Andahar. As soon as he had it removed, he bade the unicorn to be gone, and he and Savahn watched the display as Andahar galloped away, becoming much smaller with each long stride, as if covering great distances indeed, until the unicorn simply disappeared.

"Let us go and have breakfast with your daughter," Savahn offered.

Drizzt nodded and walked up beside her, letting her lead him back toward the door. "While we walk you can promise me again that you will take great care of her, and with her, while I am away."

Savahn smiled widely and bumped into him playfully. "Maybe she will surprise you when you and Catti-brie return, and show you a few tricks of a fighting monk that even you have not yet mastered."

"Then she's her mother's daughter," Drizzt agreed, and both laughed.

And Drizzt ducked away suddenly, pulling Savahn with him, in surprise as a huge shadow crossed above them. He looked up and glanced all around, but the sky seemed clear.

"You saw that?" he asked.

Savahn shook her head and started walking for the door once more, but Drizzt didn't move. He dropped his bag and stood there on his guard, hands on his weapons.

"It was nothing," Savahn said. "Just a cloud."

"Hardly that" came a voice from the east, and the two turned to see Grandmaster Kane walking around the corner of the monastery.

"Well met, Drizzt," he said. "Come, we must hurry. The storm approaches faster than I expected."

Drizzt chuckled helplessly, glanced at Savahn, and lifted his unicorn whistle to his lips to retrieve the magical steed he had just dismissed, but Kane held up his hand and shook his head. The monk started to explain, but he didn't need to, as a pair of women came walking around the corner behind him. One was tall and distinctive-looking, with a thick shock of copper-colored hair bouncing about her shoulders and striking blue eyes that were a bit too large for her angular face. She wore a fur-collared robe fastened by a single button at her waist and apparently little else, her long legs bursting free of the folds with every confident stride.

The woman behind her was a bit shorter and quite a bit softer in appearance, with strawberry-blond hair shot through with more than a little gray. She wore a simpler robe, fastened more modestly, though much shorter. And again, her bare legs sticking out below it led Drizzt to believe that the robe was all that she wore.

And he understood why.

And he understood the shadow that had swept past him.

"I believe that you know—" Kane began.

"Ilnezhara and Tazmikella," Drizzt finished.

"Kimmuriel came to me again this morning and bade me to go to them," Grandmaster Kane explained. "Their destination is your destination, and so there is no need for you to summon Andahar."

"To the Hosttower in Luskan," the copper-haired Ilnezhara said.

"Adbar," Drizzt corrected. "It will be easier to use the fiery portals."

"The Hosttower," said Tazmikella. "It won't be any faster to take the tunnels and portals. Do not underestimate us."

Drizzt offered a respectful bow. The last thing he wanted to do was anger these sisters.

"Are you ready to leave?" Kane asked.

"I would already be gone if Savahn of Winter hadn't stopped me."

Kane nodded and trotted up to the drow and monk. He pulled Savahn aside and whispered something to her that gave Drizzt some pause, for he noted the concerned expression on her face.

She grimaced briefly, but then rushed over to give Drizzt a kiss on the cheek and bid him farewell, and promised again to give Brie the very best attention. She offered a quick smile and bow to the visiting sisters and hustled into the monastery.

"She seems troubled," Drizzt said to Kane.

Across the way, the sisters began walking back around the corner of the monastery toward the large, wide field, dropping their robes as they went. Ilnezhara called back to Drizzt over her shoulder, telling him to make sure he collected them.

Drizzt couldn't help but snort in surprise when a tail sprouted from Ilnezhara's bare buttocks, and he shook his head as the sisters fell one after the other to all fours, the transformation already well under way. By the time Ilnezhara had rounded the corner, her tail was twice as long as Drizzt was tall.

Kane and Drizzt followed.

"I told Savahn that I was asking your permission to travel with you," Kane explained to the drow when they got to the corner. The dragon sisters were fully re-formed now into their more natural forms, lean and sinewy, more than thirty feet long counting their serpentine necks and tails, and covered in coppery scales that shone brightly in the morning sunshine. Not as brightly as their eyes, though, turquoise orbs that seemed to emanate light more than reflect it.

"You will join with me in my mind again?" Drizzt asked, thinking of the gnolls' cave. Drizzt winced at the thought, but he couldn't deny the possibility that he'd come out of the other side of the journey with an even greater understanding of himself and the world around him. "I cannot say that I enjoy our melding, but—"

"No," Kane interrupted, and he moved to one of the sisters, whom Drizzt recognized as Tazmikella, as she was the older of the two and some of her scales had taken on a greenish tinge of verdigris now, like the graying of her strawberry-blond hair when in human form.

Kane lifted a small saddle from the ground, stuffed Tazmikella's robe inside a saddlebag attached to it, then hoisted the saddle up high to set it on the low-crouching Tazmikella's shoulders.

"I am coming with you, mind and body," he announced. "There is little left to excite or inform me in this world now, my friend, and when the opportunity arises for me to see something new, I will not turn away."

Drizzt didn't quite know how to take that, but he moved to gather the other fallen robe and stuffed it into the bag of the saddle Ilnezhara had put on the ground beside her.

"With your permission?" he asked the dragon, who swiveled her head around to position her huge reptilian face right before Drizzt's.

"With my pleasure, you may ride me, Drizzt Do'Urden," she said in a voice that was more husky than hissy.

"Do take care when you are high in the sky," Tazmikella told Drizzt as he was climbing up into place and setting his pack before him. "My sister prefers to be on top."

Both dragons laughed, or hissed, or something between the two.

Drizzt sighed and shook his head, and hadn't even strapped himself securely in with the thick laces of the special saddles when Ilnezhara leaped away, beating her wings furiously to climb into the cold morning sky.

"And any man who rides her would do well to hold on for his life!" he heard Tazmikella shout behind him.

Drizzt appreciated the levity, as it took his mind off his continuing worries for his wife and friends. Soon enough, he also appreciated the view, the world opening wide beneath him. It would have taken his breath away, except that the freezing air was already doing that. He bent low on the dragon's shoulder to avoid the rush of the wind, but then he thought of the training Savahn had offered up on the mountainside. He fell within himself and felt his blood coursing through his body, carrying warmth. He smiled, not nearly as cold as he had feared.

He eyed the approaching storm, but only for a short while, as it became obvious that the dragons had little trouble outrunning it. Already they were descending out of the Galena Mountains, and Drizzt could see the sun shining on the waters of the Moonsea, ahead and to his left.

He took a deep, deep breath and tried to let go of his fears and concerns, tried to be in the moment, just this moment, and take in views that few people could ever enjoy. The perspective of the world was so different from on high! He saw cities in the distance and knew they must be grand, but from up here, they seemed small things, after all.

It was all relative. Size was relative, as was time, as was importance. He always tried to keep that in mind, reminding himself of his own epiphanies regarding perspective. How connected all the world seemed from up here, while how disjointed was the reality down below.

From up here, if they went farther to the west in the dark of night, Drizzt might see the fires of Waterdeep and Luskan all at once, yet how many people would live their whole lives in one of those cities without ever going to the other, without ever knowing anything beyond the broadest details, perhaps no more than the name, of the other?

"Why do you ever land?" he called out to Ilnezhara.

"For the entertainment," the dragon answered, swinging her face about. "The pettiness of lesser beings amuses me."

"Do you know why we're flying to the Hosttower?"

"Because Jarlaxle has returned from the north promising adventure and pleading for help."

"Jarlaxle has returned?" Drizzt said, his mind suddenly spinning so much that he almost forgot to hold on. "Who was with him?"

"I know not. He came to me and my sister through the powers of Kimmuriel and asked us to help him. We thought it amusing and so we are here." She started to swivel her head back out in front, but Drizzt called to her.

"My wife was with him," he said.

"It was just Kimmuriel when he came to inform us and ask this of us," she replied, and faced forward.

"No, in the north," Drizzt explained. "My wife was up there with Jarlaxle."

Around came Ilnezhara's head again. "Interesting," she said.

Drizzt had nothing to add. He prayed that he would find Catti-brie waiting for him when he landed in Luskan.

He feared that he would not.

THEY FLEW FOR MANY HOURS, THE LAND ROLLING OUT BE-low, the Galena Mountains already receding far into the distance behind them. What struck Drizzt the most in this journey was the silence, or rather, the continual and even level of noise from the wind rushing past. The dragon flight seemed so effortless—he couldn't re-call the last time Ilnezhara had even beat her leathery wings.

He watched the sun descending before him, the western sky lighting up in orange and pink and purple and yellow, the undersides of distant clouds brightening, glistening, glowing, as if they were on fire.

Twilight fell, the quiet light only emphasizing the silent, gliding flight, and despite the worrisome news from the west, Drizzt found himself at peace, losing himself between the campfires and home fires coming to life below him and the stars coming out to twinkle above. He lost himself there, in a state of beautiful meditation, the same serenity he had known so often atop Kelvin's Cairn.

Kelvin's Cairn.

The last time he had climbed that lone mountain in Icewind Dale, he had gone there to die—and there, he had been reborn in the midst of his beloved friends, so unexpectedly, nay, shockingly!

He wanted to go back there someday soon, his friends beside him . . . or no, maybe alone, or with Bruenor alone, or with Catti-brie alone.

That last stream of thought broke into his consciousness, reminded him of his great fear, and pulled him from his meditative state.

Only then did he realize that Ilnezhara was much nearer the ground, and fast descending, which surprised him, because he had almost convinced himself that the dragons would fly all the way to the Hosttower in a single journey.

With surprising grace, the dragon set down on a wide field, Tazmikella and Grandmaster Kane landing right beside them.

The dragon sisters wandered off while Drizzt and Kane shared a meal.

"It will be a short sleep," Kane warned. "We'll be flying up high again long before the dawn."

Drizzt nodded.

"And before we settle for that rest, I would ask you to allow me into your thoughts again. We will do battle with Ilnezhara and Tazmikella as you seek the harmony of your disciplines."

"I will fight a pair of dragons," Drizzt replied with a chuckle. "At least you had the good sense to put an easy task before me as I struggle through this new discipline combination."

"How many gnolls should I round up to keep you engaged for a long enough period that we might make some progress? Five? A dozen? A hundred?"

"This fight might be shorter than if you went and collected only a single gnoll," Drizzt said. He looked to the side and nodded his chin to lead Kane's gaze across the field to the approaching dragons, now in their human forms. They carried the heavy saddles and saddlebags as easily as a true human might hold a small purse, only emphasizing Drizzt's last statement.

Kane laughed and rose from his cross-legged position, standing up without touching the ground with either hand, which Drizzt found remarkable for a human, particularly for one of such an advanced age. Kane simply lifted, his legs still crossed, from sitting to standing, almost as if he were on the end of a marionette string.

Kane collected his pack and fished around inside, producing a pair of small wooden cylinders. He flicked one wrist, then the other, the items telescoping out to become three-foot lengths, which Drizzt soon recognized as practice swords.

"Do you wish to dine first, or shall we begin?" the monk asked the sisters as they neared.

"Let us be done with our dance," Tazmikella said.

"I would fight hungry," Ilnezhara agreed, locking her glowing turquoise eyes on Drizzt. "That way, if Drizzt excites me with a strike, I'll just eat him."

Kane walked over and handed the practice swords to Drizzt, who climbed to his feet still staring at Ilnezhara, trying unsuccessfully to figure out how he might decipher the meaning of the dragon's words.

Yes, that one flustered him, and frightened him, and not only because he knew she could kill him.

Kane walked away and plopped back down on the ground. "Try not to trample me in your . . . dancing," he said, and he nodded at Drizzt. "Are you ready?"

Soon after, Kane was in Drizzt's thoughts, inconspicuously and in the background, but surely there. Drizzt moved to a proper defensive balance as the two women circled him, measuring their steps, talking to each other, taunting Drizzt.

Tazmikella leaped forward, slapping her hand across. Drizzt met it with a stinging rebuke from his right-hand blade, and countered fast with a roll and stab, and a sweeping strike with his left.

He shortened the attack and rolled aside, though, sensing the rush of Ilnezhara behind him, and that one, too, he met with proper parries and ripostes, forcing the sisters back into their steady circling.

Drizzt heard his daughter's plaintive cry.

Stop it! he demanded of Kane.

The stakes are high, came the internal response. *Your wife's life might be in jeopardy here if you cannot properly champion her in her time of need.*

What do you know? Drizzt demanded, but he was drawn back to the situation at hand as both sisters came at him, left and right.

He dove forward into a roll, came up in a leap, and spun about to face the pursuit.

I know nothing, Kane imparted.

Then Brie cried out as if in pain or fear.

Become the Hunter.

Stop it!

Your wife is in danger. Your friends will be lost to you.

Stop it!

Brie cried, shrieked.

Become the Hunter!

"Stop!" Drizzt yelled, and his thoughts turned outward as his voice bellowed forth, just in time to take a clipping slap on the shoulder that threw him forward and had him rolling again. He came up flexing the arm, trying to ward off the pain.

The sisters charged.

Brie cried out.

The Hunter leaped and spun, kicking Tazmikella squarely in the chest. Drizzt sprang away, for the dragon didn't move from the blow, but he landed lightly in a turn and went right back in.

He visualized a move, a leap and somersault right over Ilnezhara, striking and turning as he descended behind her, and he even started the jump.

But the Hunter, the warrior, knew such a leap was impossible, and so denied him. Yes, he leaped, but neither high nor low, a simple, ridiculous, straightforward spring that brought him straight in at the dragons.

Tazmikella slugged him before he landed, and then he wasn't landing.

No, then he was flying.

He crashed down in the grass, his weapons lost, his right arm wrapped tightly against his bruised left side.

You must trust in your ki was the last thought he garnered from Kane before he was lying on his back, staring up at the stars.

"Well, sister, that was rather boring," he heard Tazmikella say.

"And you broke him before I could properly play with him," Ilnezhara added.

Drizzt thought the stars were particularly pretty, and that it was a good time to sleep.

"WE WILL TRY AGAIN TONIGHT," GRANDMASTER KANE told Drizzt when they climbed onto the copper dragons and began to ascend into the predawn sky. "Tonight, I will control the movements of Drizzt, and he will feel the beauty of the harmony, and Drizzt will come to trust."

The drow replied with a glare.

He wasn't in a particularly generous or congenial mood. Between the manipulation by the mimicking of his daughter's distressed cries, his fears for his wife, and the sudden confusion within him in his deepest fighting stance, the world seemed unbalanced to him. Or more particularly, his own place seemed out of kilter, and his great joys suddenly tentative.

He managed to put the dark thoughts aside as the day wore on, as the world rolled out beneath him, but when they landed that second day, it all chased Drizzt back down to the earth.

He hopped off Ilnezhara's back before she had even settled to the ground, storming across the field to confront Kane as Tazmikella put down.

"This could be interesting, sister," he heard Ilnezhara say behind him, and he glanced back to see that she was already transforming into her human form. "Perhaps we should let Drizzt and Kane do battle while we sit back and enjoy the show."

Drizzt ignored her, though he silently cursed himself for so obviously revealing his anger here.

"Be at ease, my friend," Kane said, reinforcing that notion. The grandmaster hopped down easily from Tazmikella's back. "We will push through this discordance."

"Let us begin at once," Drizzt said.

"A meal?"

"Later."

Kane laughed and shook his head.

"Now," Drizzt argued.

"It has been a long day and we will both perform better if our growls come from our throats and not our bellies."

Drizzt started to retort, but he bit it back. For all of his simmering anger and fear at that moment, he had to remind himself of the gravity of this man standing before him. Drizzt's frustrations, not Kane's actions, were driving this anxiety. His training with the monks had been beneficial to him in so many ways—he would have been obliterated by the retriever and would be long gone from this life had it not been for Grandmaster Kane.

The man was asking for trust. Drizzt owed him that and more.

They ate a quick meal and went back to their trials, with Kane melding into Drizzt's consciousness and taking control, as they had agreed, when the dragon sisters attacked.

This time he heard the distractions for what they were—distractions. And instead of listening to them, he listened to Kane . . . and to himself. Even just a bit.

Drizzt couldn't sort where Kane ended and he began, and similarly, where his monk training ended and his warrior training and primal instincts began. His body flowed in perpetual motion, leaping and spinning, always ahead of the two attackers, sometimes over one to strike from behind on the descent, sometimes turning a logical parry into a sudden and devastating offensive response.

Even the dragons seemed impressed at the sheer number of strikes Drizzt was delivering with those practice swords, and from every conceivable angle. His leap right over Tazmikella, backhanding her as she turned while he descended, drew a cheer of applause from Ilnezhara.

It proved to be a much more satisfying exercise for Drizzt that night, opening up new possibilities and greater heights, both figuratively and literally. If he could find that harmony between the two fighting styles, making them complementary instead of competitive . . .

He even accepted Kane's use of his deepest emotions and fears, the cries of his young daughter, the unknown dangers his wife might be in, as necessary—an exercise he thought akin to when the drow tortured students at Melee-Magthere to make them resistant to such brutal techniques should they ever be captured.

Indeed, the only thing Drizzt found disconcerting at all during that session were the sounds Ilnezhara made whenever a practice sword struck her, for they seemed more to be gasps of pleasure than exclamations of surprise or yips of pain.

He thought of her. He thought of Jarlaxle. He could only shake his head.

Drizzt replayed that successful sparring session all during the flight the following day, considering the harmony he had witnessed between his two fighting forms. Witnessed, and not enacted, however, for that had been the effort of Grandmaster Kane mostly, and thus, while the session had helped to somewhat alleviate his fears that this critical barrier between the styles was coming at exactly the wrong time, the trepidation remained.

He had to trust in Kane, he told himself repeatedly as he and Ilnezhara glided through the morning air. Kane had promised that Drizzt would push through the limitation—unexpected by Drizzt, but not by Kane—quickly.

He believed the supremely accomplished monk.

Still, he kept his focus on the sparring session, replaying it over and over again, burying himself in his work so he didn't have to entertain his frustrating, unanswerable fears regarding his wife.

Drizzt found himself caught between anxiety and emotional hunger when they set down later that day. Determined to be in the moment through every punch, kick, spin, and block, he knew that he had to be at his best for the expected session.

"This time, you will summon the Hunter without my help," Kane told him. "I'll not mimic your daughter's cry, nor remind you of potential troubles with your friends or wife. When the sisters attack, it is up to Drizzt to place us in that place of the pure warrior."

Drizzt nodded and watched the approach of Ilnezhara and Tazmikella, his fingers rolling on the grips of the practice swords.

Kane moved his physical body off to the side, sat down crosslegged, and began his meditative chant. Drizzt felt him as if he were knocking at the door of Drizzt's mind, begging entry.

The drow ranger, drow monk, closed his eyes and complied.

As soon as he opened his eyes again, the sisters were upon him, viciously and violently.

But the Hunter came forth. His movements with the bracers flowed beautifully with speed and precision, his wooden swords parrying and countering every attack in the barrage. He let one slap get through in exchange for a crack of his sword on Ilnezhara's face so violent that the dragon's yelp wasn't playful that time, and the practice sword, for all of its fine craftsmanship and even the bit of magical strengthening, broke in half.

The Hunter did well to be already in motion to accept Ilnezhara's slap, and even then was launched several feet away, falling into a trio of rolls to further absorb the shock.

The reminder wasn't needed, but these were indeed dragons, however lithe and human they might now appear. He came up to his feet out of the third roll and threw the broken sword to the side.

The Hunter didn't need it.

The dragons stalked in pursuit, but that was met with a leaping, spinning charge, stabs and slashes and punches flying all about, raining on one sister after the other.

Had these been real human opponents, real humanoids of any sort, and not dragons in disguise, the fight would have ended quickly and decisively, but as it was, the Hunter hit them dozens of times while avoiding or mitigating any and every attack either sister might make.

There was no conscious thought, and yet it was all conscious thought, Drizzt's mind and body moving faster than he could consider.

He would not be the one to yield this time, he was certain in the quiet part of his mind. He would not tire, his strikes would not slow, and the dragons would have to relent.

He felt their frustrations building—he could sense it in the unsubtle changes of the sisters' fighting stances and techniques. They were getting sloppy, and they were getting hit more often because of it.

And then Ilnezhara blew forth a breath weapon—not the acid that would have melted a victim, but a conical cloud of heavy gas that tried to cling and slow the Hunter.

But the Hunter evaded it, then evaded Tazmikella's similar attempt.

And he came rushing in right behind the blast and landed a leaping double kick against Tazmikella's face and chest. He bounced off, rolled, came up in a spin, and circle-kicked the closing Ilnezhara, surprising her, clearly, then even more when he stabbed her rapidly three times about her neck and mouth.

The dragon spat blood. Her eyes went wide with fury.

And she began to transform.

Drizzt let go of the Hunter and fell back, hands raised.

He saw Kane running in from the side, which surprised him, for he hadn't felt the monk's life force leave his body.

Kane and Tazmikella both intercepted Ilnezhara and calmed her down, and Drizzt relaxed when she reversed the transformation and laughed loud and lewdly.

"Such a feisty one!" she said.

"Well fought," Tazmikella told Drizzt.

"Brilliantly fought!" Ilnezhara said.

Drizzt nodded and apologized for that last overexuberant strike, then turned to Kane and said, "We did well."

"We?"

Drizzt looked at him curiously, but only for the moment it took him to sort out the truth.

Kane hadn't joined him in this fight at all. His movements, the harmony of the fighting styles, the summoning of the Hunter and the blend with his monk forms, were all his own doing.

"You have pushed through it," Kane said.

Drizzt considered that for just a few moments, then replied, "Let us eat and take our rest. I want to find my wife."

CHAPTER 25

What He Did for Us

G alathae adjusted the fit on her harness and checked the set of Bluccidere, her blue-ice-bladed sword. She glanced at her shield, which was lying to the side, for it would not easily fit down the narrow shaft the miners had dug.

She looked behind her to skinny and young Allefaero, who was said to be among the most powerful wizards in all of Callidae, and took a deep breath to steady herself as she watched the aevendrow man squirm uncomfortably in his harness, a reminder that this one, for all of his magical prowess, was far less than proficient in anything resembling athletics, or even basic coordination, it seemed. At least he didn't weigh a lot, she thought, and that mattered because he was tied to the same rope as she, and would descend only ten feet or so behind her.

"One whistle and we'll have you quickly back up the shaft," Ilina said, startling her, for she hadn't even noticed the priestess's approach. She looked to her friend, then followed Ilina's gaze to the capstan that had been brought into Cattisola and secured to the ground near the shaft. The thick silken rope holding Galathae and Allefaero was wrapped about the drum, below the five evenly spaced hand spokes. The hauling team—a pair of huge orcs, a muscular dwarf, and an ae-vendrow couple who battled as center guards for the Ardin Tivatrice—were just off to the side, rubbing their hands with chalk and stretching their shoulders and arms, while another pair of dwarves checked the long bolts securing the pulleys that would guide the rope over the edge of the shaft and prevent any fraying.

Galathae took the whistle from Ilina and looped its chain over her head. It was loud, she knew, and magical, so no matter what might happen far below, the priests up here would hear the call.

"Keep the descent steady and not too fast," she reminded them, and directed Ilina's gaze to Allefaero. "If he reactively reaches out and grabs at a jag in the shaft, you will surely pull his arm off."

Her tone showed that she was half joking, at least, and Ilina chuckled, then whispered, "His magic is his strength."

"He knows what we fear down there," Galathae agreed, nodding and reminding herself as much as speaking to Ilina. It was hard to gain confidence from just looking at the man, who seemed too young and too weak. "He has properly prepared."

The haulers moved into position, the dwarves gave the signal that the pulleys were set, and Ilina kissed Galathae on the cheek for luck and stepped away.

"You are ready?" Galathae asked the wizard, who nodded shakily, then yelped in surprise when he was pulled up into the air as the haul-ers wound the ropes more fully. Up, up went Allefaero, and out over the seemingly bottomless hole, his jaw locked in what seemed to be the beginnings of a silent scream.

The paladin hid her smile until she had fully turned away from the poor, terrified young man, then dismissed it almost immediately as she rolled her legs over the shaft's lip, bent at the waist to secure herself until the rope tightened, Allefaero now nearly ten feet above her. The haulers kept the rope taut, with just enough slack for Galathae to get over the lip and down into the shaft. It went very slowly for the next few moments as everything straightened and settled. Then began the descent, the haulers reversing direction. Allefaero didn't relax quickly enough, and his flailing had him bouncing about for the first few feet, jolting Galathae as she dangled below him.

"Just keep your hands on the rope and your legs straight out beneath you," she called up to the wizard.

Allefaero nodded but hardly complied, as he kept reflexively reaching out for the side of the shaft.

Galathae repeatedly told herself not to scold him, and that his nerves would settle. She hoped that to be the case, because the protective spells Ilina and the other priests had put on them wouldn't last for very long and a slow descent would cost them valuable time to truly consider what awaited them far below.

Apparently, that last thought was being discussed up above as well, for the speed of the descent suddenly and dramatically increased. Allefaero bounced and twisted about through a series of several jarring short drops before things steadied. Galathae figured that the timid young man must have finally convinced himself that reaching out was not the best thing to do here—or perhaps he was just clutching his hands too tightly on the rope and keeping his eyes squeezed shut as the darkness closed in about them, the hole up above fast receding.

Soon enough after that, Galathae could feel the heat rising from below and knew they were nearing the end of the shaft and the entry through the ceiling of the large crystal chamber. She felt about her belt for the small magical lantern she had secured there, preparing to bring forth its bright light.

She sensed the walls of the shaft fall away about her, felt the hot breezes of the underground chamber. It wasn't completely black as various reddish or orangish glows showed here and there in the distance. Galathae's senses told her that this cavern was very large—some of the glows seemed very distant.

She held off on the light, confident that she wasn't about to land or crash into something, or someone. Up above, Allefaero called to her softly. "Galathae? Galathae, the light?"

She wanted to wait a bit longer, but she wanted more for her companion to shut up, so she pulled back the blocking veil of the magical lantern.

A thousand sparkles greeted the intrusion of light, like visual gasps of surprise. Galathae, too, felt like gasping, both from the stifling heat and the images that came back at her. They had told her that there were crystals down here, but the paladin was in no way prepared for *this*.

Because these multicolored crystals were huge, some thicker than she was tall. And throwing heat—the same heat that had carved out the canyons that served as boroughs in the city.

"By the gods," she heard Allefaero exclaim above her, far too loudly for her comfort.

She looked up, caught his gaze, and put a finger over her pursed lips. Then she turned her attention to the floor, or rather, to the rounded top of an enormous crystal not far below. She stepped onto it and guided the wizard down beside her, then held him steady as the team far above, feeling the lessened weight, took up the slack on the silken rope.

"What did Jarlaxle call this?" Allefaero quietly asked.

"The breathless rooms."

"Without the magical protection, we would already be suffering," said the wizard. He went down to his knees, then put his hands on the crystal and bent his head lower, peering under the span of another nearby formation.

Galathae knew that they weren't alone in this place. She scanned all about, then asked Allefaero, "Anything?"

The wizard shook his head.

"Hold still," Galathae told him, and she dropped the lantern veil, stealing the light.

Several nearby glows before them cast shadows through the lines of crystals—and what was glowing was clearly moving.

Allefaero awkwardly and shakily climbed to his feet. "The light, the light!" he begged, and he launched into some arcane chanting.

Galathae did as requested and understood the wizard's urgency when a young polar worm crawled over a crystal not far away.

Then another to the side of the first, and a third trailing.

Galathae drew Bluccidere, but even with the protection from heat, the last thing the paladin wanted to do was engage a remorhaz—

striking them, even being near one, would expose her to enough heat to curl the flesh in severe burns.

She set her feet, took up her sword in both hands, and grimaced as even more of the monsters came into view.

Then came the flash, a tremendous burst of lightning flying forth from Allefaero's waggling fingers. The nearest remorhaz disappeared, blown away, taking the second with it, and the one to the side, though it held its footing, began shaking weirdly, clearly distressed.

Allefaero began casting again, but he stopped and gasped, and Galathae didn't have to ask him why, for she, too, saw the newcomer, not far behind the others, a gigantic, full-grown polar worm, some twenty feet long and thick enough to swallow an aevendrow whole!

Galathae stuffed her whistle between her lips and blew wildly, as did Allefaero.

On came the worms, and more and more of all sizes showed themselves, crawling about the crystals, coming for the intruders.

Up went Allefaero, and in came the nearest worm, the one wounded by the lightning bolt. It reared like a serpent, mandibles clacking, and swept forward in a strike.

Wisely, Galathae didn't hold her ground, falling back off the crystal to the end of the rope. Up she went, though, as those above continued their hauling, right back where she had been standing as the worm came even closer. She swept Bluccidere across desperately, her blade clicking off the worm's head and turning its attention—fortunately, as it was about to bite the rope!

Her hands burned from the strike, then from her second, third, and fourth stabs as she rose before the polar worm, up, up into the cavern, soon out of reach of that little one.

"Faster, faster," the paladin begged, for the adult remorhaz closed quickly. With shocking speed, it rushed to where she had been standing and reared up more than half its body length, small dragon-like wings beating furiously to help elevate its head, then snapped its mandibles high.

If Galathae hadn't instinctively tucked her legs under her, she'd have lost a foot, at least.

Up the two aevendrow went, higher and higher, then back into the shaft and higher still. Galathae pressed Bluccidere tight against her breast, clutching the hilt of her holy sword, left arm wrapped tight across the blade to lock it in place. Above her, she heard Allefaero whispering, words flying rapidly and seemingly nonsensically. He was just muttering, spouting fears and expressions of disbelief.

The paladin used that absurdity as a balm to calm herself. For all of his magical prowess—and the lightning bolt's strength left no doubt that he was powerful—this wizard had never known true battle.

Listening to him throughout that long ascent, Galathae got the feeling he never wanted to see battle again.

She didn't blame him.

The climb stopped a long while later, with Galathae still hanging in the shaft as those above pulled Allefaero to solid ground. Then up she went again, and felt the hands grabbing her. She tried to move about to help them, but took great care not to lose her precious sword.

When she got out and managed to sit up, she just sat quietly, letting the rambling Allefaero describe the monsters below to those gathered around. His clear and unabashed terror conveyed the truth of that crystal cavern more than her measured explanation could ever hope to do.

SEVERAL DAYS PASSED BEFORE GALATHAE ONCE AGAIN ENtered the long corridor leading to Cattisola, with Ilina and the wizard Allefaero beside her. The paladin's hands were still wrapped as her burns fully healed from her attacks on the polar worm. The priest's healing spells had greatly reduced the pain, but Ilina had advised her to keep the hands wrapped because her skin was still blistered and raw.

"I reminded the Temporal Convocation repeatedly that the warning of Jarlaxle had led us to this discovery," Galathae was saying, having already recounted her entire presentation to the congress to Ilina.

"She did," Allefaero agreed, as he had been there sitting beside her throughout the entire meeting.

"I will go to them tomorrow," Ilina said. "We are offering estimates of the number of polar worms we believe to be crawling about that chamber."

"Too many," Allefaero mumbled, and he shivered as if a cold wind had just blown through him.

Ilina smiled at that and tossed a wink at Galathae, the two of them quite enjoying the inexperienced wizard's first true encounter with a dangerous adversary.

"Two less because of your initial effort," Ilina replied to him. "We pulled the half-eaten corpses of a pair of juvenile remorhazes from the room. Clearly, the polar worms aren't particular in their diet and are not above cannibalism."

They heard a rumbling up ahead in the corridor, around a bend, and hurried to determine the source. A caravan, they discovered, mostly of dwarves and orcs, rolling huge capstan drums they had brought in from the tunnels north of Ardin.

Galathae was reminded of how critical this work in Cattisola would be to Callidae, since it appeared as if most of the city's miners were bringing their precious gear to the spot.

"We'll be carrying some crystals and crystal dust with us to address the congress," Ilina predicted. "We are retrieving some crystal bits from the chamber that have been broken and chewed by the polar worms. The visual of those broken bits will reinforce the warning. This was how Cattisola was lost, and we fight now and hold them back or all of Callidae will suffer the same fate, as Jarlaxle warned."

"Such a diabolical plan," Allefaero remarked. "The slaadi play the long game. If we hadn't been warned, would we have ever discerned why Qadeej was overrunning Callidae?"

"All of Callidae," Galathae agreed. "We know they were, and likely still are, breeding more and more of the beasts. We can expect that the encroachment of the glacier would only speed up as the monstrous ranks thickened and as those remorhazes already at their destructive work grew larger and stronger."

"It is fair to say, I think, that our guest from the south saved Callidae," Ilina said.

"You should tell that to the congress," Allefaero said.

"Repeatedly," the priestess agreed.

"It looks as if you're moving most of our mining equipment," Galathae said to a dwarf when they caught up to the caravan. She said it lightly, but the dwarf looked at her with a most serious expression.

"All of it."

Galathae slowed and fell back in line at the rear of the caravan with her friends. "You heard him?"

"Apparently the congress took your presentation to heart," Allefaero said.

They came into Cattisola soon after, to find many shafts under construction, with capstans already in place at most. The whole of the chamber bristled with activity, buckets coming up from every shaft, ropes hauling, mounds of soil and rocks growing. Off to the side, a squadron of aevendrow and dwarves practiced their coordinated movements, forming a line, aiming wands, and pretending to throw lightning bolts one after another.

The three friends meandered about, stunned and pleased by the amount of work that had already been completed. The first shaft had been widened considerably, all the way down to the crystal room, one orc explained to them, and now had three separate rope systems to feed into it, each set with three harnesses. They intended to stagger the drop and get nine wand-wielders into the chamber together in short order.

Over beside the ice pile lay several remorhaz bodies. A group of aevendrow poked about at them, then began stringing them onto long poles so that they could be carried away.

"Their glands can be distilled into powerful potions," Allefaero explained.

"The meat is tough, but tasty," said Galathae.

The other two looked at her curiously.

"Out on the ice pack, one cannot always be selective," the paladin explained. "Yes, I have eaten remorhaz—some parts cook themselves if you fold them properly immediately following a kill."

"I'm sure Ayeeda will come up with something to accompany it in a fine presentation," said Ilina.

"Oh, there they go," Allefaero said, pointing past Galathae, and the two women turned to see the dwarves and aevendrow harnessing up at the main shaft.

Quickly and efficiently, they began their descent, the haulers verily running before the push poles, letting the strike team fall down the shaft much more quickly than Galathae and Allefaero had descended, so it seemed to the two.

The three friends moved nearer but stayed safely back, not wanting to distract any in this precise operation.

Galathae gripped her sword. Ilina began preparing healing spells, just in case.

The ground began to rumble, sharp retorts echoing from far below. A scream emanated from the shaft, but it was clearly not the type of sound that might come from a dwarf or aevendrow.

"One less beastie," said an orc walking by the three friends.

The subterranean explosions of lightning continued, nine retorts five separate times.

After that fifth barrage, the commander of the surface group spun her finger in the air and the haulers began swiftly marching, turning the capstan drums to rewind the rope and retrieve the strike force. Up they came, crawling out one after another, nodding and clapping.

The last dwarf out carried a heavy rope, which she had been letting out below her in her ascent.

"Three dead monsters," she told the commander. "Last one's a big one. Real big." She handed the rope to an orc hauler. "Won't fit up any shaft but this one."

The capstan teams went quickly to work, securing the remaining length of rope on one of the drums. Then the haulers doubled up and put their backs into it, trying to get the contraption turning. They weren't going nearly as fast this time. One hauler after another fell off to the side, to be replaced by a fresh body. Across the way, an orc drummed out a slow cadence, the beats urging the team on in coordinated, steady fashion.

And when the remorhaz finally appeared, then came up to the rigging set above the hole, the three friends and everyone else in the room understood and appreciated the effort, for the hooked head of the beast was truly enormous, with mandibles as long as an aevendrow was tall and as thick as a dwarf. The head was nearly ten feet up above the shaft entry, and less than half the remorhaz was visible.

"Wasn't the biggest one down there, either," said a dwarf as he walked by the gawking threesome.

"We're in for a long fight here," Galathae told her companions.

"Allefaero will go down there and clean them out," Ilina replied with a wink.

The young wizard looked as if he might fall over.

GALATHAE FOUND HERSELF STRANGELY NERVOUS AS SHE approached the Chamber of War in the Siglig. Certainly, the room was not often used, reserved for immediate threats to the city itself and only when such threats required a great mobilization for response. She hadn't been surprised when summoned by the mona for this meeting, of course, for she had seen for herself the sheer amount of effort being put into the troubles beneath Cattisola. A council of war was clearly called for.

Her steps came hesitantly. She felt a bit of sweat on her brow.

She looked out the corridor's wide windows at the Merry Dancers, swirling in the open sky above, and she nodded, admitting to herself the cause of her unease.

The last council of war had sent the original exploratory expedition to the caverns beneath the frost giant fortress, the same expedition Galathae had led to the disaster that had precipitated the doomed rescue attempt by the strangers from the south. The pain filled her, having been so obviously reiterated with the loss of Azzudonna and three of the visitors.

She reached the door and forced herself not to hesitate, pushing through.

"Ah, good, we are all arrived," Mona Valrissa greeted her.

"Am I tardy?"

"No, of course not."

"All of the others were already in Mona Chess when the meeting was announced," Alviss of B'shett explained. "Indeed, all five of the borough representatives were meeting with Mona Valrissa when the council of war was agreed upon."

"It is an urgent one, then," Galathae presumed, taking her seat at the near end of the table, opposite the mona's chair. The five representatives sat along the side to the right of her at the long and narrow table, with only a single clerk on the left side, seated right beside the mona. The other seats on that side were for invited speakers, usually experts and scouts. Most often, those chairs were occupied by Burnook oroks—or Kanaq or some other dwarf from the city's main entry hall of Cascatte.

"We're not sure of the urgency," Mona Valrissa replied. "Certainly, the fighting in Cattisola will not soon end."

"We must hope it will not," said Alviss, drawing a surprised look from Galathae.

"What information am I missing here?" the paladin asked. She noted several of the others exchanging concerned glances then. Galathae hadn't been in Cattisola in a few days, not since her trip with Ilina and Allefaero, and she had gone down below the chamber and into the crystal caverns only that one time.

"Cattisola is a large borough," said Haveloisia, an old aevendrow who lived now in Scellobel but had been, and still was, the leading member of the Cattisola delegation in the Temporal Convocation. That delegation had diminished greatly in membership now, but it still remained, and retained a full seat at the various committee councils. "Nearly as large as Scellobel."

"Yes, of course," Galathae politely replied to the elder and much-respected representative. She had known Hahvy, as Haveloisia was commonly called, for many years.

"We cannot easily dig shafts down to any area but the eastern-most, the entryway," Hahvy explained.

"Of course." Galathae honestly wondered for a moment if the old woman might be showing the mind confusion that sometimes manifested in the last decades of an aevendrow life.

Hahvy's returned smile told Galathae that Hahvy had caught on to her concern.

"No one can remain in that underchamber beneath Cattisola for any length of time," Hahvy clarified. "You know that, *of course*."

"So, how're we to fight the durned worms that ain't in the borough's east?" Alviss interjected.

"How large is the subchamber?" Galathae asked. "Even with our light and the flash of lightning bolts, it was hard to determine."

"That chamber of crystals is why Cattisola existed," Mona Valrissa reminded her. "We expect that it mirrors the dimensions of the entire borough."

In the press of recent events and the shock of finding the remorhazes, Galathae had hardly considered that obvious truth, or the implications of it.

"Similar chambers are why all of Callidae exists, we now believe," Mona Valrissa continued. "And the River Callidae and the connecting tunnels. If all of the chamber beneath Cattisola is filled with giant crystals . . ."

"Then that cavern beneath it is miles deep and wide," Galathae finished.

"Yes," said Hahvy, "and we know that not all of the crystals even far to the west have already been consumed. A wizard's magical eye and priestly divination have confirmed it."

"Thus, the polar worms remain thick even far in the west, beyond the reach of our strike teams," said Galathae.

"Unless we start sending many priests along with them," Mona Valrissa confirmed. "And we untether them once they're down. I need not tell you the danger of that."

No, she certainly did not, Galathae thought. Wandering into that chamber without a sudden escape available back up the shafts was no expedition she would care to lead, as it was almost certainly destined to end in tragedy. She looked hard at Mona Valrissa, expecting the woman to order exactly that.

Instead, though, Mona Valrissa turned to her right and called out, "Wizard!"

A door to the side of the chamber opened and, to Galathae's shock, Allefaero entered and took the seat immediately to her left.

"I did not expect to see you here," she said as he settled, putting a stack of parchments and large books on the table before him.

"Allefaero is Callidae's foremost expert regarding remorhazes," Mona Valrissa explained, eliciting an arched eyebrow from Galathae.

"I didn't know that you had ever left Callidae," Galathae said to the young man.

"I haven't . . . well, other than to the rink above for cazzcalci, of course. I mean, I've seen a few of the battles . . . I mean."

"Then where have you previously encountered polar worms?"

"I've never seen one . . . I mean, never a living one, at least not before you and I went down into that cursed chamber."

Galathae turned her doubting expression over Mona Valrissa and the representatives.

"They are in here," Allefaero blurted, grabbing at the books. "These are all about Callidae, when our people first arrived in the ice canyons under the Merry Dancers. Remorhazes were the greatest threat in those early days, and our ancestors battled them continually for many years. Ardin was the last settled borough, you know, and only because . . . well, the bard Amiciferus Obbleivieri described the battles in the 'most fertile canyon,' some hundred years after construction had begun on the Siglig. But of course, they had to win out in that fight, and not only because of the potential of Ardin's bounty, but, as the historian Beladaeeva, who was the thirteenth . . . no, fourteenth mona, also explained, Ardin provided the best opportunities to get out under the sea ice to gather the very best blue—"

Allefaero was thumbing through an ancient book as he rambled, and he kept going for a long, long while. He held up the book to show the others some text and sketches, and finally looked back to Galathae, to see her staring at him, mouth agape.

"Yes, well, you see that I have read almost everything ever recorded by our predecessors regarding the remorhazes," Allefaero said, obviously embarrassed. "I find the polar worms quite fascinating."

"And, when it's not a sketch or a dead one, quite terrifying," Galathae replied with a wink.

That brought a smile to the wizard's face, but a short-lived one as he realized she was mocking him here.

"Yes," he admitted, and lowered his eyes.

"And yet," Galathae said, then addressing the entire council, "when we faced the polar worms, Allefaero here showed himself admirably. I do not believe I have ever witnessed a more impressive lightning bolt in my many years of battle."

"Now you understand why we sent him down that hole behind you," Mona Valrissa explained. "He is powerful not only with magical evocation but with knowledge as well. Do tell Holy Galathae what you explained to me regarding the ecology of the polar worms, Allefaero. Explain to her how they eat and reproduce."

"Sometimes both," the wizard said in an attempt at a joke. He cleared his throat before an audience of six grim expressions. "They eat their young," he explained to Galathae.

"Good."

"Well, some of their young, and they have many at a time. Litters of dozens have been recorded."

"There isn't likely much food in that chamber other than their young, I suppose."

"There may be," said Allefaero. "We landed on a crystal, but the floor might well have been far, far below us. Even with the stifling air and the heat, I would not be surprised to find quite a large variety of animals and monsters lower down in the chamber. But it doesn't matter anyway. Remorhazes are voracious. They'll eat anything they can break apart, as you can see with the damage they're doing to the crystals."

"Some arktos oroks brought up a huge broken crystal," Mona Valrissa added. "The bite marks were quite extraordinary."

"Aye, the durned squigglers bit huge chunks out o' them," Alviss agreed. "Won't be much left if we can't clear the vile beasties out!"

Hahvy sighed heavily.

"But they don't have to eat," Allefaero excitedly explained

when Mona Valrissa had hushed Alviss and bade him continue. "If Amiciferus Obbleivieri is to be believed—and the third-century in-ugaakalikurit scholar Minik Kikakik seems to confirm . . ." He reached for a different tome, shuffling through it, then another, a pole of parchments, and a third book, before Mona Valrissa refocused him.

"Just *tell* her, please, master Allefaero," she said.

"Of course; my apologies," the nervous young wizard replied. "It is not often that I get to talk about—"

"Please?" Mona Valrissa asked, and Allefaero cleared his throat.

"They don't have to eat," he said directly to Galathae. "Not often, at least. They grow as they age even if they go decades without a meal. There is one other scourge that shares similar dietary . . . freedoms."

"Dragons," Galathae said, and the wizard nodded.

"The polar worms are perhaps a distant relative of dragons," Allefaero said.

"They do not need to eat, but they chew crystals?" Galathae asked them all.

"They seem to take pleasure in that," Allefaero said. "Perhaps for nutrition, perhaps to sharpen the edges of their mandibles, but certainly some manner of pleasure, or training. You saw them."

Galathae had indeed, and she understood that this war with the polar worms was going to be far more difficult than she had first believed. "Pleasure? Training? Why would you think that?"

"Their ecology is one of devouring. They are at true rest when eating, so the scholars say—they have even been known to make noises akin to a cat's purr . . . And they train their teeth, of course, like a rodent burrowing through wood. It is pleasurable and it is practical. I can think of no creatures more perfectly designed to suit their purpose, if that is the proper word, in life. Like the great sharks who swim and eat, procreate and swim and eat. So, too, with the polar worms."

Galathae tried to work through all the implications of that. If Allefaero was correct . . .

"Their numbers will only increase, as will their size," the wizard warned them all, as if reading her mind. "The destruction of the subterranean crystal caves will accelerate. Perhaps there are polar worms lurking beneath other boroughs, perhaps even under the Siglig as we sit here."

"For us to search it all out is a daunting task," said Galathae.

"An impossible task," Mona Valrissa agreed.

"We have to fight them there in the eastern reaches of Cattisola," Galathae suggested. "Perhaps we begin other teams chipping away at the vast ice pile, and removing all they can in the borough so that we can dig shafts farther into the canyon."

Mona Valrissa was shaking her head. "That wouldn't matter, though. We need to find a way for our strike teams to remain down there for longer periods of time. Much longer. I have the wizards, priests, and alchemists researching such possibilities as we speak."

"That is good," Galathae replied, but in her mind, she didn't think it that good at all. She had been in that chamber and had felt the stifling, damaging heat through all the magical protections Ilina and others had cast upon her. The aevendrow were experts at battling the extreme cold, but excruciating heat?

Not so much.

CHAPTER 26

Curiosity Killed the . . .

The sun was high above when the dragons began an unexpected descent the next day.

As they glided lower and slowed greatly, Drizzt, shaking his head, yelled out to Kane for some explanation. The drow certainly recognized the area now, for they were almost directly south of Longsaddle. If the dragons had climbed high enough, Drizzt was fairly certain that he could have seen the Sword Coast. On the ground, they were still a long walk or ride to Luskan, but he thought that the dragons could make the city before twilight, or before twilight turned to night, at least.

"Why?" he asked when they were down to the ground, an open series of bare hillocks lightly dusted with snow. He leaped from Ilnezhara's back, moving to Kane as the monk calmly descended from Tazmikella. "Are we not meeting the others at the Hosttower?"

"We are."

"Are you fearful of the dragon sisters showing themselves in the sky above Luskan? Stranger beasts than they have landed at the gates of the Hosttower!"

"He called us strange, sister," Ilnezhara remarked, transforming out of her dragon form.

"And beastly," said Tazmikella, similarly beginning her transformation.

"He is a feisty one!" Ilnezhara exclaimed. "I do quite like that. How about you, sister?"

"I believe I haven't tasted drow in many years," Tazmikella replied. "It is quite delicious, if I remember it correctly. Perhaps we should let the fool keep talking."

Drizzt looked from one to the other, then turned back to Kane, narrowing his vision, focusing only on the man as if to give the sisters some privacy as they became human women—at least until they could don their robes.

"Perhaps you're correct, sister," he heard Ilnezhara say behind him. "For all of Drizzt Do'Urden's heroic swordplay and derring-do, he does seem a bit too modest . . . no, boring, for my tastes."

"For some tastes," agreed Tazmikella. "With proper condiments, drow flesh can be quite spicy."

"Hmm," they both said together.

"Why have we landed?" Drizzt asked Kane directly, trying to block out the distraction of the playful murderers. "The Hosttower is within our reach."

"We are landed because I asked the sisters to set us down in this very place," Grandmaster Kane replied.

"We will walk, or ride, from here to Luskan?"

"No, no. They will fly us shortly to join with our adventuring party."

Drizzt shook his head and just shrugged in confusion.

"There is one last fight," Kane explained.

"But why? You said that I had mastered the harmony and pushed through the problem. Was I not alone in yesterday's battle?"

"You were, and you have, yes to both," Kane explained. "I am not sure that I have anything left to teach you, Drizzt Do'Urden. You have mastered transcendence and your fighting skills are above reproach. There is more you will learn, but these are things that you will need to discover on your own, and incorporate into your life force, whether in fighting style, or mystical revelations, or simply in how you come to view the world. This future growth is yours to find, and yours alone."

"After one last fight," Drizzt said, perplexed.

"Before," Kane corrected. "This fight isn't for you."

"For them?" Drizzt asked in surprise, looking at the sisters.

"No," said Kane.

"Then what?"

"Before I explain, I desire something from you. A favor. Two favors, actually."

"I am more in your debt than almost anyone I know," said Drizzt. "You need merely ask, of course."

"Promise me that you will not return to the monastery and challenge Mistress of Winter Savahn in her ascent," said Kane.

Drizzt started with surprise and for a moment felt as if a slight breeze might have knocked him over. He had never imagined doing any such thing. "Her ascent?"

"To become the Grandmaster of Flowers," Kane explained. "Savahn is extraordinary, but she is not young. With the passing on of Master Afafrenfere, her path to the pinnacle of the Order of St. Sollars is soon enough clear, as it should be. Master of Spring Perrywinkle Shin is even now taking his vows to serve as Grandmaster of Flowers, but that will be but a temporary thing. He is an old man, and unlike me, he has no desire to extend his tenure in this existence. I envy him his contentment!"

"He will become Grandmaster of Flowers while you are away with us, you mean," Drizzt stated.

Kane shook his head. "I have relinquished the title altogether. It is time."

"Grandmaster Kane," Drizzt murmured.

"Grandmaster no more." The monk shrugged and Drizzt could see clearly that his smile was warm, content, and sincere. Kane was at peace. Drizzt wanted to argue. He thought the monastery and the world were better off for having Kane as its Grandmaster of Flowers.

But it didn't really matter what he thought, he recognized and understood in looking at the expression worn by the old monk. Kane was at peace in this moment, and it was a peace well deserved indeed.

"You are still coming on the journey to the north?"

"Of course! Perhaps it is exactly this opportunity that has shown me that I am no longer content in wiping the snot off the faces of students at a quiet monastery!"

That brought a laugh from Drizzt, which Kane joined.

"Grandmaster Perrywinkle is a fine leader and will serve the Order well," Kane said. "He won't be internally challenged—not now, at least, for there are more pressing matters before the brothers and sisters. But, as I noted, neither will he remain in his post for long. Mistress Savahn will almost surely be next—there are none left who could begin to challenge her in single combat."

"So—"

"None except for Drizzt Do'Urden," Kane finished, staring hard at the drow. "And I ask that you do not do that. You have been a fine student, a fine friend, and a finer ally. But you are not of the Order of St. Sollars the Twice-Martyred, and though you are forever welcome at the Monastery of the Yellow Rose, it is not and never will be your home. So, I ask you for your promise that you will not challenge Savahn when the time comes, and that you will instead support her and be a friend and ally to her as you have been to me."

Drizzt took a moment to recall the images of Savahn playing with Brie, his smile widening throughout the memories.

"That is perhaps the easiest favor that has ever been asked of me," he told Kane. "It is, of course, what I would do even had you not requested it."

Kane nodded.

"Then we should take back to the skies?" Drizzt asked.

"I said two favors."

"Ah, yes. I am to battle the dragon sisters once again?"

Kane slowly shook his head.

Drizzt cocked his head to the side. "What?"

"Remove all of your magical gear," Kane explained. "Strip down to your least garments."

Drizzt didn't move.

"The second favor," said Kane. "We will fight as monks, with our bodies alone."

"Fight against who? *Each other?*"

Kane, the former Grandmaster of Flowers of the Monastery of the Yellow Rose, wore a most wicked smile.

"OO OI!" PIKEL BOULDERSHOULDER SAID FOR THE TENTH time, and he pumped his stumped arm up into the sky with enthusiasm.

"Bah, but ye're not tellin' me all, are ye?" Ivan Bouldershoulder asked Regis, who had come to Bleeding Vines bearing the invitation for Pikel to join the expedition to the north.

"I am," Regis insisted. "That is all I know. The three who went with Jarlaxle are trapped and need our help. Catti-brie needs our help!"

"Bwee bwee," Pikel said, and giggled. "Hehehe."

"And ye'd take me brother—"

"Me brudder!" Pikel roared.

Ivan blew a sigh of exasperation. "Ye'd take me brother—"

"Me brudder!" Pikel yelled before Ivan could stop him.

Another sigh.

"And ye'd take him . . ." Ivan paused and shot a glare at Pikel.

"Oooo."

"But ye won't take meself? Bah!"

"Were it up to me, I'd take the both of you, and Pwent and Athrogate as well," Regis told him. "But this is not my expedition, nor King Bruenor's. Jarlaxle determined the team he would have around him, and gave Bruenor few options."

"Bwuenor and Bwee!" said Pikel. "Hehehe."

Regis turned a concerned look from Pikel to Ivan.

"The older he's gettin', the more he's actin' like me brother from when we were dwarflings," Ivan explained.

"Me brudder!" roared Pikel.

Regis suddenly found himself rethinking the entire expedition. He even briefly considered going back to Bruenor and Jarlaxle and advising them to replace Pikel in the ranks.

"He's still got his spells," Ivan assured him, as if reading the halfling's mind. "Spells from the old time. And for all the silliness ye're hearin' now, me brother . . ." He paused and glared at Pikel, as if daring him to echo the phrase. "Me brother seems all the stronger with them spells every year."

"Me brudder!" Pikel howled, and at Ivan's growl, he added, "Hehehe."

"We need him to protect us from the winter's frozen breath," said Regis.

"Aye, he can do that for ye, and more," Ivan said. "Ye'd think it a spring breeze and nothin' much. Seen it meself more'n once in the years we spent in Damara."

"You can do it, Pikel?" Regis asked.

"Hehehe," the green-bearded dwarf said, nodding so hard that his lips flapped through the response.

"I'm not happy seein' ye go without me, and happy less that ye're taking Pikel along," Ivan grumbled. He started to say more, but choked up and plopped his hand on Pikel's rounded shoulder. "We been through a lot, but a lot together and little alone, if ye get me meanin'."

"I do, and I completely understand. We would never have asked if there was another way, or a way to take you as well. But this is for Catti-brie."

"Yerself could stay and I could go," Ivan noted.

"This is for Catti-brie," Regis restated. "I would never stay behind, no more than you would if we were going to rescue your bro—" He glanced over and saw the sparkle in Pikel's eyes. "To rescue Pikel," he finished.

"Oooo," a clearly disappointed Pikel whined.

"Aye, I'm hearin' ye. But ye promise me, Rumblebelly. Ye promise me that ye'll throw yerself in the path of a ballista bolt flying for Pikel!"

"It would then just take the both of us, I expect," Regis said with a wry grin. "Would you settle for a crossbow bolt?"

"All kiddin' left for dwarflings. Ye promise me, Rumblebelly, ye promise me now, that ye'll keep me brother safe."

"Me brudder!" a happy Pikel boomed.

"Of course I will," said Regis, and he threw a wink Pikel's way as he added, "as if he was me own brudder!"

"Me brudder!" yelled Pikel.

The three of them laughed, but Ivan sobered quickly and offered a grateful nod to Regis, whom he trusted dearly. He turned his head curiously then and noted the hand crossbow hanging across Regis's chest.

"Ye said there were monsters up there like a walkin' block o' ice, eh?" Ivan asked.

"That's what Jarlaxle told me, yes."

Ivan held up a stubby finger, then trotted off to the back of the small room and began fishing through a large wooden chest. He returned a few moments later bearing a small box, which he held up before the halfling and slowly opened.

It was full of hand-crossbow quarrels, but not any mundane bolts. Regis had seen similar quarrels before. The priest Cadderly had invented them and had used them to great effect, and Ivan had carried on the practice—and had even requested that Regis, a skilled alchemist, supply the needed potion. The bolts were of normal size, but the centers were open, with just a trio of narrow metal strips connecting front to back. Snapped in between those strips, the bolts would hold tiny vials that contained the desired clear liquid, an explosive brew known as oil of impact. When the bolt struck a target, it would collapse in on itself, the sudden shock setting off the fluid.

"Got a couple dozen," Ivan explained, handing the box over, then rushing back for a second one. "Use 'em. Use 'em all if it'll keep yerself and Pikel safe."

Regis nodded with true gratitude. He hadn't even thought of these darts—he hadn't seen them in a long time—and when he had insisted on going along to the north, he had truly wondered if his regular weapons, whether the typical nonmagical quarrels for his hand crossbow or his rapier or his dirk, would prove to be of any real effect against the types of monsters Jarlaxle had described. These, though, gave him a lot more confidence.

"Ye keep him safe and bring him back to me," Ivan said again, gently placing the second box of bolts atop the first that Regis was holding.

"On my life," Regis promised.

"I believe ye, Rumblebelly. I believe ye."

"Come along, Pikel," the halfling said. "We've a tram to catch to Gauntlgrym and a portal waiting to take us to the Hosttower of the Arcane."

"Oo oi!" Pikel yelled, pumping his stumped arm, and he leaped over and wrapped Ivan in a great hug. Then he rushed to the side of the room and grabbed up a magical cudgel, shouting, "Sha-la-la!"

He hoisted a huge pack, dropped it back down, and fished about in it, finally producing a cooking pot, which he plopped atop his green-haired head with the handle sticking out to the side. He skipped back to the other two, going right past them, catching Regis with his good hand, and pulling the halfling along.

Before they left the modest cottage, though, Pikel stopped again and cast a spell, drawing a large set of what looked somewhat like a pair of red lips in the air, where they hung and seemed to pucker.

As Regis watched with amazement, Ivan groaned, and Pikel cast a second spell, a gust of wind that sent the lips flying back across the room to smack Ivan in the face so hard that the tough old dwarf staggered back three steps.

"Me brudder!" Pikel roared.

"Me brudder!" Ivan roared back, failing miserably as he tried to seem more perturbed than sad, as Regis and Pikel left the house.

"WHY?" DRIZZT ASKED AS KANE BEGAN STRETCHING AND removing his extraneous clothing and gear.

"Are you not curious, Drizzt Do'Urden? Don't you want to know?"

"Know what?"

"Who would win."

"No," Drizzt blurted, but he realized it was a lie as soon as he said it. His mind went back to his early days with Artemis Entreri, when they had been avowed enemies. Throughout many years, the assassin remained obsessed with battling Drizzt—Entreri clutched a self-destructive need to prove himself better than Drizzt. The drow had called him out on that unhealthy fixation, even after he had come to understand that Entreri needed to prove he was the better fighter because the mere existence of Drizzt was giving lie to Entreri's entire way of life. How could anyone fight as well as Artemis Entreri without possessing the inner rage that consumed the man?

Surely, though, such could not be the case with Kane!

Drizzt tried to dismiss the comparison, which seemed absurd on the surface.

"Now that I have your promise never to unseat Savahn, I am not afraid to let you see your true skills as measured against a former Grandmaster of Flowers," Kane explained.

"You claim to do this as a favor to me?"

"No," Kane stated flatly. "I do this because I am curious. I have never trained anyone with your particular combination of skills and your natural martial ability. Your third fight with the dragons was a thing of beauty to behold, a better row than the one in which I participated."

"I don't want to fight you," Drizzt said, but he knew that, too, to be untrue. He had only said it out of deference and respect for the old monk. Privately, Drizzt couldn't deny the curiosity.

"Oh, you really don't," Tazmikella agreed.

"Oh no, dear sister," purred Ilnezhara. "I think the drow has a dancer's chance."

"A bet, then, sister!" Tazmikella said. "If Drizzt wins, you may take him for your own physical . . . competition. If Kane wins, I'll eat the drow!"

"Splendid!" Ilnezhara agreed.

"They're joking," Drizzt told Kane as the two walked away toward a flat and open bit of ground, and he certainly hoped he was correct.

"One never knows with dragons," the monk replied.

"YOU HAVE THOUGHT THIS THROUGH?" KIMMURIEL ASKED
Jarlaxle that blustery morning outside the Hosttower of the Arcane.
The wind whipped across from the ocean, breakers slamming the
rocks all about the coast, the spray flying far and wide to wet the faces
and cloaks of the two drow. Not far from them stood Dab'nay with Azzudonna, Bruenor, and Wulfgar, while Gromph remained inside the
tower awaiting the arrival of Regis and Pikel.

"I don't see a choice before me," Jarlaxle replied. "We will need the
power of the archmage in that chamber, I don't doubt."

"Even with the others you've assembled?"

"His spells will keep the cante and n'divi away while we free the
prisoners, and if the giant slaad returns, we'll all be glad that Gromph
Baenre is there to confront him."

"The one you think Ygorl?"

Jarlaxle nodded.

"But can Gromph be trusted beyond that fight?" Kimmuriel asked.
"He could well reveal those you are determined not to betray."

"He won't."

Kimmuriel didn't respond, but Jarlaxle could see that he was not
convinced.

"It is what Gromph has wanted for most of his life, as with most
of us," Jarlaxle said. "Only he is too proud to admit it. When the civil
war in Menzoberranzan explodes, do you have any doubt as to which
side Gromph will support?"

"I think he'll stay out of it and congratulate the winner."

Jarlaxle shook his head. "He threw the lever in the Hosttower to
return the magical powers to Gauntlgrym in their time of need. He
chose his side in that moment."

"He reversed his own actions to remove his influence from the
battle," Kimmuriel corrected, but again Jarlaxle shook his head.

"The yochlols personally instructed him to shut down the flow
of power. In reversing that, he openly defied Lolth's own handmaidens."

"We do not even know Lolth's ultimate play in all of that," Kimmuriel reminded him. "Beyond chaos and strife, I mean."

"But we know Gromph's choice."

"You're taking a great risk."

"I don't think so. Not with him or you or Drizzt or Dab'nay."

"Just us, then?"

"Yes. Or those of us among that select group who manage to survive." Even as he said it, Jarlaxle was thinking he might amend his choice, though, for there was one other who might prove quite valuable.

Kimmuriel said no more and Jarlaxle pulled his cloak tight about him, and tugged down the brim of his great hat. Behind them, Gromph came out of the Hosttower, Regis and Pikel in tow.

Jarlaxle looked to the eastern sky. He had thought that the dragons and their riders would have arrived by now.

THE SUDDEN EXPLOSION OF STRIKING, PUNCHING, KICK-ing, flipping, leaping, and spinning elicited repeated gasps from Ilnezhara and Tazmikella as they watched the fight from the side. The combatants moved in a blur, reversing their positions with every other step, one leaping, the other rolling, then both turning about to engage in a brutal flurry once more.

At one point, Drizzt spun left in a circle kick at exactly the same moment Kane executed a mirror attack, both of them far wide of the moving mark. Each came down in a wide split, going right down to the ground with legs out wide, and each lifted right back out of the drop as if pulled by a string, turning right into a reverse circle kick to bring their legs crashing together.

The two men threw themselves into each other, grappling, punching, neither falling into a roll taking them out of range. Such a blur of motion that the dragon sisters couldn't tell where one combatant ended and the other began!

"Perhaps they will meld," Ilnezhara offered. "Two crashing together to become one, and we will have a new species. I will name it a druman!"

"I don't think it quite works that way, sister," Tazmikella replied.

"And as well, haven't Drizzt and Catti-brie already created your new being?"

"Ah," Ilnezhara replied, then both women winced and half turned away, chorusing "Ooh" as a stunning kick got past the defenses to snap a head back viciously.

"He is still up!" Tazmikella cried, seeing the victim return a brutal and continuing flurry—no doubt to keep the other at bay while the birds stopped tweeting between his ears.

In mere eyeblinks, the opponents were squared up once more, the wild and vicious barrage resuming with even more ferocity.

The heads of the sisters moved in unison, left, right, up, and down, both keeping a close eye on the fast-flowing battle. But then both stopped the movements with a start of surprise as the fighters across the field suddenly broke apart and stood facing each other, mimicking each other's motion as they clenched their fists in front of their chest, then slowly lowered and retracted their arms before thrusting their palms forward as if throwing some invisible missile at the other, coming to a point where their fingers brushed.

Then they each stood in place, and both began trembling and swaying, both grimacing clearly.

"Oh, sister, I believe this is the Way of the Open Hand!" Tazmikella exclaimed.

"Quivering!" Ilnezhara agreed. "I hope they do not kill each other! Have you studied the healer's kits as Grandmaster Kane bade us?"

She cut the question short as both fighters pointed at each other, then clenched their fists, halting the vibrations in the other, and both cried out in pain, with Drizzt even falling to one knee and Kane stumbling back several strides.

"Splendid!" Tazmikella cried, slapping her hands together.

The combatants seemed to fly, great leaps throwing them together once more for a continuing barrage of punches, kicks, even a head butt that sent a resounding retort across the field, followed by mutual grappling that led to mutual rolling about on the ground, every turn leaving bloody stains in the white snow.

Tazmikella shook her head, fast losing her enthusiasm. "They are such silly creatures," she said. "Sometimes I think the red-scaled wyrms have it correct with these mortals. Cook them and eat them in the same breath."

"I find them rather entertaining," Ilnezhara disagreed, her wicked grin beaming.

"Does Jarlaxle wrestle you so?"

"Are you jealous?"

Tazmikella looked back at the field and snorted derisively. "I would be sorrily disappointed if that was the best he could do in our . . . sparring."

Both laughed, then both again winced and shuddered.

"That punch truly hurt," Tazmikella said.

"Come, sister," Ilnezhara agreed, "and do bring the healing kits Kane gave to you."

CHAPTER 27

And We Sent Him Away

Galathae's lead line back to the main rope was quite long this time, allowing her to move much deeper into the vast cavern of crystals below Cattisola. Five strike teams of ten were down there now at the same time, combinations of wizards and priests, mostly, but with a few supporting fighters, particularly paladins, like Galathae.

Magical lighting had been created everywhere, reflecting off the crystals in every direction in a dazzling myriad of colors, and, of course, lightning bolts brightened it all every few moments, thunderous roars shaking the huge crystals beneath the feet of the fifty Callidaeans. Like the other warriors in the teams, Galathae had her shield strapped high on her arm, but she kept Bluccidere sheathed. Her main duty, she came to realize, was to haul up dangling team members who stumbled off the crystals, or to begin triage and healing any wounded members, and to carry them back to the extra guide rope by the main line beneath the shaft for quick extraction if necessary.

She had already done that twice, her team now down to only eight battling members.

And still, that team was the most intact of the five currently in the crystal-filled chamber. Polar worms were not stupid creatures— Galathae recalled Allefaero's remarks that they might be related to dragons—and were not coming at the teams in clear view, as in the earlier encounters. No, they were mostly running under the crystals with their sticky footpads, getting near enough for a quick and devastating strike before a lightning bolt blew them from the battle.

She saw that very thing now, off to the side, a juvenile remorhaz scrambling along the underside of a crystal and bearing down on a pair of priests who stood atop the natural beam.

Up leaped the paladin, wrapping her arms about that higher crystal. She called out to the priests, but several thunderous retorts sounded at precisely that moment and they didn't seem to hear. She tugged herself up to the top and kneeled, lifting her arms and waving wildly at the pair. Then, when they at last took note of her, Galathae pointed down to indicate the approaching remorhaz, then waved for them to run to her, yelling for them to hurry.

She started to climb to her feet, but changed her mind, as the crystal beam was not so wide, and instead turned sideways on it, fully prone and instructing the approaching priests to step over her and keep going.

By the time the second did so, the polar worm had come up to the top of the crystal. Its small dragon wings beat furiously, lifting its head up high above the paladin.

Galathae went up to her knees, then fell to a sitting position, legs gripping the crystal beam as if she were riding a fat horse. She threw her shield arm up before her as the remorhaz struck. She felt the heavy impact and went sliding backward under the weight of it, but she kept her legs about the crystal enough to hold her seat.

It took her some time to manage to draw Bluccidere, though, and to her surprise and horror, the polar worm didn't let go, instead clamping hard and thrashing its head about.

Galathae felt an explosion of hot pain as her left shoulder popped out of place, and she feared that she would be thrown from the crystal, or that her arm would simply be torn off! This was not a large worm, barely ten feet long, but the strength of the monster could not be denied.

She had no choice, and was glad of the design of her precious holy sword then, which she herself had fashioned. For one of the arms of Bluccidere's crosspiece was bladed and quite sharp, and she hooked that against a shield strap below her flailing left arm and thrust the blade skyward. She severed that strap and nearly the second one, as well, though she inadvertently gashed her arm in the process. Waves of pain swept through her from that shoulder as the worm continued to thrash, but Galathae managed to bite and growl the pain away enough to angle the arm and extract it fully from the shield.

The remorhaz continued to flail, now wider to each side since Galathae was no longer resisting. It took the beast a few more swings to apparently realize that the prey on the other side of that buckler had broken free, and by that time, Galathae had managed to creep nearer and align Bluccidere.

The shield went flying, the remorhaz's clacking mandibles came back to center and opened wide—just enough for Galathae to stab right between them, into the mouth of the polar worm, into the soft flesh beneath the creature's hard carapace. As she felt her sword sink in, the paladin called on the power of her god to divinely smite the beast.

The remorhaz retracted its head quickly, back and up high, wings beating wildly now, desperately. But the brutally wounded beast couldn't steady itself and leaned weirdly to Galathae's right for a long, long moment, before tumbling from the crystal and crashing to the one below, then rolling about that and falling again, bouncing and flopping lower and lower until out of sight.

Galathae slapped her sword hand down to the crystal, bracing herself against the pain from her left shoulder and the newest injury, a severe burn on her right forearm from the furnace-like heat of the polar worm. Her sleeve had burned away, her skin bright red and already blistering. But she had to ignore the pain, for her left arm was almost useless and she had to keep it tucked in close.

She closed her eyes for just a moment, trying to settle herself, to find her calm and her balance, but even in that darkness, Galathae couldn't block out the escalating sounds all about her: lightning, bolts, cries for retreat, screams of pain, hissing roars of the polar worms.

She pulled her left leg under her, balanced on it and her right hand, and forced herself up to her feet.

"We have to leave!" called a priestess somewhere behind her, and she recognized the voice as one of the two she had just saved. Nodding and turning, she noted the woman, fighting a retreating action with four other members of Galathae's team. She thought to go to them, but caught sight of a dwarf off the other way, flat on a crystal, crawling, a polar worm in pursuit.

Galathae doubted she could get to him, and even if she could, how could she hope to properly battle this new beast?

Common sense told her to retreat; her team members behind her yelled for her to retreat.

But she had been named by the mona and the Temporal Convocation as Holy Galathae, and that had to mean something.

She stood straight and tall, saluted her team members with her sword, turned to the side, away from them, and leaped to the next crystal, then to the one after that, running along it toward the crawling dwarf and the pursuing remorhaz.

And when she got to the end of her silken rope and saw that she remained too far away for the dwarf to get to her, Bluccidere swept down behind her, severing the tether, and Holy Galathae ran free.

"BY THE FROZEN BUBBLES IN THE DEEPEST ICE, WHAT IS that?" Emilian asked Vessi, who was working with a crew pushing about a huge metal tripod contraption, some twenty feet tall with a chain and hook hanging beneath its apex, the chain feeding through and down one of the legs to a large box that held the remainder of its coiled length.

"For securing the shafts," the out-of-breath aevendrow replied.

"It's a puncher," answered a stocky dwarf, whom Vessi introduced to his friend as Wohnik. Both aevendrow wore perplexed expressions at Wohnik's proclamation.

"When we're digging deep and run into a stubborn obstacle—stones, frozen ground, roots—we drop a puncher down the shaft to break through," Wohnik explained.

"They haven't run into any of that here, as far as I have heard," said Emilian. "The shafts are all dug, and all went smoothly."

"This one's not for obstacles then, but I'm thinkin' they might be thinkin' 'bout what might be coming up the hole," the dwarf said with a wink. He looked to Vessi and added, "Ye go and get some rest and food, but stay close and be ready. And bring yer friend if ye're called."

The aevendrow pair nodded as Wohnik walked off to join some others.

"We dragged that all the way from B'shett," Emilian explained.

"Looks heavy."

"Wait until you see what they intend to hang from it." He nodded across the way toward the entrance to Cattisola, where a pair of muskoxen were coming in pulling a long wagon with thick walls and double wheels, which groaned with every turn. In the low-sided elongated bed, the friends could see a large coffin-shaped box.

"That's the hanging piece?"

"Where is Ilina?" Vessi asked. "And aye, that is the puncher, as Wohnik called it."

Emilian pulled his gaze from the wagon. "Come on. She's working, though I expect she'll be trying to sleep soon enough. The fighting below has been terrific this day, with many wounded, and many of those seriously so."

"Deaths?"

"I don't know," Emilian answered honestly. "Some close to passing, at least, last I heard—"

He stopped short as shouts came from one of the larger shafts over to the southern side of the clearing. Ten haulers leaned against the poles of three separate capstans, digging in and driving to turn the drums and haul up the lines.

"Faster!" the team leader implored them. She was lying beside the shaft, peering over. "Oh, faster, friends! The worm isn't far behind, and it's climbing faster than we're hauling!"

Many people nearby rushed about, some coming over out of curiosity, others moving near to the capstans, lending a shoulder where they could to get the drum turning faster. Priests, Ilina among them, ran over to join litter-bearers in setting up a small triage area right near the shaft.

"Doesn't look good," Vessi remarked, following Emilian toward the fracas—but only for a few moments, before Wohnik bellowed for his team, spinning Vessi, then Emilian, about.

Emilian kept glancing back over his shoulder as he went, to see the first expeditioners come up from the room below. Battered and exhausted, many showed large bloodstains and had to be helped out of the hole, with most crawling only a few feet to the side before collapsing upon the floor.

By the time the two aevendrow got back to the puncher's framework, Wohnik and some of the others were already dragging it toward the shaft. Vessi took his spot and set himself in a way to allow Emilian to grab on right beside him.

"Hurry! Hurry!" came the cries from that busy shaft area, followed by a high-pitched, booming shriek that carried equal parts dragon roar and serpent hiss.

"By the north winds," Vessi murmured.

"A polar worm?" Emilian asked with a shrug. They had heard Galathae's stories, of course, but the sheer power of that shriek was beyond anything they had imagined from the descriptions.

Wohnik rushed over to them. "Take yer friend and go help with the wagon!" he said. "Tell the drivers to get it here and get it set up! Oh, but be fast, friends, for we've no time and none are wanting to fight that beast up here!"

"Get what set up?" Emilian asked as he and Vessi sprinted for the wagon.

"Another capstan and the spear!"

"The spear?" Emilian stopped running as he asked, caught by surprise. But Vessi had him by the arm in an eyeblink, dragging him along.

They ran to the back of the surprisingly long wagon and put their shoulders against it, pushing with all their strength. Emilian noted the drum and poles then, set to either side of the huge box. The poles held his gaze, as he thought them huge spears at first, for they were made of pressed white ice and were longer than the hauling poles on the other capstans set in the room.

He hardly found the time to sort it out, though. When they neared the commotion, the well-practiced team went into furious action, a pair of orcs dragging out the capstan's base and throwing it into place farther back and between two of the three already turning at the shaft. Aevendrow and dwarves rushed over immediately, setting long spikes—spikes as tall as an aevendrow!—in the framework's securing holes and pounding the base into place with heavy hammers.

Emilian and Vessi were tasked with pulling out the hauling poles, only three, but long enough, Emilian then realized, to slide right through holes cut through the shaped stone drum and thus serve the haulers on both sides of the hub. So skilled and precise was the team that they had already aligned the wagon and rolled the heavy drum to its back lip with levers by the time the two had set the poles on the ground.

"Get clear! It'll flatten yer feet to make ye swim like a water gull, it will!" Wohnik warned, and out rolled the drum, crashing down with a thud that shook the ground. A group of technicians were at it as it landed, keeping it up on its rounded edge and putting new levers to work immediately to get it close beside the spindle set in the middle of the base—upon which they promptly tipped it.

"Pull them out!" came a cry from the shaft, as more aevendrow and dwarves and orcs came forth from the hole, all of them looking even more ragged to Emilian now that he was up close, with some of the last ones obviously grievously wounded.

"Oh, hurry!" the hauling team leaders cried repeatedly. "Bend your shoulders, team! Turn those drums!"

"Clear the lines and clear the way!" Wohnik yelled, his giant tripod contraption nearing. As the team dragged it about the shaft opening, Wohnik climbed one of the legs with amazing agility, grabbed the hook, pulled a peg, and hopped down, dragging the lead of the chain with him. He ran to the back of the wagon and scrambled in as others pried off the bottom of the long box, while still others joined Emilian and Vessi in setting the poles in place through the drum. A pair of strong miners dragged the heavy chain out of the box and fed it to the drum.

"Fill them!" ordered the aevendrow team leader. "Left you go to wind that chain!"

Vessi, Emilian, and nearly three dozen others—six gathering on each end of the exposed lengths of each pole—crammed into position.

"Hold for Wohnik's call!" the team leader said when that chain went tight. Emilian looked at it curiously, for it ran straight to the heavy pulley at the top of the sturdy tripod, then down and back to the wagon and the hidden payload.

"Now! Push!" the team leader said, and the haulers bent low and drove on. As the turnstile came around, Emilian and Vessi noted the incredibly heavy payload—a huge, thick weighted spear—sliding out of the box and off the back of the wagon. They kept turning, dragging it to the edge of the shaft, then partly out over the shaft, where the back end rose, lifting the giant spear diagonally.

"Put your backs into it!" cried the team leader, and he, too, joined in, waving others beside him. As soon as that spear fully cleared the ledge and swung vertical over the hole, Emilian understood why others had rushed to add their shoulders, for the jolt of the thing had the team briefly skidding backward.

As they resumed the turning, lifting the spear up a bit higher, the team leader grabbed a long bolt from another hauler and rushed to the drum, sliding it into place before climbing up onto the drum. With the drum locked, the haulers were waved out of the way, three pausing to remove the long poles.

"Clear that durned hole!" Wohnik yelled. "Oh, for all the lights that're dancing in the sky, clear that hole!"

"Almost there," one of the dwarves leaning over the shaft and pulling out the battered expeditioners replied. "One more. Just one more!"

"Should be four," Vessi noted, counting the others who had come up on that particular rope. He understood when the dwarf hauled an aevendrow over the lip and dragged her away from the hole, the shred-ded end of the rope coming up and over behind them.

At least two of that strike team's members were still down there, cut off from the rest and likely dead.

"By the gods, that's a big one!" yelled Wohnik, who went to the edge of the shaft and peered over. "Big one and coming fast! Drop it! Drop it now!"

Another remorhaz shriek came from the shaft, so much closer now, roaring up from the hole and echoing throughout the chamber. All the work stopped then, desperate Callidaeans rushing for weapons.

The team leader on the drum hopped up, grabbed the handles of the bolt, and pulled it free, then leaped from the capstan as the spear plummeted, the drum spinning to let out the chain. The spear hadn't gone in far when it stopped suddenly, the chain near the drum falling slack.

Then it began jumping, the chain above the hole whipping back and forth.

Shrieks came from the hole, screaming so overwhelming that Emilian covered his ears.

It stopped as abruptly as it had started, and the drum began to spin as the spear resumed its descent.

"Run clear!" Wohnik cried, and everyone scrambled aside.

The chain went out to its end and there jolted so powerfully that the capstan nearly upended, the long and thick bolts farthest from the hole pulling up from the ground, and one tab securing the device snapping off cleanly.

But the contraption held, and the team was back at the capstan with their heavy hammers, resecuring it.

Emilian just stared at the tripod, which was bowing a bit under the weight, the chain swaying from the apex to the shaft.

He found himself mesmerized as he wondered what monster might be on the other end of that chain, and so buried was he in thought that all the places at the six spokes on the capstan were full, haulers bending and straining before he even realized that the poles had been put back in place.

His turn came soon enough, for they had to replace haulers constantly as they labored to bring the spear and the catch back up. After every third step, the team leader slipped in the locking bolt to give the team a break.

It took a long and grueling time before the back end of the spear finally showed above the rim, and Emilian and Vessi strained their necks to keep their eyes on that spot as it was lifted farther, until finally the head of the dead polar worm came into view.

It would take much longer than that for gaff crews and the other capstans to finally haul the beast out of the shaft—and what a monster it was, more than thirty feet long and with mandibles that could cut a muskox in half!

With the dead beast still radiating great heat, Wohnik's team dragged it over to the side of the glacier and pressed it lengthwise against the ice.

"That'll feed half the city, haha!" roared the dwarf, who seemed very pleased with their efforts this day.

For others, the celebration was muted, though, with a shredded guide rope serving as a grim reminder of the cost.

GALATHAE LEAPED OVER THE FALLEN DWARF, CHARGING straight into the pursuing remorhaz, Bluccidere whipping back and forth before her to force the beast to stop. Its wings beat wildly, lifting its head and upper body from the ground, swaying back as the paladin bore in.

It moved to strike, a slight and telling uplift of its midbody from the crystal, but Galathae beat it to the punch, rushing ahead and stabbing hard, again calling on her god to enhance Bluccidere's already potent sting. Ignoring the pain of the intense heat, the paladin pushed forward, and when the polar worm began to thrash, she again was one strike ahead—or one retraction, at least, as she brought back her sword, continued forward, and swung it in a powerful slash right to left.

She hit the remorhaz hard, the blue-ice blade bashing through the solid carapace and into the fleshy skin beneath. The worm tried to pull away, instinctively retracting, but it was too far to the side and fell tumbling to the lower crystals.

Galathae nearly stumbled off the crystalline plank, too, as she had reflexively taken up Bluccidere in both hands, briefly, for that side strike. Her consciousness flittered in and out from the sudden hot agony flowing from her ripped shoulder.

She started to call upon her god for healing hands, but glancing back as she did, she realized that the poor dwarf needed it more than she. He lay on the crystal now, blood flowing out from under him, streaming down the rounded side and dripping, a small flow, far below.

Galathae crawled to him and grasped his wound, invoking her goddess Eilistraee. She felt the warmth in her hand and saw the color return to the wounded dwarf's face.

But almost at once, it seemed all for naught.

For another polar worm came up before them on the crystal, and another pair pursued from behind, and yet another showed almost directly under them, squiggling up the side.

Galathae pushed the dwarf back down low and leaped up, ignoring the waves of dizziness. She had no time for that.

She had no time for pain.

She lifted Bluccidere in both hands and went into a leaping, slashing, stabbing frenzy, up ahead to drive that small worm back, then down to the side to stab at the climber.

While down low, she grabbed the dwarf by the collar and dragged him behind her as she charged the single opponent ahead. She dropped him unceremoniously to his face at the last moment, forced that left arm to do as she demanded, took up her sword in both hands, and smote the monster, once and again.

Her eyes burned, she could barely see, but she kept swinging wildly, focusing ahead, determined to clear the path for the dwarf before she died.

A shriek behind her disabused her of the hope, and she had to turn back, then charge back, to intercept mandibles descending for the poor dwarf.

She noted flashes behind her turning body, though she had no idea of what they meant and no hope that they portended anything important regarding her own fate.

For now she faced three remorhazes: the one she had just driven back from the dwarf, a huge one behind it, and the one from the side, stubbornly resuming its climb and now high enough to lift its head up and back from the beam, within striking range.

All three of them could snap at her . . . and all three did. She managed to stab the one on the side of the beam, shortening its lunge, and her slash across caught the descending attack from the huge worm in the rear.

But she missed the one in the middle, and it didn't miss her, its terrible mandibles clamping on to her already wounded left arm just above her elbow. Galathae felt the skin tearing, the bone cracking, and knew that if she tugged back, she would lose the limb. She retracted Bluccidere and bashed the monster repeatedly, wildly, anything to get that vise off her arm, anything to get away from the killing heat of the remorhaz.

She knew she was screaming. She heard the dwarf screaming and crying.

She saw the huge worm in the back rise up again and line her up for a killing bite, but she couldn't retreat and couldn't dodge, and couldn't even take Bluccidere from its work on her monstrous captor.

"Run, dwarf!" she managed to gasp between screams, until there came a hot and blinding light, a flash and darkness, and a hard thump as she fell facedown on the crystal.

The tug ended—the remorhaz had pulled off her arm, she thought. She felt her grip loosening on Bluccidere, but she stubbornly clasped it, determined to die with her holy sword in hand.

"Galathae!" she heard distantly, and thought that maybe it was her dead father, or a friend she had lost long ago, beckoning her to the next existence.

She felt weightless, free of the pain and the limitations of her corporeal form.

Until a hand grabbed her, and a voice said, "Galathae! Galathae!"

The paladin didn't want to open her eyes, but she did. She didn't want to feel that pain again, the burns, the tears, the torn shoulder and broken arm, but she did.

And she saw a familiar face, Allefaero's face, very close to her own.

"Come!" he begged. "Please, get up! I cannot lift you! Hurry!"

She tried to make sense of his words.

He pleaded and pulled.

"They're coming back!" Allefaero shouted, and the sheer terror and desperation in his voice brought Galathae back enough to remember who she was. And remember, too, her sworn duty. She couldn't let Allefaero die without trying to save him.

She forced herself to her knees. She stabbed Bluccidere's tip down onto the crystal as a brace and staggered to her feet, and even took a stubborn step toward the huge polar worm as it came back up onto the crystalline beam, its side blackened and smoking, seared as if by lightning.

But barely had the brave paladin strode forward when a hand grabbed her right shoulder tightly, and she felt herself pulled to the side, falling from the crystal.

Not below, though, for just to the side, she and her savior fell into a dimension door, and when they crashed down through the planar tunnel, they fell in a heap atop the wounded dwarf.

Galathae tried to make sense of it all, but she was beyond that now, slipping into a delirium of agony and a great weakness beyond anything she had ever known. She felt many hands grabbing at her, heard herself cry out as her left arm was twisted and slipped through some loop.

Bluccidere was pulled from her. She moaned in protest and blindly reached out, grasping for her sword, for something, for anything.

Then she found herself being dragged, then lifted.

Rising, rising.

She thought it her spirit, ascending to sit beside her god.

GALATHAE WOKE UP SOMETIME LATER, HER VISION COM-
ing into focus with the high ice walls to either side of her. She sensed
that she was moving, as if floating, long before she realized that she was
being carried along a glacial chasm.

Many more heartbeats passed before the paladin figured out that
she was being brought back from Cattisola to Scellobel.

She tried to sit up, thinking to protest. The battle was the other
way!

Barely had she lifted her head, only starting to crane her neck,
when she realized that she was out of the battle for the time being, for
the wave of fire that rolled out of her left arm and shoulder from that
minor effort had her lying flat once more, gasping for breath.

When she finally managed to open her eyes again, she found Emilian walking beside the litter, staring over her.

"Vulture," she tried to whisper.

Emilian looked at her curiously.

It took Galathae several broken syllabic gasps to complete her
joke. "Are you a vulture waiting for me to die?"

"If I were, I would have pecked your eyes from your skull when we
first dragged you up to the camp in Cattisola," her dear friend replied,
laughing. "For surely we all thought you dead."

Galathae looked away physically, and mentally returned to the last
moments down in the crystal chamber. Her arm and shoulder ached in
merely thinking about it. As did her sword hand. She curled her fingers
against her palm and slowly rubbed them across, finally exhaling when
her burned skin didn't pull off behind them.

She turned back to Emilian suddenly. "The dwarf? I went to help
a trapped dwarf."

"We have him, though alas for his companion, for she was not
recovered."

Galathae closed her eyes again, replaying the wild scenes all about
her. She knew then the scope of the task before Callidae if they hoped
to stop the destruction of the subterranean crystals, and thus halt the
encroachment of the icy death grip of Qadeej throughout the city.

We barely made a dent, she thought.

The caravan came into Scellobel a little while later, Galathae's litter rolling to a stop by the signpost on the borough's main boulevard, just south of the stone prow that cut Scellobel in half.

"Do you feel well enough for a meal?" Emilian asked, coming back over to Galathae. "Vessi said he would meet me in Ibilsitato, and Ayeeda is already preparing a fine feast for us."

Galathae nodded and managed to pull herself to a sitting position. She took Emilian's offered hand and slid off the litter, thanking her porters.

"Be quick in your healing, Holy Galathae," one of them said to her. "Your righteous brilliance brings hope to our fight."

The humble paladin took the compliment in stride and leaned on Emilian all the way to the table Ayeeda had ready for them in the inn's common room. Ayeeda joined them, demanding a recounting of the day's events—all the city was whispering about the vicious fighting under Cattisola.

Vessi arrived soon after with a surprise addition. Allefaero seemed uncomfortable when Vessi escorted him over and asked for another chair, but Galathae wasn't about to let the shy young wizard leave.

"To Allefaero," she said, hoisting a glass of ice wine. She paused and—slowly and painfully—stood up, commanding the attention of the entire room. "Allefaero," she shouted, "who saved me and saved the doomed dwarf. Were it not for Allefaero, Holy Galathae would be holey in an entirely different way, I fear!"

"Allefaero!" the dozens in the common room shouted back.

Galathae winked at the blushing young wizard. "Accept it, my friend. You have earned the applause of the whole of Callidae."

"You bring us hope that we will find a way to defeat the remorhaz menace," Vessi agreed. "Perhaps we might even dare hope that we will find a way to reclaim Cattisola."

"Where is Ilina?" Galathae asked, for the priestess usually joined them at their Ibilsitato dinners.

"Still in Cattisola," Emilian replied. "As are most of the priests of every borough. They will find little rest. They cast their protections and all of their healing, then go straight to bed to gather their strength to cast the spells again."

"The whispers say that the fighting is terrible," Ayeeda added.

"Two dead today," Emilian somberly replied. "Three more gravely wounded, not even counting our paladin friend here."

"Not so gravely," Galathae insisted. "I will be back to Cattisola soon enough." She looked to Allefaero. "What say you, wizard? How is our progress?"

The young man didn't disguise his emotions very well, and his expression wasn't overly promising. "I fear there is *no* progress as of yet," he said with a tremor in his voice.

They sat there, quietly absorbing that, before Galathae said, "I don't believe that."

"What?" the wizard said.

"We fought them. *That's* progress. Just days ago, we didn't even know we were under siege."

"And now we do," Emilian said. "And we will stop them."

"Because Jarlaxle warned us about this very thing," Vessi agreed. "You must have faith, Allefaero. Knowledge is power, is it not? And we know what we must do."

"Yes . . . but not how to do it," he said miserably.

"But we will figure that out," Vessi said. "Just as we figured out they were there in the first place." She raised her glass. "To Jarlaxle! He may have saved Callidae over the coming decades with his clever insight, and because he cared."

"Yes, for us," Ayeeda agreed. "Jarlaxle cared for us."

"And we sent him away," Galathae quietly added.

CHAPTER 28

Under the Merry Dancers

J arlaxle and Kimmuriel intercepted Pikel, Regis, Bruenor, and Gromph as they came out of the Hosttower. The mercenary leader waved Bruenor and Regis over to the others who had gathered outside the Hosttower, but bade Pikel to stay behind with the three drow.

"You have your scribes ready?" Jarlaxle asked the archmage.

"They are ready, for whatever good it may do."

Jarlaxle nodded and turned to the one-armed dwarf. "You understand that we will need your magic to keep us safe from killing cold?"

"Brrr," Pikel answered. "Yup yup."

"Good, and you have a spell that can do that? Against the coldest weather in all the world?"

"Hehehe, yup yup."

"Good," said Jarlaxle, nodding to his drow companions. "Then I want you to cast it now on my dear friend here," he explained, wrapping his arm about Kimmuriel. "Then go with Gromph into the Hosttower. He has scribes waiting with prepared parchments for you to make some scrolls of this most wonderful spell."

Pikel looked at him curiously, and Jarlaxle wasn't sure that he understood. Nevertheless, the dwarf launched into a dance, singing what seemed to the others to be a ballad of complete gibberish. He ended in a sudden leap and spin, thrusting his one hand out against Kimmuriel and waggling his fingers as if he were playing a dulcimer.

"Hehehe, brrr!" the dwarf roared.

"I don't feel any different," Kimmuriel informed the others.

"Pikel, it is done?" Jarlaxle asked.

"Yup yup."

"It will last all day?"

"Yup yup."

"You're certain?"

"Brrr," said Pikel, shaking his head, though whether he was saying that no, he wasn't certain of the spell, or of its duration, or that he meant that Kimmuriel wouldn't go "brrr," Jarlaxle couldn't be sure.

Gromph snorted a chuckle and Kimmuriel shook his head and sighed.

"Come along, little dwarf," Gromph said, grinning wickedly at Jarlaxle and Kimmuriel, reminding them that this whole thing was but a game to him, and he took Pikel by the hand and led him back into the tower.

"Well, that is reassuring," grumbled Kimmuriel.

"The dwarves swear that he is powerful," Jarlaxle replied. "But I'm not sure what he just did."

"He cast a spell, as you asked," Kimmuriel answered. "At least, he believes that he did."

Jarlaxle looked at him curiously.

"You didn't think I would risk going to the frozen north without protection on the words—words that no one can even understand!—of a green-bearded dwarf who fancies himself a druid, did you?"

"Doo-dad," Jarlaxle corrected.

"What?"

"Never mind. It doesn't matter. Let us be on our way to prepare Gromph's teleport sigil." He stepped next to Kimmuriel and conjured an image into his thoughts, focusing on it intently and allowing Kimmuriel into his mind so that he could see it as clearly as Jarlaxle could remember it.

A moment later, the world began slipping past them. Day became night, so it seemed, and the pair walked out of Kimmuriel's psionic teleportation into a high-walled ice canyon, with several domed structures of ice scattered about before them.

"Are you cold?"

Kimmuriel shrugged, considered it, and shook his head.

"Hehehe," Jarlaxle laughed in his best Pikel imitation. "Doo-dad!"

"I will leave you here forevermore," Kimmuriel warned the annoying mercenary.

"THERE THEY GO," PENELOPE HARPELL SAID, POINTING TO the area before the Hosttower where Jarlaxle and Kimmuriel wisped away to nothingness. She stood with Wulfgar and Dab'nay as Azzudonna, Bruenor, and Regis neared, and then all followed her to see at least the end of the disappearance.

"I do not understand," said Azzudonna. Her accent remained, but her words were spoken in fluent Common thanks to the spell Penelope had placed upon her.

"Jarlaxle and Kimmuriel travel to the north to prepare the glyphs that will guide Archmage Gromph's teleportation spell," Penelope said.

"They are back near your home," Dab'nay quietly told the aevendrow, who chewed her lip with obvious concern.

"They will return very soon," Penelope assured her. "And you will all go."

"Th' elf's not here yet?" Bruenor asked, walking up.

That brought a puzzled look from the two drow and Penelope, but Wulfgar and Regis knew exactly to whom Bruenor was referring.

"He should be arriving presently, so we were told," said Wulfgar. "We're watching for him."

"Eh?" Bruenor asked.

"Isn't he coming in through the gates in the Hosttower, from Mithral Hall to Gauntlgrym to here?" asked Regis.

"Jarlaxle promised a different manner of arrival, coming in from the east," the big man explained, and led their gazes back out to the skies over Luskan—all but Azzudonna, who continued to stare where Jarlaxle and Kimmuriel had been standing before they had disappeared. All of them were nervous, of course, but Azzudonna most of all. Jarlaxle was already back in the north? And with another person not of Callidae beside him?

How was this not a betrayal, she wondered.

The woman clenched her jaw as she considered the amazing circumstances that had brought her here, the amazing road apparently before her, and, mostly, the undeniable threat to her beloved home of Callidae.

It didn't get any less nerve-wracking—in fact, Azzudonna nearly jumped out of her magical sealskin, silk, and hagfish-mucus boots when a gate opened right before her and Gromph Baenre stepped out, followed by a disheveled little green-bearded dwarf with a cooking pot on his head and only half of one arm, which he had folded against his side, holding a jumble of parchments.

"They approach," Gromph announced.

"Jarlaxle?" Bruenor asked.

Gromph nodded to the east. "Drizzt."

For a while, they saw nothing, then two black specks in the distant sky, growing with every passing heartbeat.

Azzudonna watched curiously, squinting against the daylight. Her expression changed as the forms became more distinct, and more recognizable.

The aevendrow's purple eyes widened in surprise and horror and she whispered, "Dragons?" as she faded back, step by step.

"They are friends," Dab'nay told her, Penelope joining in.

"You are friends with dragons?"

"Not all wyrms are evil," Wulfgar told her. "These two are sisters, and are quite . . . interesting. They are longtime friends to Jarlaxle, and mean no harm to anyone who doesn't deserve it."

Azzudonna heard him, but distantly, her gaze locked on the sky as the great wyrms descended, their copper scales shining brilliantly in the daylight, riders coming into view on their backs.

She didn't know what to think—about any of this. She ran her fingers through her thick, wind-blown hair and shook her head repeatedly, helplessly, as the world spun about her, seemingly uncontrollably.

She heard the cries of alarm rising from the huge city just two bridges across the way—apparently the folk of this place called Luskan didn't share her present companions' opinion of the dragons.

Not that the city could do anything against them anyway.

Down they drifted, lowering, lowering, coming in to a gliding and running landing to stop right before the eight gathered on the field outside the Hosttower, a drow man and an old-looking human leaping down from their respective mounts. Azzudonna kept her eyes on the wyrm, and wide those purple orbs went again when the copper dragons transformed right there on the field, becoming women—human women.

"What in the Nine Hells happened to ye, elf?" Bruenor demanded.

"This is Drizzt," she heard Penelope saying, and knew when she blinked back into the conversation and registered the woman's words that it wasn't the first time Penelope had said that to her. She only then realized that the drow man had walked near to her and was now staring at her with eyes very similar to her own. Except that one was wickedly swollen, nearly closed. And that was but a small bit of the bruises and cuts showing on him.

"Husband of Catti-brie," Penelope explained. "And this is Kane, Grandmaster of Flowers of the Monastery of the Yellow Rose."

Azzudonna acknowledged both with nods, though she had no idea at all of whatever the Grandmaster of Flowers of the Monastery of the Yellow Rose might mean. It sounded like a title, and from the way Penelope had spoken it, one which should impress her.

"And those are the sisters Ilnezhara and Tazmikella," Penelope finished. "Though I know not which is which. And this is Azzudonna," she said to Drizzt and Kane, "who came to us through the magic of Guenhwyvar, somehow, though she has not the figurine."

Azzudonna noted that the drow named Drizzt was staring at her quite intently, almost threateningly.

"Where is Jarlaxle?" he asked.

"He and Kimmuriel will return soon," Penelope explained. "And then you all can go."

"You're not coming?"

"No," Penelope replied. "I am here only to make sure that you were properly introduced to our guest, and that you fully understand that Azzudonna is no enemy."

"I would speak with her," Drizzt said, before refocusing his gaze on Azzudonna and clarifying, "With you."

"We shall," Penelope agreed. "Right now."

"Let me heal you first," Dab'nay emphatically insisted, but as she stepped toward Drizzt, the man introduced as Kane intercepted her.

"Don't waste your spells," he said. "For you may need them before this day is done. Go and find another priest from Ship Kurth, if you would. Both Drizzt and I could use a bit of invigorating magic!"

"So I can see! What happened?" Dab'nay asked.

"Aye, flap yer lips, elf, if they're not too swelled," Bruenor demanded.

"Nothing to worry about," Kane promised, and he exchanged knowing smiles with Drizzt.

"That's not an answer," Bruenor growled.

"No . . . it's not," Kane said, and then strolled away.

When Dab'nay promised to be right back, Penelope took Drizzt by the arm and walked him past Azzudonna, motioning for the aevendrow visitor to follow.

"YOU FEEL NONE OF THE COLD?" JARLAXLE ASKED, LEADING Kimmuriel out of the glacial rift toward the ice pack, where the wind roared and flakes of snow and ice blew past in a howling and blinding fury.

"None," Kimmuriel replied. "It is a strange sensation. I hear the wind, of course, and see the cold anger of the land, but none of it bites at me."

Jarlaxle paused and reached into his magical belt pouch, producing a cup and a wineskin. He poured water into the metal cup.

"The magic of my boots keeps it warm enough while I hold it," he explained, and Kimmuriel nodded.

Jarlaxle tossed the cup carefully into the air. A bit of the water spilled and immediately froze into a small cloud of ice. Jarlaxle caught the cup and presented it to Kimmuriel.

A metal cup with a block of ice frozen inside.

"It would seem that our strange little dwarven ally is as potent as those around him have claimed," Jarlaxle said.

Kimmuriel nodded again, then motioned his chin to the open end of the rift and the raging wind beyond. "Let us hope that he is full of tricks, then," he said. "Whether we are freezing or not, traversing the terrain out there seems a daunting task."

"I won't disagree, but we'll find our way. We may have to wait for the storm to abate. An orc once told me that it's different up here. The land itself wants to kill you. I cannot disagree."

"You really believe that they are alive?"

Jarlaxle took a moment to consider it. "We freed a couple who were similarly entombed, and had been so much longer than our three friends. They were alive, though perhaps on the edge of death—we couldn't get to them fast enough to truly discern. But even in that event, Dab'nay has spells that would revive our failing friends before Death could grasp his bony hand about them.

"We are only a couple of hours' travel to the rift and tunnel that will bring us to them," Jarlaxle went on. "Let us finish our task, then go and retrieve our party. We can wait and plot here until the wind slows enough for us to quickly pass."

He turned about and started back to the igloos, his hand in his pouch to retrieve the magical beacons Gromph had given him to mark the location. Kimmuriel grabbed him by the arm, though, and stopped him.

"Where is the other place?"

"To the right and far along Qadeej. Several days of travel, but broken by encampments like this one. Our friends up here are resourceful, I assure you."

"Friends?"

Jarlaxle nodded. "Come."

"Then let us go and retrieve the others and be done with this."

"AS I SAID, THIS IS DRIZZT, SON OF ZAKNAFEIN, HUSBAND of Catti-brie," Penelope told Azzudonna. "We have told you much about him, of course, but I wanted a formal introduction before you fly away to the north."

"Fly? On the backs of dragons?"

"No, no, I meant that figuratively, of course. You will be taken to the north by Kimmuriel and Archmage Gromph and their respective magics, not on the backs of dragons."

"The sisters Ilnezhara and Tazmikella are not evil, nor enemies to us," Drizzt added. "And you will find them to be great allies if a fight lies before us."

"A fight certainly lies before you, before us, if you plan to enter the caverns beneath the giant fortress," Azzudonna said.

Drizzt looked to Penelope for an explanation, and when the woman shrugged, he turned back to Azzudonna.

"Jarlaxle knows more than I do," Azzudonna told him. "He was in the room when Zaknafein, Catti-brie, and Artemis Entreri were lost. I fought in that same room many months ago, in the time of Conception Verdant, to similarly disastrous results. I begged them not to go, all of them."

"But they went, and now my wife is lost to me, perhaps forever," Drizzt replied rather sharply.

"You are not the only one who lost someone you loved because of that," said Azzudonna, not impressed by his sole worry, and that gave Drizzt pause indeed. He looked to Penelope and found her nodding.

"Azzudonna is correct when she says that Jarlaxle knows more than she. I am certain that he plans to fully explain that which lies before you in the north."

Drizzt looked back to the aevendrow.

"But enough of this," Penelope added. "I wished for you two to meet—I think it important for the coming days. But do not squabble, I beg. Drizzt, I tell you in all confidence, and Jarlaxle confirmed it, that Azzudonna here was not at all responsible for the tragedy that happened in the north. I expect that Guenhwyvar brought her here in hope, not in an arrest."

"*Was* it Guenhwyvar?" Drizzt asked the aevendrow.

Azzudonna shrugged. "I believe that it almost certainly was. I was leaving the tunnel and was tackled from behind. I traveled across the world, so it seems, and landed in a room that I am told belonged to you and Catti-brie at the house Penelope rules. They said they saw the great cat."

"Have you ever heard of such things regarding the panther?" Penelope asked, and Drizzt nodded through every word.

"On occasion. What you describe is not unknown to me. So you know of Guenhwyvar and of the others, that much is clear. How? Tell me your story of your time beside my wife."

Azzudonna's jaw went very tight. "I was beside them for many tendays," she said. "They became dear friends to me and I fear they're lost, and will grieve for long years if they are not recovered."

"That's all?"

The woman didn't blink, and Drizzt narrowed his eyes.

"She cannot talk of it," Penelope interrupted. "Jarlaxle knows more," she continued, taking Drizzt by the arm and redirecting his gaze to the mercenary, who only then returned with Kimmuriel, the two appearing over by the Hosttower.

"Let us get you and Grandmaster Kane properly healed and prepared, that we might all get our answers quickly." She paused there and stared at Drizzt, even reached up to touch his swollen, nearly closed eye. "What happened?"

"Nothing" was all that he replied. There was no smile when he said it this time.

WITH GROMPH USING THE MAGICAL BEACONS JARLAXLE had set, and Kimmuriel using Jarlaxle's memories again, combined with his own, the two transported the group to the rift nearest the entrance to the tunnels. Beyond that channel, the wind roared and the snow blew about, but the sky was clear, and the thirteen party members stepped out of their teleports under a majestic sky of swirling green light, with purple and blue and red flares showing at the edges of the gyrations of the Merry Dancers.

Ilnezhara and Tazmikella remained in their human forms. They weren't bothered by the cold, nor were Jarlaxle with his boots, Gromph with some magical item of his own that he did not disclose, or Azzudonna, dressed in her sealskin, silk, and hagfish-mucus traveling gear. For the other eight, including himself, Pikel Bouldershoulder cast the enchantment to protect them from the elements, even once more upon Kimmuriel, to extend the durations of the earlier dweomer.

Even that brief moment standing on the ice demonstrated to them all just how serious a danger this land presented.

Jarlaxle assigned groups to various igloos, but first gathered all of them in the largest of the structures. In there, with help from Kimmuriel, who scoured his memories to garner accurate images, then telepathically gave them to Gromph, and the archmage, who then replicated those images by creating illusionary models of the place, they were all given a complete layout of the tunnel and cavern, even the locations of the trapped people inside.

They studied it and studied it. Kimmuriel used his mind magic to put them inside the place in their imaginations, letting them see it and feel it. One sight in particular brought a gasp from Azzudonna, for a bit deeper into the cavern from those pillars holding the captives stood the remnants of several other such pillars.

"The Companions of the Hall will remain together, of course," Jarlaxle decided. "Your coordination in battle is legendary, after all. I would ask Pikel to stay with you in support."

"Aye, stay close, me druid friend," Bruenor agreed.

"Doo-dad!" shouted Pikel.

"Dab'nay with me," Jarlaxle said. He held up the hilt of Zaknafein's sun blade. "We'll extract the ice-encased prisoners. Kimmuriel will watch over us?"

The psionicist nodded.

"As for the others," Jarlaxle asked as much as stated, and he held up his hands. "Where do you fit?"

"Wherever I choose," Gromph said.

"Exactly," Jarlaxle replied. "I would no sooner try to dictate the role of Archmage Gromph or Grandmaster Kane as I would for a pair of dragons. You'll see our enemies all about. I trust that you'll all find ways to put your . . . skills to the best use."

"I haven't eaten giant flesh in years," Ilnezhara said.

"A bit tough and stringy, if I recall," Tazmikella agreed.

"And what of my role?" Azzudonna asked.

"That is for you to decide," Jarlaxle answered. "Not in the battle, but right now. This is our fight. We go to rescue our friends."

"And mine. Those who remain."

"What do you mean?" Drizzt asked.

"The broken pillars," Jarlaxle explained. "And the number of captives we saw. More of Azzudonna's friends went in there than remain, I fear."

"Almost half are gone," Azzudonna agreed.

Several around her sighed and nodded.

"We will get those who remain," Jarlaxle promised. "But this recent trouble is our doing and our responsibility. You didn't come in there with us when our friends were caught, on order of your mona. I wouldn't make you risk your life now for this. If you wish to return to your home, we can send you well on your way immediately, with our best wishes and deepest gratitude—and from myself, Azzudonna, my heartfelt thanks for your friendship and the good you did for us in . . . well, during out time together.

"*Perte miye Zaknafein*," Jarlaxle ended with a wink.

"Your politesse is indeed boundless," Azzudonna answered, staring at the mercenary with a little smirk on her face. "That night under the Merry Dancers was the most magical moment of my entire existence, and that magic was not created on a whim or a hope. Yes, Jarlaxle, *perte miye Zaknafein*. It was an expression of devotion and loyalty and desperate passion."

"Of love," Jarlaxle said, and Azzudonna didn't argue.

"Because of all that, you know that I am not leaving," she told him, told them all. "I'm going into that room with you. If you fail, I fail. If you fall, I fall, but know that, like you, I do so with an open heart. It is worth the risk, even if Qadeej himself awakens and comes against us."

"We're not losing, elf," Bruenor put in. "That's me girl in there."

"Bwuenor!" shouted Pikel, and the group in the igloo shared a laugh, even the dragons, even Kimmuriel Oblodra.

Not Gromph, though.

And not Drizzt.

CHAPTER 29

In the Lair of the Slaad God

I sense that there are many whites up here," Ilnezhara said to Tazmikella. They stood together outside the igloo after the group had fully rested. Pikel Bouldershoulder remained near the structures, casting his spells of protection against the deathly cold air on all who needed them. The wind howled through the glacial rift, while beyond its sheltering high walls, a storm roared in blinding fashion.

"It is indeed their kind of place, isn't it?" her sister replied.

To the side of the dragon sisters, several others overheard, including Azzudonna, who looked to the two curiously and with obvious alarm.

"White dragons," Drizzt explained to her.

"There are some, yes," Azzudonna confirmed. "We have taught them to avoid . . ." She stopped and shook her head, mad at herself, clearly.

Drizzt looked at her for just a moment, then, realizing he was making her uncomfortable, guessing that she had just almost revealed something she should not, he called the pertinent information out to the sisters, warning them that, yes, there were white dragons in this general region. Ilnezhara and Tazmikella walked over, making Azzudonna even more visibly uncomfortable.

"You have seen them?" Ilnezhara asked the aevendrow.

Azzudonna hesitated and glanced back and forth between the dragons and Drizzt.

"Are you friendly with them?" Tazmikella added slyly.

Azzudonna's shocked expression denied that without her saying a word.

"Ilnezhara and Tazmikella waged a great battle with a pair of white dragons over the mountain that housed the home of King Bruenor," Drizzt explained.

"Against or beside?" the aevendrow asked.

"Against!" Ilnezhara sharply replied. "Oh, dear drow woman, do you know nothing of dragonkind? Why would you think that we would fight beside any of the chromatic beasts?"

"Chromatic?" Azzudonna quietly echoed, clearly confused.

"A truly frightful and wicked notion, sister," Tazmikella agreed.

Poor Azzudonna seemed quite lost by it all. "I . . . I did not . . . I only know of the dragons who are sometimes encountered in this region. White-scaled dragons, yes," she carefully stammered. "I . . . are there others besides them and you?"

"Ah, dear sister, no wonder the poor lass is so afraid of us," Tazmikella said.

"Dear girl, do speak with Jarlaxle before you draw upon such prejudices," Ilnezhara added. "You may discover that we are worth knowing. And playing with."

A flustered Azzudonna stammered again but didn't reply, and the dragon sisters walked away, giggling and bumping against each other in a playful manner that seemed more appropriate for human teenagers than for polymorphed great wyrms.

"Always keep in mind that any of those playful bumps you see from them now would send you flying away," Dab'nay told the aevendrow, walking up to join Azzudonna and Drizzt. "Be glad that they're here, and gladder that they're on our side."

Drizzt laughed and offered a confirming smile and nod to Azzudonna.

"Has Jarlaxle made his decision yet?" Drizzt asked Dab'nay. "Are we going, or must we wait for the storm to abate?"

"I think he wanted to wait," Dab'nay answered, before looking at Azzudonna and adding, "until our host here told him that it could be many, many days before that happened."

"We cannot know," Azzudonna explained. "Storms in the night can blow through fast or they can linger."

Pikel Bouldershoulder went hopping by them then, singing and dancing his way out toward the end of the glacial rift.

"What is that strange little one about?" Dab'nay asked. She looked back, as did the others, to see the rest of the team moving forward from the igloos, following Pikel. The three drow and the dragon sisters fell in line with the others.

Pikel stopped at the very edge of the rift, his light green robes flapping wildly in the howling wind. Those coming behind couldn't even hear their own voices then, so near to the fury of the storm, but somehow, Pikel's singing continued in their ears, and even more strangely, the wind itself seemed to become the music carrying Pikel's tune.

The dwarf danced in a circle and hopped in a spin, waving both his arms, with lines of various colors streaming from his stumped arm, spinning up into the air and forming into a rainbow of large magical birds, which flew away into the clouds.

"What is he doing?" Dab'nay shouted, though even those very near to her could hardly hear her. "He might draw danger to us!"

"I don't think so." Drizzt understood her confusion, but unlike Dab'nay, he had seen enough of this strange dwarf to offer his trust here that whatever Pikel was up to, it would probably lead to something good.

The dance continued for many minutes and Pikel's song increased in volume.

Or no, they all came to realize slowly. It wasn't that his voice was getting louder, but that the wind around them was quieting.

"He's calming the storm," Dab'nay uttered in shock.

Drizzt nodded at her, then smiled reassuringly to Azzudonna, who seemed quite overwhelmed by the druid's display.

"Mounts!" Jarlaxle shouted. He pulled out his obsidian figurine and summoned his hellsteed. Kimmuriel followed suit, as did Dab'nay.

Drizzt lifted his scrimshaw whistle and brought forth Andahar. Bruenor dropped his own figurine, one Jarlaxle had given to several of King Bruenor's elite Gutbuster Brigade, and summoned a hell boar.

"We'll lead the way," Ilnezhara said, and dropped her robe and began her transformation. Beside her, her sister did the same.

"Fly low, sister," Tazmikella said. "We've no time to attract a white and do battle."

"But I would so enjoy it."

"Our friends need us."

Ilnezhara, now almost fully in wyrm form, made a grumbling sound of discontent.

"And Jarlaxle will reward us," Tazmikella added, and the other dragon stopped growling and puffed a bit of acid out of her nose, as if to say, "Hmm."

"I will run alongside," said Kane. No one argued with this.

Gromph surveyed the group, then cast a spell to create spectral steeds for Wulfgar and Azzudonna, nearly translucent ghostly white horses with long flowing manes and tails. Then he conjured one for himself (which was unlike the others and very much like Jarlaxle's hellsteed).

The aevendrow backed away, though, shaking her head, clearly unsure.

"She doesn't know how to ride," Jarlaxle announced, recognizing her hesitation and considering her background.

Drizzt pulled himself up on Andahar and paced the unicorn beside Azzudonna, reaching down his hand to her. She took it and he pulled her up behind him.

"You'll be safe," he assured her. "Andahar will not let you fall."

With a typically disgusted sigh, Gromph began to dismiss the extra horse, but Regis dared to reach up and grab the great wizard's arm, stopping him.

"Can you make it a bit smaller?" the halfling asked. "I can ride it as is, but make it a pony and I'll take Pikel with me."

Gromph glared at the halfling's hand upon his arm until Regis wisely pulled it away. The archmage turned to the horse, considering the question for a few moments, seeming intrigued, as if he had never thought to do that before. In the end, he shrugged and cast another spell, and the spectral horse diminished before their eyes, becoming a spectral pony.

Up went Regis, who had become an expert rider in his years with the halfling highway band known as the Grinning Ponies. "May I name him?"

Gromph looked at him with an expression somewhere between disgust and disrespect. He walked away shaking his head and grumbling.

"Onward, Rumblebelly," Regis said, loud enough for Gromph to hear and react with another muttered curse. More than Regis grinned at that result. He guided the pony over beside Pikel.

But the green-bearded dwarf was having none of it. Laughing hysterically, Pikel sang again and, before their eyes, transformed his body into that of a giant bald eagle, except that its head feathers were green, not white, and one wing was shorter than the other.

"By the gods," Azzudonna breathed behind Drizzt. "What manner of warriors, what assortment of curious and strange creatures, have come to this land?"

"Allies," Drizzt assured her.

She didn't respond verbally, but Drizzt felt her arms around him squeeze just a little bit tighter.

Out of the rift swept the troupe, led by two copper dragons and a wobbling and chanting eagle, continuing his spell to calm the winds and even to turn them favorably for the journey. With nightmares, spectral horses, and a hell boar galloping, and an old man miraculously running to pace them, onward they charged, the glacial wall to their left, the next rift and the entrance to the caverns fast approaching.

They covered the miles in a matter of minutes, not hours. The dragon sisters and Pikel led the way around the bend and down the ice canyon. They dropped down and came back to their humanoid forms, all three, and stood beside the corpse of a fallen frost giant, frozen solid and dusted with ice and snow.

"My retreat was less than clean," Jarlaxle admitted when he and the others arrived. He moved to the tunnel and peered in.

"Seems quiet enough," Ilnezhara remarked beside him.

"The cante are silent and all but invisible," Azzudonna told them. "They could be spread about the floor and walls even as we stand here and we would not know."

"They can be revealed as magical," Jarlaxle said, speaking to the spellcasters. He drew out a wand and cast a spell upon himself from it to detect such magic, as Gromph and Dab'nay similarly enchanted themselves. Pikel did something as well, but Jarlaxle couldn't be sure of what, since the audible components of his spell were all seemingly gibberish.

Kimmuriel, meanwhile, stood very still. Too still, as if his body was simply frozen in place.

Jarlaxle looked to him and nodded, then told the others to await the psionicist's return.

A few moments later, the physical form of Kimmuriel blinked its eyes as the spirit of the drow came back to its physical host.

"The chamber is quiet and as you described," Kimmuriel told Jarlaxle. "But I sensed a hush in there, and a general feeling of . . . sentience."

"Qadeej," breathed Pikel, but no one paid him any heed.

"We may be walking into an ambush," Kimmuriel warned.

"I wouldn't doubt it," Jarlaxle said.

"Then let's be done with it," said a seemingly unconcerned Gromph. "I am weary of this frozen place already."

Jarlaxle nodded. "As we agreed," he said, and Gromph began a spell, as did Dab'nay.

And Pikel began one as well.

Gromph's ball of flame appeared right in the tunnel entrance, burning brightly. Then came Dab'nay's, of lesser size and intensity, but still formidable.

Then came a third one, blazing brightly, catching them all by surprise, and even Gromph looked over at Pikel with something between shock and respect.

"Qadeej," the green-bearded dwarf said again, smiling widely, his light gray eyes sparkling in reflection of the intense balls of fire.

Side by side, floor-to-ceiling and wall-to-wall, the three summoned globes led the way down the tunnel. Hisses and shimmers of retreating translucent liquid informed the party that the path had indeed been guarded in a waiting ambush. Now the cante were being consumed or chased before the hot flames.

"We're going to be fighting as soon as we enter the main hall," Jarlaxle warned. "Just secure a perimeter about the stalagmites so we can get our friends . . ." He paused and looked at Azzudonna and clarified, "So we can get *all of* our friends free."

The fiery orbs moved slowly along the corridor, but they were doing their job, quite obviously. The three spellcasters kept them spaced to fill the tunnel, and as the troupe made their way along, no cante or any other monsters rose to challenge them.

Drizzt slipped down from Andahar, Azzudonna following, but he didn't dismiss his magical mount. Wulfgar and Regis, too, dismounted from their spectral steeds and fell in beside the drow, who moved beside King Bruenor on his hell boar.

"If I get down, the thing'll run wild," Bruenor explained. "Jarlaxle says the little fire beastie will serve us well inside."

"Here's hoping we won't need it," Drizzt replied.

"When has that ever happened to us?" Wulfgar asked.

Regis laughed, then glanced all around, at the dragons, at the archmage, at the Grandmaster of Flowers. "If our enemies understood us, they would be hoping the same. And hiding in deep holes."

"Giants and slaadi may also be about," Azzudonna warned. "They fear little."

"Slaadi," Bruenor huffed. "Durned frogs. Just frogs. Here's hopin' they're tasty as their little cousins."

That brought a scrunched face from Azzudonna, an expression both curious and disgusted, but she didn't reply.

"Side chamber coming up on the left," Jarlaxle said, and raised his arms to hold the others in the front rank back while the fiery orbs continued to sweep the corridor before them. He looked to Gromph, who nodded and began casting.

As predicted, the orbs rolled past an opening on the left-hand wall, and another orb of fire, this one much smaller, flew behind the three right as they continued on their way along the main corridor, angled perfectly to soar right through that opening.

A moment later, there came a great rush of hot air, flames filling and spouting from the side chamber.

On went the group, confident that nothing in that room would have survived Gromph's blast, moving to only a few feet behind the orbs.

"We're nearing the end of the corridor," Jarlaxle announced only a short while later. "When it opens, move the flames aside, then put them back behind us to seal the tunnel. The cante are all about us now, flowing among the cracks within the glacier. I can sense their magic. They'll find their way out soon enough."

The dragon sisters moved in front, the three spellcasters in a line across the corridor behind them. As soon as they saw the room opening up before the moving balls of fire, Gromph and Dab'nay tightened their magical grips on their respective flames, pressing them against opposite walls.

Pikel, though, went into a short, skipping dance, singing again, and his rolling flame seemed to swirl and spin within itself, fires of different colors roiling within it.

"What's he doing?" Regis whispered from behind.

"Durned if I'm knowin'," Bruenor admitted.

Gromph's ball of flame went out left suddenly, Dab'nay's disappearing to the right, but Pikel's sat there at the entrance to the vast cavern just a moment longer, transforming from a ball of fire into what looked like a horse of fire, orange, yellow, and white, before leaping straight up into the room, out of sight above the tunnel.

The dragon sisters were already running into the room, transforming as they went.

In went the spellcasters.

In thundered Jarlaxle and Kimmuriel on their hellsteeds, Jarlaxle leading Dab'nay's and handing it off to her just inside the vast chamber.

In ran Kane and Azzudonna, the Companions of the Hall close behind, Bruenor's hell boar puffing flames with every stride.

"Form a perimeter!" Jarlaxle ordered as Dab'nay brought up a magical light in the middle of the icy stalagmite mounds, the illumination showing the ghostly forms of those trapped inside.

Jarlaxle entered that chamber full of hope, expecting that he and his powerful friends could get the captives and be out of there in quick order.

As soon as he exited the tunnel and got a good look around at the chamber, though, he realized that such would not be the case. His eye went first out to the left, across the uneven, stepped ice floor to the distant, nearly translucent circular window, and any relief he might have had to see that neither Ygorl or any other slaadi were over there was quashed immediately by the veritable army—scores and scores of cante—that arose from that icy surface. And as he scanned back toward the stalagmite prisoners, he saw the charge of the undead n'divi, coming out from the tunnel up at the ledge on the wall opposite from him. A train of the ice-encased zombie creatures, ice golems animating a corpse within, streamed to the frozen waterfall slide and threw themselves recklessly down it, skimming fast to the chamber's main floor.

Frost giants! So many frost giants rose from the floor of that ledge running nearly the length of the wall across the way that they seemed to make the vast cavern smaller, lifting boulders and huge weapons, while more behemoths poured out of the tunnel alongside the n'divi.

And slaadi—now Jarlaxle and the others saw them, in force, up on that ledge directly across from the tunnel he had just exited and all the way down to the right to the corner of the roughly rectangular hall of ice.

The giants and the slaadi knew they were coming. Their enemies were waiting for the rescue attempt. Were, in the case of the frost giants rising from the shelf, literally lying in wait.

Jarlaxle's mind whirled as he tried to sort it all out. Had Ygorl or some other powerful slaad detected Kimmuriel's psionic intrusion? Had Qadeej, the wind god whose body had given this glacier life, somehow informed the giants? Was it the cante in the tunnel, serving as lookouts?

How had they known?

And more importantly, of course, what were Jarlaxle and his band of heroes to do now?

The mercenary spun around, trying to conceive a new plan.

He saw immediately that he didn't need to.

Ilnezhara and Tazmikella were already sweeping past him, roaring their dragon roars, running and half flying fearlessly toward the enemies on the shelf.

Gromph was deep into spellcasting, aiming—if Jarlaxle correctly measured the archmage's gaze—somewhere down to the left.

The Companions of the Hall followed the charge of King Bruenor—who began hopping his hell boar, each landing of the beast's hooves sending powerful blasts of fire—and the flight of Aegis-fang, which shattered one, then another, then a third, of the nearest cante in a single, spinning throw. Andahar was there, too, barreling in, running down the small enemies swarming nearby, horn and hooves so very lethal.

Drizzt broke off from his three friends, joining with Grandmaster Kane, who seemed to almost fly while springing from icy pillar to pillar, atop trapped prisoners, leaping, soaring, into the throng, hands and fists exploding into striking, spinning, kicking action.

Dab'nay and Kimmuriel came past Jarlaxle on their hellsteeds, skidding up to mounds, spinning their mounts about and kicking at the ice to break the prisoners free, even as Azzudonna joined Jarlaxle in going to the nearest victim, Artemis Entreri, with Jarlaxle working the sun blade to finish the work started by Kimmuriel's mount.

Jarlaxle's heart soared when Entreri's head moved, an eye half opening in acknowledgment.

And his heart sank when he looked up to call for Dab'nay, for then he realized that still more cante were close by, rising from the floor directly ahead of him and over to the right, behind the dragon sisters, and with nothing between him and them except a pair of stalagmites—one restraining Zaknafein, the other Catti-brie.

"Perimeter!" he started to cry out, his voice a near shriek of desperation.

But the word caught in his throat, lost in astonishment, as the last of the party, who all thought the least of the party, made his entrance. Jarlaxle noticed a flash back behind him to the right, and heard a rumble, and it only occurred to him that it was the sound of hooves as the magical spectacle came into sight.

"Me king Bwuenor!" roared Pikel Bouldershoulder, standing at the flaming crossbar on a chariot of fire, holding the reins of a team of horses also composed, it appeared, entirely of fire. The shouting dwarf sped out across the way, leaving a line of blazing flames in his wake. Past the mounds he went, before cutting hard to his left and continuing out until he encompassed all of the stalagmites, circling them, coming back around behind toward the tunnel they had entered.

Drawing a perimeter of fire, circling and circling, running cante down into puddles and flying chips and bursts of spreading steam.

Jarlaxle handed the sun blade to Azzudonna. "Now you know what to do!" he yelled. "Free them fully!"

"What are you going to do?"

His answer was to run toward his nightmare, leap up, and begin his weave, the diabolical mount kicking at every mound they passed, the fiery hooves breaking the foundations of the prisons.

Jarlaxle winced with every strike, fearing that such a brute-force attack instead of carefully extracting the captives could prove disastrous to the poor souls trapped within. But they had no time, a point drummed into him, almost literally, as a giant-hurled boulder spun past his face.

Pikel's perimeter run was holding back the cante and n'divi, but the shelf was lined with range fighters—giants with boulders, slaadi with large spears . . . and spells! A lightning bolt struck Jarlaxle as he turned back toward the wall showing the entry tunnel, the bolt catching the hellsteed on the flank and sending it spinning.

"Stay straight!" Jarlaxle growled at it through shivering teeth, and he tried to hold firm the reins through the violent muscle spasms of the energy clicking through his body.

Another boulder bounced past him, skipped on the ice floor, then ricocheted off the next ice stalagmite in line, spinning and flipping into the face of Dab'nay's riderless hellsteed. Always difficult to control, always on the edge of demonic fury, that riderless nightmare mount went into a sudden frenzy, leaping and spinning, bucking and kicking.

"Dab'nay!" Jarlaxle roared.

The riderless hellsteed leaped and double-kicked, both hooves smashing into a mound, blasting it apart and launching its prisoner out the other side to the floor, where she went skidding along, facedown.

Jarlaxle tried to pull up and turn his horse to regard the fallen form. But he stopped abruptly and sucked in his breath in fear, recognizing the victim.

GRANDMASTER KANE AND DRIZZT CRISSCROSSED IN MID-air in their flips, Kane landing in a slide, popping up to a circle kick that halted the shambling approach of an n'divi, stopping the ice-encased zombie cold. Cracks spiderwebbed out from that impact, the ice then just dropping away.

The remaining zombie orc just stood there for a few moments before falling forward in true death, facedown to the ice.

Drizzt landed across the way, dropping to his knees and not slowing the slide, gliding between a pair of n'divi, his blades crossing before him and bashing the slow-turning monsters in the sides. As he slipped past, Drizzt stabbed a backhand over his shoulder, driving Vidrinath into the back of one enemy, catching fast and sending the drow turning left in a spin that brought him back to his feet.

He yanked out the scimitar even as his other blade, Icingdeath, glowing fiercely in the cold air, descended, cracking through the ice and cracking through the skull, destroying the undead monster. Drizzt turned for the second, but Bruenor Battlehammer came hopping past him, the hell boar spouting flames and taking the dwarf beyond the other n'divi Drizzt had gashed.

Bruenor's many-notched axe finished the job. And the hell boar never slowed, barreling into a cante that rose before the dwarf king, shattering it, then shattering a second that tried to rise behind it.

"By the gods, elf!" Bruenor roared, yanking hard on the reins, pulling up the ferocious hell boar.

The dwarf's cry and sudden stop caught Drizzt by surprise, until he heard Wulfgar yell, "Too many!" behind him.

He spun farther to his left to see Wulfgar and Regis, and the stalagmite mounds behind them within the ring of Pikel's continuing fire. Aegis-fang exploded a cante, swatted aside an n'divi, and came crushing down so hard on the top of the head of yet another n'divi that both the ice and the zombie inside it just seemed to explode and drop flat under the weight of the blow.

"Too many!" Wulfgar yelled again, pointing past Drizzt, who whirled about.

And knew doom.

Dozens, scores, hundreds of monsters, cante to n'divi to frost giants to enormous, hopping bipedal frogs, red and blue, swarmed the edge near that higher tunnel, moving toward and down the waterfall now.

Drizzt tore his gaze away in surprise as a crossbow bolt flew past him to strike yet another cante, one cleverly rising right beside the drow ranger, and even flowing over one of his boots. The crossbow bolt ended that sneak attack, however, collapsing in on itself and exploding in a sudden and violent burst to shatter the monster to bits.

Drizzt wanted to thank Regis, and wanted more to urge the Companions of the Hall on, to fight for Catti-brie, for Zaknafein, for Artemis Entreri, for all trapped within this cavern of cold and ugly death. But he couldn't tear his stare from the spectacle of the approaching army, a force too powerful.

Simply too powerful.

How did we so underestimate this threat?

That inability to look away, though, gave Drizzt the best seat in the cavern to witness the bared power of those who had come with him. To see Grandmaster Kane fearlessly flying forward in great leaps and bounds and somersaults and killing kicks, destroying everything in his path, though his amazing efforts seemed a pittance against this force.

Not so with the magical strike of another, however.

They appeared in the air one after another, or two at once: small balls of burning rock, lava in the air high in the cavern, plummeting down, glowing angrily and growing as they fell, meteors crashing and exploding all over that area of the cavern. Splattering monsters, melting cante, tossing aside giants and slaadi alike.

Falling, falling, on the frozen waterfall slide, melting it, shattering it, dropping it and the hundred monsters upon it crashing to the floor below.

Drizzt snapped his head about, looking back upon the archmage of the Hosttower of the Arcane, standing with his arms outstretched, bringing forth more and more swarming meteors, their fires reflecting in his eyes as if they were his children sent to war.

And a cry the other way had Drizzt and the others spinning farther, looking past Gromph, past the flaming ring and the work on the icy tombs, and back to the corner and the wall opposite, where stood the dragons, Ilnezhara and Tazmikella, battered by stones, stuck with thrown spears, but resilient in the way only dragons can be.

Ilnezhara snapped her head to the side, launching the chewed and broken corpse of a blue slaad through the air.

Tazmikella just clenched her jaw tighter on the frost giant she had plucked from the shelf. Its legs fell from one side, upper torso and the rest of it from the other.

More missiles flew in. More monsters rushed to the front of the shelf to launch their weapons.

"Now, sister!" Tazmikella roared, the sound of her dragon voice alone stopping the enemy throwers in shock.

And together, the dragons breathed, cones of acid flowing forth, melting ice and skin alike as the great wyrms swayed their heads on serpentine necks, back and forth.

"Well now," Bruenor muttered, and even his energetic hell boar seemed muted by the sudden display of outrageous arcane power.

"Chase the retreating tide!" Regis yelled, rushing past his friends and raising his hand crossbow. He lifted his bent arm before him and set his right wrist upon his left forearm, taking quick aim and letting fly.

More crashing, more screams, more tumult flowed from behind, where the dragon breath was dropping half the great shelf in the room, but the gracefully arching quarrel seemed immune to the shaking ground, seemed as if flying through a separate dimension, quiet and serene.

Until it struck the back of a retreating giant and collapsed in on itself and exploded, the force throwing the massive frost giant forward and to the floor.

"We've got them!" Regis growled. "We've got them all!"

Bolstered by the halfling's cry, the Companions of the Hall started forward, Kane beside them, ready to embrace the sudden swing of fortune.

And then fortune swung again.

For out of the tunnel up on the remaining shelf flew a slaad, giant and dark, like living smoke enwrapping a skeletal frame. Just seeing it caught the cheers in Regis's throat, and stopped the charge of the others, and stopped the retreat of their enemies.

Just seeing it filled the rescuers with dread, for such was the effect of this god-being, Ygorl.

The greatest slaad flew up high in the cavern and cut at the air with its unholy scythe. Ygorl's weapon tore the air itself, it seemed, leaving glowing lines in its every cut and turn, and when the god flew on past, soaring above the front line of companions, focusing its ire on another, the glowing lines remained, burned into the air for all to see.

A symbol.

Unholy, unclean, agonizing.

Bruenor roared, or tried to, his cry caught in a gurgle as he rolled off his hell boar. Regis dropped to the floor, vomiting and shaking. Wulfgar doubled over, then roared against the pain and stood straight—almost—before doubling over again.

Kane locked his hand in a meditative pose, fighting, fighting, as did Drizzt. And they were resisting, but it would take more than that, they realized, for the cante, the n'divi, the giants, the slaadi were not so ill affected, no. They were emboldened.

And the monstrous tide was coming back in.

GROMPH BAENRE, NO NOVICE TO SUCH SYMBOLS AND DARK magic, blinked through it, maintaining enough concentration to watch the flight of the god-being and begin a spell of his own. He grimaced and shook his head when Ygorl threw a storm of ice and wind over at the stalagmites, all but extinguishing Pikel's fiery ring and the chariot, as well, when the dwarf turned and couldn't stop himself from driving right under the deluge.

"Oo oo oo oo oo oo!" Gromph heard the green-bearded druid yelp in rapid succession as the hailstones pelted him.

They were doomed.

They were all doomed.

Unless . . .

Gromph growled through his spell even as Ygorl turned on him, flying fast and raising that diabolical scythe.

A lightning bolt flew out from the fingers of the archmage, such a blast that would have felled a giant, a titan, or even one of the dragon sisters. It flashed up at Ygorl, striking the smoky slaad, which made Ygorl itself look like a thundercloud, the arcs of lightning flickering about ribs and bones within the dark cloud of the being.

The flight stopped fast, right there, Ygorl hanging in the air, jolting, sparking, trembling.

But not falling, and as the residual shocks dissipated, the slaad's scythe began to spark—black and not blue—and almost as if transforming, channeling, and redirecting Gromph's own bolt, the slaad god sent it shooting down from above, a black flash that struck the archmage and threw him back against the wall near the entry tunnel.

Gromph battled unconsciousness, and saw Ygorl flying in for him, and thought his life at its end.

But then Ygorl shuddered and stopped again, the god-being lurching out to the side, turning and then fleeing, profoundly stung.

And Gromph, fighting to stay awake and alive and ready to fight, came to understand when Ygorl reached out a hand behind across the empty space, erasing his own symbol!

Gromph rolled his head to the side.

Kimmuriel was there, not far away, astride the hellsteed, unbothered by the mind-melting illusionary agony of the symbol, and now assaulting Ygorl's mind with the power of his own psionics.

Gromph looked down at his hands, still sparking with black lightning.

But not hurting.

Kimmuriel had shielded him, had almost certainly saved his life.

The archmage reached out at the retreating Ygorl, flying now for the circular window of ice far across the way, and threw forth the energy still crackling about him, his bolt chasing and catching Ygorl, and stinging the empyrean being profoundly.

But Ygorl flew through the jolt, and when Gromph tried to move forward to pursue and lash out at the god-being again, he stumbled and fell back against the wall, more wounded than he had realized.

JARLAXLE WATCHED OUT OF THE CORNER OF HIS EYE, THE flight, the glowing symbol . . .

The mercenary doubled over in sudden, shocking pain, the sheer agony of it bringing his thoughts careening back to his younger days in Menzoberranzan—on those not-so-rare occasions when he had angered a matron.

And there, in those distant memories, Jarlaxle found the strength to fight back, to tear his gaze from the glowing, burning lines Ygorl had written in the air. He dropped from his hellsteed, huddling, blocking the symbol with the nightmare's bulk.

He peeked out and followed the god-being's flight, and instinctively held up his hat, turning it into an umbrella just in time to fend off the pelting ice of Ygorl's storm. He held his breath, looking to Dab'nay and Azzudonna pleadingly, looking to Entreri, who was squirming on the floor, desperately covering up against the onslaught of the storm, looking across the way to the shattered mound and beyond it to the form of the poor woman who had been ejected so brutally by the double-kick of Dab'nay's uncontrolled hellsteed.

Doum'wielle, lying so very still, reacting not at all to the frozen elemental barrage.

Through the swirling ice and sleet, he saw his mighty brother strike out, and he knew hope, then saw Ygorl reverse the bolt and throw the great and powerful Gromph back against the wall, like a child or a toy.

And Jarlaxle knew dread.

He glanced left, thinking to flee, and saw Kimmuriel sitting tall on his hellsteed, strong and resolute, unbothered by the pelting ice, focused with illithid-like intensity on one target alone.

And the ice storm stopped, and Jarlaxle saw that it was the doing of Pikel, little Pikel the doo-dad, dancing and singing beside the diminishing chariot of fire, countering Ygorl's magic with his own. How could the likes of Pikel Bouldershoulder hope to match the power of the bared god of the slaadi?

But somehow, impossibly, he was doing so.

It made no sense to Jarlaxle, but he wasn't about to question the good fortune of it—especially when he knew such fortune could be fleeting. He needed to move.

Across the way from the door, the dragon sisters fought for their lives, and Jarlaxle gasped aloud when he realized their predicament. For their breath had melted the shelf, but the tide of water had rushed down about them, and there had refrozen, leaving Ilnezhara and Tazmikella trapped by their legs and tails as the giants and slaad, the cante and the n'divi, swarmed them.

The dragons bit and beat their wings, thrashing and fighting to the end.

"To her! To her!" Jarlaxle called to Dab'nay and Azzudonna, pointing to Doum'wielle. "Oh, hurry!"

The two ran past Jarlaxle, Azzudonna tossing the sun blade back to the mercenary leader as she went to the woman she, too, had once known as a dear friend.

Jarlaxle hoisted the blade and looked to the mound that had once held him, remembering his portable hole still trapped there.

Could he perhaps escape this catastrophe?

He even took a step that way.

But no, for behind him, not far, stood Zaknafein, and beside him Catti-brie.

He led his hellsteed to the nearest, Zak, and started to mount, but stopped and moved aside when another hellsteed moved in, guided by Artemis Entreri.

"My friend," Jarlaxle murmured.

He didn't need to direct the clearly battered man, who deftly turned his mount and kicked at Zak's stalagmite, then turned again and paced away, cracking the ice shell holding Catti-brie.

Jarlaxle went to work on Zak's tomb immediately, the sun blade shaving the ice so easily and methodically. Entreri came back beside him.

"Free them all," Jarlaxle instructed, and he allowed himself to hope once more that they would rescue these poor victims and get away.

When he glanced back, though, he knew that any hope was premature, surely, for he realized only then that Ygorl was flying fast for the circular window.

And if the creature got there, Jarlaxle knew what would happen next.

"Stop him!" Jarlaxle screamed above all the noise. "Stop him or we cannot win!"

He jumped up, stabbing his finger to the left wall of the room. He winced when he heard Zaknafein breathe his name, and feared that his efforts here would only cause his friend even more profound pain when the cyclones of ice came swirling through once more.

"Stop him!"

ABOVE IT ALL, THE CRASHING ICE, THE ROARING DRAG-
ons, the thunderous spells, Drizzt heard that single call.

He had learned through many years the wisdom of Jarlaxle.

Jarlaxle knew this place.

Jarlaxle understood.

Thus, when Jarlaxle yelled, Drizzt looked to him and followed his
gaze, and heard in the rogue's voice a level of panic and terror so very
rare coming from that one. He didn't question, he didn't hesitate.

He knew.

He whistled to Andahar and began running, then leaped upon
the magnificent unicorn when it charged up beside him, urging it
across the cavern with all speed. A cante rose before them, but Andahar, unbidden, lowered its horn and shattered the beast, running right
through it.

A pair of giants tried to come in from the side to intercept, but
Andahar veered and left them sputtering, far behind.

A pair of slaadi, blue-skinned, huge, and formidable, appeared as if
out of nowhere, simply blinked into existence, right before and beside
the charging unicorn, locking their clawed hands onto Andahar before the unicorn or its rider could even realize their sudden presence.
Andahar thrashed and stubbornly pressed forward, but the slaadi were
strong, their claws sharp and long.

Drizzt started to draw his blades, but he had no time for this, hearing the echoes of Jarlaxle's frantic plea. He leaped up to stand on Andahar's broad back, then flipped forward over the unicorn's head as the
powerful slaadi finally stopped the forward motion. He landed on his
feet, running with all speed, his focus fully ahead, fully on that smoking dark form.

"Hold them, Andahar," he whispered, confident that the unicorn
would fight the slaad to the last.

More cante rose around him, another slaad blinked into position
before him—a trick of the greater being, he knew—but Drizzt had
no time for them. He leaped atop a cante and sprang off, even as the
strange weird-like creature turned its head from ice to liquid, trying to
suck him in.

He fell sliding to his knees, then exploded upward as the blue slaad swiped across with a gigantic two-handed sword, tucking his legs as he rose and flew forward, the blade flowing harmlessly beneath him, then kicking out hard into the slaad's face, sending it staggering backward. It shook its head, making a strange intermittent croaking noise, and readied its sword defensively.

But Drizzt was already long gone, running, leaping, sliding along and up the uneven floor, finding pathways in the broken blocks of ice and focusing, always focusing, on that godlike being. He sprang over blocks of ice, calling upon his ki to lift him impossibly high. He leaped for an icy shelf sticking out from the wall, turning about as he flew to put his back to it. He went in just beneath the lip, reaching up, hands facing back, to catch the thick lip. He held fast as he rocked under it and back, and on that return swing, tugged hard and kicked upward, flipping himself backward onto the shelf.

The giant slaad being saw him coming now and a black lightning bolt shot out at the ranger, clipping him and sending him spinning to slam against a shelf of ice.

But not stopping him. Indeed, hardly slowing him.

The great and terrible creature knew of his intent and Drizzt wasn't surprised when the monster lifted its dark scythe and drew another symbol in the air, the glowing lines attacking Drizzt's very life force with an aura of negative energy that nearly laid him low.

Nearly, but Drizzt heard the panic in Jarlaxle's voice.

Nearly, but Drizzt knew that his father was back there, entombed in the ice.

Nearly, but Drizzt knew that his friends were all here, and that, if he failed, all could be lost.

Nearly, but Drizzt knew that Catti-brie was in that ice behind him, a victim of this very creature. His wife, his love, his purpose, Brie's mother, his life.

Nearly, but he understood all the terrible implications of defeat here, and so he heard again his daughter's cries.

Jarlaxle had warned him. He could not fail.

He ran right through the power of that symbol of death.

He felt the burning pain, denied the burning pain, and closed, Icingdeath and Vidrinath in his hands, jaw clenched.

The Hunter.

But no, more than the Hunter, as Kane had shown.

He sprang lightly, soaring, calling upon his ki to lift him, shelf to shelf, up and up, to the last ledge, then rushed in at the creature and knew its name, as if it was telepathically telling him.

Ygorl!

And he knew he should be afraid, and he knew that he could not win.

Catti-brie was back there. The Companions of the Hall were back there. His father, his friends, his mentor were back there.

He hit Ygorl with a flurry of fury and precision, his blades rolling, stabbing, striking in left and right in such a barrage that could not be blocked or parried or dodged or turned aside in any way. Even a marilith demon, with six arms holding swords, could not have avoided the strikes. This was as near perfection as Drizzt Do'Urden had ever known, a symphony of movement and balance and sheer power beyond the Hunter.

That perfect combination Kane had shown to him.

And he hit Ygorl, more than once, his heavily enchanted blades cutting through the heavy smoke, clicking off slaad bones.

Ygorl!

The slaad god took the strike and did not wince, did not fall away. Across came that scythe in a blinding black flash of movement, and Drizzt spun only just before it, the deadly sickle coming close enough for him to smell the murderous magic on its blade.

One touch . . . Ygorl!

He knew that Ygorl was imparting these thoughts to dispirit him, to make him falter and know he could not win, but he didn't doubt the truth of this last communication.

To get hit by the power of that scythe would bring a swift end.

Back it came the other way, lightning fast, and Drizzt had to throw himself into a sudden retreat . . . a retreat that turned almost as soon as it began, and in he went again, scimitars biting hard, furiously. He had to be perfect.

So he would be.

Or he—and everyone he loved—would die.

CHAPTER 30

In the Heart of the Wind God

A zzudonna slid down beside Doum'wielle, gently rolling the half-elf, half-drow woman over onto her back. She supported Doum'wielle's neck as she did, then pulled her own hand away to find it covered in red.

"No, no, stay with me," Azzudonna pleaded. "You're almost free."

Doum'wielle coughed up a bit of blood and opened her eyes, staring confusedly at the woman who was leaning over her for just a moment before uttering, "Azzu . . ."

"Stay with me!" Azzudonna begged. Beside her, Dab'nay began casting, but before she could send forth the healing word, Doum'wielle's eyes fluttered and her head lolled to the side.

"No, no!" Azzudonna protested.

Dab'nay pulled her off Doum'wielle. "I have her," she said. "I'll get her back! Go to Jarlaxle now!"

And Dab'nay began another spell, a more powerful one by far.

Azzudonna stumbled away, watching, trusting.

Dab'nay brought forth a small diamond and waved it over Doum'wielle's eyes, chanting, calling to her spirit before it could flee the mortal form. The diamond glittered and sparkled, and seemed to send some of those sparkles into the eyes of the dead woman.

Who blinked and was not dead any longer, arching her back in a great heave of breath.

A word of healing came fast behind, and Doum'wielle blinked repeatedly, suddenly awake again and even beginning to prop herself up on her elbows.

"To Jarlaxle," Dab'nay told Azzudonna again, the aevendrow standing and staring.

Azzudonna stumbled around, then gasped in relief, it seemed, when she noted Jarlaxle easing from an ice mound the wonderful man she had come to love. She rushed for Zaknafein and helped extricate him fully, hugging him close as he came back to his senses.

WITH THE AGONIZING MAGICAL SYMBOL ERASED FROM the air, the Companions of the Hall quickly regrouped. Kane was far ahead now, charging at the two slaadi that had intercepted Drizzt and now battled a valiant Andahar. Their claws ripped at the unicorn's flanks, tearing its magical skin. Andahar did not bleed, not liquid blood at least, but every cut showed a brilliant line of light, escaping the summoned steed as surely and as detrimentally as the blood of a real unicorn.

Bruenor and Wulfgar took the front, with Bruenor calling his hell boar back to him. The wild demonic beast wasn't obeying, however. It leaped and charged, bored and snorted flames at any enemies that came near, running back and forth simply because it couldn't seem to stop.

"Come on, boys," Bruenor told his two friends. "Let's show these beasties who they're fightin'!"

In reply, Wulfgar lifted Aegis-fang back over his head with both hands and sent it flying end over end at the nearest enemy, a charging red slaad. Up the slaad hopped and in went the warhammer against its chest, and it was a long time before the slaad came back to the icy floor, a lot farther back—and a lot less alive—when it finally landed in a heap.

Even as Bruenor taunted the next before them, a frost giant, a second giant came rushing in from the side. A popping explosion preceded the behemoth's yelp of pain and a desperate grasp at its shattered knee, and its charge became a tumble and slide, bringing it face-first near Bruenor.

The dwarf king's many-notched axe gained another chip as he cleaved the giant's skull. Bruenor tore it free and battered the giant again and again about the head and neck, then leaped up on the shoulders of the dead thing, lifted his bloody, brain-dripping axe and shield high, and roared, "Battlehammer!"

The dwarf spun to meet the charge of the giant he had been taunting. It came in roaring, both hands holding a gigantic axe, then suddenly and reflexively dropped one hand to its belly and gave an "oof" of surprise.

The hand-crossbow dart's explosion turned that gasp into a scream of protest and pain.

Bruenor charged in, chopping at the behemoth's legs. Down came the giant's two-headed axe, but off balance and weakly, for it was held in just that one hand, and the cut proved easily avoided by the veteran warrior king. Bruenor jumped back, then forward as the axe swept down and about before him. Then he leaped right back in, shield-rushing the giant's lowered arm—not to do any damage, and certainly not to push the behemoth back, but to get his shield up against the forearm. For this was Bruenor's long-used round shield, emblazoned with the foaming-mug standard of Clan Battlehammer, but it was more. Catti-brie had combined it with Orbbcress, a powerful drow creation named after a spiderweb. On Bruenor's command, the buckler grew in size, spiraling out like a spiderweb, and, like a web, it stuck fast to that forearm.

Up into the air went Bruenor as the giant stood straight and raised its arm to shake the troublesome dwarf free. Up he went even higher, as the giant intended, and as Bruenor had expected, to throw him halfway across the chamber. The behemoth meant to lift Bruenor up over its head, but as Bruenor rose past the brute's shoulder, he whipped his axe across into the giant's face, taking its lips and several teeth, and widening its mouth considerably.

Bruenor let go of the weapon, leaving it stuck in place as he casually reached behind his shield and summoned a tankard of ale from it, then gracefully drank that tankard as the giant fell forward, taking Bruenor down along with it.

He hadn't quite finished his drink when he hit and bounced, releasing his shield's magical hold on the giant's forearm.

"Bah, ye bastard son of an umber hulk and a drunken orc!" the dwarf yelled in protest as the ale flew all about. He flung the tankard into the giant's eye, took up his axe handle in both hands, braced a boot against the giant's face, and yanked the weapon free with a great cracking and splattering sound.

"Where's yer mother?" he yelled at the giant, putting his axe into its skull for good measure. "Bah!"

"To Wulfgar!" Regis yelled to him, rushing up and trying to pull him along. "Wulfgar!"

Following the halfling's gaze, Bruenor saw his large friend, some distance ahead of them now and battering a blue slaad with a barrage of hammer strikes that simply blasted through any defense the slaad tried to offer.

But that slaad was hardly alone, and Wulfgar, deep into a bloodlust, seemed unaware of two others, both red-skinned, coming at him in long leaps from opposite sides.

GRANDMASTER KANE TRIED TO KEEP TRACK OF DRIZZT'S run across the room. He traded a leaping circle kick into the face of a blue slaad for a gash of its claws on his leg. He felt the sheer uncleanliness of that strike and understood what it might mean, but he paid it no heed, landing lightly as the slaad fell away, then spinning back to leap right up and over Andahar's broad back, crashing down upon and grappling with the second slaad that had ripped the unicorn's flanks.

Andahar stumbled forward, going for the now-distant Drizzt, loyal to the end, but only a few strides along, another blue slaad leaped upon the unicorn, savagely tearing at the mount's back and neck.

Andahar seemed more light than solid unicorn now, but still stubbornly strode forward after Drizzt, as if too confused to even fight back against the slaad.

One shaky step followed another, but only a couple of times before the magical steed simply dropped, legs splaying wide, the powerful blue slaad tearing with abandon.

Kane's fists pounded his current opponent into the ice in short order, the monk's eyes never leaving the spectacle of Andahar's fall. He rushed away from the battered and dying slaad, a last attempt to get to Andahar, but when he realized he would be too late, that the unicorn was already destroyed, he instead ran for Drizzt and Ygorl as they now squared up before the huge circular window.

Kane didn't take the same route Drizzt had, though. He ignored the broken ramp Drizzt had improvised and ran straight for the window, fully aware that it was at least twenty feet up from the floor and not caring in the slightest.

GROWLING, GROMPH FOUGHT THROUGH THE FOG IN HIS mind, cursing the huge slaad being who had thrown such power against him. The only psionic power the archmage had ever felt greater than this assault was the collective strength of the illithid hive mind.

He had realized from the beginning that this was no ordinary slaad, not even a great and powerful slaad, but now he understood the true might of this creature that had come against him, against them all. And Gromph knew fear, for this was a supernatural force far above and beyond the hulking froglike creatures.

Perhaps even above and beyond *him*.

He looked to the distant demigod standing before the circle of ice set into the far left-hand wall. He saw Drizzt there battling fiercely, and futilely, surely, and noted the charge of Grandmaster Kane, still far away. They were both doomed, Gromph realized, and he turned his attention back to the situation nearer at hand.

They had to get out of there, and quickly, and that meant he needed to remove the continuing pressure on those trying to free the prisoners. He launched his most lethal spells, flinging fireballs and lightning bolts at the slaadi and giants pressing the trio of Bruenor, Wulfgar, and Regis, even putting a line of blazing fire between those three and the monsters that kept rushing for them.

Doing so made him a target, and a pair of slaadi turned their attention to Gromph, throwing spells his way.

But they were not Ygorl, and the archmage's magical shields and wards held their dweomers at bay while his return barrage quickly finished them.

ILNEZHARA BREATHED AGAIN, AT THE FLOOR AND AT HER sister, before freeing her limbs.

Tazmikella paid no heed to the acid, other than to gauge its melting effect on the ice that bound her. With a great leap, she exploded free of the floor and went wild, a dragon unbridled, launching giants and slaadi with her thrashing tail, beating n'divi and cante to bits with her wings, leaping and stomping with all four legs like a terrified washerwoman stomping rats.

She spun fast, whipping her tail behind her to launch a giant through the air. Her front claws caught a blue slaad, lifting it high, where she bit it in half.

"Thank you, sister," she said as the pieces of her victim fell from her maw.

"Repayment, if you please," the battling Ilnezhara asked, still stuck.

Tazmikella's back legs kicked aside her attackers. She beat her wings, launching her into a fast turn, tail trailing and whipping farther along to sweep the legs out from under a group of giants and slaadi, sending them all sliding back across the icy floor.

"Of course," she calmly replied, and breathed from on high at Ilnezhara and those monsters pressing her.

Freed from the ice—and her nearest foes felled by her sister's acid—up into the air leaped Ilnezhara. She and her sister now lifted up above their enemies, dropping on them at every opportunity, and melting them with acid whenever their deadly breath weapons returned.

But they, too, were looking to Jarlaxle's group and the progress there, and, now, as they climbed above the blocking flames of Gromph's roaring wall of fire, they also took note of Drizzt's fight over at the circular window.

"I think he needs us, sister," said Ilnezhara.

"Indeed," came the answer, and the two breathed acid one last time, finishing their current battle, and turned fast for the far-distant left-hand wall of the vast cavern.

WULFGAR WENT DOWN HARD UNDER THE WEIGHT OF THE red slaad that had flanked him. He slid his hand up the handle to the base of Aegis-fang's heavy head and began punching it hard into the face of his attacker.

The blue slaad was still there, though, not dead and coming back in. Wulfgar felt the sudden heat as Gromph's wall of fire came roaring to life, but it was behind that second attacker, and Wulfgar felt, too, the warmth of his own blood rolling down his side from the digging claws of the red slaad atop him.

A small missile flashed above him and above the red slaad, and he understood when he heard the explosion, turning his head just in time to see the blue slaad thrown backward into that wall of fire by the exploding hand-crossbow dart, the creature screaming in high-pitched croaks.

And suddenly, the slaad atop him seemed to get even heavier, and then jerked suddenly and unexpectedly.

Bruenor, standing on its back, leaned forward to regard Wulfgar from over the top of the now-dead slaad's head. "I can tell ye were trained by Drizzt," the red-bearded dwarf said with a wink. He yanked his axe free of the slaad's skull and jumped down to the side, then pushed the giant frog off his friend. "Here's hoping these things're better tasting than a yeti."

Regis rushed to join them as Bruenor helped Wulfgar to his feet, and the halfling wasn't alone, with Pikel Bouldershoulder running beside him, hopping with every step and pointing frantically ahead. "Drizzit Dudden!" the green-bearded dwarf yelped. "Drizzit Dudden!"

The companions turned, all three yelling to Gromph to drop his fire wall. The archmage replied with a magical message, one that was fired into the minds of all on this side of the wall of fire: *Retreat!*

Bruenor yelled back a denial, but Gromph paid him no heed and was already heading back toward the exit tunnel. And others were following, those rescued from the icy stalagmite tombs supporting each other and stumbling along.

Back the other way, Bruenor took hope, for the dragon sisters flew past, coming over the four near the fiery barrier, and over the wall itself.

"Drizzit Dudden!" roared Pikel. He never slowed as Regis joined Bruenor and Wulfgar, the dwarf hopping right past them.

"Pikel, no!" Regis yelled, thinking his friend about to be incinerated.

But Pikel didn't hesitate at all, plunging into the roaring blaze of Gromph's mighty barrier of flame, disappearing from sight.

Regis and the others gasped, but then looked to each other with surprise when they heard Pikel's receding voice, "Drizzit Dudden!"

DRIZZT CONTINUED HIS BARRAGE, UNRELENTING, FORCing Ygorl to stay with him. He could hear the wind beyond the circle of ice, could feel the cold even through his magical protection, and given Jarlaxle's explanation of what had happened the first time, he understood clearly the potentially disastrous price they would all pay if he allowed the slaad god to remove that fragile barrier.

Ygorl kept up with his myriad strikes almost as if the god was anticipating Drizzt's every twist.

Indeed, Drizzt realized immediately, it was doing exactly that.

The drow clenched his jaw and clenched his mind against Ygorl's telepathic intrusions. He would not allow Ygorl in.

The results were immediate, with Icingdeath slipping past Ygorl's attempted parry to plunge into the smoky flesh of the giant slaad, cracking off a rib bone. Drizzt hoped the scimitar would "drink" there, hoped that his sword's cold magic would perform its typical feast on the fires of a lower-planar creature.

But no, Ygorl was not a being of fire, Drizzt realized immediately and retracted. He had stabbed the god-being solidly, but had he even really hurt it?

Ygorl's movements didn't slow, and across came the scythe in a great horizontal sweep, left to right before the drow, forcing Drizzt back—but not too much, because he had to make sure he was close enough to block that swing before the scythe smashed the ice window.

So he leaned back instead of scampering back, bending low and backward and twisting to get Icingdeath in line, and when he realized that his scimitar wouldn't get far enough to halt the scythe, he instead fell flat to his back and thrust his right foot up and out, just ahead of the scythe's swing, hooking the weapon just below the blade with his foot and calling upon his ki to render himself immovable.

But Ygorl wasn't trying to move him. No, the slaad god reversed the swing and rolled the scythe almost immediately upon contact with the foot, turning it over, bringing it back the other way, and now in a manner where it would easily slice off Drizzt's foot and lower leg.

The drow sucked in his breath, expecting the amputation.

But the weapon didn't cut through him, and instead, Drizzt was spun about on the ledge, nearly tumbling over. He didn't understand until he felt the energy, the cut and power of Ygorl's strike, crackling about him, and as he tried to rise, he quickly glanced to his left, back across the cavern.

He saw the dragon sisters closing from the left, near what remained of the shelf and the frozen waterfall. He saw Pikel hopping and screaming just beyond the wall. He saw Kane drawing near, and saw, at the end of Gromph's great wall of flames, Kimmuriel Oblodra sitting astride his nightmare.

The riddle was solved.

Kimmuriel's kinetic barrier had saved him, he knew.

Not that the information mattered in the moment. For Ygorl's reversal wasn't about his leg, or about him at all. No, the slaad god whirled completely around the other way, that mighty scythe crashing into the circular window, shattering it.

The polar winter rushed in on hurricane winds, so strong that Drizzt, just outside the torrent, saw Ygorl's form stretch weirdly, the smoky "flesh" of the being extending out to the side, leaving Ygorl's bones momentarily exposed. For a brief and hopeful heartbeat, Drizzt thought that Ygorl might have inadvertently destroyed itself, but no, the form came back whole, the wind continuing, the barrage of icy hail and shattered sheets of the window blowing into the chamber. Ygorl lifted a hand and called forth a spell, enhancing the hurricane, creating swirls, creating power, creating tornadoes.

And Drizzt couldn't get to Ygorl. Whatever power of his ki, whatever strength of his training, body, soul, and control, he understood that to move before that broken window would launch him flying across the room in short and violent order.

He could only huddle and watch.

He watched the broken shards of the window fly off, spinning missiles, many flying about Grandmaster Kane. He saw his mentor, his friend, dodge and kick one aside, then go spinning back, around and down as many more went pounding through, shattering with every contact.

Drizzt couldn't see much through the hurricane, but saw enough to know that Kane had just lost his right arm!

He stared at the monk, who rose the moment the large missiles were past, stumbling forward once more. He wanted to focus there, to draw strength from fearless and mighty Grandmaster Kane, but his attention was drawn back toward the wall of fire, the roiling flames hissing and battling the onslaught. And more than that, his attention was caught and held by the dance of Pikel Bouldershoulder.

Pikel stood tall before the onslaught, silhouetted by the flames close behind, rocking back and forth, waving his arms and screaming his spells, though Drizzt couldn't begin to hear the chant. The floor all about Pikel began to roil and wave like an ocean swell, leaving a horde of cante in its wake.

Drizzt turned back to Ygorl, still in the center of the inrushing storm and bothered little, if at all. The slaad god lashed out at the dragons as they struggled against the hurricane winds. They were far enough to the side of the main blast to still come forward in their flight, which gave Drizzt some hope, but he also worried they were slowed too much.

That fear was confirmed when a bolt of black lightning reached out from Ygorl, forking to strike at both. A second followed right behind.

As much as he had come to respect the power of this being before him, he gawked in surprise when that magical lightning found its mark. These were dragons, among the greatest beings in the Realms, yet Tazmikella and Ilnezhara dropped to the floor in heaps, and the wind sent them sliding back, back across the ice.

As it pushed their bodies back, the ice storm also roared against Gromph's wall of fire, which battled against the assault. The flames would lose that fight, though. Which meant everything Drizzt held dear would lose, too.

Because his dearest friends, his dear father, his beloved Catti-brie were all on the other side of that wall of fire.

JARLAXLE THOUGHT THE FIGHT OVER, THOUGHT THEM all doomed, when he heard the crash of the circular window down the far end of the cavern and heard the wind rushing in. He had seen it all before.

He glanced to the remnants of the stalagmite mound that had captured him on his first journey into this cold hell, and wondered briefly if he might somehow get his portable hole free of the ice and perform his trick a second time.

But there was no chance.

Except . . . it wasn't ice that assaulted Jarlaxle, but rain. It stung indeed, and the wind buffeted him and the others wickedly, but the ice wasn't yet able to form and entomb them. At one point, Wulfgar went sliding by, Bruenor and Regis riding him like a sled, with Bruenor's hell boar giving chase—a scene so absurd that Jarlaxle laughed aloud despite the imminent doom (though his laughter went unheard in the roar of the wind).

His light mood died fast, though, when he noted that Wulfgar was leaving a wake of blood.

Get them out! All! Now! Jarlaxle heard in his thoughts, and he saw Kimmuriel riding his nightmare toward the tunnel.

Everyone on this side of the flaming wall, at least, heard that call, for all but Gromph were already moving. Azzudonna supported Doum'wielle. Dab'nay and two other freed prisoners supported each other. Jarlaxle ran to do the same, pulling Catti-brie fully free and hoisting her over his shoulder. He started out, but paused, scooping Taulmaril from the base of the broken stalagmite.

Entreri brought his mount to Zaknafein and took the weapon master's hand. Neither had the strength to get Zak up, though, so Entreri just held on and let the mount drag the man.

More than a score, rescuers and victims, battled the wind and moved to escape.

Jarlaxle veered past his old ice prison, hoping to see the black cloth of his portable hole. He spotted it, but the ice had it, and as much as Jarlaxle treasured that item, he treasured the woman slung over his shoulder far more. "Farewell, my favored home," he said. "We have been through a lot together, alas."

He glanced back to Gromph, who stood before his flame shield, casting again and again, raising another wall of fire, then a third, determined to defeat the hurricane of Ygorl.

Jarlaxle knew in his heart that it was hopeless. That the hurricane was too much. But maybe, just maybe, Gromph's rage-filled casting would give him and the others enough time to flee. So he focused on the tunnel, leaning against the wind, struggling to keep his feet in light of the howling winds and the pelting rain.

Kimmuriel came back out of that tunnel then, turning fast to the side.

And behind him came a horde of cante, pouring into the main chamber, but turning the other way from Kimmuriel, turning to Jarlaxle's right as he approached. They rushed at a group of retreating, helpless victims, most of whom were now crawling, and flowed among them, and Jarlaxle's heart fell.

Only for his dread to turn to confusion. For the cante flowed among them, but not over them. The watery, icy weirds didn't climb up to encase any, but simply went past the group, rushing to the nearest end of Gromph's wall of fire and flowing around it toward the far end of the great chamber.

To the call of the slaad god Ygorl, Jarlaxle believed, and he closed his eyes, hugged Catti-brie a bit tighter, and whispered a prayer for Drizzt, for Kane, for Pikel, and for Ilnezhara and Tazmikella.

He was already plotting to bring another party here, a stronger party. As he began making his way toward the tunnel once more, he noted Gromph walking backward, cursing, pausing every few moments to throw yet another spell at the relentless onslaught. Kimmuriel sat astride the nightmare beside him exiting the room, and he said something to Jarlaxle. But the rogue didn't really hear it, too lost in the fantasy as he imagined four dwarven armies and the Bregan D'aerthe host finishing the grim business that had begun in this chamber.

He imagined not a rescue, but revenge.

JARLAXLE WAS WRONG ABOUT THE CANTE. THEY DID NOT hear the call of Ygorl at all.

Pikel Bouldershoulder was on the front side of the wall of fire, so Ygorl's tornadoes of binding ice were neither diminished nor melted by Gromph's enchantment when they reached him. And unlike Kane, he wasn't near enough to the far wall to be mostly under the force of the storm. The green-bearded dwarf should have been taken already, entombed in a stalagmite of ice, as Jarlaxle's band had been taken in their first battle here those many days ago, as Galathae's first expedition, including Doum'wielle, had been taken at the time of the spring equinox.

But he wasn't. His beard was frosty, certainly, his teeth chattering as he sang to a god. Not a dwarven god, not Moradin or Dumathoin or

Clangeddin. Nor to one of the druidic gods common in the southland, like Catti-brie's own Mielikki.

No, Pikel sang to a god he felt very near, and every line, every chant, ended with an emphatic "Qadeej!"

Qadeej, a Wind Duke of Aaqa, one of the great Vaati celestials, who had chosen this place to abandon his physical coil and pass on to the other side of existence, thus creating this very glacier.

This chamber, this exact spot, was the tomb of the wind god Qadeej, Pikel understood, for he felt the spirit of the celestial being resonating all about him. The cante were of Qadeej, the n'divi were of Qadeej, the storm Ygorl had sent into the room was of Qadeej.

But Ygorl was not Qadeej.

Qadeej of the wind, and so of nature, and so of balance.

Pikel's song, Pikel's spell, Pikel's plea was a call for that balance, the dwarf's curious mumbling claiming in the manner of a magistrate that one creature here, and one alone, was destroying that very thing treasured in the realm of Nature.

The wind rose before little Pikel, rolling before him like a funnel cloud lying on its side, taking ephemeral form, like a darkening thunderhead. It grew and the pelting ice could not get through it, and the tornadoes approaching Pikel were unspun by it, and Pikel stood tall, calling to Qadeej, demanding of Qadeej.

Qadeej heard.

The cante, a hundred cante, swarmed at the green-bearded dwarf.

IT WAS HARD TO TELL WITH A CREATURE THAT SEEMED more insubstantial smoke than flesh, but Drizzt clearly sensed that Ygorl was confused by the dark cloud that had arisen halfway across the room, a countering wind that not only stopped the furious wintry hurricane in its path but was now flying fast the other way.

Drizzt ducked tighter against the wall when that countering windstorm howled through, sounding like a chorus of a dozen ancient dragons roaring out in unison. He felt the initial push of Pikel's storm, but the wind was aimed more specifically, and to the side of the window, there was far more noise than actual squall. Drizzt dared to peek out under his covering arm, to see Ygorl standing in the middle of the second hurricane, that awful black scythe raised in both hands above its head. The slaad god yelled back, it seemed, but the wind took the cries of protest right out through the large opening in the wall.

It took Ygorl's storm, too.

It was powerful, but not enough to take Ygorl.

Drizzt fleetingly thought to leap upon the distracted monster then, but if he got in the path of that gale, he would simply be launched out the window before he ever got near to his intended target.

He crouched there, flustered, helpless. He wanted to help—he knew that he had to—but how?

And then it all stopped.

It happened so abruptly that it took Drizzt a moment to even understand that the air within the vast chamber was very still.

Ygorl was still staring hatefully at the little dwarf so far away. And Drizzt was still tingling with the energy caught by Kimmuriel's kinetic barrier.

No longer sidelined, no longer unable to act, Drizzt rolled to his feet and leaped at the slaad, bashing with Vidrinath and releasing the power of Ygorl's murderous strike back into the slaad god.

He had destroyed Demogorgon once with a similar strike, though that one had carried the power of nearly all the drow of Menzoberranzan with it.

This time, his enemy was hardly vanquished, but Drizzt had hurt Ygorl . . . at least, he *believed* he had, from the strange croaking shriek that came forth in response.

Ygorl staggered back several steps.

Only for Drizzt to retreat several steps when Ygorl came back at him, the scythe working with furious speed. He had no kinetic barrier now—getting hit meant death, most certainly.

This, though, was a fight he could understand. Still, every block from Drizzt came in the form of crossed blades, for the strokes of the slaad god were too strong for him to parry now with only one scimitar. Even then, the weight of the blows from the side sent him half spinning, and those coming down nearly buckled his knees with their power. He couldn't even think of countering any attacks that he blocked.

He needed Ygorl to miss.

One sidelong cut had him turning left and stepping back. He took the chance and retracted his blades, the scythe just barely missing as it passed. Drizzt intended to reverse and go right in, seeing a small opening, but he hesitated, for on the cavern floor below the ledge came Grandmaster Kane, quickly closing across the last expanse with mounting speed in the absence of the windstorm.

Ten feet away, with Ygorl still focusing on Drizzt, Kane leaped, his remaining arm extended before him, and almost seemed to fly, higher and higher, eclipsing the ledge twenty feet up.

For only a brief moment, Drizzt thought Kane meant to barrel into the slaad god to push it out the window as Pikel's storm had failed to do. But before Kane had gone halfway in his great leap, Drizzt recognized that no, such was not the monk's intent.

For Kane began to transform in that leap, his physical being becoming sparkles of light, shimmering and threatening to flutter away as if he had turned into a kaleidoscope of glittering butterflies.

Drizzt understood.

He wanted to cry out, to deny Kane's choice, but the words caught in his throat, and wouldn't have mattered anyway.

For Grandmaster Kane was transcending, becoming both less and more of his physical being, becoming one with the multiverse around him, becoming one with everything, starstuff, the harmony of the cosmos.

And that form, those butterflies of light, didn't crash against Ygorl.

They went *into* Ygorl's smoky form, and there they remained.

Drizzt stepped back even more, staring, his jaw hanging open at the spectacle before him, for the smoky, vapory body of the slaad god truly seemed like a distant cloud at that moment, a thunderhead with sparkles of lightning erupting within its grim darkness.

Those points of light *were* Grandmaster Kane, and every spark clearly stung and shook Ygorl, who roared in defiance and pain.

Drizzt had the opportunity to rush in and batter Ygorl, but how could he? For Kane was a part of that being now.

The drow gripped his weapons, watching, confused.

PIKEL PAID NO HEED TO THE MOUNDS OF LIVING WATER flowing at him, then past him. He just kept yelling "Qadeej!" at the end of every line of his new song, while he danced and twirled about. Everything about him became irrelevant as he basked in the moment of communion, as he felt the beauty of the wind god and welcomed Qadeej into his heart.

The cante, though, surely paid heed to Pikel. The dwarf seemed only vaguely aware of that as they rushed past him and flopped and slopped down to the floor, one atop the other, piling and forming in a great blend of their sustaining energy, going from a hundred separate magical beings, or constructs, or whatever animated them, into a single growing column before the dancing, green-bearded dwarf.

And that column took more definite form, becoming a gigantic, towering arm, and a hand, with fingers stretching.

A god taking form.

"Oooo," said Pikel, coming out of one pirouette and finally seeing the singular creation standing majestically before him. "Qadeej?" he asked.

He had no idea of what he had just awakened. But he did resume his dance, eliminating the twirls and singing a song dominated by the refrain of "half'n'halfen, half'n'halfen, half'n'halfen," crying out for the beauty of balance while rocking side to side with his arm and half arm outstretched, as if trying to mimic the pan holders of a large scale.

DRIZZT WORKED WILDLY WHEN YGORL CAME ON AGAIN, the points of light that had been Grandmaster Kane gradually dissipating within the dark boundaries of the slaad being.

The drow ranger tried to deny what he had just seen before him, almost as if trying to excise Kane from the hulking Ygorl with his scimitars.

Drizzt had lost Kane. He had lost one of his dearest friends and mentors.

All the distractions faded away. He became the Hunter and more. All of his training, years and years, centuries even, with the blade and his heightened understanding of his life force and this physical coil he wore came together in perfect harmony.

He was as Grandmaster Kane had hoped he would be.

Every movement, no matter how subtle, heightened that which followed. Icingdeath slipped past Ygorl's defenses. Vidrinath followed, once and again.

A spin and duck got Drizzt's foot up to kick Ygorl in its frog-like face, a blow that would have thrown Wulfgar across the room.

Then again on the completion of the turn came the scimitars, one and another, slipping past, striking his enemy hard.

And Ygorl was diminished. There could be no doubt. The strikes by Gromph, the kinetic release of deadly magic by Drizzt, the wind of Pikel, and mostly, the sacrifice of Kane, had profoundly wounded the deific being.

Still, it became apparent to Drizzt in those very first exchanges after resuming the fight that he remained impossibly overmatched. Even though he was getting his attacks through Ygorl's defenses and avoiding that deadly scythe, he became convinced that his scimitars, for all their enchantments, were doing only minimal harm to this great and godlike Ygorl.

He had to be perfect, so he was, as close as he had ever been.

It didn't matter.

"Run away, all!" he cried out for Pikel and the dragon sisters, and any other allies still close enough to hear. He continued his work, determined to keep Ygorl engaged fully for as long as possible. As Kane had sacrificed for him, so would he for his friends.

"Catti-brie is out," he told himself, and that brought him hope and acceptance.

More of his strikes got through, but it gave Drizzt little encouragement, for the giant slaad being wasn't even trying to stop them, obviously convinced now that they couldn't really hurt. Absent that distraction, Ygorl fell into a rhythm that Drizzt could not interrupt. Growing confident and full of rage, clearly, Ygorl took up its weapon in just one hand, still defending, while drawing another agonizing symbol in the air with its free hand.

Drizzt clenched his jaw, desperate to fight through the debilitating magic. Frustrated that his perfection was so casually dismissed.

But Ygorl came on suddenly, a great overhead chop that Drizzt could not hope to deflect or block, striking so quickly that the drow's only escape was to simply throw himself backward, half turning as he went.

Ygorl hit him with a swirl of wind, a sudden and wicked cyclone, that spun the drow in midair and altered his flight to slam him against the glacial wall to the side of the circular opening.

Drizzt struggled to maintain consciousness. He knew that he had to get up and ready his blades, knew that Ygorl would close fast and kill him with a single blow.

He found his focus on what appeared to be a giant arm. A pillar of ice, it seemed, a hand reaching up from the floor like the limb of some gigantic creature that lay below the icy surface.

The arm swayed away from him, then came back suddenly, punching across, and Drizzt sucked in his breath, expecting to be squashed.

But the blow didn't land.

The hand punched at Ygorl, not at Drizzt, striking the slaad god with the force of a Vaati celestial, slamming the smoky giant and driving it through the opening behind the press of its giant translucent fist.

That fist stopped at the circular window and quickly de-formed, flattening itself there and releasing dozens and dozens of cante to stretch and rejoin, re-forming the icy window, sealing out the winter storm, sealing out Ygorl, at least for the moment.

Once again the vast chamber fell silent so suddenly it nearly took Drizzt's breath away.

Far across the chamber, Drizzt saw Gromph's fire wall die to smoky wisps. He noted the dragon sisters back in human form, stumbling for the exit tunnel.

"Oooo," he heard Pikel say, and he turned his attention to the dwarf on the floor below him, and, more importantly, to the giant forearm that swayed back and forth before the doo-dad.

"Oooo."

They both watched as that towering pillar of ice fell over away from Drizzt—fell over Pikel, rushing down, pressing the dwarf below it before flattening out across the floor, a new and slick glaze of ice, like an Icewind Dale pond fast freezing on a late autumn night when the winds turned to blow from the north.

Drizzt pulled himself up from the floor of the ledge on that far wall of the vast chamber. He looked to the ledge before him, in front of the circular window, where a pile of clothes, Kane's robes, remained.

He moved over and picked them up, holding them reverently.

He had seen this before.

He closed his eyes and thought of the sparkles of light, the butter-flies of Grandmaster Kane's corporeal being, internally warring with Ygorl. Flickering and fleeting, transcending, leaving this life behind, selflessly. Giving himself, quite literally, for the sake of Drizzt and the others.

With a heavy sigh, Drizzt rolled off the ledge and dropped the twenty feet to the floor below, noting the sheen of the new ice, glisten-ing green from the glow of the Merry Dancers twinkling in through the nearly translucent window.

"Pikel," he whispered repeatedly as he approached, searching all about.

He found nothing.

Tears streamed down Drizzt's face as he pressed the robes of Kane near to him and stared down at the area where Pikel Bouldershoulder had been lost.

He believed that his wife was outside. He was fairly certain that his father, too, had been rescued. And Entreri, and a dozen others.

He understood the cost, and hated it, even as he nodded.

For this was what they did. This was the price of friendship, the loyalty that bound them all and gave strength to them all.

But Kane!

But Pikel!

The gain could not be denied, but neither could the pain of the losses.

Drizzt sheathed his blades and moved slowly and deliberately across the floor, almost hoping that a cante or a hundred cante would rise up to challenge him, hoping that more slaadi and giants would return to the chamber to hinder his passage.

Because in that awful moment of loss, Drizzt Do'Urden just wanted to hit something.

EPILOGUE

Carrying Catti-brie over his shoulder, Jarlaxle followed the others down the tunnel, right behind Bruenor and Regis, who were dragging a barely conscious Wulfgar. Jarlaxle studied the man's wounds, first staring at the great gash on his side and wondering if it might prove mortal, but then looking more closely at a wound Wulfgar had taken on one arm, a wound that looked painfully familiar to Jarlaxle in the way it was showing on the man's skin. How glad he was that Catti-brie was there, with her understanding now of how to cure the slaad disease.

Jarlaxle looked ahead of that trio to Entreri, leaning low on the hellsteed, holding on to Zaknafein's hand as the man half stumbled, half dragged himself alongside.

Up in front, Kimmuriel led the way on his hellsteed, stomping its hooves and sending gouts of flame out to the sides, the breadth of the tunnel. Jarlaxle could only hope that the swarm of cante that had come forth represented the whole of them in that passage, though, for among this battered, retreating group, not many could hope to defend themselves.

Behind Kimmuriel came Gromph, walking steadier with each step, a mask of outrage growing on his face, Jarlaxle noted as he kept looking back to the trailing line of rescuers and rescued.

Jarlaxle was glad to see that look, and was not surprised when Gromph stepped up beside Kimmuriel and filled the tunnel before them with a fireball, then launched a second one into the same side room he had blasted when they had entered.

Finally, they came out into the rift, where the storm had quieted and the Merry Dancers shimmered in the sky above. Coincidentally, the strike team had rescued a dozen and one, a *verve zithd*, who had been lost in the spring raid led by Galathae. Half of them aevendrow, the other six comprising three arktos oroks and three kurit dwarves, and, of course, Doum'wielle.

But five of his own thirteen were still in there.

"We got to go back!" Bruenor roared.

Jarlaxle turned back to the dwarf, who stood with Regis over the prone Wulfgar, with the big man stubbornly trying to rise as he clutched the garish wound at his side.

"Th'elf's still in there!" Bruenor said. "And Pikel. Form up!"

"They'll get out or they'll be killed, King Bruenor," Gromph countered. "We cannot win in there. The fight is ended."

"Yer fight, might be!" Bruenor shouted back. "We ain't for leavin' our own!"

"Then go and die. And perhaps the next dwarf who takes the throne of Gauntlgrym will prove wiser than their predecessor."

"Let's go," Wulfgar said through his gritted teeth, and he forced himself to his feet—almost. He tumbled back to the ground.

"Dab'nay!" Jarlaxle yelled, but it was Catti-brie who rose beside him and made her way first to the fallen Wulfgar. She even waved away Dab'nay, who was busy trying to bolster the battered prisoners.

"I have my spells," she explained to Jarlaxle, who moved beside her. "As surely as I had them when I was frozen in the chamber. It's as if time stopped in there."

"Red slaad and a blue," Jarlaxle explained, and Catti-brie nodded, understanding the implications.

With Jarlaxle's help, she got to Wulfgar and immediately began to cast.

She stopped, though, and reached into her pouch, producing the onyx figurine. She called to Guenhwyvar and nodded to Bruenor as the panther began to form.

"Let's go!" Bruenor said, and hopped onto his hell boar. Regis ran up and fell into place behind the dwarf.

And another mount came pacing by, heading for the tunnel. Atop his hellsteed, Artemis Entreri nodded to Jarlaxle and Catti-brie.

Catti-brie grabbed Taulmaril from Jarlaxle and pulled off her quiver, tossing both up to the man.

Guenhwyvar charged for the entrance, Bruenor and Regis right behind.

Entreri gave chase, galloping the hellsteed full out, and was the first one back into the tunnel.

Jarlaxle just stood and stared, hoping against hope. He reminded himself that they were not safe yet, and so looked around.

Catti-brie tended Wulfgar with her spells. The man looked better already. He lifted his hand and called back into the cavern, and Aegis-fang appeared.

"Get me a mount," he told Jarlaxle, though sheer stubbornness wouldn't get him through this now, for he certainly wasn't nearly ready for such a charge quite yet.

Jarlaxle scanned the group, watching Dab'nay and Azzudonna as they worked from orc to dwarf to aevendrow, helping, healing, reassuring. He noted Doum'wielle, Little Doe of the Moonwood, sitting and staring at Gromph, clearly terrified.

Jarlaxle moved to her.

"He won't hurt you," Jarlaxle assured her.

Doum'wielle gawked at him, obviously unconvinced.

"You're going home," Jarlaxle told her.

"No!" she growled back at him. "Never!"

After a moment of confusion, Jarlaxle understood and clarified for the poor woman. "Home to Callidae, not Menzoberranzan," he explained.

Doum'wielle stared at him for a few heartbeats, then exhaled and burst into tears.

Jarlaxle wrapped his arm about her. "We came to rescue you," he whispered to her. "You deserve this. You deserve Callidae. You are welcomed there and beloved there."

Doum'wielle just hugged him tight, and it felt good to him.

Doing this for her felt very good indeed, and reminded him of the reason they risked so much.

This was not the way of Menzoberranzan, not the way of Lolth.

This was the right way.

A few calls and the movements of all around him looking back toward the tunnel turned both Jarlaxle and Doum'wielle.

A pair of human women emerged from the tunnel, leaning on each other, covered with more blood than clothing.

Relief flooded through Jarlaxle at the sight of Tazmikella and Ilnezhara, but it was tempered by the obvious pounding they had taken, a reminder that these foes were formidable, an army of great power, and that none of them were yet safe.

"THE COPPER DRAGONS," WULFGAR EXPLAINED TO CATTI-BRIE. "Jarlaxle did this, all of this, to rescue you and the others. But the cost."

"We do not yet know the cost," Catti-brie cut him short. "Drizzt is not dead."

Wulfgar couldn't speak past the lump in his throat. He pulled his dear Catti-brie closer, nodding to her claim.

The hell boar rushed out of the tunnel, Bruenor and Regis astride. Entreri charged out of the tunnel on his nightmare, Taulmaril in hand. Both mounts were pulled up abruptly, spinning about.

Catti-brie held her breath, then burst into tears when her husband appeared, Guenhwyvar by his side.

As it always should be.

She leaped up and ran over, Wulfgar staggering to follow. She rushed in for a great hug, but stopped short, noting the bundle Drizzt carried so reverently.

"Grandmaster Kane is no more," Drizzt announced.

"Where's Pikel?" Regis blurted.

Drizzt looked to the halfling and slowly shook his head. Then he swayed as if he was about to fall over, but Catti-brie caught him and held him and whispered into his ear that she would never let him go.

"GROMPH IS RETURNING TO THE SOUTHLAND NOW," JARL-axle announced a short while later, after the healing was completed and the troupe was ready to move. "King Bruenor, Regis, Wulfgar, and my dear dragon friends will go with him."

"Wait now . . ." Bruenor began to protest, looking to Catti-brie and Drizzt.

"This is not an invitation to debate," Jarlaxle said. "This was pre-determined. We know what we're doing, and this is the only way. The six of you must leave—now. We will join you shortly."

"You'll need help getting them folks we rescued home," Bruenor argued.

"Every extra person slows us down, and we must indeed be away, and at once," Jarlaxle replied.

"Then me girl and Drizzt come with us."

"Catti-brie cannot, because of a promise that she must keep." Jarlaxle looked to the woman as he said that, and she nodded.

"I canno', me da," she added. "I must do something first, on me word." She glanced over at Azzudonna and the two shared a nod.

"Nor can Entreri, nor Zaknafein," Jarlaxle explained, and the two men nodded. "And Drizzt won't leave Catti-brie's side, I am sure."

"I wouldn't let him," said Catti-brie.

"Kimmuriel will return us when we have fulfilled our promise, and Dab'nay will tend to the wounded as we make our way."

"Yer way where?"

Jarlaxle sighed and stared at the dwarf.

"Ah, so ye're not for tellin'," Bruenor reasoned. "And that's part of yer deal, eh?"

"Trust us, me da," Catti-brie begged the dwarf, moving right before him. "We'll be home. We'll all be home, soon. I promise. On me word as a Companion of the Hall. We're not for leaving any behind, nor breaking our vows, aye. As ye came for me, so I'll be back for yerself."

"Of course. Ye're me girl," he said, as if that was enough for what they'd all been through.

And she knew, for him, it was, and she smiled as she said goodbye.

He wasn't happy about it, but Bruenor just threw up his hands, muttered something about gratitude, and moved back to join Regis and Wulfgar.

The dragon sisters and Gromph joined them, Jarlaxle whispering, "Igloos?" to the archmage as he passed, to which he responded with a nod.

A moment later, a door appeared in the air, and the six travelers stepped through, returning to the Hosttower of the Arcane in the City of Sails.

"Now we just have to figure out how we're going to get out of here and back to the first rift," Jarlaxle told the remaining group.

"The journey will take hours, even with your mounts," Azzudonna reminded him.

"Longer than you believe, I fear, and more dependent on the weather's mood," Jarlaxle replied. "You wear your protective clothing, but some of us are shielded from the killing cold by spells alone, which will expire, and the caster was lost to us in the cavern."

"Pikel," Drizzt explained to Catti-brie, Zak, and Entreri.

"I can help with that," Catti-brie told them. "But the duration of my protections is not long, and we've many days of travel ahead."

"Then please let us begin," Kimmuriel interrupted, and he summoned his hellsteed. "I am weary, but if it becomes desperate, I can bring some ahead to the rift."

Drizzt lifted his whistle and called to Andahar, hoping that the unicorn would return, given the true beating it had taken in the cavern—he had not before seen Andahar destroyed and so dismissed due to a battle. He breathed a great sigh of relief when the mount came charging up from afar, growing larger with every stride.

Off they went without hesitation, but even with the mounts, it did indeed become desperate in short order, as the storm came up anew beyond the rift. Using his psionic powers, Kimmuriel wind-walked the group, a few at a time, to the rift, where they found Gromph waiting for them.

They huddled in the igloos and hoped the storm would abate.

"The slaadi used the frozen prisoners as hosts, we believe," Azzudonna explained to the visitors from the southlands. "They took the ones we did not find one at a time, and from them created more of their foul kind."

"They followed no pattern," Doum'wielle added. "Just every now and again, they would come and take one. I cannot tell you the horror. I—we—could see, but we couldn't move. We couldn't act. We couldn't blink. We were just there. We just . . . watched."

"Watched and existed with the world going on about us, like ghosts trapped between life and death," Catti-brie added. "The enchantments I had cast did not expire, the spells I had prepared did not slip from my mind. It was unlike anything I have ever known."

"And nothing I ever want to know again," Entreri remarked. He wore a mask of disgust and shook his head. "I'd take the wasps in the cocoon before I'd go back to the black of emptiness."

That brought more than a few raised eyebrows from those who knew of Entreri's ordeal in the painful hell he had endured at the severe judgment of conscience personified.

"We will get you back to Callidae," Jarlaxle promised.

Azzudonna stiffened at the mention of the city, and looked around to those from the south who had not been there before.

"We're bringing them—or rather, they're likely bringing us," Jarlaxle insisted. "This was the price of the rescue."

A cold look passed over the aevendrow's face, the realization that a greater cost might soon be realized. She couldn't deny her happiness at the rescue of thirteen lost Callidaeans, nor at the rescue of Catti-brie, Entreri, and, of course, Zaknafein.

But the rules of the city, the needed secrecy, could not be so easily dismissed. She looked to Jarlaxle, reminding herself of his promise, reminding herself that he had earned her trust. Or had he? Wasn't the mere act of him bringing the others north a betrayal? Azzudonna didn't know what to think here, but as she had no options open, she had to hope and let it play out.

"The other three were not subjected to the ritual," Jarlaxle told Kimmuriel and Gromph. "Their memories of our destination are clear, I am sure. Access those with your mind magic and you will see clearly, and we can be in Callidae . . ."

"I won't do it," Entreri announced, and he stared at the archmage.

"Nor I," said Zak.

Catti-brie didn't respond, but she, too, turned a wary eye upon Kimmuriel, Dab'nay, and particularly Gromph.

"Better that I died than betray them," Entreri stated.

"There you have it," Zak agreed.

Gromph chuckled and snorted. "It's good to see that you've thought this through," he told Jarlaxle.

"It doesn't matter, and they won't have to betray their word," Jarlaxle told them all. "It is possible that I have recovered enough of my memories for Gromph and Kimmuriel to locate the city and get us there. The plan hasn't changed."

He turned to the three who had been frozen beside him. "I didn't wish to do it this way, but there were only so many options available. And even those became more limited with the loss of Pikel, who could protect us through the storm as we traveled conventionally."

"But once you have brought them, the ritual won't protect my home, obviously," Azzudonna said.

"Haven't we earned your trust?" Jarlaxle asked.

"Some of you have."

"You can trust Drizzt Do'Urden, perhaps more than any of the rest of us," Artemis Entreri put in.

"Enough of this," said Gromph. He turned to Azzudonna. "Are you going to have your rescued kinsmen, the orcs and the dwarves, attack us?"

"Of course not. We are not ungrateful."

"Aren't you, then?"

"Gromph, you do not understand," Jarlaxle said.

"If you're lying, please come on quickly, so it can be settled quickly. I grow impatient."

"I beg you all to simply shut up," Kimmuriel intervened, and he stepped in between the groups and turned his attention to Azzudonna.

"Hear me well, Azzudonna of Callidae," he said. "Your city is not unknown to me, not any borough of the place. For it is not unknown to the hive mind of the illithids, where I am no stranger. They have known of it since its inception, but fear not, for they care not enough to ever bother with you and yours. They are no threat.

"Nor are we. On my word. I need to witness this place you call home. Gromph Baenre and Dab'nay need to witness this place, for the sake of hope, and for circumstances beyond Callidae that involve the life of your distant kin who have lost their way. And Drizzt Do'Urden needs to see this place, and above all others here, deserves to. You can trust us.

"More, you *must* trust us. You live in Callidae, yes, but you also live in this world. We will do all in our power to protect you and your secret, but there are larger things at play."

"So I once thought," Doum'wielle muttered, and she was staring at Gromph, the wizard who had so casually and callously thrown her through a portal into the desolate north.

"We *will* go to Callidae," Kimmuriel told her when Azzudonna continued to show doubt. "With or without you. You can no longer hide it from us. That is a promise, but no threat, for there is no threat here. I tell you simply and honestly, we are no threat to your home. You must believe—"

He stopped and nearly fell over as the ground beneath them began to violently shake. Cries from beyond their shelter's walls told them that it wasn't just this igloo, either, and they all scrambled outside before the structure simply collapsed upon them.

The shaking ended as abruptly as it had begun.

Outside, Jarlaxle and the others stopped and stared, as those who had exited the other igloos stopped and stared, for before them in the glacial rift lay a great block of ice, glowing not merely in the dim reflection of the Merry Dancers, but as if with an internal light.

The block split suddenly with a loud crack and the halves fell aside, leaving a single diminutive figure standing there, then shaking wildly, his dwarven lips flapping, to get the ice chips off his thick green beard and light green robe.

"Pikel?" Catti-brie murmured.

"Oo oi," said the dwarf, and he reached up for the pot he wore as a helmet and pulled it from his head, and it took his friends a moment to realize that he was using his left arm—the arm he had lost decades before!

Except it wasn't his arm—not the one he once had, at least—for it wasn't of flesh and bone, but a limb of blue-white ice.

He brought the impromptu helmet before him and banged the sheen of ice from it with his other hand, then plopped it back on his head.

"Hehehe," he said.

Drizzt and Catti-brie ran to him, the others close behind.

"How?" Catti-brie asked repeatedly.

"Qadeej!" Pikel shouted, and he pulled back and began to twirl. "Qadeej, me brudder!"

Me brudder? Catti-brie mouthed.

"Don't ask," said Jarlaxle beside her. "Better not to know."

The score of onlookers stood and stared as Pikel continued his dance, singing to Qadeej and reaching for the sky above, calling for an end to Ygorl's storm.

The clouds parted, the Merry Dancers shone brightly, but Pikel continued his dance, reaching up, beckoning them, and indeed, the sky almost seemed to respond, green swirls reaching down at the dwarf, coming right to the ground beside him and swirling, spinning, taking shape.

"Qadeej, Sustarre," Pikel said, as if introducing two celestial beings the others could not see.

"He's making another chariot of flames," Jarlaxle realized, and it soon became quite obvious, except that this one was much larger and wasn't conventional fire, but green, like the Merry Dancers. And it was pulled by a team of eight horses, or horselike images at least, swirling and ethereal.

When it was completed, Pikel leaped up and took the reins, then held his arm of ice out to invite the others, all of them, aboard.

"I'll never understand that dwarf," Jarlaxle remarked. "And that, I expect, is a good thing."

"No one does," Catti-brie agreed. "And yes, that's a good thing."

"The gods surely seem to," Jarlaxle corrected. "Is there any god of nature, even a Wind Duke of Aaqa, who doesn't rain favor on that one?"

"Let's hope not to find out."

They set off soon after, all of them riding in Pikel's chariot of celestial light, which seemed to be speeding above the ground, not upon it, for not a bump or jolt was to be felt.

"Can you take this atop the glacier and over it?" Jarlaxle asked the dwarf.

"Hehehe," came the reply, and up the side of the glacier they climbed.

After the sounds of surprise quieted and the others caught their collective breath, Jarlaxle turned to Azzudonna, Catti-brie, Entreri, and Zak.

"I want to go in through the outer cavern of Cascatte," he explained. "I want my friends to first glimpse the city the same way we did."

"I cannot argue with that desire," said Zak. "Like you, I knew at once."

"Knew what?" Drizzt asked.

"That we had come home, my son. That we had come home."

Catti-brie hugged Drizzt closer and tried hard not to weep. "If only Brie were here," she whispered into his ear.

"Besides," added Jarlaxle, "it will be worth the detour just to watch the look on Gromph's face as he rides the slide into Callidae."

The archmage scowled, and the four who had been to the ice city laughed.

PIKEL DROVE THEM ON A WILD AND EXHILARATING RIDE, squealing all the while. He guided his magical chariot right up and over the glacier, then into the rift far to the east, near the edge of the ice cap. Into the tunnel warmed by the small flowing stream, in the same oasis area where Jarlaxle and his three companions had lounged and watched the family of foxes before being captured by the Callidae patrol.

There, Pikel dismissed the chariot and the group set off on foot, down the tunnels and into Callidae. The southerners' weapons were not taken this time; they weren't dressed in robes and marched forward. Rather, they all continued as a group, past the cheers of the kurit and arktos oroks who lived in Cascatte, who recognized some of their lost fellow Callidaeans (and Jarlaxle and his three friends as well) and into the tunnels beyond. Despite her reservations, or perhaps because she simply could not reconcile them any longer with the evidence these strangers had repeatedly put before her, Azzudonna now happily and proudly led the way.

Now Jarlaxle stood at the end of the tunnel before Scellobel, blocking the path to the ledge that overlooked the wide borough. Several of the rescued Callidaeans had already gone through, including Doum'wielle, who seemed to want to get as far away from Gromph as possible, but Azzudonna remained, standing hand in hand with Zaknafein.

"Would you like to take Drizzt out to the ledge?" Jarlaxle asked Catti-brie.

Not needing to be asked twice, she pulled her husband along by the hand, brushing past Jarlaxle and out onto the high ledge above the vineyard.

Scellobel rolled out wide to either side, split down the middle by that prow-like stone.

Drizzt froze, unable to find his voice for many heartbeats. His lavender eyes soaked it all in: the artwork of the bridges and buildings, the ice walls reflecting the swirls of the Merry Dancers, the multitude of people below, of drow, aevendrow. And of others, the blue-skinned kurit dwarves, the orcs, the round-faced humans. He couldn't make out the details from up here, but he could sense the heartbeat of the place clearly enough. And he could hear the songs from below, joyous and light, and smell the delicious aroma rising up from the vineyards.

"To Lolth's contempt," Kimmuriel said breathlessly, coming out behind them.

"To the Nine Hells with that ugly spider," said Gromph from the tunnel. Drizzt turned to watch the sour archmage come forth, and took great pleasure and great hope in seeing the man verily transform at the sight, as if the tension and anger were suddenly simply falling away from him as he looked upon the wonder of Callidae.

"It was worth the journey, yes?" Jarlaxle asked him, and Gromph couldn't respond, and he didn't have to.

Pikel came bobbing out of the tunnel beside Dab'nay, who immediately slapped her hand over her mouth, her eyes, like those of the other newcomers, misting with tears of joy.

"Hehehe," said Pikel, bouncing along and taking it all in. "Dere?" he asked Catti-brie, pointing to the descending slide at the right-hand edge of the ledge.

Catti-brie nodded and said, "Yup yup," in her best Pikel voice.

For the next few moments, all they heard was the receding "Wheeeeee!" of the green-bearded dwarf as he flung himself down the slide, winding and snaking to the city below.

Then they heard the moan of the unceasing polar wind, sounding magical indeed under the swirling lights of the sky above.

Somewhere down in Callidae, some group started singing.

Drizzt was not surprised. It simply fit.

There was no other way to describe it. Here, in this place, the sound of voices lifting in song, happy, joyous, somber, reflective, simply fit.

He turned to his wife and kissed her deeply.

"We have to get my granddaughter up here sometime soon," he heard Zaknafein say.

Indeed.

Dramatis Personae

Along the streets of Menzoberranzan . . . the drow.

Matron Mother Yvonnel Baenre: Also known as Yvonnel the Eternal. Ruled the house and the city for two thousand years. Killed by King Bruenor Battlehammer when she led the city against Mithral Hall more than a century ago.

Quenthel Baenre: Daughter of Yvonnel the Eternal and current Matron Mother of Menzoberranzan, ruling from the seat of House Baenre. Gifted with the memories of Yvonnel the Eternal by the illithids so viscerally that they are as much a part of her as they were to her mother. Through them, discovered the deception of Lolth and helped create the Great Heresy against the Spider Queen.

Sos'Umptu Baenre: Yvonnel the Eternal's daughter, mistress of Arach-Tinilith, former first priestess of House Baenre and current high priestess of the Fane of the Quarvelsharess. Remains fervently loyal to Lolth, putting her at odds with Matron Mother Quenthel and House Baenre.

Yvonnel Baenre: Daughter of Gromph Baenre and Minolin Fey Branche. Like Quenthel, she was gifted the memories of her grandmother, Yvonnel the Eternal, only for her, it was performed in utero. She is only a few years old, but was born with full consciousness and two thousand years of memory. Perhaps the most powerful drow in Menzoberranzan, she used magic to age herself into a young drow woman. She admires Drizzt, secretly loves him, and, with Matron Mother Quenthel, facilitated the Great Heresy, leaving the city of Menzoberranzan on the verge of civil war.

Matron Zhindia Melarn: Zealot of Lolth, led the assault of the Sword Coast of Faerun against Luskan, Gauntlgrym, and Bleeding Vines, and seemed on the verge of victory until the Great Heresy of Quenthel and Yvonnel stole her drider army out from under her.

The Blaspheme: An army of some eight hundred driders returned to life on the Material Plane to serve Matron Zhindia Melarn in her surface war. But when Yvonnel and Quenthel fashioned the magical web to remove all curses, even the Curse of Abomination that eternally tormented them in their half-drow/half-spider form, they rushed through to become again true drow, now following House Baenre in opposition to Lolth.

Mal'a'voselle "Voselly" Amvas Tol: Mighty warrior from another age, the long-dead House Amvas Tol, where she ranked as weapon master. The powerful, broad-shouldered woman serves as Blaspheme field commander.

Aleandra: Another of the Blaspheme and a friend of Voselly since their days fighting side by side in House Amvas Tol in ancient Menzoberranzan.

Dininae: Another of the Blaspheme and one of the few who lived in recent years in Menzoberranzan. His true identity is Dinin Do'Urden, elder brother of Drizzt. He was turned into a driver by his sister, Vierna, and met his death at the end of King Bruenor Battlehammer's many-notched axe.

Along the streets of Callidae . . . the aevendrow.

Azzudonna: A young aevendrow woman, proud warrior of the Biancorso cazzcalci team, hero in the most recent match. A fierce fighter, Azzudonna has found a strong bond with Zaknafein.

Holy Galathae: Paladin of Eilistraee, Galathae is a leader in the defenses of Callidae and was instrumental in accepting the four strangers—Jarlaxle, Catti-brie, Artemis Entreri, and Zaknafein—who happened upon the city.

Aida'Umptu, "Ayeeda": The innkeeper of Ibilsitato in the borough of Scellobel in Callidae. With unusual blue eyes, mostly blue hair, and a perpetual smile and joy for life, she became friends with the four strangers, particularly Jarlaxle, who spent their nights in Callidae in her establishment. She is very close with Azzudonna, Ilina, and Alvinessy.

Allefaero: A young bookworm and wizard, this mage-scholar is the city's expert on much of the flora and fauna of the region. Preferring to spend his days in the library, Allefaero is quite nervous that his understanding of the dangerous environ will almost certainly put him on the front lines of a great struggle.

Ilina: Priestess Ilina was one of the earliest to accept the four strangers, as her god is quite similar to that of Catti-brie, Mielikki. With an indisputable reputation, Ilina's vouching for the outsiders was an important voice in their acceptance.

Alvinessy, "Vessi": Best friend of Azzudonna, the short wiry man plays dasher for Biancorso. Like Azzudonna, he is young and full of life and hope and dreams.

Doum'wielle Armgo: Daughter of a drow man and a moon elf woman, Doum'wielle found her way to Menzoberranzan and a place as a noble in Barrison Del'Armgo, the city's Second House. She ran afoul of Gromph Baenre and was thrown through a portal to the far north. Jarlaxle convinced his three companions to go north primarily to find her, and learned that she, too, had stumbled upon Callidae, and had been accepted by the aevendrow, but now, alas, was seemingly lost forever.

Mona Valrissa Zhamboule: The current mona, or governor, of Callidae, Valrissa carries the weight of great responsibility on her shoulders.

A savvy politician and decent woman, she balances the responsibilities of office and leading the Temporal Convocation with the responsibilities to her heart, and that which she knows is right.

From the Sword Coast . . .

Gromph Baenre: Yvonnel the Eternal's oldest child, former archmage of Menzoberranzan, and now the archmage of Luskan's Hosttower of the Arcane. Considered among the most powerful wizards in the world.

Kimmuriel: Co-leader of Bregan D'aerthe with Jarlaxle, Kimmuriel has ever been an enigma to his roguish counterpart. For Kimmuriel is a powerful psionicist, a master of mind magic who spends quite a bit of time with the strange illithids at their hive mind. He is older now, and more introspective, asking the larger questions of his life.

Dab'nay: The drow priestess has served Jarlaxle in Bregan D'aerthe for many decades. Once a lover of Zaknafein, always a friend to him and to Jarlaxle, she often questioned why Lolth was seemingly granting her divine spells, since she has no love for the evil Spider Queen. Her prominence within Bregan D'aerthe has grown in recent years as she has become integral to their handling of their rule in the city of Luskan.

Jarlaxle: A houseless rogue who began Bregan D'aerthe, a mercenary band quietly serving the needs of many drow houses, but mostly serving their own needs.

Drizzt Do'Urden: Born in Menzoberranzan and fled the evil ways of the city. Drow warrior, hero of the north, and Companion of the Hall, along with his four dear friends.

Catti-brie: Human wife of Drizzt, Chosen of the goddess Mielikki, skilled in both arcane and divine magic. Companion of the Hall.

Regis Topolino (Spider Parrafin): Halfling husband of Donnola Topolino, leader of the halfling community of Bleeding Vines. Companion of the Hall.

King Bruenor Battlehammer: Eighth king of Mithral Hall, tenth king of Mithral Hall, now king of Gauntlgrym, an ancient dwarven city he reclaimed with his dwarven kin. Companion of the Hall. Adoptive father of both Wulfgar and Catti-brie.

Wulfgar: Born to the Tribe of the Elk in Icewind Dale, the giant human was captured by Bruenor in battle and became the adopted son of the dwarf king. Companion of the Hall.

Artemis Entreri: Former nemesis of Drizzt, the human assassin is the drow warrior's near equal or equal in battle. Now he runs with Jarlaxle's Bregan D'aerthe band, and considers Drizzt and the other Companions of the Hall friends.

Guenhwyvar: Magical panther, companion of Drizzt, summoned to his side from the Astral Plane.

Andahar: Drizzt's summoned steed, a magical unicorn. Unlike the living Guenhwyvar, Andahar is a purely magical construct.

Penelope Harpell: The leader of the eccentric wizards known as the Harpells, who oversee the town of Longsaddle from their estate, the Ivy Mansion. Penelope is a powerful wizard, mentoring Catti-brie, and has dated Wulfgar on occasion.

Grandmaster Kane: A human monk who has transcended his mortal coil and become a being beyond the Material Plane, Kane is the Grandmaster of Flowers of the Monastery of the Yellow Rose in far-off Damara. He is friend and mentor to Drizzt as the drow tries to find peace at last along a turbulent road.

Thibbledorf Pwent: A walking weapon in his spiked and sharp-ridged armor, Pwent is a battle-hardened dwarf whose loyalty is as strong as the aroma emanating from him. He led every seemingly suicidal charge with a cry of "Me king!" and gave his life saving King Bruenor in the bowels of Gauntlgrym. His death was not the end of Pwent, though, for he was slain by a vampire and became a vampire himself until being freed of the curse by the same magical web that freed the driders of the Curse of Abomination.

The Brothers Bouldershoulder, Ivan and Pikel: Ivan Bouldershoulder is a grizzled old veteran of many battles, mundane and magical. He's risen to a position of great trust as a commander in Bruenor's Gauntlgrym guard. More eccentric and extreme than Ivan, the green-haired Pikel fancies himself a druid, or "doo-dad," and helped Donnola Topolino create wonderful vineyards in Bleeding Vines. His limited and stilted vocabulary only adds to the deceptive innocence of this quite powerful dwarf.

Kimmuriel Oblodra: A powerful drow psionicist, Kimmuriel serves as co-leader of Bregan D'aerthe beside Jarlaxle. He is the logical foil to the emotional Jarlaxle, and Jarlaxle knows it.

Eternal Beings

Lolth, the Lady of Chaos, the Demon Queen of Spiders, the Queen of the Demonweb Pits: The mighty demon Lolth reigns as the most influential goddess of the drow, particularly in the greatest drow city, Menzoberranzan, known as the City of Spiders for the devotion of its inhabitants. True to her name, the Lady of Chaos constantly shocks her followers, keeping her true plans buried beneath the webbing of other more obvious and understandable schemes. Her end goal, above all, is chaos.

Eskavidne and Yiccardaria: Lesser demons known as yochlol, they serve as two of the handmaidens of Lolth. The pair have proven so resourceful and skilled that Lolth gives them great rein in walking the ways of the drow and making a glorious mess of everything.

Ilnezhara and Tazmikella: The dragon sisters are longtime friends of Jarlaxle and Artemis Entreri, having met the duo in the Bloodstone Lands more than a century before. They are copper dragons, but spend much of their time polymorphed into the form of human women. Greedy and lustful, they covet treasures and pleasures. Is it any wonder they have bonded with Jarlaxle?

Ygorl, the Lord of Entropy: Huge and terrible, with a body of dense smoke over his giant slaadi skeleton, the god of the slaadi wields a terrible scythe and magic more terrible by far.

Qadeej: One of the Vaati, or Wind Dukes of Aaqa, a group of godlike beings opposing chaos in the cosmos, the legend of Qadeej claims that he lay down on the north pole of Toril and there died, and that the great glacier that now houses Callidae on one end, and the frost giant and slaad castle on the other, arose from the magic of his body.

About the Author

Thirty-four years ago, R. A. SALVATORE created the character of Drizzt Do'Urden, the dark elf who has withstood the test of time to stand today as an icon in the fantasy genre. With his work in the Forgotten Realms™, the Crimson Shadow, the DemonWars Saga, and other series, Salvatore has sold more than thirty million books worldwide and has appeared on the *New York Times* bestseller list more than two dozen times. He considers writing to be his personal journey, but still, he's quite pleased that so many are walking the road beside him! R. A. lives in Massachusetts with his wife, Diane, and their two dogs, Dexter and Pikel. He still plays softball for his team, Clan Battlehammer, and enjoys his weekly *DemonWars: Reformation* RPG and *Dungeons & Dragons* 5e games. Salvatore can be found on Facebook at TheRealRASalvatore, on Twitter at @r_a_salvatore, and at RASalva Store.com.